JEHU:

Regicide

JEHU:
Regicide

A Novel

J. L. WILDEBOER

RESOURCE *Publications* · Eugene, Oregon

Resource Publications
An Imprint of Wipf and Stock Publishers
199 W. 8th Ave., Suite 3
Eugene, OR 97401

www.wipfandstock.com

PAPERBACK ISBN: 978-1-6667-4141-4
HARDCOVER ISBN: 978-1-6667-4142-1
EBOOK ISBN: 978-1-6667-4143-8

APRIL 18, 2022 3:46 PM

To Jean

Regicide:

1: a person who kills a king

2: the killing of a king

MERRIAM WEBSTER COLLEGIATE DICTIONARY,
11TH ED., (2003)

The term "regicide" denotes both a person who brings about the death of a king, and the act of bringing about the death of a king. Both concepts apply directly to Jehu, a commander of the army of Israel who was anointed by a prophet of the Lord to bring an end to Israel's House of Ahab.

However, the concept of regicide applies not only to Jehu, but to the entire era of Jehu. In the biblical and parallel accounts of Jehu's time, at least eight separate regicides are noted, including not only kings and queens of the Kingdoms of Israel and Judah, but also kings of Aram and Tyre. Indeed, one king of Israel is condemned for not putting an end to a king of Aram captured in battle, and the prophet Elijah is charged with anointing not only Jehu as King of Israel, but also Hazael as King of Aram, for the express purpose of committing regicide.

The regicides include not only kings and queens, but also army commanders, a eunuch, a priest of Astarte, a High Priest of Jerusalem, and even an unwitting archer.

CONTENTS

DISCLAIMER

THIS is a work of fiction.

This novel is based primarily on the events portrayed in the Bible, specifically I Kings 9 through II Kings 11 and II Chronicles 10 through II Chronicles 23. The historicity of the events described in the biblical narrative is assumed.

An effort has been made by the author to describe the events portrayed as they may have logically proceeded within the biblical narrative.

All of the characters portrayed in this novel are based on individuals either identified by name, title or role in the biblical narrative. All of the named characters in this novel, except for King Phelles and King Baal-Essen II of Phoenicia, are based on characters named or identified in the Bible narrative. No fictional character is introduced in this work.

However, the motivation, intent, speech and thoughts of many of the individuals portrayed in this novel and many of the events described in this novel are speculative and inventions of the author. Much of the narrative and statements attributed to characters in this novel are an invention of the author. Statements of individuals included in the biblical narrative are faithfully recited in the novel, but additional dialogue and statements attributed to the characters are inventions of the author.

The "Index – biblical Sources for Chapters" at the end of this work identifies as the first entry the passage of the Bible from which the events portrayed in the chapter are taken, if the chapter is based on events portrayed in the Bible, and the subsequent entries identify the biblical passage from which biblical references or events referred to in the chapter are taken. All historical events described in this work as relate to the Israelite peoples are derived from events described in the Bible, or inferred from those events, although the significance and meaning of the events described may be an invention of the author.

THE FLIGHT OF AN ARROW

Jehu

I will make my arrows drunk with blood. Moses,
Deuteronomy 32:42

T HE arrow sprung from the string of my bow, splitting the currents of the winds and tracing a slight arc in the air as it flew toward its target. For but a moment, suspended between heaven and sheol, the flight of a thin shaft of cedar tipped in bronze and guided by the feathers of a falcon determined the course of my life, the life of my King, and the path of a kingdom.

A wild-eyed, breathless youth of a prophet of the Lord had set me down this path only a day earlier, followed by the chariots I commanded. We were assaulting the fortified, walled city of Jezreel with a handful of soldiers. Should my arrow miss its mark, the King's chariot would pick up speed and escape behind the gates of the city. The chariots following me would scatter, fleeing from the King's vengeance, and I would stand alone, a nameless regicide ignored by the King's scribes.

WISDOM FROM AN ARMY'S CAMPFIRE

Jehu

He will take your sons and make them serve with his
chariots and horses, and they will run in front of his
chariots. I Samuel 8:11

THERE is much wisdom to be had around the campfire of the army.
If you wish to rise quickly in the ranks, become a charioteer; they
have blazing speed, inspire awe and are the first into action; a guarantee
to be noticed by the king and his commanders. If you wish to be the first
of your village to be killed in a battle, become a charioteer; they have
blazing speed and inspire awe and are the first into action; a guarantee to
be noticed by the enemy archers.

If you do not want to fear the king, become the king. If you want to
fear everyone else, become the king.

What sort of wisdom is this? It is the wisdom of fear and death—
qualities as pervasive and as ignored as the acrid smoke from the army's
campfires. Few soldiers in the army of the Kingdom of Israel have come
to the army for the glory of battle or to cheat death. Most do not like going into battle. They have come into the army because they do not want
to hide in caves and gullies with their families and flocks while armies of
other nations sweep through their fields and villages. They would rather
face the enemy with a sword in their hands than a threshing fork.

It is a strange time we live in. Perhaps metal workers are to blame.
Their arts in working iron have surpassed their predecessors' arts in tin

and copper, and every generation seems to see even stronger iron created and more deadly armies conjured from their fires. Gone are the
days when after six or seven blows your sword is a useless club and the
battle reverts to the brute force of rocks and cudgels. Arrows now pierce
through layers of leather that used to protect us. Battle has become more
deadly.

Not only has battle become more deadly, kings and armies have
become more deadly. Every kingdom seeks to devour its neighbor. The
smallest kingdom seeks territory and villages from its smaller neighbor
to grow stronger and resist its larger neighbors. The enterprise of every
kingdom is to enlarge its borders and enrich its treasury. The armies have
become fiercer because they are paid by their plunder of crops and herds
and treasure and slaves. Is the Kingdom of Israel and its previous dynasties, the House of Jeroboam and House of Baasha and House of Omri
and Ahab, any different from the other nations? Is the House of Jehu to
be different?

And yet even in the midst of a deadly battle I would still see some
beauty in the eyes of even my adversary. Were they not men like me?
Even after they were pierced and bleeding, uttering some vague curse or
blessing for a deity I did not know, I would see an unwitting creation of
the Lord and I would pity them.

Some of the old stories and the old traditions still live on. We are
the children of Abraham, chosen of the Lord. And yet we still have an
army. A chosen people? Chosen for what? There are now two kingdoms
of Abraham's children, the Kingdom of Israel and the Kingdom of Judah.
Are we both still chosen? The Temple of the Lord remains in Judah. A
few prophets of the Lord still scurry about our kingdom haranguing and
cajoling, perhaps waiting on the House of Jehu. It was a prophet who
anointed me King of Israel, but since that time they have become silent,
so I am left to my own counsel. Our victories seem to be followed by
defeats, and even our strong neighbors are being overwhelmed by their
even stronger neighbors.

There will be other voices in this history, taken by other scribes. My
scribes have told me this must be a king's history; it must be a story told
by the King alone. I have seen kings' histories. I have heard of the blustery
pillar of Shalmaneser of Assyria, boasting that I sent him some golden
bowls, and that I bowed down before him. Did I not send golden bowls
also to Edom and Tyre and Aram and, yes, to Assyria? Did I not receive
golden bowls and other gifts in return? Does he not know that I received

that same golden bowl as tribute from Ammon? Gifts to other kings, yes; for treaties, for trade, for coronations, for the birth of an heir, yes, even for tribute. I was not born a king, so I do not intend to boast like a king. I am, after all, only a soldier, and bragging and boasting has led to many a defeat. So there will be other voices in this history.

As for King Shalmaneser, in payment for his lies every year I behead two of his army who remain my captives, and send a mule with my presents into his kingdom. I am waiting for the glorious King Shalmaneser to inscribe these gifts on his pillar. I have not been at the beheadings in the last few years. I do not know if there remains any glimpse of beauty in their eyes as the last of their blood seeps out of their lives.

JEROBOAM'S REVOLT

Jehu

My father scourged you with whips, I will scourge you
with scorpions. King Rehoboam, I Kings 12:15

How did I come to this wisdom, or lack of wisdom? I was a young
man when all of this started, but at the time I was oblivious to the
fact that anything was starting. As a youth, I did not know what prophets
and priests did to keep themselves busy, but the House of Omri kept the
army employed. I began in the army as an apprentice charioteer during
the last years of King Omri and rose to commander of chariots during the
twenty-two years that Omri's son Ahab reigned as King. Even in my last
years as commander of the chariots, there were few that could outrace
me, and even those that could, could not upset my chariot in a race.

King Baasha of Israel had unwittingly groomed an able military
King in his commander Omri. King Baasha in his twenty-four year reign
waged almost constant war against King Asa of Judah, the sister kingdom
of Israel, created when King Solomon's great kingdom split in two. Commander Omri's share of King Baasha's warring with King Asa became
greater and greater as Omri proved his abilities in the field. King Ahab
followed in his father King Omri's footsteps. He was often in the army
camp with his father before Omri became King. Ahab was well versed in
the ways of the military.

It is fitting then that through King Omri, King Baasha, a regicide
who killed King Nadab, son of King Jeroboam of Israel, also trained me
as well. The army of Israel that I served in was still very much King Omri's

army. I knew Ahab well before he married Jezebel of Sidon and before
he became King, and I knew he had more interest in the army than in
palace intrigue before his marriage to Jezebel. Temples and gods were live
and let live with Ahab. With Jezebel, gods were the road to power, and
ultimate power was the throne.

I talk much with my old scribe—too much he says - about tales our
fathers told us of the times before King Omri and King Baasha. We lived
in different worlds than our fathers. King Omri built Israel into a strong
kingdom after Baasha's wars bled us dry. My old scribe says my history
cannot be understood without knowing what happened before King
Omri; why our kingdom was so loyal to the House of Omri for so long.

No one fears the King anymore, not even my scribe. He knows it
has been years since I have run over an adversary with my chariot. I will
reward my scribe by mentioning him in my history—but I will not give
his name. I will have his scrolls read to me when he is done. My scribe
has his own tales. He says he is descended from a long line of Hittite
scribes. He tells me of the extensive archives of the Hittites in their capital
of Hattusa where his forebearers worked. I have been to Hattusa in my
travels as a youth with my father. I tell my scribe that the Hittite archives
of parchment, papyrus, vellum and hides have been used in the campfires
of the armies of Assyria and Babylonia; only the clay tablets of the Hittites remain to this day, those which have not been smashed by drunken
soldiers. Such is the lot of the history of kings long forgotten.

When Ahab succeeded his father Omri as King of Israel it had been
sixty-two years, according to my scribes, since Jeroboam's rebellion severed the ten tribes of the Kingdom of Israel from King Solomon's kingdom. While only a stump of two tribes remained with Solomon's arrogant
son Rehoboam, the royal house of King David, not to mention the Temple of the Lord, had too strong of a hold on the capital city Jerusalem for
Jeroboam to overstep the bounds of the prophet Abijah's commissioning.

King Solomon had put Jeroboam in charge of the entire labor force
of the kingdom. This was a sign of the remarkable success of Solomon,
that one of the most powerful officials in the kingdom was not a military
leader or a member of the royal family, but a public works official, building palaces, walls, roads, fortification, ports, granaries, market places and
temples.

Ruling the Kingdoms of Israel and Judah required a special skill not
required in other kingdoms of the time. Our neighboring kingdoms had
their share of priests and seers of their numerous deities, but their priests

and seers operated out of temples financed and controlled by the royal palace. If a king wanted to impose a new tax levy or attack a neighboring kingdom, the new policy would be presaged by new visions and oracles from the temples. In Israel and Judah, it was not enough to deal with foreign kings, or subjects, or member of the royal family who may be pretenders to the throne, or the Levites or priests that controlled the Temple in Jerusalem, or the merchants or traders; the kings of Israel and Judah also had to deal with the self-proclaimed prophets of the Lord, heirs of Moses they claimed, as they pronounced "the word of the Lord."

Support by the prophets gave the kings credence with the people. King Solomon could build on the reputation of his father David who had been anointed King while barely an adult by the prophet Samuel. Solomon himself was anointed King by the prophet Nathan.

In Jeroboam's case, the agent of the rebellion against King Solomon was the prophet Ahijah of Shiloh. Being from Shiloh gave Ahijah a mystique of authority. Shiloh was the home of the prophet Samuel who had anointed David King. Ahijah took it upon himself to anoint Jeroboam King over Israel. And why? Because, according to Ahijah, Solomon had taken to worshiping Asherah, the Sidonian goddess Astarte. If that wasn't enough, he also worshiped Chemosh, god of the Moabites, and Molek, god of the Ammonites. And those temples Jeroboam was in charge of building? Those would be for Asherah, Chemosh, Molek and others.

Solomon was a great temple builder. He first built the great Temple to the Lord in Jerusalem - the centerpiece of Jerusalem, the focus of worship, pilgrimage and celebration for the entire kingdom. Several times a year, large segments of the entire nation made their way to Jerusalem and the great Temple. While there, the masses also marveled at Solomon's palaces, The Palace of David, The Palace of the Forest of Lebanon, The Palace of Pharaoh's Daughter, the Hall of Justice, the great city wall and its magnificent gates, and other public works the likes of which their fathers had never seen. Jerusalem under Solomon was a far cry from the tales related by the priests and elders of the Israelites hunkering down in pits to grind their grain to hide their harvest from their avaricious neighbors. Under Solomon, the descendants of those once dominant neighbors pilgrimaged to Jerusalem to pay their tribute to Solomon and once again pledge their fealty to Solomon and renew their trading treaties.

Jerusalem had truly become a cosmopolitan city. And how better to receive the foreign dignitaries and solidify their loyalty than to build temples to their deities as well? Their gods had now taken up residence in Solomon's capital and were demonstrating their loyalty to Solomon the magnificent. And yes, even Solomon would enter their temples with the dignitaries after graciously receiving their gold and silver, and offer sacrifices to their gods. Solomon was truly one of them. They were not required to abjure their gods and sacrifice to some foreigner's god. That truly took the sting out of the heavy tribute he exacted. It was far better to enjoy the benefits of partnering with the rich and prosperous Solomon than to be shut out.

But King Solomon's cosmopolitan ways stuck in the prophet Ahijah's craw. Ahijah would wonder aloud, "How many wives did the King need?" Ahijah would also ask whether Solomon's foreign wives had more to do with Jeroboam's temple building than solidifying his suzerainty over the neighboring kingdoms.

Prophet or not, word of Ahijah anointing Jeroboam did not sit well with Solomon. Solomon probably doubted that Jeroboam was so pious as to take Ahijah's pronouncements at face value. If he was such a loyal servant of the Lord, wouldn't he have refused to build all those temples to the gods of other nations in Jerusalem? What really angered Solomon was Jeroboam spreading the claim by Ahijah that if Jeroboam was loyal to the Lord, Jeroboam's dynasty would be as enduring as the dynasty the Lord established for King David. For such a wise King, in the end I think Solomon allowed his own magnificence to take him in. Did not Jeroboam see the grandeur of King Solomon's kingdom? Who did that bricklayer Jeroboam think he was? Solomon had no cause to sit around an army campfire. If he had, he would have recognized the wisdom of the army; a king has cause to fear everyone.

I often wondered about Ahijah's prophecy; "as enduring as the House of David?" Perhaps both Solomon and Jeroboam failed to recall that during David's life the House of David looked more like a tottering tower, not something secure or enduring. Did Jeroboam have any memory of Solomon's half brother Absalom murdering his oldest half-brother Amnon for raping half-sister Tamar and then staging a rebellion against his father David? Or Solomon's half brother Adonijah pronouncing himself King while King David was still living? And the power grab when David died that almost left the memory of youngest son Solomon a bloody mar on the floor of the royal palace?

Years later, when a wild, breathless prophet drenched me in oil at Ramoth-Gilead, I already knew the tale of Jeroboam's anointing. I took no great comfort from it. Jeroboam's kingdom still survived, but Jeroboam's son was struck down by a usurper. Anointing oil on the head of a king makes the crown a slippery item.

Jeroboam was quick and smart enough to escape Solomon's plan to quickly excise Jeroboam from the kingdom and from life itself. Once King Solomon died, it was safe enough for Jeroboam to return from exile in Egypt and to reestablish his contacts to easily outmaneuver the arrogant to the point of stupidity heir apparent King Rehoboam.

Jeroboam knew all about temples, and not just the architecture and the number of quarrymen, oxen teams, stone dressers, carpenters, silversmiths and tapestry makers it took to put one together. He knew how many priests and celebrants and servants it took to operate one. He knew about pageantry and awe, processions and pronouncements, incense and altar flame. And he knew the draw that temples could be and the loyalty they could inspire.

With Jerusalem firmly in King Rehoboam's grasp, Jeroboam knew it was only a matter of time that Rehoboam, if he had half a wit about him, could turn Jeroboam's adherents against him as the Israelites dutifully pilgrimaged to the Temple in Jerusalem several times a year. If a temple is needed, if a site for a pilgrimage is desired, Jeroboam could provide that. After all, hadn't he just been anointed by the prophet Ahijah? Hadn't he just been promised a dynasty as enduring as King David? Who better to be able to decree a few new temples? Based on his years of experience, and relying on a little historical imagery for those not given to critical thinking, Jeroboam provided not just one golden calf, but two; one at Bethel and one at Dan, and hired some priests to provide whatever unction was due to lend a chimera of sacredness. Bethel was at Israel's southern border, almost within sight of King Rehoboam's rump Kingdom of Judah. Why travel all the way to Jerusalem when you are already at Bethel? Dan was close to our northern border.

Jeroboam recruited the Levites, the national priest class, to run his temples. He found few takers. The Levites all answered to the High Priest, appointed and seated in the Temple of Jerusalem, who was very protective of the dominance of the Temple in Jerusalem. Once word got around what type of temples Jeroboam was building, there was an exodus of Levites from Jeroboam's realm to Jerusalem and environs. Jeroboam did nothing to discourage them from leaving. If they would not support his new religious polity, they would resist it, and he was better off without them. Jeroboam did not need a rebellion of Levites in front of his new temple. It only took a handful of willing Levites to train the ambitious would be priests to operate Jeroboam's new temples.

And festivals? Yes, just like in Jerusalem. What good is a temple without a good draw? Jeroboam designed the necessary assembly points, processional ways, gathering places, columns and platforms, marketplaces and raised public altars to help the worshipers forget about Jerusalem. And since he was now a national leader who needed to curry favor with potential allies, Molek, Asherah, Baal and Chemosh did not go wanting for their own temples.

The emigration of Levites from King Jeroboam's new kingdom left the Israelites in Jeroboam's control searching for an identity. They were Israelites, sons and daughters of Abraham, Isaac and Jacob. They had been slaves in Egypt until Moses led them out and delivered them to the promised land. They invaded the land behind Joshua. They suffered and scratched out an existence under the itinerant Judges who ruled the land before our kings took over. They had been part of King Solomon's dominion. They pilgrimaged to the Temple in Jerusalem and wondered at the marvels of King Solomon's city. But now Solomon was gone, and Jerusalem was no longer part of their realm.

King David had appointed the Levites as officials and judges throughout the land since they were no longer needed to carry the tabernacle around from campsite to campsite. The Levites had remained in place in the land under Solomon, even after the new idols had been introduced to the Temple. They continued to instruct the people in the Laws of God. But in the new Kingdom of Israel under Jeroboam, the Levites were gone, and new laws pleasing to King Jeroboam were being announced in Jeroboam's new temples. Some of the laws sounded very familiar, some of the laws sounded very strange. Some actually laughed at the new laws. They remembered the old laws. "These are not the Laws of Moses!" they would scoff. But their new priests would explain why things had changed. "God did not stop writing laws at Mount Sinai. God's law is not frozen in stone tablets. The old laws were good for the old times, but look how much has changed. The land has been subdued. We trade with other lands. King Solomon is gone. The Lord now has two kingdoms of Israelites."

Not everything the new priests said agreed with what other new priests said. And some new laws would be announced, only to be changed the next year. The people would say that that was not the Law of the Lord they remembered. But there were no Levites to consult. A generation grew up that had not been to Jerusalem, a generation that had only heard old stories of King Solomon, who knew only of two kingdoms, Israel and Judah. "Why are our temples wrong?" they would ask. Gradually, only a few hold-outs remained on the periphery, where they preferred to live. It was safer. They lived like the entire nation had when they were under the thumb of the Philistines. I imagine that was not what the prophet Ahijah had bargained for.

THE SUCCESSION OF ASSASSINS

Jehu

Many servants are breaking away from their masters
these days. Nabal, I Samuel 25:10–11

M Y scribe tells me my thoughts on Jeroboam are interesting but
tiresome. I guess I am old and doddering enough now that
even a palace scribe can argue with the King. I told the scribe that King
Shalmaneser of Assyria would cut off his hands for disagreeing with the
king's history. The scribe asks me if I would like him to read to me the
inscription on King Shalmaneser's pillar if I so revere a king's history. My
scribe knows me too well.

Still, my scribe cannot tell me why this Kingdom of Israel was created. A prophet of the Lord had anointed its first King, but what was
the purpose of this nation with the Temple of the Lord and the House
of David still in Jerusalem? As the time grew closer to the time I was
anointed as King, I could not help but feel that the tumult of those earlier
times was starting to repeat itself under the Kings I served - Omri, Ahab,
Ahaziah and Joram. The House of Ahab had grown out of the House of
Omri, but it was not the same.

King Jeroboam's reign and dynasty was a pale reflection of King David's kingdom. King Rehoboam of Judah was mustering troops to regain
possession of Jeroboam's domain when he was confronted by a prophet
of the Lord, telling him not to fight against his fellow Israelites. Having
lost most of his domain out of arrogance must have humbled Rehoboam

as he listened to the prophet and sent his army home, the closest he came to resembling the wisdom of his father.

King Jeroboam did not share Rehoboam's brief encounter with wisdom. Jeroboam, sensing weakness in Rehoboam's wisdom, called on Pharaoh Shishak, who had given Jeroboam refuge when he fled from Solomon, to give him an advantage over King Rehoboam. Shishak obliged, requiring Rehoboam to ransom Jerusalem from a siege by stripping the Temple in Jerusalem of most of its gold, the bounty used by Jeroboam to lure Shishak to invade Israel. The Pharaoh also saw fit to roam into King Jeroboam's realm, reaping more pillage from cities in Israel, an unanticipated cost to King Jeroboam of Egypt's intervention. Having been ravaged by Shishak, their armies bloodied and weakened, the realms of Jeroboam and Rehoboam took an involuntary respite from their anger and glared at each other over their borders. As for Pharaoh Shishak, he saw nothing in the rugged hill country of Judah or the dusty plains of Israel that enticed him to control the land, so he returned to Egypt, happy with the riches he carried away.

King Rehoboam's son Abijah tried to avenge his father's losses at the hands of King Jeroboam's erstwhile ally Pharaoh Shishak, and also tried to reclaim all of Israel for the House of David. After eighteen years of Jeroboam's reign over Israel, King Abijah confronted Jeroboam and routed Jeroboam's army with massive casualties, even to the point of taking one of Jeroboam's temple towns, one of the towns with Jeroboam's golden calves, Bethel, away from Jeroboam for a time. There was war between the Kingdoms of Israel and Judah throughout King Abijah's reign. King Jeroboam, the builder of majestic buildings and manager of a large force of enslaved workers under King Solomon, did not have a good grasp of the army. King Jeroboam died while still under King Abijah's thumb, leaving Jeroboam's son King Nadab with a kingdom in decline.

After reigning for two years in a kingdom severely weakened by the losses under King Jeroboam, Jeroboam's son King Nadab was killed by the usurper Baasha, who made himself King. King Nadab, during his short reign, at least tried to do his duty as King. King Nadab was pushing back against the incursions by the Philistines, the same loose affiliations of cities on the coast of the great sea that had been hammered by the jawbone of an ass wielded by Judge Samson. At the time of Baasha's rebellion, King Nadab was besieging the Philistine town Gibbethon. What better time to mount a rebellion in the capital city when the King is tied down in a siege days from the capital by horseback?

Rather than a dynasty like David's, the dynasty of King Jeroboam was followed by a succession of assassins. Baasha was thorough enough. Not only did the regicide Baasha assassinate King Nadab, he also dispatched everyone who was related to King Jeroboam, eliminating any heir of Kings Jeroboam or King Nadab who may have a claim to the throne. It was probably Baasha's thoroughness in eliminating the previous dynasty that allowed him to hold on to power for twenty-four years. Any rallying point for a successive rebellion had been eliminated.

Despite becoming a King, I am a soldier, first, second and last, so perhaps I have no business speaking of history. But as a soldier, having battled or skirmished with the Arameans almost every campaigning season, I always sought to understand why Aram became our most belligerent neighbor. King Solomon's domination of the region since the time of his father King David left all of the neighboring kingdoms quiescent; it was better for them to reap the benefits of working cooperatively with the power of Solomon that to risk being left out.

After Jeroboam's rebellion and the division of King Solomon's kingdom, it did not take too long for neighboring kingdoms, accustomed to working to please King Solomon, to realize that once Solomon's Kingdom had been broken in two the remaining halves did not equal the whole, especially when the halves continually weakened each other by waging war against each other. Rehoboam and Jeroboam continually warred against each other until exhausted. King Rehoboam's son and successor Abijah resumed the warring against King Jeroboam, and when Abijah died and was succeeded by his son Asa, King Asa and King Jeroboam warred against each other during their reigns. When Baasha took the throne of Israel from the House of Jeroboam, King Baasha and King Asa warred against each other during their reigns.

I believe that the Kingdom of Aram saw the constant warring between the siblings Judah and Israel as an invitation to probe for a weakness that could be exploited. Since the Kingdom of Israel bordered the Kingdom of Aram, acting as a buffer between Judah and Aram, Israel took the brunt of Aram's probing. Each Kingdom, Israel and Judah, believed it should be considered the rightful heir of the glory of Solomon, so they battled each other bitterly for the mythic crown, and weakened each other in the process. Along with outright warfare, King Baasha also tried to cut off trade between Judah and Aram by fortifying the city of Ramah on the trade route between the Aramean capital of Damascus and the Judean capital of Jerusalem.

With Ramah blockading the trade that would be funneled from Africa and Egypt through Jerusalem and up to Aram and into the Euphrates and Tigris valleys, the traders and merchants sought out different routes, drying up the international trade that had filled both King Asa's Judean coffers and the Aramean treasury in Damascus, by bypassing the trade monopoly on the seas held by the Phoenicians ports of Tyre, Sidon, Byblos and their sister cities. It was this trade blockade that invited the Kingdom of Aram to contend with the Kingdom of Israel, and would lead eventually to the many battles I would be involved in as an army commander against Aram. It was in the middle of one of these contests with Aram that my rebellion against Israel's House of Ahab began.

King Baasha had entered into trade treaties with the Kingdom of Aram. Baasha also had treaties with the Phoenician trading ports of Tyre, Sidon and Byblos along the great sea, the same Phoenicians who were important trade allies of King Solomon. Trade which would normally pass through Jerusalem was pinched off at Ramah and was redirected to Tyre, Sidon and Byblos, and shipped by the Phoenician fleets to the Nile and Egypt and Cairo, choking off Jerusalem's control of this trade.

So how does a trade war between kings bring into play an old soldier like me? Trade routes are controlled by armies. King Asa conducted a diplomatic offensive to recapture Ramah. And his army in this offensive was his treasury. King Asa emptied out every scrap of gold silver and bronze he could lay his hands on in the treasury of the Temple in Jerusalem and in the treasuries in his royal palaces, loaded it on as many camels as he could find in his kingdom, and sent it to King Ben-Hadad in Damascus. Along with all of the gold and silver in Jerusalem, King Asa sent a message to King Ben-Hadad:

> Let there be a treaty between me and you as there was between my father and your father. See, I am sending you a gift of silver and gold. Now break your treaty with Baasha King of Israel so he will withdraw from me.

Aram had been a thorn in King Solomon foot throughout Solomon's reign, but when Jeroboam's kingdom broke away, Aram no longer shared a border with Judah, and Aram would play one sister kingdom against the other. King Asa's ploy used Aram's duplicitousness to his advantage. It would have taken Ben-Hadad's armies years of relentless warfare to pillage and plunder enough cities and kingdoms to equal the wealth being bestowed on him by King Asa, just for making and breaking a trade treaty, and the treasure of Asa came to Ben-Hadad without the loss of one chariot or one soldier.

King Asa's treaty with King Ben-Hadad did require Ben-Hadad to take action against the Kingdom of Israel. But Ben-Hadad could do this without touching his own treasury. He equipped an entire army with the largess from King Asa and marched against the Kingdom of Israel. King Baasha of Israel was not prepared for this sudden challenge from Aram. He had treaties with Aram and was engaging in a booming trading relationship with Aram as he strangled Judah's trade. King Baasha's border with Aram was essentially unprotected and unprepared for the onslaught from King Ben-Hadad's new army. Ben-Hadad sent the commanders of his forces against the towns of Israel. He conquered Ijon, Dan, Abel Beth Maakah and all Kinnereth in addition to Naphtali. These were not glorious military victories, but they brought their own glory. The small border guard forces that King Baasha had stationed in these outposts were politely ushered out of town by Ben-Hadad's overwhelming forces and sent packing. By the time King Baasha was able to muster his own forces, the towns and the territories were gone. Not only did King Ben-Hadad have a fully financed new army that did not come out of his treasury, he now had the plunder and trade from the newly conquered territories.

King Baasha had been outmaneuvered. His dreams of defeating King Asa and reclaiming the throne of Solomon came to a crashing end. King Baasha had spent some of the largess from his trade with Aram in building a new trading town. When Aram turned on him, Baasha essentially abandoned Ramah and retreated behind the walls of his capital of Tizrah. After years of bitter warfare against the Kingdom of Judah, Baasha was bested by a trade treaty.

❋   ❋   ❋

By the time King Baasha died, the Kingdom of Israel had been significantly weakened, inspiring Zimri, the commander of half of the King's chariots, to believe that he could make as good a King as Baasha's son and successor Elah.

It did not help that toward the end of King Baasha's reign the prophet Jehu bar-Hanani proclaimed an end to the House of Baasha:

> I lifted you up from the dust and appointed you ruler over my people Israel, but you followed the ways of Jeroboam and caused my people Israel to sin and to arouse my anger by their sins. So

I am about to wipe out Baasha and his house, and I will make your house like that of Jeroboam son of Nebat. Dogs will eat those belonging to Baasha who die in the city, and birds will feed on those who die in the country.

We Israelites are studiously interested in the history of our nation. We claim to be a people chosen by the Lord. Why we may have been chosen over any other people seems to be glossed over by our historians. As a chosen people we carefully keep track of our generations, perhaps a sign of an ingrained insecurity of being mistaken for some other, non-chosen people.

I have to assume that the next usurper, Zimri, was one such student of our nation's history. Zimri studiously observed that Baasha staged his successful rebellion against King Nadab within two years of Nadab succeeding his father King Jeroboam. Student of history Zimri most likely also observed that King Elah had undertaken another siege of the Philistine town of Gibbethon. King Nadab, Jeroboam's successor, was besieging Gibbethon when Baasha assassinated King Nadab. Usurper Zimri was the commander of one-half of King Baasha's chariots, not a palace position, but one that gave him a fighting force that he could command and coconspirators under his command.

King Elah of Israel ascended to the throne in the twenty-sixth year of King Asa of Judah. In the twenty-seventh year of Asa, King Elah found himself getting drunk in the home of Azra, the man in charge of the King's palace in Tizrah, the capital city of Kingdom of Israel. Zimri brought the forces under his command from the siege at Gibbethon to the capital of Tizrah, where the King was drunk from revelry. A king who sends his army into battle while he remains in the capital city to engage in revelry is not much of king. The fact that his drinking partner was the administrator of the royal palace suggests the quality of people the King had surrounded himself with. A year of King Elah's reign may have established that this was Elah's style of rule, and Zimri would have none of it.

Although the name Zimri has become a byword for traitor in our kingdom, Zimri should be better known for his greed and arrogance than his treachery. Zimri assumed that if he was the one that struck down the King, he would be entitled to the throne. Zimri made his move against the King without consulting the other commanders in the army who commanded forces more powerful than he did. Perhaps Zimri felt he could leap over his more senior commanders by striking first.

Zimri withdrew his forces from Gibbethon to support his move on the royal palace, leaving commander Omri to maintain the siege at Gibbethon. On learning that Zimri had gone off by himself to strike down King Elah and declare himself King, the army proclaimed Omri the new King. Omri lifted the siege of Gibbethon and led his troops with its siege machinery to the capital Tizrah and besieged the city with Zimri in it. With only a small force to support him, Zimri retreated to the citadel of the royal palace and when no other commander stepped forward to support him, burned down the royal palace around him.

As a young charioteer in the last days of King Omri, I would hear tales King Omri would relate regarding Zimri's rebellion. "The king must be close with the army. A rebellion will not succeed if the army does not support it. And beware of an unhappy army. A commander with a following in the army is a dangerous man."

King Omri, the old soldier, died in his sleep in the palace, the last place he had ever expected to die. We all assumed it was a peaceful death, since that was how it was announced by the royal household. Years later, in the light of more recent events, it is possible to question anything that happened in the palace. He had reigned for twelve years.

It was during King Omri's reign that the events that led to me being anointed King of Israel began to unfold.

THE DISPOSITION OF KING PHELLES OF TYRE

Ethbaal I

In the pride of your heart you say, "I am a god; I sit on the
throne of a god in the heart of the seas." Ezekiel 28:2

O UR regrettable late King Phelles sought to choke off the treasury
of the Temple of our great Goddess Astarte, and so I returned the
favor. With the treasure that our ships of Tyre brought in, there was no
call for the King to be so stingy. But that was not his only crime. Our
Temple to the Wondrous Astarte was the center of the Kingdom. King
Phelles imagined that he could rule Tyre from his royal palace and ignore
the visions and oracles of the priestesses of Astarte. The Great Astarte had
built up this kingdom and its wealth and the strength of the King, but the
King foolishly tried to hoard the credit for these wonders for himself. The
will of the Goddess Astarte is not something a mortal king can ignore.

Decree after decree issued from the Temple of Astarte from the
mouth of the Sacred Goddess to the royal palace. The headstrong King
Phelles had the temerity to question these decrees, to send messages asking respectfully that the Goddess amend Her decrees to suit the royal
will, and even to go so far as to blaspheme Astarte by saying again and
again that the Divine decrees were the words only of the priestesses or
the High Priest.

I, Ethbaal, as the High Priest of Astarte, by the will and grace of
the Goddess Astarte, was bound by duty to my Goddess to rebuff the
King's blasphemy. Great public ceremonies and sacrifices were staged in

the streets outside of Astarte's temple in Tyre, pleading to the Goddess not to withhold her beneficence to our great city due to the ignorance of King Phelles. The unrepentant Phelles sought to respond by withholding from the Temple of Astarte the city's obligation to the Temple. Such intransigence could be expected from Phelles as the last of four brothers to rule after they had killed their father. Phelles himself had displaced his last brother as King by having him strangled. Astarte's priestesses had divined that the time was ripe to challenge Phelles. Phelles had murdered his brother the King a mere six months earlier, and the citizens of Tyre remained shocked by his actions.

Greater ceremonies and processions from the Temple of Astarte even to the gates of the royal palace were held, only to be met by the palace guard. Despite my exhortations for peace, despite my calling on the name of the Great Goddess Astarte that the King not defame the Goddess or this great city, several of the priests and priestesses of Astarte were struck down and murdered by the palace guard, and more would have died had I not personally thrown myself between the procession and the guards.

The Goddess Astarte decreed that I was to bring peace between the royal palace and the Temple of Astarte. As the son of King Ahiram of Byblos, I was able to recruit an embassy of the palace guard from Byblos. A compact between Tyre and Byblos had seen me installed as the High Priest of the Temple of Astarte in Tyre, as a means to maintain good relations between the cities. King Phelles graciously received our humble procession of priestesses and priests at the gates of the royal palace, ready to receive our obeisance and tribute as had been promised. As soon as Phelles showed his face outside the gates of the royal palace, he was seized and bound by my guard and brought to the Temple of Astarte, where the appropriate rites were performed to restore the grace of Astarte to our city. At the conclusion of the rites, I strangled that dog Phelles on the altar of Astarte with my own hands, my priests holding his arms as my priestesses flayed the still struggling King. When taking control of a kingdom, the new king should leave no doubt as to who is in control and who should be feared.

Having established my rule in Tyre, appropriate treaties with Sidon and Byblos were renewed, which eventually led to my control of those Phoenician cites as well. The late King Phelles, as the fourth heir of his murdered father, felt that he was entitled to the great wealth of Tyre as a birthright. He ignored the looming threats outside our borders and over the seas, feeling that our treasury could solve any problem. To an extent it could. Rather than war, plunder and pillage which some of our neighbors practice as the extent of their art of diplomacy, our Phoenician cities made their way through the world with trade and far flung colonies and trading posts. Our accomplished ships and sailors gave us a great advantage over other cities on the sea, whose ships rarely dared venture out of sight of land.

Great wealth flowed into Tyre and Sidon, but to invade and besiege our cities would choke off our shipping, and dry up our wealth. But we were not defenseless. Attacking us risked offending our many trading partners who would come to our defense to protect the benefits they received in trade with us. Our ships were all Phoenician, the better to keep our skills to ourselves, but our populace consisted of merchants, traders, artisans, craftsmen, shipbuilders, warehousemen, diplomats, linguists, scribes, dock workers, draymen, slavers, silversmiths, jewelers, caravan leaders, musicians, singers and revelers. Our trade consumed all of our people, and to conscript our craftsmen and workers for our army would reduce the amount of trade we can handle and reduce our treasury, so we hired our army from our trading partners.

Our mercenary army was not large, but we could move our soldiers from province to province swiftly, depending where the greatest threat appeared. Many generations earlier Tyre protected itself with its trade and treaties, providing King Solomon of Israel with artisans and materials to build his royal city Jerusalem. Solomon's powerful kingdom was best dealt with peacefully, and his kingdom provided a useful buffer for us with the coastal Philistines to the south, who were more given to military adventures than trade. When Solomon's kingdom split, the kingdoms of Israel and Judah were content to war with each other. They were so occupied with their constant wars that they gave no thought to Tyre or Sidon or Byblos, allowing us to continue our trading while only manning a few isolated border outposts.

The Kingdom of Israel appeared to have no polity other than warring with the Kingdom of Judah and slaying their own kings on a regular basis. They continued to provide a useful buffer for us, pushing back against the Philistines during their regular incursions into Israel which kept the Philistines from our borders. This changed when army commander Omri became King of Israel. The wars against Judah to the South ceased, and Omri's kingdom began expanding, exacting tribute from Aram and Moab and Edom, kingdoms which had tried to push into

Israel in the past. Since Tyre and Sidon had not mounted any excursions against Israel, King Omri saw fit to let us alone.

What the unfortunate late King Phelles and his even later brother failed to recognize was that in less than ten years King Omri had built the most powerful kingdom in the region since the times of Solomon and that Tyre and Sidon had failed to establish any significant trading ties with Omri. King Omri was grateful that we could provide slaves from our provinces to help build his new capital of Samaria, but there was no sign that his influence would wane in the coming years. Sooner or later, if he had not thought of it already, King Omri would think of his unrivaled and accomplished army and with that thought he would think of the wealth that flowed through the ports of Tyre and Sidon, and realize that his capital was but a few days chariot ride away from the groaning docks in our ports.

King Phelles desired to leave well enough alone, trusting that King Omri would be content to graze his cattle and raise his crops in the fertile Jezreel valley, and never think of the wealth being unloaded each day on our docks. The Goddess Astarte is not so foolish, and her seers and divines made it known that if King Phelles failed to protect her holy city, a new king must be found who would.

King Omri was receptive to our overtures. Tribute from many nations flowed into Samaria, and now an alliance with Tyre and Sidon would allow some of our trade into his borders, while we gained the protection of King Omri's powerful army, allowing us to greatly reduce our expenditure for our mercenaries.

My daughter, princess Jezebel, had been installed as High Priestess of the Temple of Baal in Sidon. How fitting, that as her father I retained the position of High Priest of Astarte in Tyre, while my daughter became High Priestess of Astarte's consort Baal in Sidon. But Jezebel, young as she was, was far more capable than a mere High Priestess or princess. She had joined the priestesses of Astarte as they flayed the suffocating King Phelles. She was not shy in asserting the power of her god Baal.

Princess Jezebel would have made a fitting Queen of Tyre and Sidon, but her older brother Baal-Eser II had made his own reputation as a very young commander of a trading fleet and was becoming skilled as a diplomat. He would succeed me as King of Tyre. But what a fitting dowry for Jezebel, as she married into the royal family of King Omri, to have her brother waiting to assume the throne of Tyre and Sidon. Rather than relying on our mercenaries, Tyre could depend on the powerful army of

Israel, and Israel would grow even greater with its share of the trade from our ships. A land power and a sea power united. Astarte would continue to shower her beneficence on Tyre and Sidon, and Baal would show his power in Israel. My children may find themselves building an empire!

King Omri was eager to marry one of his sons to the princess Jezebel—I insisted on Omri's first born and future King. A union with wealthy Tyre and Sidon added significant prestige to the family of the former army commander. And the union with a nation with a powerful army also strengthened my position and prestige in Tyre against those who had been supporters of the short-lived King Phelles. The wisdom of the Goddess Astarte had become obvious to all.

Although accomplished in battle, the Israelites were mere junior apprentices in revelry. The rites and processions and ceremonies and feasts through temples and palaces that celebrated the union had the Israelites staggering before we had half begun. Those mutton and goat eaters had never tasted the wonder of the delicacies and wines placed before them.

❋   ❋   ❋

The Kingdom under King Omri was much more stable than under King Baasha. The incessant wars against the Kingdom of Judah had ceased. As commander of the army, Omri first found no satisfaction in battling fellow sons of Abraham, but after years of bitter conflict with the Kingdom of Judah Omri developed a deep disaffection with his distant relatives. The cessation of war with Judah did not bring a closer relationship with that kingdom. The palace, the army and the populace were content to have nothing to do with their former bitter enemy.

King Omri chose to ignore Judah, and the Kingdom of Judah was happy to return the favor. The treasuries of both countries had been strained by the constant state of war with their neighbor, which in turn weakened their stance with their other neighboring states. King Omri redirected his efforts to the North and East with great success. Years of constant warfare with Judah had hardened Omri's army to a point it was much more capable than many of the neighboring kingdoms. King Omri was very stingy with his army. A few initial sorties were sufficient to convince a neighboring kingdom that it would be better off paying Omri's price than waging a full-fledged war and risking destruction.

REFASHIONING SAMARIA

Jezebel

When your merchandise went out on the seas, you
satisfied many nations; with your great wealth and your
wares you enriched the kings of the earth. Ezekiel 27:33

T HE histories of the Israelites will not look favorably on me. Not
that they should. My history is not the history of Israel. I am of
Phoenicia, established well before Israel, and my history will extend beyond that of Israel, that nation split into two, waiting for a more powerful
kingdom to devour its remnants.

No one can give an account of Queen Jezebel except for Queen Jezebel. I am the weaver of dynasties. I am the daughter of King Ethbaal of
Sidon and Tyre, and will weave Israel and then its sister kingdom Judah
into the fabric of my dynasty. Before anyone had heard of the god of these
Israelites, our people were sailors wandering the seas. When we came
to these lands we saw forests fit for ship building; juniper for hulls and
beams, cedar for masts, oak for oars, cypress for decks. We traded with
Egypt for linen for our sails. No one could match our ships, and with our
ships, no one could match our commerce.

Tyre and Sidon have trading outposts in Cyprus, Sicily, Utica, Cadiz, Rhodes and even beyond the great sea. From beyond the great sea
we trade our glassware for gold and our purple fabric for tin, tin for the
bronze smiths. We would then trade our gold and tin throughout the
great sea, multiplying our glassware and fabric ten, twenty and thirty
fold. While our ships plied the seas, the plows of Israel plied the furrows,

and we would trade for their wheat, olive oil and honey with goods we had obtained at the cost of a few glass beads.

Sidon had created its sister city Tyre, and Tyre had a far flung empire. Sidon's old kings lost their control of Tyre. Tyre allied itself with King Solomon of Israel and grew wealthy and arrogant. I know history well. There is no place for weakness in kings. My father, son of a king of Sidon, was installed as High Priest in the temple of Astarte in Tyre and turned the tables on Tyre when he disposed of the King of Tyre, and brought Tyre and Sidon into the same fold.

My father knew that strength just as well as weakness can be exploited and Israel had both strengths and weaknesses to exploit. Israel had broken from Judah and rebelled against Solomon's son. Israel's strange god had his temple in Jerusalem and offerings had to be brought from Israel to Jerusalem. The new Kingdom of Israel built new temples, but the assassins who called themselves Kings of Israel could not hold their kingdom together. King Nadab was assassinated. King Elah was assassinated, and the assassin Zimri burned the palace down over his head when the army refused to follow yet another assassin.

The Philistines on the coast of the Great Sea bordering southern Israel were antagonistic toward Israel thanks to Israel's repeated incursions. King Nadab of Israel was assassinated by Baasha while besieging the Philistine city of Gibbethon and Israel was again besieging Gibbethon when King Baasha's son King Elah was assassinated by Zimri.

Aram from the north had attacked a whole swath of cities in Israel. King Asa of Judah, due to his experience of his wars with King Baasha, had garrisoned all of his walled cities, along with the cities in Israel that he had taken from Israel. King Asa of Judah all but strangled Israel with the treaty he made with Israel's powerful neighbor Aram.

Ahab's father, King Omri, successfully pushed back against these threats. Without a formal treaty he had let King Asa know he had no intention of continuing his predecessor King Baasha's constant wars. This freed up soldiers from Israel's southern border. Omri then selected his weakest neighbor, Moab, to the southeast, and in his first year's campaign marched far enough into to Moab to extract promises of substantial yearly tribute. Moab is still paying this tribute. With Israel border with Moab now secured, and financed with the tribute from Moab, Omri turned his attention to the southwest and pushed into Philistia. In addition to tribute, Omri collected from Philistia some border towns to provide a buffer zone. In his third year's campaign, Omri cautiously took on Aram, regaining year by year towns Aram had previously taken from Israel, and then extending his reach into Aram itself.

The cities of Phoenicia did not gain their dominance with armies on the land, but through trade over the seas and the skills of their merchants and craftsmen. Omri's expanding army and territory became a concern to us. With each year, Omri's army grew stronger, and his territory expanded. Tyre and Sidon rely on mercenaries for its army, but mercenaries drain away funds needed to grow our extensive fleet of trading ships. King Omri's domain of sheepherders and grain growers, as a result of King Asa of Judah's agreement with Aram when Baasha was King of Israel, had lost almost all of its trade routes with the outside world.

To protect Tyre and Sidon from King Omri's army, I was married to King Omri's son Ahab. My father, King Ethbaal, expanded Phoenicia's reach by establishing the city of Botrys to the north of Tyre, and the city of Auza in Libya. Both cities were ports and trading centers. With my marriage to Israel's royal house, I became the seed for a new colony of Tyre and Sidon inland. With the marriage, Israel benefited with added trade flowing into Samaria from Phoenicia. It was a marriage of a powerful army with the dominant trading fleet. It was also the marriage of two new, royal houses; the House of Ethbaal and the House of Omri. And I was the linchpin. Father Ethbaal was very artful. "Control their temples and you will control their kingdom," he told me. But their temples were far-flung, far to the south and far to the north—at their extreme borders! What foolishness. One thing the ancient King Jeroboam did not learn from his time in Jerusalem was centrality. The temple in Jerusalem was in the capital city, right next to the royal palace, near the primary markets in the city. Jeroboam built his temples in small towns; there was no reason to go to Dan or Bethel, and no reason to stay, except for the temples.

Samaria was a plum ripe for the plucking when our royal procession entered King Omri's capital after the nuptials in Sidon. King Omri had purchased this hill from some shepherd. Yes, purchased—a King purchased this land from his subject. This reinforced what I already knew about this land and its revered law. Their law decreed what transactions were allowed and were not allowed, and their law applied to all equally, King and subject alike. I understood that commerce and trade needed rules governing its transactions, but to bind a King?

The city of Samaria was brand new, and it looked like it had been built by a soldier. Ramparts and towers, impervious gates and sweeping views of the surrounding country side were its main features. The royal palace was suitably impressive for a King of Omri's stature, but utterly lacking in royal charm, grace and power.

Most notable was the absence in Samaria of anything that would have been called a temple in Tyre and Sidon. There were a few small buildings, some mere hovels, dedicated to various gods, even one dedicated to Baal, but they inspired the awe due a large latrine or small stable. Israel's first King, Jeroboam, was a renowned temple builder; first in Jerusalem for King Solomon, and then, after he rebelled from Solomon's son Rehoboam, he built Israel's temples to its golden calves, but he built his temples on Israel's far Northern border at Dan, and at its far Southern border at Bethel. It was not possible to build temples any further away from the capital. And what influence could they have with the palace if they were so far away?

Even after King Jeroboam built Israel its own temples, the people were still drawn to the temple in Jerusalem. This was a weakness that could not be allowed. Why were not those people punished for their disloyalty? And this god in Jerusalem; a god delivering its law to the people? What rubbish! The king is the law. But these people and their god! "Ask of the lord," they keep saying, "what does the lord say?" My priests will tell you what your gods say. What makes you think a god would be interested in talking to a plowman or a wool spinner? Your king will tell you what you want to know.

And their prophets! Damn their prophets! These prophets were not even from the temple in Jerusalem. Why is that allowed? Priests, if that's what those prophets are, are to be attached to a temple. How else are they to serve their god and their king? But these Israelites! They follow these prophets around, asking for a word from their god. They support these prophets, they shelter these prophets, and they hide these prophets. Is that not treason? If you want to hear your gods talk, go to the temples, you fools!

Yes, there was that temple in Jerusalem, the temple for all of these children of Abraham. But Jerusalem is so far away, and Judah was at war with Israel for so many years that fewer and fewer of my subjects continued to visit the temple in Jerusalem. And Samaria, the capital city of the nation, was a city without a temple, and without priests or priestesses.

As I said, Samaria was a plum.

My Lord Baal had to be honored, and a temple for Baal had to be built. As part of my marriage agreement, a suitable site for a temple for Baal was selected and plans drawn up. This would not be the Baal of

Samaria or the Rimmon of Damascus as they chose to call Baal in Aram. This would be the Baal of Queen Jezebel; Jezebel of Tyre and Sidon and now Jezebel of Samaria. No, I was not Queen yet, and my desire for a temple to my Lord Baal was seen as the whim of a homesick royal princess new to the House of Omri. But I would be Queen, and when I became Queen, my temple to Baal would be the Queen's Temple. What influence would those temples in faraway Bethel and Dan have when the magnificent temple to Baal would dominate the capital of Samaria, and within sight of the royal palace? My Temple would not start out magnificent, but with an understated majesty, and it would grow.

Our capital Samaria had the royal palace and the main markets of the kingdom, but I would make it a true capital by building a temple to Baal. I did not have to control the temples in Bethel and Dan. With a temple to Baal in Samaria, the temples in Bethel and Dan would wither on the vine. King Ethbaal provided me with a sizeable escort of priests of Baal to accompany me on my trip to Samaria as their new Queen. I was a priestess of Baal, and there was no one in Samaria to minister to me. And of course I a needed temple of Baal built in Samaria—close to the royal palace—I was the Queen after all—where I could worship the Lord Baal. King Ethbaal saw to it that additional priests of Baal were sent to oversee the construction of the temple in Samaria, and then more priests from Sidon and Tyre were needed to work in the temple.

The citizens of Samaria were reluctant to build a temple to a foreign god. They clung to their national gods, those golden calves, somehow connected to their mythic sojourn in Egypt. A few swore by the temple in Jerusalem. Several unfortunate courtiers found themselves outside the palace for suggesting in my presence that Lord Baal was a foreign god. "I am the Queen of Israel. Are you suggesting I am foreign to you? Are you suggesting I do not belong in the royal palace? The Lord Baal is my god. As long as I am the Queen of Israel, Baal is not a foreign god." To replace these rebellious courtiers, more priests of Baal were required from Tyre and Sidon.

As the temple grew, so did the number or priests of Baal in Samaria. All of my affairs as Queen were handled by priests of Baal. Gradually, when it was discovered that dealing with the palace required dealing with priests of Baal, more citizens of Samaria found themselves in training to be priests of Baal.

Oh how I love my temples. And soldiers. Soldiers in temples I find irresistible. I am Queen. I cannot be resisted. The good soldiers I make my personal priests. What cause has Ahab to complain? Soldiers drop like flies on the battlefields; Ahab can always find more soldiers if he needs them.

But too many soldiers and too many priests can cause problems. Only three times have I had a bastard. But power, oh what power they gave me. What awe and wonder and fear these Israelites held me in. Bow down to your gods. Bow down to me! Those little demons would shriek and wail; their limbs jerk and twist; their backs arch as their skin sizzled and spat and smoked. And the people! Thousands of them on the ground, faces in the dirt, groveling at my feet. I held them down for two hours. Do you want to live? You must bow until you hear my voice. And what a frenzy when they were let up. Worship! Ecstasy! You have been spared! My child for your god, for your kingdom, for your lives. What power!

One I spared. But dynasties must be careful. No bastard can be a pretender to the throne, a threat to the dynasty. But he was not told who he was, so he cannot pretend. And he was castrated. He has served me for years as a eunuch in the palace. He was told of the terrible fate I saved him from. Service to your Queen is now demanded for your life. Unless you want to be ungrateful. He still serves, the ignoramus. He must wonder why I sometimes laugh so hard when he enters the temple in my procession. It never ceases to amuse me. Someday I think I will offer him in the fire, and as he burns I will whisper in his ear who he is.

Samaria was well on its way to looking like Tyre and Sidon, albeit without the port or docks. There was nothing standing in the way to Samaria being pulled closer and closer to its Phoenician sisters. Plans were underway for an exchange of visits between King Ahab of Samaria and King Baal-Eser II of Tyre, my brother. Phoenicia may soon be able to claim an inland kingdom, bound by treaty and blood to their mighty port cities and their overseas possessions. And with the temple of Baal in Samaria, there seemed to be no limit in sight to the power arising from this unlikely union.

POTTERS, PROPHETS
AND DYNASTIES
Jezebel

Shout louder! Surely he is a god! Perhaps he is deep in
thought, or busy, or traveling. Maybe he is sleeping and
must be awakened. Elijah, I Kings, 18:27

I WAS well on the way to winning the battle of the temples. Ignoring
the temples in Bethel and Dan took no great art. They were supported
by royal patronage as a lure to keep our subjects from worshiping in
Jerusalem and patronage can wane. But this land was rife with prophets;
prophets that did not come out of the temples in Bethel and Dan. These
prophets could be seen in Samaria and the entire countryside when I first
came to Samaria, but they seemed to breed into a plague as the temple to
Baal was being built in Samaria, until they were worse than locusts by the
time Ahab became King.

I knew where these prophets came from. If you pressed them, and I
had many well-pressed by the time I was done with them, they would say
that their god of Israel can only be worshiped in the temple in Jerusalem.
It was subterfuge. King Asa of Judah, the keeper of that temple in Jerusalem, was known to support them, and Asa had been King of Judah for
thirty-eight years when Ahab ascended to the throne.

Under Asa's successor, King Jehoshaphat, things only got worse.
The Kingdom of Judah had grown strong and prosperous under King
Jehoshaphat. Jehoshaphat's father King Asa had been at war with King
Baasha of Israel for almost all of Baasha's twenty-four year reign. When

King Asa bribed the King of Aram to break its treaty with King Baasha, Baasha had to withdraw his forces against Judah to protect its borders with Aram, allowing King Jehoshaphat to inherit the resulting peace.

King Jehoshaphat succeeded his father Asa in King Ahab's fourth year. All of his prophets, and that land is thick with those prophets or Levites or priests, whipped the people up to support Jehoshaphat. King Jehoshaphat fortified the towns that his father King Asa captured from King Baasha of Israel; the Philistines on the coast to their south brought him silver and other tribute. The Arabs paid tribute of flocks of rams and goats. He built forts and store cities in Judah. He kept a standing army of experienced soldiers in Jerusalem, and with the reserve he could call up from the provinces, he could field an army of such size that any thought of enlarging our territory at the expense of the Kingdom of Judah was an invitation to disaster.

I told Ahab that if he did not want Jehoshaphat's prophets swaying his people toward that temple in Jerusalem after he became King, they would have to be eradicated.

"Do you want to be swallowed whole by King Jehoshaphat? He is not a friendly, harmless uncle, Ahab. He grows stronger every day. He does not have to send an army against Samaria to conquer. You may not see his siege towers growing yet, but his miners are tunneling under your walls as you sleep in your bed. It is his prophets. He breeds them in Jerusalem and they grow like mildew on your robes and rot on your timbers and when it is too late you will see your walls collapsing into the caverns he has dug under your walls.

There was one old prophet, the potter they called him, who was a constant plague. This potter was cunning. He would send his followers into the small towns and villages. "The word of the Lord," they would proclaim. They would wander over the hills, proclaiming the "word of the Lord" to every sheep herder and sickle wielder they ran into. They would chase down caravans, harangue olive growers in their groves, and weavers at their looms. Before I married Ahab, they would stand on the roads to Bethel and Dan, even at the gates of the cities and the steps of their temples and condemn the sin of worshiping Jeroboam's golden calves.

I had been content to allow the prophets to attack the temples in Dan and Bethel. They would chase the mindless sheep away from Bethel and Dan, and I would herd them into the grand temple to Baal we were building in Samaria. There could be a place for those prophets in my kingdom. But as soon as the corner stone was laid in Samaria for the temple of Baal, the prophets left their pickets at Dan and Bethel and flooded into the country side. Forgotten were the golden calves. Now they harped on the temple of Baal. No, they harped on Lord Baal himself. An abomination they called my Lord Baal. My priestesses were harlots. The rites offered to Baal they called a curse on the land. Their worst they saved for me. I was the grand whore monger; the corrupter of the nation.

The prophets forgot one thing. I would become the Queen. King Omri still thought of himself as an Israelite. The god these prophets claimed was the god of the Israelites, golden calves or not, and King Omri, so decisive on the battle field, could not bring himself to condemn them. I beseeched King Omri, on my knees with many tears, a crushed woman, humiliated and forlorn by the unfair insults of those cruel prophets.

"I have served my Lord Baal for all my life. I made a pledge to my dear father Ethbaal that I would not forsake the god of my native land, I swore on the head of my dear mother. And now these wretched men curse me for keeping my pledge to my parents."

Moved, yes, King Omri was moved, but he said that the same prophets continually chastised him for maintaining Jeroboam's temples.

"You are young, my child, you have much to learn before becoming Queen. Learn to forebear with the prophets. They have much good to say to the people, take the good with the bad. I have ignored them for years. They have given up on me. Maybe they will tire of you in a season as well."

To Ahab in our chambers I raged.

"This is not their kingdom, Ahab. They cannot be allowed to curse me once I have become Queen. I will not allow it. You will not allow it! Can a subject curse their Queen? Will you allow it? If the people see those prophets cursing their Queen and you do not stop it, they will laugh at me, Ahab! They will laugh at you! What kind of king allows his subjects to curse his Queen? If you fear to act against them, every rebel and malcontent will smell blood and we will be struck down before our first year is over. Swear to me that you will hunt these prophets down like dogs when you become King. Swear it to me, Ahab!"

And I was right. Perhaps those prophets smelled blood. Perhaps they thought that Ahab would be a weaker King than Omri, that they would be able to push Ahab around. But ever since I had first set foot in Samaria, the constant drone of the prophets became louder and louder, and as the temple of Baal rose from its foundations, their condemnations grew louder as the temple walls grew higher.

I knew of their god in the temple in Jerusalem, but now I began to call their god the cursing god. The insistent prophets began to recite every curse from their god that their scribes had written down. They began standing outside the temple of Baal as it was being built trying to frighten people away with their god's curses for following Baal; plagues, wasting diseases, scorching heat, drought and blight. They were imaginative, those prophets were. They called down curses of a bronze sky over an iron ground with a rain of dust and powder; your carcasses will be food for the birds and wild animals; curses of madness, blindness and confusion. These same prophets had harangued King Omri throughout his reign over the golden calves, but his powerful army and the wealth of Samaria made it easy for the citizens of Samaria to scoff at them. King Omri was happy to shoo them out of the city. Then they would carry on at the city gates, so we paid street urchins to hurl dung at them. I could not constantly complain to the King about the prophets, he still had his fond childhood memories of the temple in Jerusalem, and maybe harbored fantasies of being the new King Solomon. The prophets were still of "his people," and that was the problem. I will rule through Baal, and my Lord Baal is the Baal of Tyre and Sidon.

In one way I agreed with the prophets and their cursing god. The prophets wailed, "The foreigners who reside among you will rise above you higher and higher, but you will sink lower and lower. They will be the head, but you will be the tail."

"Ironic," I thought, "if only these cursing prophets knew. They may as well have been present at the councils with my father Ethbaal I, my brother Baal-Eser II and our prophets of Baal and Astarte." The Lord Baal will unite Israel with Tyre and Sidon. King Omri's army will replace our mercenaries and protect us from the rumblings we could hear growing beyond the Euphrates. But the prophets? Once King Omri died, the prophets would no longer be our "people." Rather than bother King Omri, our prophets of Baal formed their own temple guard. The streets of the capital were cleared of prophets, and there was one less headache for the King.

❋   ❋   ❋

By the time King Omri died, the original temple of Baal had almost been finished. The highly esteemed King Omri inspired even more awe with a temple of Baal from Tyre and Sidon in his capital. This alliance with Tyre and Sidon suggested he was extending his influence even over the seas. I saw it from a different perspective, but as long as the temple was being built, King Omri could think whatever he wished.

King Omri's death was timely. As Queen-in-waiting, I realized there were limits to how many priests of Baal should be seen in the palace, and how large the temple of Baal should become. King Omri's occasionally furrowed brow suggested that we had reached his limits. How fortuitous, thank you Lord Baal, that it was exactly at that point that King Omri died.

My husband Ahab had seen the temple of Baal grow under King Omri. He had seen the priests of Baal take over many functions in the palace and the city. Once King Omri was gone, there were no limits. My priests of Baal were just as efficient and effective as the Israelites they replaced. Ahab had also seen the wealth and commerce that the temple of Baal brought to Israel's capital of Samaria and the wealth that King Omri's treaties with Sidon and Tyre had brought to his kingdom. The strength of King Omri's kingdom was due in no small part to these treaties, and I was the surety. The priests of Bethel and Dan complained that they were being cut off, or maybe just ignored. But they were from backwaters in the kingdom. Samaria made the kingdom great, not those small towns.

He was a young man, ruddy, wearing ragged skins, with strong arms like a quarry man. Perhaps he was two years younger than me. He would have made a fine priest of Baal. But he was a follower of one of these prophets. Less than a week after the death of King Omri he had the temerity to climb the steps of the temple of Baal in Samaria and condemn all those entering. My priests waited until they heard his entire tirade, waiting for him to speak against the King or Queen. Perhaps he had been carefully instructed not to condemn the royal household. But he spoke against the Queen's temple and that was enough. He was brought to me in the grand assembly room in the palace where King Omri had lain on his bier a few days earlier.

"Prophet, my scribe has just read to me the words you spoke on the steps of the temple of Baal. Are those your words?"

"They are," answered the undisingenuous man of god, a look of bewildered wonder and fear on his face. Perhaps the flaccid acting King Omri made him believe he had license to blaspheme my Lord Baal.

"Do you know, young prophet, that the words you speak against the temple of Baal are words you speak against your Queen, since the temple of Baal is your Queen's temple."

"There is only one Lord God in Israel, the God of Abraham, Isaac and Jacob."

"Baal is in his temple! Have you forgotten Baal?"

"Baal is not a god. Baal is a dumb idol. Baal . . ."

"Silence! You have left me no choice. But I will give you a choice. Do you wish to be struck down here, or in the temple of Baal?" It was a brilliant idea that had just struck me. Who would not want to extend his life, if only for the few minutes it would take for him to be brought to the temple of Baal, and then I could sacrifice one of those cursed prophets on the altar of Baal.

The prophet gaped at me open mouthed, I would not give him time to curse me.

"Speak! Here or Baal?"

"Baal? Never Baal. I would . . ."

"Strike him! Now! Strike him down!"

When taking over a kingdom, one must leave no doubt who is in charge and who is to be feared.

It was a waste of blood to see it flow on the floor of the palace rather than on the altar to Baal, but the prophet's words could not be left unchallenged. Ahab still thought of himself as one of these children of Abraham, Isaac and Jacob, and I could not allow these rabble time to sway Ahab. If Ahab was swayed, then the prophets would have time to sway the people, and if the people were swayed, then Baal would be questioned.

If I allowed Baal to be questioned, then Tyre and Sidon would remain to be seen as foreign nations. If Baal is accepted, then Samaria, Tyre and Sidon would become sisters, and Jerusalem would be a solitary orphan lost in the wilderness. The life of a worthless prophet was a small price to pay.

One does not receive a burial for sedition and blasphemy. The body of the prophet was dragged outside of the walls and deposited in the dung heap built up by the oxen on the grounds of the threshing floors during harvest season. His wailing brother prophets were beaten off until the deceased had been properly endungeoned. How fitting to have them clamber through the mire to claim the fruits of their labor.

The prophets were fittingly quiet for the next several seasons. I had hoped it was fear, but it may just have been a period of mourning. But it was refreshingly quiet in the city without those cursing prophets.

With the prophets quieted, the temple to Baal continued to expand. Not only did Baal's temple increase, so also did my own temple—my dynasty. My daughter Athaliah was married to Jehoram, King Jehoshaphat's son from the vaunted house of David and Solomon. Three dynasties—the House of Ethbaal, the House of Omri and now the House of David! The Phoenician cities of Sidon and Tyre, Israel and Judah all joined together, and I am the linchpin, securing Phoenicia to the Kingdom of Judah. Athaliah is truly my daughter. She understands dynasties and she detests weakness. Old King Jehoshaphat of Judah, Jehoram's father, gave his other sons cities to rule and treasuries. He was a kind-hearted, weak old fool. So many royal sons with so much power is less power for the king. A little wine, a few days at a festival, a comparison of grievances, underlings with too much to gain prodding their masters on and you have a rebellion. Matters would have to be attended to in due time. There could be no chinks in the wall of my dynasty.

❈　　❈　　❈

After Athaliah left for her kingdom in Judah, word came to Samaria of this old prophet reappearing - the potter - and he was actually a potter. A potter! A master of clay! Filth under his fingernails, back bowed from bending over the wheel, eyebrows singed from peering into the kiln. A potter of all things! And not just a potter, a teacher. What sort of idiocy he teaches I could not say, but he had a school of sorts, or at least he had a ragged band of adherents that saw to his needs and hung on his every word. I had pushed the temples at Bethel and Dan into the background, but this potter swore by the temple in Jerusalem. And the temple of Jerusalem has no room for other gods. Has this potter forgotten whose kingdom he treads on? Jerusalem is not the capital of the Kingdom of Israel. But the temple of Jerusalem and this potter-prophet says that my subjects are the Lord's people. The Lord, always the Lord. "Thus says the Lord," this maker of pots is wont to say. Do his pots speak to him? Does the whirling of his wheel entrance him? Do the tongues of flame in his kiln give him his mysterious oracles?

We had heard about this potter turned prophet, Elijah was his name, but had never seen him until he appeared at the gates of Samaria. Yes he was cunning. He did not venture onto the steps of the temple of Baal as his young, unfortunate follower had, but by simply showing his face at the gates of Samaria he inspired wonder in these hill-bound simpletons.

"Ahab, dispatch this blasphemer from your kingdom, or I will send to Tyre for a king who will." I was to be feared, but I could not afford to be the hated. If I sent out the guard from the temple of Baal to dispatch this potter, I would be the Queen from Sidon striking out at a prophet of their ancient god who delivered them from Egypt. The foolishness! Even their priests at Dan and Bethel told them that the golden calves delivered them from Egypt, but these goat and mutton eaters clung to their ancient superstitions. So it fell to Ahab to deal with him, a true Israelite, son of the great King Omri.

Ahab went out to the gates of the city to confront the old potter. But there was no confrontation. The old prophet did not hold forth against the temple of Baal or the Sidonian Queen or the prophets of Baal. The prophet's audience had grown as word spread that the King was on his way to the city gates. With all but half the city at the gates, the old prophet raised his staff and voice, as if pronouncing a king's decree:

"As the Lord, the God of Israel, lives, whom I serve, there will be neither dew nor rain in the next few years except at my word."

He was sly, that old potter. He spoke no treason. He issued no condemnation of the King or Queen. He simply said there would be a drought. He did not say why his deity decreed a drought, but he decreed it in the face of the King. Even these plow steerers of Samaria could divine the prophet's condemnation.

Perhaps Ahab would have said something to take the venom out of the prophet's curse. Perhaps Ahab would have shown a kindness, or cunning, by showing hospitality to the tired old traveler by inviting him to the royal palace. That would have impressed the crowds at the gate. But the old man did not wait for any response. It was clear he intended to deliver his judgment and brook no appeal. No sooner were the words out of his mouth than he turned on his heel, dashed away from the gates and was gone.

"This is treachery. This prophet is telling your subjects that you are cursed, that their god is punishing the land because you are King. And now his followers are spreading the same venom across the country side."

We fought a battle against that drought. Our soldiers were in every country and looked in every cave in the kingdom. Our swords were not silent. Many couriers delivered their lists of dead prophets to the palace.

The god of these prophets could only relent when it saw the power of my Lord Baal against its prophets. And relent it did. After pursuing that prophet Elijah for three years, Elijah suddenly shows himself to Ahab and says his god was sending rain to the land. "It is my Lord Baal that is sending the rain, Ahab. Baal has overcome that god of the Israelites. We have destroyed its prophets; we have shorn its power."

The old potter Elijah had been around from the days of King Baasha, and all during Omri's reign. He may have fashioned himself as a spokesman for his deity, but prophet or not, he was an agent for the Kingdom of Judah. His god! Always his god! And who was his god? The god of the temple in Jerusalem. If the prophets of the god of the temple in Jerusalem wanted to rule it over Israel, that was treason. Ahab had to know that to pander to these prophets was to abdicate his throne. And Ahab? These Israelites cannot get this god thing out of their heads.

Omri had been an army man. He did not plan or scheme to be King. He understood that as the army commander his duty was to his King, but he did not grasp what being King meant. He maintained the army; he moved the royal palaces from Tizrah to the more defensible Samaria. One thing Omri never mastered was control of the nation's temples. These Israelites and their strange golden calves; "worship these; it's the same as worshiping the god of Israel in Jerusalem."

"Jerusalem, you drunken, senseless children, that's your enemy! Have you forgotten King Baasha's wars with Judah?" My father King Ethbaal could see that Israel was a field ready for plowing. Ahab knew that he was a rudderless ship. He would allow himself to be driven onto the reefs of his peoples' old fables of burning bushes and smoking mountains and old potters speaking for the only god they dared acknowledge. Despite inheriting his father Omri's powerful kingdom, now strengthened further with access to the wealth of Phoenicia, Ahab could not part from the legend of their strange god setting this people apart from the rest of the peoples. What arrogance from a tribe of sheep shearers and grape pressers. As long as Ahab allowed the prophets of that god to roam the countryside, these people would remain married to their hills and valleys and resist transforming this kingdom into something truly great. I did not consent to being married to Ahab so I could hold court with rough sandaled prophets and wheat threshers.

But Ahab had not learned to control his country or his temples. "It's the God of Israel," he would lament. And I could not help but to scream at him: "The god of Israel is in Jerusalem! Are you the King of Jerusalem?

Your old kingdom is over. Your god did that! Didn't some old prophet of your god anoint that rebel Jeroboam? *You* are the King of Israel! Do these prophets support the King of Israel? No? Then *Kill* them!" Ahab could only wring his hands. He knew what had to done, but he could not do it. So I did. I taught those prophets who was King.

But Ahab! He just could not strap on his sword and deal with it. The army. He was comfortable with the army, maybe too comfortable. He had spent a lot of time with his father in the camp. He became a capable commander, but outside the camp he was adrift. "You have to deal with this, Ahab!" Left to himself, Ahab was a child. And Elijah knew it.

"A contest between that prophet and my priests? There is no contest! Kill him! Had you left your sword at the palace? He was right in front of you! And you couldn't kill him?"

No he couldn't. So he let Elijah put on a show and wins over the crowd.

"And killed my priests? All of them? They were my priests, Ahab! Mine! Why did you let that happen? I don't care where the fire came from, you fool! I can make fire! If you let them kill my prophets, why shouldn't they kill you?"

So Elijah incites the people to kill four hundred and fifty of my prophets, including some of my dear soldiers. These men had been carefully chosen and groomed to haul the ship of Israel off of its isolated hills and launch it onto the seas, and now they all lie slain.

"But Ahab, you were out to kill him." Ahab could only hang his head. Pathetic. How long can he remain as King if he is allowed to be baited like that? The god of Israel! Those magicians play on these old superstitions.

I sent Ahab out hunting for Elijah and his followers, with the master of the royal household, Obadiah. We had already put a good number of their prophets to death. If they were not dead, they were in hiding. But Elijah had fled. If we had killed him, we would have known. We had messengers and spies travelling to every nation we knew of. If their king was not friendly they would find their kinsmen temple worshipers. "Has Elijah come this way? Have you heard where he is?"

But I am Queen. I sent my own royal decree out. "Do you think you no longer have to hide because you murdered my prophets, Elijah? Were you in fear for your life when Ahab was searching for you? You have not felt fear yet, Elijah. You will be as dead as my prophets by tomorrow, or may my gods strike me down." He knew he could not bargain or persuade or fool me with his showmanship. So he fled. I burn every time I think of that magician still being alive. But he is in hiding. And his followers, if there are any left, are in hiding also. So he is as good as dead.

I would have kept searching for Elijah until I found him, but King Ben-Hadad of Aram attacked, and for two years we were in fear of losing our kingdom.

AHAB PONDERS

Ahab

One who puts on his armor should not boast like one
who takes it off. King Ahab, I Kings 20:11

QUEEN Jezebel just will not tolerate the prophets of the Lord. And
why not? From Moses to the Judges, from the time of King Saul
and King David and King Solomon there have been prophets of the Lord
with our people. But she will not accept this. "We are kings and queens,"
she says, "we will not hand our kingdom over to those diviners and
soothsayers." Maybe she is right. If the prophet Ahijah saw fit to anoint
Jeroboam to take the kingdom from Solomon's son, maybe our people are
meant to be divided. This is our land and we shall rule it. And if Ahijah
anointed Jeroboam, and Jeroboam saw fit to make our calves to worship,
aren't these prophets who harp on and on about our calves destroying
what Ahijah and Jeroboam built? Should we worship in Jerusalem? That's
laughable. It has been over sixty years since Jeroboam became King, and
the small trickle of people that continued to go Jerusalem for the festivals
has all but dried up. Worship in Jerusalem? My people do not know what
that means.

My father Omri would listen to the prophets. Most of the time he
would laugh. But he liked the old traditions. He could remember going to
Jerusalem as a child. Sometimes as often as three times a year. He would
tell us stories. We would have liked to see the Temple in Jerusalem. It
sounded wonderful. Was not Solomon our father too? Were we not all
Israelites then? But father Omri reminded us sternly that he was now

King of Israel. He did not strive to be King, but once he was acclaimed as King he would fight to protect his kingdom and his throne to the last drop of blood.

My father Omri was a hard man. He had spent his life in King Baasha's army, fighting battle after battle with King Asa of Judah. He had lost many a good soldier in those wars. He had lost his taste for Jerusalem during the bloodshed. So many darts and arrows and spears had been hurled at him by King Asa's soldiers that he stopped thinking of them as Abraham's children. His chariot had been upset so many times in battle that the only tradition he wanted to share with his brother Israelites was that of the slaughter. But he still had his boyhood memories. Somehow he kept those separate. It was like he lived in two different worlds at times. I envied my father's memories, but I did not share them. We had a common history with that kingdom to the south, we had shared common traditions, but that was gone. They did nothing to sustain my kingdom.

And the prophets? I think they shared the same memories as me and my father. And they used those memories for their own purposes. Jezebel is devout. Life for her is her temples. I do not bother to tell her about the memories of my father. She would not recognize them. She knows who her gods are, and they certainly are not the gods of the people in Jerusalem who year after year fought us. "Gods are not like that," she says. "They are either for you or against you. They are not on both sides at the same time." I cannot argue about gods with her. But I do listen to the prophets. I will listen to what the prophets of Baal and Asherah say as well, but I find I do not think like them. They know nothing of our ancestors Abraham, Isaac and Jacob, and do not care for my stories about them. But with Jezebel and the alliance with the cities of Phoenicia, the wealth and name of this kingdom have grown. Maybe Jezebel's gods had something to do with that.

My father Omri told me to keep an ear turned to the prophets. A prophet said that the Lord was going to bring the House of Baasha down, and shortly later Zimri kills Baasha's son King Elah. And not just King Elah, the entire house of Baasha. Whoever may have tried to claim the throne by invoking the name of Baasha met the sword, along with anyone who would try to invoke sympathy for the house of Baasha for their own advantage. My father would tell me, "The kingdom fell to me on the word of a prophet. Someone could try to take it away the same way. Listen to the prophets."

But Elijah was impossible to listen to. "Do away with the Baals," he would say, over and over again. I think he meant to get rid of Jezebel. And our children too? That would be his next demand. He would never be satisfied. Should I just surrender the kingdom to Judah? After Jezebel lost her prophets at the hands of Elijah she was consumed with tracking down Elijah. Her only comfort was detailing the ways she would end his life, and the life of anyone that gave him a night's rest in a bed, or a drink of water, or directions to the next town, and how she would pull their house down and fill their well. Elijah fled into the wilderness. Some reports had him going in the direction of Aram. Strange that he would not seek out his god in the Temple in Jerusalem, but then he knew we had our spies in Jerusalem night and day.

I suspect Elijah did flee to Aram, since within months of Elijah fleeing, King Ben-Hadad of Aram descends on us with an alliance of thirty-two other kings, leaders of cities and provinces beholden to him. Wherever Elijah had fled to, I had to give up the search. If he had been in Aram, he must have left Aram by the time Ben-Hadad was dragging his siege engines over our borders. There were no demands from Aram to tear down our temples or the Baals Jezebel re-erected after Elijah fled. No, Ben-Hadad just wanted gold and silver, and my wives of his own choosing, and my brightest children. I think the demand for children was just to humiliate me; they would have been put to the sword or sold as soon as they were delivered.

But I capitulated. We were stripping the palace and the temples of gold, silver and bronze to meet Ben-Hadad's demands for plunder. For Ben-Hadad, he would not have to exhaust his army and treasury in a lengthy siege. First, Aram's army would have had to battle over the plains surrounding Samaria to force us behind the walls of Samaria. Then they would have to start their siege of the city. With the size of the army accompanying Ben-Hadad, it would be less than a week before we would be forced behind the walls, but sieges could last for months, if not years, tying down Ben-Hadad's entire army. As for Israel, we would become a little poorer, but Samaria would be saved, its walls and gates would not be undermined or battered, its citizens would not be starved, and Aram would withdraw, allowing us to go back to our fields and pastures.

But capitulation was not enough for this Ben-Hadad. Before we could deliver our gold and silver another courier from Aram's army is at the city gate with a new demand:

> At this time tomorrow I am going to send my officials to search
> your palace and the houses of your officials. They will seize ev-
> erything you value and carry it away.

I knew what this meant. I was willing to pay Ben-Hadad his tribute
or plunder or extortion to keep his army from sweeping through the city
and pillaging it, but now he wanted me to let his army into the city and
ransack it without having to breach the wall and fight his way in. The
people of the city were terrified. They had heard tales from relatives in
our border towns that had been besieged and then burned to the ground.
So I summoned the elders of the city and put the question to them. One
cannot hold a city under siege if the people are in rebellion. The elders
concluded that to let Ben-Hadad's army into the city would have the same
result as if they had breached the walls. If Ben-Hadad wanted us to issue
him a license to rape, pillage and burn, he would have to fight his way in.
The message I gave to Ben-Hadad's couriers was concise:

> Tell my lord the King, your servant will do all you demanded the
> first time, but this demand I cannot meet.

Ben-Hadad's reply was swift in coming. We could see his tents from
the towers on the city walls. Ben-Hadad was also concise:

> May the gods deal with me, be it ever so severely, if enough dust
> remains in Samaria to give each of my men a handful.

The Aramean couriers were smug. They were grinning like jackals
as they glared around the palace at the treasures they planned on ripping
off the walls and hoisting over their heads once the entire Aramean army
was let through the gates of the city. Their glares were not limited to treasures. They raped every woman they saw with their eyes, nudging each
other as they pointed out their claims. Theirs was a studied avaricious-
ness. Their display was for the benefit of me and my army commanders,
to convince us that the battle had already been decided.

I was putting on my own display. My army commanders were not
with me in the throne room as I received these Arameans. I had let the
Arameans in the city rather than receive them in my tents in the army's
camp to give them the impression they have already conquered. I rounded
up some bedraggled sheep herders, old men and even a few beggars and
put them in commanders' armor, and put some emaciated youths behind
them as soldiers. The Aramean forces already had the advantage over us,

but I needed these couriers to take back reports to King Ben-Hadad that Samaria was at his mercy.

After Ben-Hadad's scroll that the couriers brought in was read to me by a scribe, I asked that the scribe hand it to me. I did not ask my scribe to take down my capitulation as the Arameans expected. Instead, I looked at the scroll in my hands as if studying every mark on it. I then looked up at the Aramean couriers, still smirking rather undiplomatically at me, and tossed their scroll at my feet, keeping my gaze on the couriers. The couriers tilted their heads curiously, wondering why this soon to be chained former King was acting so strangely. Then I spoke directly to them.

"Tell your King Ben-Hadad this. One who puts on his armor should not boast like one who takes it off."

The couriers grinned back at me, waiting for more. They had expected me to get down on my knees and beg for mercy. They waited longer, waiting for me to dictate my capitulation to my scribe. I continued to return their stares, saying nothing. Finally I flicked the back of my hand at them, as if shooing a fly, dismissing them.

THE ROUT OF THE ARAMEANS

Ahab

If they have come out for peace, take them alive; if they
have come out for war, take them alive. King Ben-Hadad,
I Kings 20: 18

T HE palace and the city were silent as the Aramean couriers were
ushered out of the city gates. We had kept our dignity, but there
was a deep sense of dread. I led my commanders back to the army's camp
to prepare for battle, but there was little hope that we would be able to
hold off the Arameans before we retreated behind the gates of Samaria
to endure a siege. And the siege? No one dared speak of how we would
be able to survive a siege with the number of kingdoms, tribes and cities
allied with the Arameans against us.

As I arrived at my tent in the army's camp, I was told that I had a
visitor waiting for me. Perhaps an answer to our pleas to Jerusalem for
aid? Instead, waiting for me in my tent is Elijah who looked like he had
crawled out of some hole where he was hiding. He had made it to a sentry
outside my camp, and chariot commander Jehu had him ushered into
my tent. This Jehu still put stock in these prophets. This prophet would
have never dared to show his face at the palace as long as Jezebel and her
prophets were there. Now this prophet now stood face-to-face with me.

"The word of the Lord," he says. "Now God is on my side?" I wonder.
"You don't want me to tear down my Baals? You are here to help?"

"Here's how to battle Ben-Hadad" he says. But Jehu was taken aback
once this prophet laid out his plan.

"Could this be a trap, my lord," Jehu wondered. "The prophets of the Lord have cause to see you harmed. The Queen has pursued them mercilessly."

I just didn't have that feeling. No prophet of the Lord had ever hesitated to condemn me to my face if that was the message he was tasked to deliver. And one thing I had learned, offensive as these prophets of the Lord could be, they did not deal in subterfuge. The prophet's plan, if that's what you could call it, did give me reason to question his honesty. But I have learned to respect the prophets, even though they condemn Jezebel. Besides, Jehu insisted on personally guarding me with his chariots. If the prophet's plan was a ruse, Jehu's chariots would be standing by to snatch me out before any ambush could be sprung.

I always wondered about some of Elijah's prophecies when we were out in the field. Some of his prophecies came out as outlandish strategy and tactics; were these the words of his god, or was he just a wily old man? But what did he know of military tactics, and how did he know how Ben-Haddad and his allies would react to his trickery? I think this prophet just hatched a clever trick and Ben-Haddad fell for it. So we did what the prophet told us to do. We assembled the youngest striplings from each of our 232 provincial commanders; some of these weren't even soldiers; some were old enough to be armor bearers, some were a year or two from being soldiers, and then certainly not in the vanguard. They spent most of their idle time in the camp getting used to the heft of a sword or lance, the pull of the bow.

But Elijah had them advance on their own, right up to the pickets of the Arameans. When Ben-Hadad's scouts reported the advance, he was sure it wasn't an attack.

"Children! Does he think we'll be exhausted from hacking their children to death that we can no longer fight?" It was pure scorn, and bewilderment.

No one had ever heard of this happening. Ben-Haddad and his thirty-two kings and satraps had been assembled in Ben-Haddad's tent getting drunk; all decided to stay and keep drinking. A wave of relief swept over the Aramean front lines and into the reserves. Word of an unexpected advance by the Israelites had sent the entire camp scrambling; strapping on armor, looking for their commander or their troops, running to find mislaid weapons, rounding up startled horses, moving the baggage wagons out of the way. Now comes word that the kings are drinking, celebrating the beginning of a great victory! There was to be no battle today! They were not assembled, no one was in formation. They stood watching to see how victory would unfold.

Then laughter, relief, mockery. "Two hundred? A line of two hundred? Boys? Not a man among them?" There was to be no battle, no wounds, no shed blood. King Ben-Haddad's directive filters through the camp: "If they come out for peace, take them alive. If they come out for war, take them alive." Whoops go up. Hostages will be taken. Then terms for their release and for surrender. Horses were released, weapons laid down or stacked up, bets placed, calves and goats rounded up for the feast.

I was in my chariot within sight of the young men as the Arameans ambled out to round up the youngsters, Jehu and his chariot is to my right ready to turn me around and run me back behind our front line if they rush me. "What foolishness," I think, "How did I get talked into this?"

"Is the army ready, Jehu?"

"Yes, my Lord, just behind your chariots."

The chariots were lined up behind us. Should the Arameans charge us through the thin line of young boys we had sent ahead, the chariots could blunt their charge and give the army the time to advance and give me time to join with the army.

Then something caught my ear, the young boys were singing as the Arameans got within spear range of them; a children's song, with the tune going up and down the scale. I could hear the Arameans laughing, jabbing each other in the ribs, "What fools these Israelites," they must be saying. They stopped within an arm's length of the boys, laughing and smiling, waiting for the impromptu concert to end. Their hands were at their hips. None had a weapon in hand.

The boys' song built up to a crescendo, the boys were smiling broadly, ending their song with a shout. And at the shout, the cue, their swords, daggers and lances were loosed, cutting through arms, knees and ankles, thrusting through necks, slashing exposed faces, smashing against helmets. Half of the Arameans fell before the boys' shout was over. Those still standing that did not turn and run were set upon by the entire line as they grabbed fruitlessly, trying to unsheathe their daggers. The boys were already all over them, too close for a sword or a lance to be of any use.

Jehu's chariot jolted forward as the first blow fell, before any Aramean had time to hit the ground. His nominal driver waving Jehu's banner, the signal for his line of charioteers to follow, Jehu yells over his shoulder, "The army, Ahab, the army!"

"The army, my lord," my driver exclaims.

"Yes, the army," I say in wonder, amazed at the sight before me; the line of boys bending over the last of the Arameans, waving Aramean swords and helmets over their heads, whooping; arrows flying out from Jehu's chariots striking the fleeing Arameans, charging straight toward the Aramean line, the rattle and pounding of the line of chariots behind me following Jehu's lead.

"Yes, the army," I finally say, my chariot wheeling around, picking a space between Jehu's charging chariots, and heading toward my army, the main part of which was hunkered down behind hillocks and in valleys, some distance behind the chariots.

"First line, advance. Follow the chariots! Second line, flank their camp, forward!"

By the time my footmen got within sight of the camp of the Arameans, we could see the dust raised by the chariots criss-crossing the camp, creating chaos and panic, the chariots tearing through handfuls of soldiers as they try to form up, cutting and collapsing tent lines, stampeding horses. There were no pickets to grapple with, there was no advancing line of footmen, no arrows arcing toward us.

It was a rout. I had no occasion to raise my sword. Ben-Haddad and some of his court escaped on horseback, along with some of his chariots. There were so many scattered Aramean soldiers and their allies that we would have exhausted ourselves trying to round them all up. All that was left in their camp, their entire baggage train, was ours.

JEHU'S MISSION TO ELIJAH

Jehu

Let the discerning get guidance—for understanding
proverbs and parables, the sayings and riddles of the
wise. Proverbs 1:5–6

A FTER the rout of the Arameans, King Ahab sent me on a mission. "Commander Jehu, the prophet Elijah is leaving camp. I want you to walk with him as he leaves."

"I will send an escort of my men to accompany him. Will he ride in one of the chariots?"

"No commander, I want you to walk with him by yourself."

"By myself, my Lord?"

"Yes, Jehu. You have spoken with him before have you not?"

"I have my Lord."

"Then speak to him again. He came to my tent last night. His words were, "Strengthen your position and see what must be done, because next spring the King of Aram will attack you again." He would not say more. See if he will tell you where Aram will strike."

"My King, that old man speaks in riddles. I cannot understand half of what he says sometimes."

"I know. But he hates me. Maybe he will tell you more. I would like to know how to fight the Arameans before they are descending on us."

"My King, I will walk with him, but the man will only speak of what is on his mind. I have ridden mules that were better company."

A rider from the King's company located Elijah and brought me to him. The old prophet's sandals were raising their own trail of dust as I approached him. He did not stop as I dismounted next to him. I ran to catch up to his steady pace.

"Greetings, prophet."

Looking straight ahead and not slowing his pace he responded, "Have you decided to join the prophets, soldier?"

"I have not heard any voices, prophet. What would I prophecy? That the wind is from the West?"

"If you follow the way of your kings, you are chasing the wind. Is that a good strategy for a soldier?"

"Prophet, King Ahab has sent me. You probably already know that."

"I know it now that you have told me. Is that astonishing enough for you?"

"I have a simple question for you, prophet. I do not want to do battle with you."

"It matters not if you battle me. Do you battle the Lord?

"Prophet, I just have a question. I do not wish to be difficult."

"A question from that King you serve. King Ahab. And you do not wish to be difficult? Have you visited any of the caves I have hid in?"

"I would rather be battling the Arameans than dodging your stones. It is a simple question. How will the Arameans attack us next year?"

"That is a good question for a soldier. But I am not a soldier. When an enemy is approaching you send out scouts to learn the high ground, the ravines and the fords do you not?"

"Yes."

"Well I have been scouting this land all my life soldier. And I am scouting it now."

"What are you looking for prophet?"

"What am I looking for, soldier? I am looking for the same thing Abraham was looking for, and he did not see it either. He left to live in tents as a stranger in a strange land. Did he find what he was looking for? I do not know. Maybe I am looking for the same thing Sarah was looking for, a child. And yes, I am as old as Sarah and just as sorry and hopeless. But I keep on looking. Maybe I am hoping that the Lord will raise this dead kingdom we call Israel; looking for a ram caught in a thicket that will save our lives as it saved Isaac. I have not seen that ram. A promised land? Yes, I keep searching for that promised land. Is it here or someplace else? I do not know. Maybe my hope is like that of Joseph;

that descendants I do not know will dig up my bones and bring them to the place I am looking for. Maybe my hope is that of Moses. Maybe I hope I will call things into being if I am mistreated, just as our people are mistreated, rather than prophesying to please the King. Hope? I have the same hope as Gideon, Barak, Samson, Jephthah, David and Samuel. Where are they now?"

The old man stopped walking, and turned to look at me for the first time since we had been walking.

"And where are we now? Where are we going?"

"Prophet, we are on the road to Mt. Carmel. You are on the road from Samaria."

"Ah Samaria, the home of slaves and the impoverished, of ivory palaces with sumptuous feasts, of the sanctuaries of Baal. Then we are going in the right direction."

"Prophet, I never know what you are talking about or if you mean what you say."

"I am talking about what road we are on, I thought that was clear."

"No, you were talking about Samaria and Baal."

"So I will repeat my question, Commander Jehu. Where are you now? Where are you going?"

"Are you playing the fool to mock me? I told you what road we are on."

"And you are on the same road that I am. Are we going in the same direction?"

"Your riddles, prophet, would make a madman flee his madness."

"And yet you flee from my riddles. Would that you flee from that King of yours."

"I stand with the King of Israel, prophet. I have taken an oath."

"An oath to the King of Israel, or an oath to King Ahab?"

"I am a soldier, prophet. I am not a judge, not an elder, not a prince, not a scribe and certainly not a prophet; a soldier."

"Yes, once again you become a soldier. It is your shield from my stones and arrows. But you are a troubled soldier, and some day you may have to become something more than a troubled soldier. I will say one more thing. You do not need to respond. I will be silent, and then we can part ways."

"Finally the old haranguer provides a blessing!"

Elijah stopped walking once again, gazing at the road lying before him. He slowed his breathing and spoke slowly and softly.

"There are many soldiers in the army of Israel and many commanders; commanders of horsemen, of archers, of chariots, of footmen. And yet on this road, it is only one soldier that walks with this old prophet of the Lord. Think of why that is, Jehu. Think of why that is."

With that the haggard old man walked off, veering off the road and on to a barely visible path. I stood still watching him disappear into the undergrowth, never looking back or to the side.

"How did an old fool get to be a prophet?" I thought to myself. "I walked down the road with him. There is no wisdom in that. One of us is witless. It is not good for the kingdom to have a witless prophet or a witless commander."

THE BATTLE OF THE VALLEYS

Jehu

Their gods are gods of the hills. King Ben-Hadad's official,
I Kings 20:23

THE next year, the Arameans resolved to have their revenge. They had been embarrassingly routed at Samaria, but their force had not been seriously damaged. Our army had been dug in to defend Samaria, ready to retreat behind the wall, and when the rout developed out of nowhere; we were not equipped to give chase. My chariots started the rout, but our defensive lines were not ready and not eager to give pursuit, and chariots can only pursue so far before we are exposed and unsupported. We did capture almost all of their baggage trains and supplies which had been abandoned by the fleeing Arameans.

But strategy and logistics are only minor considerations in the waging of war. The Aramean army had been humiliated and in some disarray. Some of the Aramean provincial governors debated with King Ben-Hadad over the wisdom of another campaign a year after such a thorough rout. There was little enthusiasm in the countryside for paying the King's levies to resupply the army for another campaign. But a humiliating rout, especially when the rout was pulled off by a trick that the King fell for, can lead to dangerous whispers in the palace and at the army encampment. More than the King's ego was at stake. And a king's ego will prod the king to listen to any source that promises to allow him to keep his head.

I do so much appreciate it when the palace hierarchy and army councils of our neighboring kingdoms play theologians. To protect themselves from recriminations for their part in last year's defeat, they placed the blame on the gods. Well did they know that their patron King Ben-Hadad needed to convince his subjects that he was not a fool for being routed, especially when word started going around that the rout was arranged by a trick sprung by a prophet of one of their gods. So King Ben-Hadad's officials, after garnering support from some pliable priests and prophets, convinced him that the god of Israel was the god of the hills and that if they fought Israel in the valleys next year they would prevail. I'm not sure which god the Arameans thought was the god of Israel. We have had the temples of the golden calves since the days of Jeroboam, but we also have our companies of prophets across the countryside reminding us of the God of Abraham, Isaac and Jacob. I'm sure any Aramean dignitary visiting Samaria would believe that Baal or Asherah or any number of deities worshiped by Queen Jezebel were also our gods. But as little as I pretend to understand the way of our rough hewn prophets, I can only laugh at those palace theologians in Damascus.

As a soldier, I kept my head down when the prophets went head to head with our royal family in their constant harangues regarding religion. The army as a whole was the army of Israel and identified in a general way with the God of Abraham, Isaac, and Jacob, but I could find supporters of a number of deities around any campfire. Nor did I allow myself to get pulled into arguments when an army commander would argue that the God of Israel should be worshiped in the Temple in Jerusalem. Most were content with worshiping at the temples in Dan and Bethel.

"Was not the first golden calf erected by the Lord's first High Priest Aaron, the brother of Moses?" they would argue, "Yes, they should have waited for Moses to return from Mount Sinai, but their calf was not evil itself. Would Aaron have misled the children of Israel? Was Aaron struck down for the calf? If the calf was evil, he certainly would have been. They are still the calves of our people. Is it so bad that we worship the calves? Was not the Lord honored also? The Lord was almighty. But the calves delivered us from Egypt. Our people did not always have the Temple in Jerusalem, and we did not always have the golden calves in Dan and Bethel. But now we have them. Does that make them evil? Besides, other than being made of gold and being calves, these are not the same as the golden calf worshiped in Sinai, made in a foreign land. These are the calves of the sin offering. Even the first High Priest Aaron offered a calf as a sin offering. The people from Jerusalem are simply jealous of our calves."

I had heard these arguments since I was a child. I found them hollow, but I left that to the prophets. My duty was to the army and my chariots, and I would let those that favored the Temple in Jerusalem know that the army cannot be divided, and that they should save their arguments for their village or the marketplace, not the encampment.

Israel was well supplied. The rout of the prior year had allowed us to capture a large portion of the Aramean baggage train, including supplies, weapons, horses, chariots, and captives, which were sold or ransomed. But there was little enthusiasm for taking the field a second year in a row; we had hoped that Aram would not challenge us again for a long time. They had been bled dry. But an attack must be answered.

The army that King Ahab mustered to answer the Arameans was smaller than the one that had routed the Arameans the previous year. We knew the losses the Arameans had suffered, and we knew of the effort that would be required to reprovision and reequip an army, and the problems any king would have in recruiting or impressing new troops to replace those missing from the rolls following a significant defeat. Our overconfidence was shaken when we started getting reports from the advance guard of the size of the Aramean army forming in front of us.

Rather than arriving with a smaller concentrated force extracted from Ben-Hadad's most experienced forces as we had expected, the Aramean force was engorged with a massive army of foot soldiers. Their ranks literally covered the valley in front of us. Riders were sent out to find out with whom Ben-Hadad had allied himself. These certainly could not be all Arameans. Our first surprise was that all of our riders made it back to camp safely. None had been overtaken by chariots or horsemen, or shafted by archers. Our second surprise was that our riders reported that the Arameans had too few horsemen to give pursuit. Their few chariots and cavalry were held far to the back, near what was assumed to be King Ben-Hadad's command. Covering the ground like locust were unaccompanied footmen. Only a few detachments of archers were seen scattered around a few of the regiments. Nor was there any sign of any other king or prince allied with the Arameans. This was a feint of a massive scale. "He has scoured the countryside for shepherds and servants. He's put shields in the hands of slaves and children," was the consensus around King Ahab.

King Ahab had summoned a concentrated extract of his most able, seasoned troops to the battle, hoping a mere show of force would dissuade Ben-Haddad after last year's rout. But compared to the massed troops of

Ben-Hadad, the small army we had brought out looked like a few flocks on the hillside. Ahab conferred with his most experienced commanders, men he had seen as a child fighting under his father King Omri, but they split into two camps. One argued that the masses of Ben-Hadad's weak-armed amateur foot soldiers would be no match against Ahab's best charioteers, cavalry, archers and our experienced footmen with lances, spears, swords and cudgels. The masses of Ben-Hadad's green ranks would break and run under attack by our chariots and cavalry before our footmen would be called upon to engage. The other faction argued that our foot soldiers would wear themselves out striking down the hordes of Ben-Hadad's army, and their sheer massive numbers would absorb and overwhelm any chariot and cavalry charge.

We met Aram in the open plains, exactly as Aram's prophets and priests had desired. We stood encamped against them for seven days. We mounted parades and demonstrations, feints and raids to try to convince them to reconsider. But with each demonstration, their priests would stage more and more elaborate productions, with larger, louder sacrificial demonstrations.

King Ahab had other reservations about a direct frontal assault against the Arameans. He saw the predicament King Ben-Hadad's councilors, priests and prophets had put himself in. I told King Ahab that Ben-Hadad had put himself in his predicament by adopting the interference provided by his recruited priests to cover last year's rout.

"He will not withdraw, my brother Ben-Hadad," announced King Ahab. "His priests have told him to fight on the plains. After being defeated in the hills, he would look like a coward if he failed to follow the guidance of Aram's gods. His army would see to it that he would be the priests' next sacrifice."

We sat in camp for three days while King Ahab wrung his hands out of concern for his fellow sovereign. To his mind, Ben-Hadad's predicament called to his mind the times he butted heads against Queen Jezebel's prophets of Baal when they would support some outlandish demand from the Queen.

On the fourth day at camp, word came from our pickets that one of the young prophets had reached them with word that none other than Elijah was on his way to see King Ahab. As troublesome as that man could be, this was welcome news to me.

It was Elijah's words from the Lord that had broken the Aramean siege of Samaria last year. King Ahab no longer echoed Queen Jezebel's venom against Elijah for putting Jezebel's prophets of Baal to the sword. If anything, Ahab seemed to welcome the peace that came with the absence of Jezebel's provocateurs. Jezebel's new prophet recruits did not have the same insolence in standing up to King Ahab at Jezebel's insistence. Jezebel's vitriol toward Elijah was still there, but she kept it under wraps in the presence of the King. "Where was Baal when we routed the Arameans?" Ahab would throw in Jezebel's face when she insisted that Ahab take some action against someone who had withheld something Jezebel said Baal was demanding.

ELIJAH RUMINATES

Jehu, Elijah

Go up this mountain in the Abarim Range and see the
land I have given the Israelites. Numbers 27:12

Jehu

I WAS delighted to be able to ride out of camp after days of sitting in
camp with no plans to advance. While Elijah could find his own way,
I made it my mission to meet him. It was a great relief to have a reason
to ride out of camp in my own chariot with only my driver and a young
attendant. In battle I would ride with an experienced archer or lancer or
slinger, depending on the nature of the battle, but these youth needed
their experience hanging on for dear life as if in battle, and I was happy to
give it to them. I was interested in finding out what this old prophet was
going to tell King Ahab, but I was more eager to talk to this man who said
he spoke for the Lord God, the creator of the worlds. What army would
not want him on their side?

We reached our sentries and got word that Elijah was expected to
come on the road from Jezreel. We were still in sight of the sentries when
we came upon an old straggler raising a stream of dust behind him on
the road. He looked like a ragged flag flapping on a post, but there was no
mistaking his dogged progress, as if he was moving the earth under his
feet rather than just stepping over it.

He did not bother to stop or slow down as my chariot approached him. Nor did he bother to glance in my direction or greet me as I pulled the chariot to a stop alongside of him. By the time I jumped off the rear of the chariot, Elijah was down the road not slowing or glancing over his shoulder. I was a little irritated that I was short of breath by the time I caught up with him, his walk a step or two faster than mine.

"My father, I can take you to the King."

"I will see the King soon enough commander."

"It is still a good distance."

"Maybe the King will be gone by the time I arrive, if the Lord wills it."

"I thought you were here to see the King?"

"I will see who the Lord sends me to see, soldier."

Now I was irritated. I respected this old man as a prophet of the Lord, and admired him for his fight against Jezebel's Baal, but I thought I would receive at least a nod of acknowledgement from him.

"So prophet," I said, "what word do you have for the King?"

Elijah stopped suddenly and gave me a hard look, pausing for a moment.

"So Jehu, what do you think Moses saw from the mountain at the end of his life?"

"Moses, my father? Moses is a long way off. The Arameans are close."

"Moses, soldier, Moses. What did Moses see from the mountain top?"

With that the old prophet took off walking with no warning. I had to run several steps to catch up with him to proffer my response.

"Moses? The priests and the scribes tell us he saw the promised land."

"No, what did he really see? When he was denied entrance to this land, what did he see happening in the land once he died?"

"Joshua was his commander. He saw Joshua conquering the land."

"Did he see the battle of Ai? A defeat in only the second battle?"

"How would he know? He could not tell how every battle was going to go. He saw the land flowing with milk and honey, a rest for his people, a people more numerous than the stars in the sky. A mighty nation for the chosen people. Maybe he could see the temple being built."

"Did he see Jephthah or Deborah? Saul and David? Rehoboam and Jeroboam? Did he see Baasha and Zimri?"

"Prophet, why are you asking me these questions. I am a soldier. Tell me what Moses saw from the mountain."

"He saw all of this. That is why he was happy not to have to go to the promised land."

"Why would he be happy not to go to the promised land after wandering in the wilderness for forty years?"

"He would have been happy if he saw all of this, everything that has happened since he died. He would have been happy not to wander in the promised land for three hundred years."

"He would have seen King Solomon's kingdom, he would have seen tribute and trade flooding into Jerusalem, with peace in every village. He would have seen Solomon's palaces and Solomon's Temple."

"Soldier, where is Solomon's kingdom now?"

"Solomon's Temple and his palaces are still there, in Jerusalem."

"And what is inside of Solomon's Temple as we speak?"

"Why do you trouble me with these questions, prophet? I'm just a soldier. I'm sure you'll tell me."

"Oh, I will most certainly tell you. There are Baals and Asherahs and Chemosh and Molech and a hundred other gods and devils in the Temple. Gods of rock and trees, gods of thunder, wind, sun and stars in the Temple wage a war for space for their altars and priests. Such a war that surely the heavens themselves must shake. Is that why Joshua carried the Ark of the Covenant into this land of promise, because there were not enough gods to fight with in Egypt?"

"You speak in riddles, prophet. At least Jezebel's prophets can tell you when the sun is going to rise."

"That they can, but only after many incantations and fires and some gold or silver in their trays."

"True enough, but the Temple is still Solomon's Temple and the Temple is still in Jerusalem."

"I know where the Temple is, soldier, but where are the gleanings left for the gleaners? Has a year of Jubilee been celebrated? Have your servants been freed? Have the debts been forgiven?"

"Those are old traditions prophet. Things change."

"Why did the Lord send our people to the promised land, soldier?"

"Because a promise is a promise, prophet. By the village of my grandmother, you are a tiresome soul!"

"Did he send us here to wage ceaseless war, to go on raids after every harvest, to trade for slaves?"

"Of course not, prophet."

"Then why do we wage ceaseless war, soldier? Why did Zimri kill King Elah?"

"Cease prophet, be still! You wear me out with questions no one can answer."

"Your people wear me out, soldier. I am a tired man. You have given me no rest. The Lord has given me no rest. Tell me soldier, is this the promised land?"

"Cease, prophet, cease! Yes, this is the promised land, the land promised to Abraham!"

"And is there a patch of ground where Abraham could graze his sheep where the grass will not taste of the blood of innocents killed for their land, of fathers killed for their daughters, of sacrifices to Molech, from the edge of a sword seeking nothing but conquest . . . ."

Elijah

Jehu flung his staff to the ground in disgust and walked away from me while I was still talking. His young attendant bent over to pick up the staff as Jehu jumped into the chariot and jerked the reigns from the driver's hands. The youth had time to stand up with the staff and turn around, only to see Jehu's chariot dashing off, the helpless driver hanging on with both hands.

"Left behind again, son?"

"Yes, master. A least there is a path back to camp this time."

I do not know why Jehu came out to meet me that morning. I do not know if the Lord sent him. Perhaps it was simply Jehu being Jehu, always dashing from place to place, unable to sit in one place for long, driving his chariot as if he was racing to beat the wind to its destination.

I do not know why I felt like I had to chastise him for the history of his people or the kingdom he served. But it felt like my questions were coming out of his heart; I was asking him questions he could not bring himself to ask.

THE CAPTURE OF
KING BEN-HADAD
Jehu

Look, we have heard that the kings of Israel are merciful.
King Ben-Hadad's officials, I Kings 20:31

I WAS not too far from our sentries when I left that wretched old man. I told the sentries to bring Elijah to the King's tent when he reached them. I left my chariot with the driver, washed my face, and was sitting off to the side of King Ahab when the old prophet was brought before the King. I was curious to see if the old prophet asked the King the same questions he hurled at me.

Elijah did not open with a condemnation of the Baal worship in Samaria under Queen Jezebel. Elijah dealt with King Ahab exclusively as the man who was King of Israel.

"Do you see, King, the ignorance of those fools the King of Aram regards as prophets of their false god? Do you see the path these prophets have led King Ben-Hadad down? Do you see the foolishness of the King and the Arameans in even listening to or considering what those evil men say to him? Can you see now how a king can be brought low by the false prophets of this locust herd of false gods? Listen now, King Ahab to what the God of Abraham, Isaac and Jacob has to say. This is what the Lord says. 'Because the Arameans think the Lord is a god of the hills and not a god of the valleys, I will deliver this vast army into your hands, and you will know that I am the Lord.'"

Elijah's words brought Ahab no comfort. Now it was the word of Elijah's god against the god of the Arameans. He had been worn down by Jezebel's priests of Baal incanting and contorting in front of him to take any comfort from some other prophet bringing some word from some other god. King Ahab had spent so much time with his Queen that he had become entirely muddle headed. It was as if he needed someone like Jezebel to shout at him: "Listen to the prophets of Baal, you fool! Are you a god yourself that you can ignore them?" But no one in the camp was going to call King Ahab a fool to his face.

The army commanders were divided on strategy. Now the gods were divided. Ahab sat like a stone, staring straight ahead. But the commanders came together after hearing Elijah. They were not all men of great faith, but they had been on the battlefield last year and watched Elijah's tactics lead the army to a resounding triumph. So many had become disgusted with the machinations of Jezebel and her sycophants that they were happy to go along with anyone willing to rub it into the face of anything Baal. As Ahab sat stewing, his commanders consulted. Finally the most senior approached King Ahab.

"King Ahab, we have heard the Word of the Lord from his prophet Elijah. Elijah is a proven prophet of the Lord. We would still be besieged in Samaria if Elijah had not delivered us."

Perhaps the King was mulling over Queen Jezebel's reaction upon learning that the murderer of her beloved priests had determined the army's strategy the second year in a row. Finally he delivered his judgment. "We will fight him. We must do it with speed, with our chariots." Then he turned to me, "Jehu, ready your chariots. When the Arameans move against us, look for their weakest line and drive a hammer through it. They do not have the chariots or horsemen to repel ours."

Ben-Hadad did attack, as best as he could, but the shouts and incantations from his priests only added to the confusion of orders once we struck hard at their center, their strongest point. When we saw their formation, we convinced Ahab that if we went against their weakest point, their center would maneuver to regroup, and even if chased from the battlefield, would maintain an organized fighting force to live to fight another day. We struck to create panic and rout, and we succeeded. As our chariots raced through their forward guard and began disemboweling their center, all of their surrounding, weaker units caved and fled, even before being challenged. The only fight they put up was in delaying skirmishes, put up to protect their King's flight from the field.

The fleeing mass of what had been the army of Aram had no control or cohesiveness. A large portion of it simply melted away. That part had never been an army to begin with.

On seeing the rout develop, Ben-Hadad held back his chariots and horsemen. They surrounded the King as he fled to the garrison town of Aphek. The King almost had to fight his way through his mass of fleeing troops to make it into the gates of the city. Their flight to Aphek was disorderly, and the town was not prepared to receive an unanticipated influx of a fleeing army.

As we were assembling our troops for an assault against their gates, and our carpenters were hurriedly building ladders to breach their walls and covering shields, we began to take arrows, stones and lances from a mass of Aramean soldiers who had mounted the walls of the city to repel our assault. But Aphek was a garrison town, not a fortified town, and the Aramean soldiers in their haste mistook the clay fronting sculpted to look like stone for a stone wall, when in fact it was only rubble packed into wooden frameworks disguised to look like a fortress. The weight of the hundreds of Aramean soldiers on the feeble wall collapsed it. The Aramean soldiers not killed or maimed in the collapse of the wall were overrun by our troops as they rushed into the dust and confusion of the collapsed wall. The Aramean flight to the city was so unexpected and disorderly, that the intrusion of our troops into the city only slightly increased the ongoing chaos, but substantially increased the blood, death and dying in the city. King Ben-Hadad and his commanders fled on foot to an upper room set against the wall.

There was much excitement among our pursuing troops inside the city. "We have their King trapped! Do we storm the building? Call for Jehu. Ask what we should do."

Of all the battles we had been involved in, we had never had this situation; an opposing King was trapped by our forces. We had won many battles. After some minor battles, perhaps our foe ceased its raiding for a few years. After some major battles, we may have won several important cities or trade routes or began to receive tribute. But to capture their King! Their entire army had been routed, and now there was no center for them to form around. Even their most able commander would have difficulty rounding up enough troops to mount at most a delaying action. The road to Damascus lay open to us.

By the time I arrived at the house built against an uncollapsed portion of the wall, after scrambling over the rubble of the collapsed wall, all the shouting and chasing had ceased. The streets were quiet, filled with our troops who were milling under the house where King Ben-Hadad and his retinue had fled. The house was silent with no sign of life. No one commander had assumed control. As I walked toward the van of our troops, they began shouting and pointing, "Look! There!" Three Arameans were walking down the stairs from an upper room. The first thing I noticed was that they did not have any weapons of any sort and had no helmets or breastplates or military trappings of any nature. Then I noticed something very curious, and very out of place. They had rags, sackcloth, around their waists, and coils of rope around their heads. Signs of mourning, or repentance, but not a recognized military sign of surrender. As soon as I saw them, I broke through our troops and began up the stairs to meet them.

"You are surrounded," I said to the first Aramean on the stairs. "Your army has fled the field. Do you intend to surrender?"

The Aramean responded first by bowing to me and then said, "My Lord, our army did retreat, as you said. We are at the mercy of your Lord, King Ahab, son of Omri. We have heard that King Ahab is merciful. We have come out not to fight, but to ask for the mercy of your Lord, King Ahab, so perhaps he will spare the life of our Lord, King Ben-Hadad."

"Is your King Ben-Hadad in that upper room?"

"As you say, commander. My master is here. He asks only that he see the face of King Ahab to ask for mercy, and to spare his life."

I felt I had no choice but to take these three men to King Ahab. The fighting had ceased and these men were not offering any threat to my men. Since King Ben-Hadad was invoking the name of King Ahab, as a soldier I could not take my King's place and decide what was to become of Ben-Hadad. As I selected a handful of men to escort the Arameans, word came that King Ahab was at the collapsed gate of the city. At the gate, Ahab was on his chariot, his guard debating whether he should move into the city. The King had only heard that several Aramean generals had been cornered in the city. As the three Arameans came within sight of King Ahab, they threw themselves on the ground before his chariot.

"Our Lord and Master, King Ahab, son of King Omri. Our army once again has been crushed before you. We submit to your will. We hear that you are a most merciful ruler and are not given to taking vengeance against those that submit to you. Your servant Ben-Hadad says: 'Please let me live.'"

King Ahab answered, "Is he still alive? He is my brother."

I could tell that these men were good at what they did. As soon as King Ahab called Ben-Hadad his brother, the men pulled themselves off of the ground, and picked up on King Ahab's words. "Yes, your brother Ben-Hadad!" they said.

"Go and get him," the King said.

I left the three diplomats under guard with King Ahab, and selected a handful of the King's men to go with me to retrieve King Ben-Hadad. It would be too much to expect the excited soldiers surrounding the upper room, after battling their way into the city and a frantic chase, to retrieve an enemy King from hiding without having their way with him.

We found King Ben-Hadad in the upper room, cowering behind his retainers, who looked like they were more concerned about saving their own skin than defending the life of their King. Ben-Hadad did not rise as we entered. Nor was he as wordy as his diplomats. We had heard of Ben-Hadad's mercy. He enjoyed hauling rebellious princes in front of him after their besieged cities had capitulated, to berate them for offending his majesty and to tell them that the gods had determined their fate before the siege had even begun. Then, depending on his mood, or the difficulty his army had had, would order his enemy's dispatch quickly or slowly, occasionally delivering the final blow himself.

"King Ben-Hadad?" I asked, although there was no doubt who he was. Ben-Hadad continued to look at me, not changing his expression and not responding to the question. I think the only thought going through his mind was whether he would raise his arms to ward off the blows, or would go down with a show of courage.

"King Ahab has asked to see you." Ben-Hadad again said nothing, perhaps wondering if this was one last jest at his expense before I took off his head to take to his adversary. When the final blow was not struck, he slowly rose to his feet, still not certain if he would walk out of the room or be carried out.

"The King?" he asked, seeking confirmation of his wildest dream.

"Come," I motioned.

Ben-Hadad gasped. This was more astonishing to him than the final blow that he had expected. His cowering posture suddenly transformed into the arrogance of regal bearing. I was no longer his feared executioner, but simply a messenger boy. He gestured forward as if giving a command, "Then bring me to him."

With two others, I escorted King Ben-Hadad toward King Ahab. As we approached, I saw that King Ahab had entered the city and was only two streets removed from the Arameans' last holdout. When King Ahab saw Ben-Hadad being escorted toward him, he motioned for Ben-Hadad to join him in his chariot that had been carried over the rubble. I could see Ben-Hadad growing in confidence with every step. As Ben-Hadad stepped up into Ahab's chariot, they embraced as if they were indeed brothers. Ahab paid no heed, or did not notice, how quiet—sullen—his commanders were. This dog had besieged Samaria the year before and would have torn us limb from limb and sold our wives and children into slavery had he not been repelled by the prophet Elijah. And this year he campaigned against us once again, seeking to wipe us off the face of the earth. We would have liked to have paraded Ben-Hadad around Samaria. It did not matter if he lived or died, but he needed to be humiliated. We could see the kinship Ahab felt toward Ben-Hadad. Ahab was the King, son of a most powerful King, married to the daughter of a King. Ben-Hadad was a fellow King. Ahab's loyalty was to his royal kin. We were not his brothers in arms, we were not fellow Israelites; we were his loyal subjects, his possessions. He had been under the sway of Queen Jezebel too long.

Immediately Ben-Hadad took the initiative before any advisor to Ahab could intervene. "Brother Ahab, you have fought valiantly. Many years ago my father's armies took from King Baasha many of Israel's fortified cities. Let me return all of them to you as your just reward. You will obtain in your own name cities that King Baasha lost and that even your father King Omri was unable to recapture. Your father King Omri was the greatest King the nation of Israel has known. His renown has spread beyond all of our borders. Now the name of King Ahab will be known as the King who conquered cities that even King Omri could not conquer. Also, you have the right to set up your own market areas in my capital Damascus. Years ago, my fathers had their own markets set up in Samaria when King Omri was King in Israel. Wealth will flow from Damascus to Samaria. The royal palaces in all the nations will agree, you are truly the son of King Omri. You have done things that even King Omri did not achieve. Brother Ahab, why pursue my armies further? If you besiege my cities, they will be ruined and your soldiers will make off with the best of the plunder. I will hand them over to you undamaged and whole. If you conquer for plunder and slaves, how much will your soldiers and commanders take before you received burned and broken pieces of what is left over? With your markets in Damascus, all of the profits will go to you. That will be your King's plunder. Why should a king share his rightful gains with his underlings?"

King Ahab was totally taken in. He had heard the prophets of the Lord say that he house of the Lord should share in the plunder of war.

"Brother Ben-Hadad, you have spoken wisely. I can agree to a treaty on the terms you propose. Why should we exhaust our treasuries to pay for more soldiers? I am building a beautiful palace entirely inlaid with ivory and the finest woods from Cush. Buying a chariot for a soldier gives me no pleasure. We will cease fighting. We will have peace. And on the basis of that treaty, I will set you free."

I do not believe King Ahab ever understood how much his army commanders resented setting Ben-Hadad free. The road to Damascus was littered with abandoned equipment left behind by the fleeing Aramean army. The bulk of Ben-Hadad's troops had fled to their villages. The Aramean commanders were scouring the countryside trying to round up enough troops to throw together a rear guard defense for the flight to Damascus. But there was no rear to guard. The cities Ben-Hadad had granted to Ahab stood undefended, their gates wide open. Rather than a right to open markets in Damascus, we would have owned the entire city. Ben-Hadad had given to Ahab what Ahab already held.

A PROPHETIC DISSENT

Bidkar

That is your sentence. You have pronounced it yourself.
King Ahab, I Kings 20:40.

O N the way back to Samaria, King Ahab was in good spirits. He had
dispatched commanders to the cities ceded by Ben-Hadad. Scribes
took down his words to be dispatched to Queen Jezebel discussing who
should be appointed governors of the cities and who should get grants for
trade and commerce. He discussed control and management of the new
markets in Damascus. In two days he had gone from expending massive
amounts of treasure to maintain an army in the field and fearing for the
future of his kingdom, to contemplating a triumphant return and dream-
ing of new sources of revenue the new cities and the Damascus markets
would bring to his royal coffers.

King Ahab's journey to Samaria had barely started when on the side
of the road there appeared a straggler from the Israelite army, with his
head bandaged and blood seeping down his forehead and over his face.
As King Ahab's chariot approached the straggler, not sure what to make
of the man, he cried out to the King, "King Ahab, I was in the thick of the
battle, and someone came to me with a captive and said, 'Guard this man.
If he is missing, it will be your life for his life.' But I was distracted during
the battle and the man disappeared."

King Ahab, as merciful as he had been with Ben-Hadad, did not
pause, "That is your sentence. You have pronounced it yourself." Mercy
to a fellow monarch was one thing, but discipline in his own army was

another. I was waiting for the King to order someone to strike the sorry soldier down, at the same time puzzled why the soldier was so eager to confess his failure directly to the King. But before an order could be given, the soldier whipped off his large bandage and approached the King closer. By now we all recognized the man as one of the company of prophets that followed Elijah. King Ahab rarely enjoyed meeting up with any prophet of the Lord. He had rarely heard anything good from them, but for two years in a row Elijah's prophecies had seen two routs of the Aramean army. He showed his reflexive alarm at being confronted by a prophet, but seemed to visibly relax, thinking maybe this would be more good news.

The prophet's angry glare at King Ahab once the prophet took his bandage off his head immediately dissipated any thought of good news. We could see that the prophet's wound was real and still seeping blood as he raised his arm, pointing directly at the King, saying, "This is what the Lord says: 'You have set free a man I had determined should die. Therefore it is your life for his life, your people for his people.'" With that, the prophet turned on his heels and strode off into the wilderness. I expected an outburst from the King. He simply stood in his chariot, silent, staring at the back of the prophet as he made his way into the bramble off of the road. Ahab's face was sullen and dark. Finally he said to no one, "How I tire of those dogs. They will turn on you with no reason."

There was little talk from the King and those riding with him on the way back to Samaria. There was much talk in the chariots of the commanders. "Your life for his life," caused much consternation among those who had heard the prophet's words. Few would dare to speak what was on their minds, "How can we follow a King who a prophet of the Lord says will be put to death," but that was certainly on many minds. There were rumblings among small, select groups of commanders about what the House of Omri was becoming. Few were full-fledged fanatics of the Temple worship in Jerusalem, but their identity as children of Abraham caused many discomfort with the foreign influence which most laid at the feet of Queen Jezebel.

Our victorious entry to Samaria was strangely muted. King Ahab remained angry and surly since being confronted by the prophet. There was a modest celebration among the commanders, but King Ahab was nowhere to be seen. He retreated to his palace and remained out of sight.

AHAB THE INNOCENT

Jehu

Is this how you act as King over Israel? Jezebel, I Kings
21:7

T HE unfortunate aspect of peace was that it left time for King Ahab
to ruminate about the glory he was due as King.

King Ahab had not lifted a finger to wrest Naboth's vineyard from
Naboth. Ahab had bargained in good faith with Naboth for his family's
vineyard, but had not been able to convince Naboth to sell it to him.
It disturbed Ahab greatly that Naboth would not sell him the vineyard.
The vineyard was located just outside the walls of Jezreel, the Kingdom's
central garrison city. The vineyard was one of the most attractive parts of
Jezreel with row after row of vines draped over the rolling hills along the
road leading to Jezreel. Close to the gates of Jezreel and pressed close to
the outside of the city wall was a network of roads and paths connecting
the vineyard with the pressing pits, the rows of small hovels for housing the workers during harvest, the open spaces for parking the wagons
full of grapes as they waited for the pressing pits, the store houses for
the wooden vats for holding and fermenting the pressed juice, and larger
store houses for holding the clay vessels and wineskins for the wine. Out
of view of the small vineyard village, and further from the city walls, was
another small village for artisans; potters for the wine vessels and their
kilns, leather workers for the wineskins and their tanning vats, carpenters and their shops for building and maintaining the wagons and carts
needed for the harvest, and large barns for storing them after the harvest

was done. The prosperity of Naboth's family had increased significantly after Jeroboam's revolt from King Solomon.

A new king and a new army needed to be supplied, and new King Jeroboam needed a place to garrison his army. During Solomon's reign, Jerusalem had been too far away to provide any business for the vineyards of Jezreel, but when Jezreel was selected by King Jeroboam as a base to provision his fighting forces, Naboth's family found themselves serving as the primary suppliers of wine for Jeroboam's new army. Once supplying the army, Naboth's family then found themselves supplying the royal palaces. And when Omri built a second royal palace in Jezreel, they found themselves as the exclusive purveyors of wine to the royal family. Years of well funded vintnering provided Naboth's family with an expertise unmatched in the region. The great expansion of the Kingdom of Israel under King Omri brought an even greater expansion to the Jezreelite vineyards. And as purveyors of wine to the royal palace, Jezreel wine became the wine of choice of princes, priests and merchants.

King Ahab was well aware of the treasure that flowed from the royal coffers to the Jezreel winery. King Omri had been well aware of the gold and silver that changed hands to arm and equip his armies. Chariot builders and metal workers received royal grants and were controlled by the palace. A loss in battle recouped to the benefit of the King as the royal levies on the land flowed to the palace to manufacture new javelins, swords, saddles and helmets. But King Omri also saw to it that his loyal subjects received the benefit of his victories, and allowed the common suppliers such as granaries, vineyards and potters to prosper while supplying the Kingdom.

❀　　❀　　❀

"You fool. Why should Naboth have the vineyard? What has he done to deserve it?" It was my misfortune to visit the royal palace on occasion now that I had been promoted as one of the commanders of the chariots. My commander would drag me along to the palace when the King would meet with his commanders. I think he just did not want to be by himself in the palace. On this occasion we got to hear what we learned from the palace servants was not an unusual dressing down of our King by Queen Jezebel.

"Is he the son of Naboth's father? What a great honor! If the girl that empties my chamber pot has a litter of bastards, do they inherit the royal palace? You say that it is the inheritance of Naboth's family. Have you forgotten the history of your people those prophets of yours enchant you with? Who owned Naboth's vineyard when your great prophet Joshua parted the Jordan River? It was not Naboth's father, I tell you that. And where is that owner of the vineyard now? The blood of the Canaanite who owned Naboth's vineyard is still fertilizing the vines. Did not that Canaanite have a father? Did not that Canaanite have an inheritance? Was he not struck down and that vineyard taken from him as plunder? Did the Israelite prophet that struck down that Canaanite ask the Canaanite how much he wanted for the vineyard? When that prophet plunged his sword into that Canaanite's neck, did he offer to exchange the vineyard for some other land Joshua was plundering?"

King Ahab waved us off. There was not going to be a conference today. I thought maybe the King was embarrassed by his Queen, more likely Ahab realized that Jezebel would not relent unless he capitulated, and the King did not want his commanders to see him surrender. We went about our business. The horses we had gone to talk to King Ahab about were too good to pass up, so several days later they were in the royal stables and our younger charioteers were learning how to train them for the chariot. A messenger came from the palace calling for two chariots to escort the King with a detachment of the palace guard. I could have dispatched anyone under my command, but I elected to go, and directed my young apprentice Bidkar to go with me. Bidkar showed a proclivity for command, and further exposure to his King would not hurt him.

When we arrived at the palace, the King and the guard were waiting, and we were instructed to lead the King's procession to the vineyards. I was a little disappointed, thinking that the glory of a charioteer should not be wasted on an agricultural tour. Young boys dashed along side of us in the streets for as long as they could keep up, delighted to be able to see the King's chariots close up, maybe hoping to impress the King, but more, to impress the charioteers.

At the vineyard, we saw the gates to the main vineyard sealed with cords and several royal seals. Just to give me an excuse to unsheathe my dagger, I stepped from my chariot and cut off the cords and broke the seals. We then entered the vineyard grounds as the King began touring the buildings within the enclosure. It was not the harvest season, but I thought it strange that there was not a soul on the grounds.

"What a fine vineyard," the King remarked with awe. "Look how well built these buildings are, what craftsmanship! Look at how well maintained these buildings are, and nothing out of place, all in order. I will swear that that old Jehoshaphat does not have a vineyard like this. Damascus does not have a vineyard like this. Not even the domains of Sidon can boast a vineyard like this."

We held our chariots just inside the gates, waiting with the royal guard, as the King toured every corner of the enclosure.

"Why such an entourage to visit a vineyard?" I asked one of the guards, a little embarrassed I had taken Bidkar out on such a domesticated mission

"This vineyard has a history, commander. They thought there may be some trouble, perhaps a thrown rock or two. Better to make them think twice if they see some chariots around."

Before I had time to think about the guard's answer, trouble showed up at the gate of the vineyard. At first I thought it was just a beggar, but then thought that beggars tried to look pathetic, not angry, and then I realized who our beggar was.

"I am here to see the King," demanded the beggar.

Before the guard had a chance to respond, I raised my hand to the guard.

"I know who this is. I will take him to the King."

Maybe the guard recognized Elijah at that point, because I expected an objection from the guard that never came.

"I will take you to him," I said to the beggar.

"I can find him," replied the beggar, who started his familiar quick walk into the vineyard without looking at me. I did not like to be ignored, but was not sure I wanted Elijah to acknowledge he knew who I was either. I trotted after the old beggar, a minor humiliation for a chariot commander.

King Ahab was in a large storage building, looking at the large wooden vats, standing between rows of storage shelves. I hustled in after the prophet, waving off the surprised guards standing with the King. As the King turned to see who was approaching, the old man shouted,

"King Ahab!"

The King scowled and slumped, the look of delight wiped off his face. It was as if this beggar had just wrested the King's fine vineyard from his hands. Elijah did not wait for the King to respond, nor did he reintroduce himself, nor did he give any preface or explanation for his remarks.

"This is what the Lord says: 'Have you not murdered a man and seized his property? Yesterday I saw the blood of Naboth and the blood of his sons,' declares the Lord, 'and I will surely make you pay for it on this plot of ground.' This is what the Lord says, 'In the place where dogs licked up Naboth's blood, dogs will lick up your blood—yes, yours!'"

I was too stunned at Elijah's words to see how the King reacted to this charge. The words of the Queen back in the palace came back to me, but before they could register, I heard the King speaking.

"So you have found me, my enemy!"

"I have found you," Elijah answered, "because you have sold yourself to do evil in the eyes of the Lord. The Lord says, 'I am going to bring disaster on you. I will wipe out your descendants and cut off from Ahab every last male in Israel—slave or free. I will make your house like that of Jeroboam son of Nebat and that of Baasha son of Ahijah, because you have aroused my anger and have caused Israel to sin.'"

I waited for the King to respond, but he stood still, glaring at Elijah wordlessly. Elijah glared back, pausing for a moment, not waiting for the King to reply, but waiting for the King to understand his words. Then Elijah continued,

"And also concerning Jezebel the Lord says: 'Dogs will devour Jezebel by the wall of Jezreel. Dogs will eat those belonging to Ahab who die in the city, and the birds will feed on those who die in the country.'"

All stood frozen, snared by the prophet's words. "You old fool," I thought. "Is it not enough that you threaten the King's life and his descendants, must you give his Queen to the dogs as well? I am standing right next to you with a dagger in my belt, and the King is going to order me to strike you down. It is your fault if you die old man, not mine"

The guards standing next to the King had their hands on their swords. Maybe their hands were there as Elijah approached unannounced. They looked from the King to Elijah and back, not certain if it was their duty to strike down this treason immediately, or wait for an order from the King. But the King continued his glare at the dusty old relic standing in front of him. Elijah continued his glare back at the King. I thought, "Prophet, you are not a soldier. You do not break into the enemy's camp on a raid, deliver your blows and then stand still and wait for him to strike back. You should be on your chariot racing away. Where is your chariot?"

Then, with the force he had delivered his words, Elijah turned around and began to walk out of the vineyard, neither faster nor slower than he had entered. The King had his guards with him, so I turned to follow Elijah, expecting an order to strike him or imprison him. Instead, all I heard was the King in back of me.

"The prophets! Damn the prophets! Damn the prophets!"

I looked back toward the King. He was still glaring at the departing Elijah, but he saw me walking and looking back, and gave me no order. As I approached the gate I reached Bidkar.

"Bidkar, I will follow this trouble maker. Look after my chariot. Come after me if there are any orders from the King."

HE DOES NOT PRIZE HIS HEAD

Jehu

I would see that they receive justice. Absalom, II Samuel

15:4

I FOLLOWED the old prophet down the paths through row after row of
grape vines. He was headed away from the city. Watchers on the towers on the walls of Jezreel could follow him for almost a half day's journey
on foot, but I had my own reasons for following him.

The old man must have known I was following him, although he
never looked back. It occurred to me that he may have been expecting my
dagger to enter his back, so I spoke to him.

"How will this happen, what you spoke of to the King?"

Elijah did not look back and did not slow his gait.

"I only know the word that the Lord delivers to me. I do not know
how the Lord moves. The Lord decreed the end to the House of Jeroboam,
and years later Baasha killed King Nadab and exterminated the House of
Jeroboam, down to the lowliest servant. Was that the Lord's doing?"

"Prophet, I do not know that. Was that the Lord's doing?"

"Why do you trouble me with my own questions? Do you think a
prophet does not have his own questions? You are Jehu are you not? And
now you are a commander of the army. So tell me Commander Jehu,
what is the mission of your army?"

"My mission is to follow the commands of my commander and of
the King. So tell me prophet, was it the Lord's affair to strike down the

entire House of Jeroboam? And is it the Lord's affair now to strike down the entire House of Ahab as you just said to the King's face?"

"The Lord's affair? What is not the Lord's affair?"

"Is not your Lord the Lord of Abraham, Isaac and Jacob? And is not King Ahab a King of Israel? How can you say the Lord will strike down the King, the King I took an oath to protect?"

"Look at the kingdoms around you, soldier. How do their dynasties rise and fall? How does a king remain seated on the throne? When all else fails, there is the sword."

"Or there is the sword first."

"Usually the sword first. And look at the battles fought between your neighbors. Blood upon blood, war after war. Look at the slave markets in Damascus and Tyre. Where do those slaves come from? How many cities have you seen in your travels whose walls have been torn down, whose houses have been burned, that stand empty, stripped of their people?"

"Many. In every kingdom I have been in."

"And is it better now or is it worse?"

"I cannot tell. It is as it has always been. But why do you not answer me about the Lord shedding the blood of the entire House of Jeroboam?"

"A household was struck down. The Lord did not wield the sword. Baasha struck down King Nadab and his family. No prophet anointed Baasha. Did the Lord do this? There is violence on all sides, in all kingdoms, it never stops. Whole cities are bled dry. Entire kingdoms are sacrificed to the whims of kings. Is the Lord unjust because the House of Jeroboam is no more? Is this thought foreign to you - justice? Should kings reign and crush the poor to enlarge their palaces and live forever? They bathe themselves in the blood they have spilled, yet you would shed tears when they come to the same end? You would have the Lord ignorant of these matters? You slice and tear at the flesh of the righteous and foul on the battlefield, but you are squeamish when the blood of the evildoer is spilled? Is the Lord blind to these things? Should Jezebel murder the prophets and live to a ripe old age? Is that the justice you seek?"

"It is for the Lord to seek justice. It is for me to follow the desires of my King."

"It is for you and your King to seek justice. But do not fool yourself, the Lord will do justice."

We walked along for some time. With all our talking, Elijah did not slow his walk or ask for a rest. Bidkar finally caught up with us in his chariot, but he had no orders from the King. He had come out to bring

me back to Jezreel. As Bidkar pulled up, Elijah kept walking, not turning
around.

"So that is Elijah," remarked Bidkar, watching the prophet's back re-
ceding from us, "how does that man keep his head on his shoulders after
what he says to the King?"

"I do not think he prizes his head that much. Sometimes I think it
may not be that well attached in any event."

"Is he brave or foolish?"

"I think he has to be a little of both."

❀   ❀   ❀

Weeks later, word came out of the palace that King Ahab had taken
to wearing sackcloth - mourning clothes, a symbol of penitence. There
was no public pronouncement, no procession to any temple, no decree
of fasting. It was a very personal declaration, but having been made by
the King word of the action spread to every corner of the city. Very little
was seen of the King in public. After two weeks, the King began to appear
in public. He sat in the judgment seat at the gates of the city listening to
his petitioners, still attired in sackcloth. The proceedings had a somber
caste, as opposed to the all but flippant irreverence by the King and his
courtiers at the city gate of years previous. There was also a rumor that
the King was fasting, but there was no announcement to that effect, and
no official pronouncement to explain the King's actions.

Queen Jezebel's very public processions to the temple of Baal continued, but with no more frequency and no more pageantry than before
as I had expected the Queen to do to show her displeasure with Ahab's
self humiliation, an act Jezebel felt a king should never take. King Ahab
did not join in these processions as he had before. On the other hand,
Naboth remained dead; his vineyard was harvested by the King's servants
and his wine drunk at the King's table. I could not see what good the
sackcloth did to restore the vineyard. None of Naboth's relatives dared
to approach King Ahab even while he was sitting in sackcloth at the city
gates. No one believed Ahab could maintain his air of solemn repentance
for long, and Naboth's family feared that they would be stuck down on
their way to the city gates should there be any suggestion they were going
to ask for redress.

From Elijah's followers, word came that Ahab's sudden humility
had bought him a stay of the execution of Elijah's sentence. "Justice," I

wondered, "the old prophet spoke of justice. This is justice?" I resolved that I would serve the King as I always had, as a soldier. If it did not involve the army, I would leave the prophets and kings to fight their own battles.

ATHALIAH

Athaliah

The eyes of all Israel are on you, to learn from you who
will sit on the throne of my lord the King after him.
Bathsheba. I Kings 1:20

MY mother, Queen Jezebel, knew from my birth what my fate was,
just as she knew from her birth what her fate was. Her father, King
Ethbaal had poured money and masonry into the ancient temple to Baal
in Sidon to support Jezebel's position as priestess in the Temple. She had
told me how survival amongst the flux and avarice of the small cities of
Phoenicia was a cut throat existence. Alliances between the cities had to
be made to ward off or please the waxing and waning kingdoms to the
North, South and East. Only the Great Sea to the West gave us any peace.
No one could out-sail the Phoenicians. But when forming alliances to
ward off the outsiders, Phoenician kings had to keep their hands on the
hilt of their swords to protect themselves against the greed of their brothers. So to great Baal offerings went up and festivals were held. Sons could
maintain a dynasty's hold on the city, but daughters were valuable for
alliances.

The Baal of Sidon was most efficacious. King Omri of Israel, my
grandfather, was creating a great kingdom. As a commander under King
Baasha, he had seen how the constant wars between King Baasha of Israel
and King Asa of Judah had bled the nation of treasure and men; how the
constant fighting neglected the crops and trade routes and impoverished
the country. There was a brotherly jealousy that fired these wars; who was

the true Israelite? Baasha had a foolish dream of taking Jerusalem and their precious temple. Judah also sought to restore their claim to all of Solomon's kingdom, which included the territory of Israel.

When made King, Omri put an end to the constant warring against the Kingdom of Judah and allowed his country's natural wealth to fill his coffers and build his army. He sent out his armies against his weakest neighbors, not to spill blood, but to negotiate under the shadow of his half-completed siege towers. He would not conquer, but would possess their fealty. His neighbors were grateful for his forbearance from their destruction and happily paid their tribute to Omri. Their armies were preserved and their troops happily returned to their fields and crops, setting aside a portion for King Omri.

King Ethbaal did not wait to see King Omri's siege towers approaching. He did not want to negotiate alliances with his brother Phoenicians at the length of a dagger. Processions and flocks, prophet and priests, virgins and prostitutes, women and children poured into the temple of the mighty Baal of Sidon. Baal was to be pleased and Sidon was to be preserved. My mother Jezebel, daughter of King Ethbaal, was to be offered to the House of Omri; not as a concubine or a secondary wife to the King, but a wife to heir to the throne, Ahab, Omri's first born. King Omri was impressed by the wealth of Tyre and Sidon, but had little affinity to the Phoenicians' great trading fleets. He declined Ethbaal's offer to take him aboard for a short cruise. The Israelites were married to the mountains and hills. Their land, they said, their promised land, according to some ancient mythology carried by their people about their strange god promising the land to them. Whatever their tales were, it involved land. The sea was not their inheritance. They were blind to the sea.

King Ethbaal traded to King Omri something he could not obtain from his army; a royal title, a pedigree, something the old, rough soldier lacked. His son Ahab was to be married to the daughter of a King. His cousins from the southern Kingdom of Judah could no longer brag that they were true royalty, descendants from their mythic King David. Now his son would be married to a Queen, his children offspring of royalty.

Mother Jezebel was intent on bringing this matter full circle. Marriage into the royal family of Judah. Now her offspring would have an unmatched pedigree. Offspring of King David only? Her children would be offspring of King Ethbaal of Tyre and Sidon, King Omri of powerful Israel, and of the royal line of David.

Was there more? Tales trickled in of powerful kings from the East - Assyria - growing more and more restless. How better to feint their armies than to offer children of impeccable royal pedigree to cement alliances and provide a bulwark against the greed of Assyria. How a mother dreamed of her progeny controlling conquering empires.

THE FICKLE PROPHETS

Athaliah

The Lord your God will raise up for you a prophet like
me from among you, from your fellow Israelites. Moses,
Deuteronomy 18:15

O THER threats to the royal household were more elusive, ones not
trapped by the trappings of royalty. The primitive Israelites could
not shake their atavistic inclination to their unseen deity and that deity's proclivity to send troublemakers out in the guise of prophets. These
prophets were not tied down to any particular temple and thus did not
depend on their livelihood from the take in offerings to that temple, or
any priestly hierarchy that could be manipulated, cajoled, bribed or deposed. These prophets made poverty and helplessness a badge of honor.
Just enough spiritual hocus pocus to bewilder widows, shepherds, and
other dregs of society to give them a base.

These prophets had been allowed to become more and more radi-
cal. Originally, these supposed holy men had been closely allied to the
Temple in Jerusalem and to their ancient rulers they called their Judges.
They even acted as royal counselors to King David. As generations
passed, they seemed to sever their connections to the King, the temple
or the royal household. They were answerable to no one. To the north,
in the Kingdom of Israel, the prophets despised the national temples in
Tizrah, Bethel or Dan. They developed their own following, their own
"schools;" devoted followers that would hang on their every word and

even provide for their needs if some idiotic vision sent them wandering over the countryside trying to get themselves executed.

These holy men, as they held themselves out, felt they operated on a higher plane, as if they were speaking directly for that god of the Israelites. If that didn't make them dangerous enough, they took some perverse delight in acting as king makers. A good word from a prophet garnered wide support from the public at all levels, and could even hold the army in check.

The prophet Ahijah from Shiloh—the one that anointed Jeroboam the first King of Israel - may have been a sign of things to come. He was not Ahijah from Jerusalem; that was Solomon's city. He was Ahijah from Shiloh. Shiloh was considered a holy place. It is where the Israelite's mythical leader Joshua supposedly set up their god's portable temple - it was a tent, of all things, supported on poles. Yet it was that rusticness that appealed to the old Israelites. The story went that the Israelites had dragged that old musty tent around the wilderness for forty years. At Shiloh, their Joshua cast the lots determining what piece of real estate eleven of the twelve tribes would receive in the promised land they were about to conquer. Their legend is that the prophet Samuel, the one that first anointed David as King, was staying in that tent in Shiloh as a child when he said he heard the Lord appointing him a prophet. Their psalm about all the complaining says that God abandoned "his holy tent in Shiloh," and "chose Mount Zion," something King Rehoboam and his successors have used ever since to their great advantage to incite hatred against the Kingdom of Israel.

Yes, I know the Psalms of the Israelites, and I know their history. Am I not their Queen? So maybe some of these prophets thought that assembling at Shiloh would give them some insight, or maybe they just thought living in that old, historic holy place would lend them some authority they otherwise would not have if they just came from rooting around in the wilderness.

In any event, Abijah from Shiloh is the one that put on his demonstration for Jeroboam, ripping his new cloak into twelve pieces and giving Jeroboam ten of the pieces, then proclaiming that the Lord had told him that the kingdom was being taken from Solomon, and that Jeroboam would be given ten of the tribes of Israel. Ahijah then anointed Jeroboam King over this non-existent country of the ten tribes of Israel. Maybe coming from Shiloh, he felt he could imitate Samuel from Shiloh anointing David King. After reigning for forty years, David was such a legend that everyone remembered his anointing by the prophet Samuel of Shiloh. Abijah allowed Jeroboam to boast that he had been anointed by the prophet Abijah of Shiloh. And wonder upon wonder, Jeroboam actually became a King!

But if Jeroboam did not realize it at the time Abijah anointed him King, he soon learned what the royal palaces in both Jerusalem and Samaria have learned all too well; these prophets are notoriously fickle and unpredictable. Abijah later turned on Jeroboam. Forget the promise of a dynasty to rival David's. When Jeroboam would not hew to Ahijah's idea of sanctity and allegiance to only the god in that temple in Jerusalem, he issued this prediction that Jeroboam's son would die. Everyone dies, but if a prophet says someone is going to die and he does, the prophet can claim to speak for his god, no matter how many times he may have been wrong in the past.

We all knew how the prophet Ahijah had inspired Jeroboam with that anointing, only to get Jeroboam's son Nadab cut down two years after succeeding his father. If Ahijah was an indication of prophets to come, the prophet to come would be Elijah. If Abijah was a plague on the House of Jeroboam, Elijah was ten plagues on the House of Ahab.

THIS TOO CAME TO PASS

Jehosheba

Terrors overwhelm me; my dignity is driven away as by
the wind, my safety vanishes like a cloud. Job 30:15.

MY grandmother the Queen, the wife of King Jehoshaphat of Judah,
told me how the terrors began. Terror was what it was, absolute
terror, from the beginning to the end. King Jehoshaphat had become a
devout man. He supported the Temple and the worship of the Lord. He
brought the priests and the Levites out to the provinces to instruct the
people in the Law of the Lord.

King Jehoshaphat saw an alliance with King Ahab as a way of reuniting the northern and southern kingdoms, of recreating the Kingdom
of Solomon under his rule. His son, and my father, Jehoram, would be
married to the daughter of King Ahab of Israel, and the sons of that union
would become King of Judah with a claim to the throne of the King of
Israel as both the great grandson of King Omri and a direct descendant
of King David.

My grandmother told me how she screamed and yelled at her husband Jehoshaphat. "This cannot be done! Have you not told me yourself
of the prophets of the Lord that her mother Queen Jezebel has pursued
and murdered? She will carry into this palace on her robes the smell of
the smoke from the searing flesh of her young brothers that her mother—
the Queen of that vaunted House of Omri—that you so much want to
be a part of - sacrificed to that demon Baal! Smoke on her robes! Jehoshaphat, if it were only smoke! She followed her beloved mother into

those jaundiced halls of that demon Baal, carrying her baby brothers in her hands—no! High above her head as she proudly paraded into that temple of death—straight to that burning, flaming altar! The blood of those children are on her hands. Did she run out of that temple to save her brothers? No. She handed those babies over to her mother—Queen Jezebel—so Jezebel could lay those screaming infants onto that burning altar. Is that not murder? Did not Jezebel insist on doing it herself? Jezebel would not hand the infant to the priests of Baal. She insisted on committing the murder with her own hands. No, those are not wild rumors. The people who brought those reports from Samaria are reliable."

I do not believe that my grandmother exaggerated the strength of her protests. If anything, she would have toned her accounts down for my benefit. The evil daughter of Queen Jezebel she was talking about, Athaliah, was my mother. Later, I learned of other horrors even my grandmother could not bring herself to share.

"It is my plan," protested King Jehoshaphat. "I sit on the throne of David. My palace looks over the Temple of the Lord. Nations bring their tribute to Jerusalem. The army of Judah is the most powerful of all our neighbors. No one dares attack us. No one is strong enough to challenge our dominion. And look at the Kingdom of Israel. King Ahab is being pulled by his Queen Jezebel to be an outpost for the Phoenicians. But they are Israelites and they will always be Israelites. We will join Israel to us under our son Jehoram and our kingdom will be as powerful as Solomon's kingdom. And Athaliah, daughter of that Phoenician Queen Jezebel will draw Tyre and Sidon into the fold. Do not honor Solomon as the greatest King Israel has ever seen. Honor your son Jehoram. He will rescue the Kingdom of Israel. And the Kingdom of Israel will belong again to the House of David."

"How can you be so blind? The House of Ethbaal mocks the Temple of the Lord. They murder the prophets of the Lord! They burn their own children in the fire! They are jackals!"

One did not talk to King Jehoshaphat that way, even his own wife. My grandfather Jehoshaphat was set in his ways. He had modeled his ways on Solomon, and, like Solomon, in his later years he sought to become more cosmopolitan. The stingy, jealous God of the Temple, as he saw it, was very helpful to him in building up his kingdom and creating loyal subjects. Subjects with loyalty to the Temple in Jerusalem would also be loyal to the King in Jerusalem. But to exercise control over other dominions with other gods, he could not be controlled exclusively by what he came to see as that jealous clique in the Temple. With the Philistines and Arabs bringing in tribute, King Jehoshaphat felt it was ungracious not to acknowledge their gods. He built places for them to worship. He would join with them in their rites at their temples in Jerusalem during their annual pilgrimages to Jerusalem to present their tribute. Had the Egyptians built them temples for these other gods?

The attitude of the Levites and priests of the Temple toward the King became noticeably cooler. Not all priests had the courage of our prophets, and it was a rare prophet who would set his face against the King. But they would not echo Jehoshaphat's enthusiasm for a broader view. His enthusiasm was met with silence in the Temple. The priesthood had been taught that the Israelites were to be loyal to one and only one God.

"After all I"ve done for you" he would exclaim, "you should see your way free to support your King in trying to enlarge the Kingdom. Am I not of the House of David? Traders and emissaries from other nations should feel comfortable in our country. It will only increase trade, increase our influence beyond our borders, and make us more secure. And will that not increase the wealth of your countrymen and fill the coffers of the Temple?"

A union with the House of Omri had been on Jehoshaphat's mind for a long time. It was just part of his "greater Kingdom" way of thinking. "We are dedicated to the Lord and the Lord will enlarge your Kingdom if we please him," was the response of the priests. But Jehoshaphat had been too long a King and too long successful. He was becoming loyal only to himself.

When he could not develop support for his ideas in the Temple, he became more and more detached. There would be fewer and fewer occasions for any advisors from the Temple to be in the presence of the King. If they would not support any of his grand schemes, he would pay less attention to the Temple. So when emissaries from King Ahab and Queen Jezebel came to the palace to discuss a royal marriage, the Temple learned of it only through servants in the royal household. Emissaries? They were prophets of Baal! The priests knew who was doing the negotiations for the House of Omri; it was the House of Ethbaal—Jezebel—making demands and setting the terms.

It was while negotiations were underway for the union between Athaliah of the House of Omri and Jehoram of the House of David that my grandmother had her confrontation with King Jehoshaphat. The King did not speak to my grandmother after that. There was no occasion for her to be called into the royal presence.

My grandmother rarely met her daughter-in-law Athaliah. Her few conversations with her son Jehoram after the marriage were restrained. After the marriage, Jerusalem became a very chilly place for her and her supporters in the Temple. Everyone knew who the crown prince was, and who would be King and Queen once Jehoshaphat died.

How I, the daughter of Queen Athaliah and the granddaughter of Queen Jezebel of Israel became married to a priest from the Temple of the Lord is a tangled web. My mother said, "Your grandmother Jezebel was told she was to marry Ahab of Israel. I was told to marry Jehoram of Judah. It is how dynasties are made. But you—you shall marry the High Priest of this god these Judeans worship in their Temple. It is the people in that Temple that truly stand in our way. Your grandmother was the priestess of Astarte in Sidon. Perhaps you can make yourself the priestess of this Judean god." I was silent. My grandmother, King Jehoshaphat's wife had taught me to respect his god like none other. Marrying a priest in Jerusalem was better than being married off to some prince in Edom or Moab. But the High Priest already had a wife and left no doubt he was not interested in another. But my Judean grandmother knew my heart, and also knew who stood in the long line to succeed the current High Priest. Both my grandmothers wanted me in the Temple and married to the High Priest.

My grandmother told me that Athaliah's retinue that accompanied her from Samaria contained a large contingent of the priests and prophets of Baal from her mother Jezebel's household, along with a smattering of loyal adherents to a menagerie of gods which Athaliah had dragged along with her. The royal palace was renovated to make room for temples to Baal. Servants of the royal household attached to Athaliah and Jehoram found it more difficult to slip out to the Temple; they were expected to worship Baal with their masters. My six uncles, the younger sons of King Jehoshaphat, were more fortunate. King Jehoshaphat was installing them in cities spread across the country with well-endowed treasuries. I would see them maybe twice a year when they came to Jerusalem for festivals. With Jehoshaphat's younger sons being dispersed throughout the kingdom, crown prince Jehoram and his wife Athaliah had the run of the palace, and by extension the run of Jerusalem, even up to the walls of the outer court of the Temple.

The terrors did not start outright at that point, but the hints of the inner terrors began immediately. My grandmother had heard what it was like living in Samaria under Ahab and Jezebel. There was no temple to the Lord in Samaria, and the people who still remembered the Lord in Israel tried to learn from the prophets. But to find a prophet in Israel - they had all fled to the most remote corners of the kingdom for their lives - was next to impossible. Word of a prophet in the Kingdom of Israel came only infrequently, and then silence. There were many prophets never heard from again. The kingdom of Judah remained prosperous, no, wealthy, during the last years of King Jehoshaphat's reign, but a silence had begun to descend over the land of Judah. We saw nothing to convince us that Judah would not begin to resemble Israel once Jehoram assumed the throne with Athaliah. Once Jehoram had become King, we began to wish that we could resemble Israel rather than what we had become.

MESSAGE TO JEZEBEL

Athaliah

King Solomon, however, loved many foreign women
besides Pharaoh's daughter—Moabites, Ammonites,
Edomites, Sidonians and Hittites. I Kings 11:1

To my most dear mother, treasure and prophetess of the most mighty Baal, greetings from the newest royal city of the Houses of Ethbaal and Omri, from your dear daughter, Queen ascendant of Judah, and future Queen Mother of the House of David.

This strange city of Jerusalem is very religious, but what peasants its observants are. They have little memory of any god but the god they call the god of Israel, a god that dwells in the temple in Jerusalem but whom no one has ever seen. The strange priests of this strange god speak only of laws, laws, laws. Regulations for eating, for farming, for marriages, for harvesting crops, for clothing, for sex, for childbirth, even for mold. It is all rather hideous. The priests of this god have their hands in everyone's affairs. But these priests have no idea of power or strength or wealth. They also speak of justice, but it is not the justice we know. The magistrates of Sidon and Samaria will see to it that commerce may be carried on, but here they speak of justice as if a king were the same as his subjects.

The King is devoted to this god of theirs, but I believe he is really devoted to his kingdom, and will serve this god to serve his kingdom.

Dearest mother, the palace is ours! Jehoram's younger brothers are all being shipped out to the provinces. Only the youngest of them have yet to go, and the King is making preparations for their eventual departure.

When my husband Jehoram becomes King, he alone will be in Jerusalem. He alone will be in charge of the army. I have sent my priests out to the cities where Jehoram's younger brothers have been installed. We have sent them gifts of friendship and alliance. We have been extravagant in our gifts, but then we will be getting all our gifts back in time. We are well acquainted with whatever advantage each prince's city gives them, so we will be well prepared when the time comes.

I have even visited their strange temple; a temple with no idol, no image of their god. Not even the King is allowed to go into what their priests call the holy place. The temple is run by their Levites. They are an arrogant troupe. They pride themselves in holding their god above all, even above the King. It is a very unwise priest who does not serve the King above all. They have a temple guard, but should their arrogance call them to question King Jehoram, two boys with swords can hold them at bay.

I have followed your advice. I have not tried to meddle in their temple or befriend their priests. They do not like that my grandfather is King Ethbaal, but they remain content that Jehoram is descended from their King David. In their mind, that seems to cure all. We are not seen as a threat, and we will keep it that way.

But even with the strangeness of this city, Jerusalem is not entirely foreign to me. Even you, my Queen Jezebel, would find a place in this city where you would feel at home. Their hallowed King Solomon is more than an ancient king. Solomon of old is hallowed, revered - one could almost say worshiped - although the closer to their temple they get the more they would deny it. Their glorious Solomon built their revered Temple, and the Palace of the Forest of Lebanon—Lebanon, mother, the Lebanon of Tyre and Sidon, the very Palace and Temple for which our revered King Hiram of Tyre provided the majestic cedar pillars and beams. The Palace is so revered it is almost a temple to King Hiram of Tyre. Solomon was a great builder and all his buildings are revered as a monument to his greatness.

But the best for last. King Solomon had a wife from Sidon. And for this wife King Solomon built a temple to the goddess Astarte, known here as Asherah! Your Lord Baal's consort from your days as High Priestess at the Temple to Baal in Sidon! And the Temple to Asherah still stands! It had been closed before and then reopened as kings waxed and waned in Jerusalem, but it was never razed. It was built by Solomon's master builder Jeroboam, as part of Solomon's matrimonial pact with Sidon, and no one would dare destroy one of Solomon's buildings. King Jehoshaphat's father Asa had shuttered the temple several years ago, but I was so homesick for the Temple to Asherah, our Astarte, that he allowed me to reopen it, so long as I did not offer any sacrifices during their hallowed Sabbath. There were a few old priests that had been allowed to stay in the temple to maintain it, and we have quietly resumed our rites and sacrifices.

Jehoram enjoys accompanying me to Asherah's Temple. He has promised that when he becomes King he will build for me a temple to Asherah's consort, Lord Baal. Jehoram's brothers are very loyal to the ways of their father Jehoshaphat, but they are being moved to their own cities outside of Jerusalem, and in any event, we have a plan for dealing with them when the time comes.

My Queen, your dynasty grows and prospers. Seeds were planted years ago by King Solomon, and they will grow to fruition when Jehoram becomes King of Judah and my children grow to become kings.

THE FESTIVAL FOR KING JEHOSHAPHAT

Jehu

The quiet words of the wise are more to be heeded than
the shouts of a ruler of fools. Solomon, Ecclesiastes 9:17

F OR three years, Aram and Israel were at peace. Aram had been
routed two years in a row and was willing to comply with the treaty
with Israel. King Ahab had little basis for seeking to raise an army against
Aram, since he had given up his chance to control Damascus when he
gave Ben-Hadad his treaty. King Ahab was pleased with the revenues
from his markets in Damascus, and from his newly recovered cities. My
impression of Ahab's complacency in the face of Jezebel's desire for a
greater kingdom, even though it went unspoken in the palace, was King
Ahab's fear of the wounded prophet's prophecy on the road back from
Aphek. Rarely would a professional palace prophet dare say anything bad
about plans a king had his heart set on. Perhaps Ahab was considering
whether to relent and resort to sackcloth as he had after Naboth's death.
Perhaps he was reluctant to show weakness by yielding to the prophets a
second time. For the first few months after returning from Aphek, King
Ahab did not show his face outside of the palace.

I would have expected Queen Jezebel to laugh at Ahab's foolishness, but I heard from the palace guard that even Queen Jezebel was
slightly cowed by the prophecy. She put great stock in the prophecies of
her prophets of Baal, at least the ones she had not conjured herself with
outright bribery, and a shocking prophecy from a prophet of any god was

something she took very seriously. I was never able to figure out how she weighed the prophecies from her competing gods. I came to conclude that Jezebel viewed her constellation of competing gods as something similar to the waxing and waning of kingdoms and empires. The King serving the most powerful gods would have the most success against Kings with weaker gods; gods could be somehow empowered by diligent, even hysterical, service and ceremony. Extreme devotion to these vain gods would awaken their lust for power and dominion. An unserved god may fade away, or lose interest in its apathetic devotees. Times of extreme crisis would call for extreme measures. Bloody, horrific rites of slashing, cutting, dismembering, impaling, weeping, wailing and outright flailing around would awaken or appeal to these hard to please deities. If an opposing god was in the ascendance, more diligent, extreme and heinous rites were called for. If a god failed to produce, a new god or gods would be appealed to, but at the risk of offending the god being ignored.

Jezebel never directly disputed the power of the God of Israel. After all, a god was a god. But Baal had provided for her native Sidon, and had taken her where she was today. The word was that she also thoroughly enjoyed the more lascivious practices of Baal's consort Asherah, and enthusiastically participated in their various rites. She was, however, thoroughly shocked at the unholy demands of the Lord of Israel. It was no secret that she would openly challenge Ahab over the demands of that so-called god of Israel. "What kind of god can become powerful if it accepts offerings of pigeons from the poor? Pigeons! Ha! A god does not become powerful with an offering of pigeons, you fool! The poor have their bodies they can offer, they have their children. Who fears a god that accepts pigeons? And how can a god become fertile if its people do not offer their fertility to it? Look what Baal has done for Tyre and Sidon and Byblos. Do you think Tyre and Sidon would have dominions throughout the great sea if Baal's priests and priestesses kept their legs crossed? Are the priests of that god in Jerusalem to be eternal virgins? And Priestesses? A god with no women priests? Where is the fertility in that?"

I do not know what private word Jezebel received from her prophets of Baal regarding the condemnation of Ahab by the Lord's wounded prophet, but within the year feelers were coming out of the palace in Samaria to the palace in Jerusalem. Kings were like gods in that respect, and needed cross-pollination and diligent tending for a dynasty to prosper. In talking to Obadiah, head of the royal household in Samaria, I heard of rumors coming from Jezebel's quarters that fear of Ahab's immediate demise prompted Jezebel to push for a royal alliance with the Kingdom of Judah. King Ahab resisted any attempt to forge a marriage alliance with Tyre or Byblos, sister Phoenician cities of Sidon. Even Ahab could see Israel being dominated by Phoenicia with such an alliance. But Ahab was open to an alliance with the Kingdom of Judah, fellow descendants of Abraham. In Jezebel's mind, if Ahab was killed, she would be dependent on her sons alone for her survival. First-born Ahaziah worshiped only wine and was resisting any suggestion of marriage. Where would she be if Ahaziah then died and left no heir? But marriage of her daughter Athaliah to the son of the King of Judah promised a never ending reward. If only Athaliah had been born as her first son, Jezebel's future would be secure.

King Jehoshaphat's first born son Jehoram, heir to the throne of David and Solomon was to be married to Athaliah, the daughter of Queen Jezebel. The marriage between Athaliah and Jehoram was an affair that could not be forgotten, either in Samaria or Jerusalem. That the marriage was proposed, arranged and consummated within a year of Israel's second rout of the Arameans suggested that the impetus for the union was Jezebel's fear of Ahab's impending prophetic death. The gloss on the wedding, which in King Ahab's mind was probably the reason behind the wedding, was Israel's renewed image of a powerful country. That Israel had routed the Arameans and gained new cities in the bargain provided Israel with significant prestige. Now, an alliance with the powerful King Jehoshaphat of Judah significantly increased that prestige. Already enjoying the increased wealth from its treaties with Tyre and Sidon, Israel's neighbors to the West, Israel's armies now proved themselves in battle against Aram, Israel's neighbor to the East.

When a second year passed with no harm coming to King Ahab, it was not difficult for Queen Jezebel to assuage Ahab's dread. "If you die twenty years from now, will it be because some locust-eating nomad said something to you? 'Your life for his life?' Really? Do we not all die? And that Naboth fool? You ripped your clothes and put on sackcloth because of what that murderer Elijah said to you. I told you it was treason. You should have struck him down on the spot for threatening the King. Those prophets are just trying to agitate your subjects on behalf of that temple cult in Jerusalem. It is all treason. You must get King Jehoshaphat to rein these people in. Tell him you do not make trouble for him in Jerusalem. Why do his people stir up trouble for you in Samaria?"

Ahab knew that Elijah and his school of prophets were not from Judah, but he was growing weary of Elijah's threats hanging over his head. Jezebel had been diligent in her service to Baal, and believed it was time for her husband Ahab to challenge the prophecies directly. What better way than to put Aram to the test for a third time. Rather than relying on trickery from the prophets in Jezebel's service and fight Aram alone, they will recruit their newly aligned ally, King Jehoshaphat of Judah, to battle Aram. A state visit was arranged for Jehoshaphat to travel to Samaria. It would be the first visit by either a King of Judah or Israel to the other's capital city. The two kingdoms had fought numerous wars and battles against each other, and suddenly, with the marriage of Jehoram and Athaliah, the two kingdoms had become closely aligned.

The welcome provided to King Jehoshaphat in Samaria was the greatest offered to any dignitary since the founding of the city twenty years ago by King Omri. Samaria resembled a slaughterhouse as the first days of the week-long festivities got underway. The temples of the various deities were overwhelmed, their priests exhausted by the constant sacrifices. The glow of the bonfires, the blood flowing in the streets and the mobs of people reveling made it look like the city had been breached, set on fire and pillaged. A walk through the crowded streets showed that the blood was from the herds of cattle, sheep and goats being slaughtered and roasted on great fires that seemed to burn in every open square in the city. At places the blood in the streets was mingled with the wine which was flowing as freely as the blood. Feasting and revelry was everywhere. After a night of feasting, the crowds would pull themselves out of bed to see the processions, ceremonies, displays and contests put on every day.

The grounds of the palace built by King Omri were impressive. Over seven thousand people could be assembled in the open spaces there, but that left room for nothing else. The threshing floors just outside the gates of the city provided much more space. When King Omri built Samaria, he also built these large threshing floors. Israelites within three days journey of Samaria were required to bring their grain and corn to Samaria's threshing floors for threshing. King Omri decreed that no threshing floors were to be constructed in the vicinity of Samaria. Those that were there before Samaria was built were broken apart and scattered. The grain of the kingdom had to be processed at King Omri's floors. The King collected his fees for the use of his threshing floors, and also charged for the use of his oxen and threshing sledges for threshing. Hauling threshing sledges and oxen for threshing was costly and impractical for the farmers coming more than a day's journey to Samaria. A large portion of the grain of the kingdom passed through Samaria, providing significant commerce for Samaria, and making it much easier for the King to collect his taxes. For those too far away from Samaria, King Omri built other royal threshing floors.

The large stone threshing floors gave several teams of oxen long straight runs for pulling the threshing sledges. Around the threshing floors themselves were large open fields used for storing the grains being brought in and the meal and flour once ground, for housing and feeding the oxen, with tents for the oxen drivers and grain handlers, tents to house the farmers waiting their turn, and fields for the oxen, mules, carts and wagons used to haul the grain to and from the city, along with space for the merchants, traders and caravans shipping the grain out.

The festivities for King Jehoshaphat took place after the planting season, while the threshing floors were vacant. The flat, stone threshing floors were ideal places to set up pavilions for the Kings and their retinues, with canopies set up to provide a stage to house the Kings, thrones, with an expansive area in front of the thrones to stage processions, ceremonies and public feasts. Every day my chariots would parade from King Ahab's palace, through the streets of the city, out of the city gates to the threshing floors, escorting the Kings and their courts to the threshing grounds for that day's festivities. We would stage horse and chariot races around the outskirts of the threshing grounds, and perhaps have one or two processions through or around the city, before we would process back into the city at the end of the day, escorting the Kings back to the palace.

A CONJURING OF PROPHETS

Jebu

Am I so short of madmen that you have to bring this
fellow here? Acish, King of Gath, I Samuel 21:15

ON a few of the festival days, the kings would hold court on the threshing floors, although it was more of a public display, with King Ahab
asking the opinion of King Jehoshaphat about the merits of a petitioner's
request. It was at one of these public sessions that King Ahab broached
the subject of reclaiming Ramoth-Gilead with King Jehoshaphat.

The subject of making war on a neighbor would typically be discussed behind closed doors in the palace. However, King Ahab's displeasure over the situation with Ramoth-Gilead was widely known. After
Ahab's treaty with King Ben-Hadad, Ramoth-Gilead was to be restored
to Israel as other cites had, but Ben-Hadad relented and kept his hold
on the city. Discussion about what was to be done about Ramoth-Gilead
was a common subject of discussion in the streets and market places
of Samaria. Ahab and his court had been urging a non-committal Jehoshaphat to join him in a campaign to take Ramoth-Gilead from Aram.
King Jehoshaphat was more intent in enjoying King Ahab's festival than
discussing foreign relations. But Jehoshaphat was also enjoying his time
spent with his fellow sovereign and the father of his son's new wife, which
inclined him to being very agreeable.

After the history of Ramoth-Gilead was discussed, and the bases
for Israel's complaints against Aram were publicly discussed, King Jehoshaphat finally said, "I am as you are, and my people as your people;

we will join you in the war." Before King Ahab could react or proclaim
more feasting and celebration on top of the feasting and celebration that
was already taking place, King Jehoshaphat added, "But war is a serious
matter. In Jerusalem, before we assemble supplies or muster our soldiers,
we call on the Lord. We offer sacrifices to the Lord in the Temple and
consult with our priests. King Ahab, before you give the order to march,
first seek the counsel of the Lord."

King Ahab held his smile in suspension. His advisors had suggested
that Jehoshaphat may make such a suggestion. This was not a foreign idea
even to Ahab, or Jezebel for that matter. Much flailing and slashing occurred in Samaria's temples to Baal when war was in the offing for Israel.
It was just that Jezebel's practice of scattering the prophets of the Lord to
the four winds made it hard to find a bona fide prophet of the Lord in
Samaria at a moment's notice.

I could only share with my closest associates such as Jehonadab
my suspicions of a darker motivation for the push to go to war against
Aram a few short years after a favorable treaty with them. "Kings do get
killed in battle. Look at how Ahab allowed Ben-Hadad to escape death.
If Ahab dies, will Jezebel have any problem controlling her son Ahaziah
who is married to a wineskin? And if Jehoshaphat dies, then her daughter
Athaliah is the new Queen in Jerusalem. There is no bad end to this war
for Jezebel."

So the threshing floor became an arena for a new, strange procession and demonstration, a festival of prophets. King Ahab emptied the
temples of Samaria of priests and prophets. In the main the assembled
prophets were from the temples of Baal, but there were healthy contingents representing a fair assortment of deities. The incense and torches,
chanting, robes and headdresses, idols carried on litters, pennants and
banners, and intense fervor and devotion put the army's horsemen and
chariots to shame. It took some time for Ahab to dampen the noisy fervor of the prophets. Apparently the prophets believed that, just like gods,
kings would be impressed by intense showmanship. There were at least
four hundred prophets on hand, although it was difficult at times to sort
the prophets from other devotees or hangers on.

Once a semblance of order was obtained, King Ahab addressed
the prime prophets of the various sects assembled. "Shall we go to war
against Ramoth-Gilead, or shall I not?" These prophets were not ignorant of Jezebel's desires, which were widely circulated in and outside the
palace. The royal summons to the temples for the prophets to assemble at

the threshing floor was accompanied by a separate message from Queen Jezebel. These demonstrative seers were entertaining if nothing else. One buffoon dressed up as a prophet, Zedekiah, brought with him a set of iron oxen horns and was running around the threshing floor in front of the kings' pavilion holding his horns on his head and bellowing, "This is what the Lord says: 'With these you will gore the Arameans until they are destroyed.'" So as not to be out done, other prophets started a chant, "Attack Ramoth-Gilead and be victorious, for the Lord will give it into the King's hand."

Ahab was truly entertained, while King Jehoshaphat looked slightly bemused at the entire proceedings. Jehoshaphat scanned the milling crowd of prophets looking for someone who looked moderately less intense than the mob in front of him. He had participated in countless consultations with priests, prophets, princes, merchants, commanders and foreign emissaries. There was always someone less enthralled with the majority consensus. Especially with the priests and prophets there would always be at least one hard-headed, stubborn rascal that stuck to some unreasonable position out of principal, even in the face of the King and his advisors. But he could not see one individual in the throng of four-hundred spittle-spraying, red-faced, cavorting prophets who looked the least bit reticent in voicing his enthusiasm.

Perhaps King Jehoshaphat was mildly chiding Ahab when he turned to his fellow monarch and asked Ahab, "Is there no longer a prophet of the Lord here whom we can inquire of?" Only a few of the prophets in the front ranks may have heard Jehoshaphat's aside, but the front-row enthusiasm gradually cooled, spreading a chill over the whole group. "Is there no longer," King Jehoshaphat said. I nodded to Jehonadab, who was standing a few rows behind the platform for the thrones, keeping watch over the bodyguard contingents. Jehonadab had heard Jehoshaphat clearly and was smiling broadly. "Is there no longer a prophet," Jehoshaphat had said. There used to be prophets of the Lord here, what happened to them? Is there not even one prophet of the Lord here? Everyone knew who had sent the prophets into hiding, at least those who had escaped the sword. That delicate subject had not been discussed in the previous days' festivities. Queen Jezebel had never been far away from Ahab's side while King Jehoshaphat was present. King Jehoshaphat had been an exemplary guest. He had reciprocated Ahab's greetings as a fellow descendant of Abraham, Isaac and Jacob, as fellow descendants of slaves under Pharaoh. Jehoshaphat was a King, not a prophet, but he was a skilled diplomat, and this well-timed, modest aside, in the face of the monstrous din of Ahab's four hundred capering prophets called Ahab on the carpet. Where are the prophets of the Lord, Ahab? Are you the King of Israel?

King Ahab stared straight ahead. Queen Jezebel sat frozen. This was her party. She wanted a fight with Aram. She wanted one or both of these kings out of the way of her dynasty. She had heard through her daughter Athaliah all that Jehoshaphat had done in service of the god of Jerusalem, and how devoted he was to that god. She had seized on Jehoshaphat's request for prophetic advice to demonstrate how glorious her prophets of Baal were. Maybe Jehoshaphat would be impressed. Maybe he would see the need for a temple of Baal in Jerusalem. She would bring the subject up to him at an appropriate time. But Jehoshaphat's dismissive aside to Ahab had brushed all of that aside. Had anyone but King Jehoshaphat made the comment, there would be threats of war if the commentator was a foreign visitor, or threats of execution if the commentator was a subject of King Ahab. I looked with wonder at the silent, stone-faced Queen. Rarely would she be silent if something at court disturbed her. I did not know what was in Jezebel's mind, but her silence convinced me that the marital alliance with King Jehoshaphat had nothing to do with restoring the glory of the Kingdom of Solomon.

King Ahab did not bother to look at Jezebel. She was silent, which meant to him that she was mortally offended by King Jehoshaphat's comment. She did not attempt to convince Jehoshaphat of the sagaciousness of her prophets, she did not protest consulting the prophets of some other god after Baal had spoken. She would be planning her revenge against Jehoshaphat. There was nothing Ahab could say that would make a difference. So Ahab answered Jehoshaphat, "There is still one prophet through whom we can inquire of the Lord, but I hate him because he never prophesies anything good about me, but always bad. He is Micaiah son of Imlah."

Jehoshaphat merely replied, "The King should not say such a thing."

Without looking at either Jezebel or Jehoshaphat, King Ahab simply motioned to one of his attendants and said, "Bring Micaiah son of Imlah at once."

So Micaiah was brought from the dungeon to the threshing floor. Some effort had been made to clean him up on the way, mainly by throwing water at him and trying to wrap some type of ill-fitting robe over him to conceal the rotting rags he had been sleeping in for the past few months. No one was aware of the particular offense that had landed Micaiah in the dungeon this time. Maybe it was a new prophecy, maybe Ahab or Jezebel remembered anew an old prophecy that reignited their hatred for him. He stood in stark contrast to the swarm of other prophets attired in their temple finery, specially augmented for their audience before two kings. The prophets of various deities thought it great sport to roll their eyes and hold their noses as Micaiah walked by and provide a running commentary about the sort of deity served by this prophet. "Look, there is a prophet for the god of the rats and cockroaches." "I sacrificed to that prophet's god this morning in the latrine." "What strange incense is that?"

King Jehoshaphat observed the proceedings without comment or expression. He had intensely studied the group of the prophets of the Lord brought forth by Ahab. Their finery was at least equal to that of the Levites that served in the Temple in Jerusalem. But there were strange additions to their garb. Leather straps around some of their wrists held small images of Asherah or Molech. Silver chains around their necks suspended images of Baal or Chemosh. Some of the prophets' hair was groomed in the fashion of the priests at the temple of Baal. Jehoshaphat could not make out if the neck of one of the prophets had been tattooed or merely painted with some design. He listened carefully to their prophecies. He waited for some of them to invoke one of the deities they carried around with them, but they all incanted, "The word of the Lord, the word of the Lord." He listened with great interest as the prophets of other deities also prophesied in accord with the prophets of the Lord.

King Jehoshaphat was not a young man any more, but I could occasionally glimpse in his eyes some of the fire and intensity with which he had ruled Judah. He rarely concealed his opinion. Any prophet or advisor or prince who appeared before him, whether summoned by Jehoshaphat or not, would face a withering barrage of questions. If a prophecy from a prophet, he would not challenge the word of the Lord, but he would inquire for more details and even challenge the prophet's credentials and authority, especially if the prophet had been in error in the past. He searched Micaiah's attire as closely as he had the entire congregation of prophets in front of him. He looked for any of the chains or straps or images he saw on the other prophets. He had heard of these cross-pollinated prophets of Israel before, but he had never seen one.

I waited for King Jehoshaphat to begin questioning all of these prophets assembled before him. I had heard of prophets of Baal that had made it into the palace at Jerusalem, only to be flayed and skewered by the King's sharp tongue and rapid wit. They would return home to Samaria and remain silent about their experience in Jerusalem. From what I had heard of King Jehoshaphat, I knew that he never remained passive about anything. But here the King was silent. He had heard of Micaiah before and wanted to see how Micaiah stacked up against Ahab's herd of prophets. He heard what he expected, but added nothing.

THE PROPHET MICAIAH

Jehoshaphat

These people have no master. Let each one go home in
peace. Micaiah, I Kings 22:17

I HAD seen the temples of Baal in the streets of Samaria and the temples
of other gods. I thought it strange that a temple to those absurd golden
calves in Bethel and Dan had not been built in Samaria. They were, after
all, the gods King Jeroboam had created for his Kingdom. But I could
see that Queen Jezebel had no interest in any god but Baal. I had seen
Queen Jezebel's prophets of Baal in her retinue at the marriage festival
in Jerusalem, but I did not understand how thick these prophets were
in Samaria until my visit. Seeing King Ahab and Queen Jezebel in their
capital of Samaria gave me a new understanding of this Kingdom of
Israel. Yes, King Ahab was an Israelite like me, but if I hadn't known who
he was I may not have realized what kingdom I was in.

Yes, I knew what was happening in Israel - I knew what was happening in all of the surrounding kingdoms - but in Samaria I expected to be
in a land of fellow Israelites. Instead, I was lost. I didn't know where I was.
But by agreeing to the marriage of my son Jehoram to Athaliah, I believed
that somehow I could bring our two kingdoms closer together.

I had many interesting discussions in Jerusalem while the marriage
was being arranged. "Repentance," said the prophets, "Israel needs to repent of their golden calves and their Baal worship."

"Yes," I said, "I agree. But why should I wait for them to repent?
Jehoram may be an old man by then, and where would his heirs come

from then?" Many prophets are very wise, but this was like a military operation. There are many ways to wage war. The best way is to fight without weapons. A son born of both Athaliah and Jehoram would have claim to both the throne in Jerusalem and the throne in Samaria. The line of David was sturdy. It had shown its endurance by the succession of Solomon. It had survived the folly of Rehoboam. It had been sustained by my father King Asa.

"And the Kingdom of Israel?" I had asked the prophets. "Was not the House of Jeroboam extinguished? Was not the House of Baasha extinguished? And Zimri? A dynasty of a week! There was great hope for the House of Omri, the strongest King since Solomon. But how long can Ahab sustain his dynasty while his Queen rips it apart with her foreign gods? God forbid it, but what happens if Ahab or his sons falter? Who will keep the throne in Samaria from collapsing? I will tell you who. The sons of Jehoram from Judah will! Israel will look for someone to save it, and the armies of the sons of Jehoram will rescue it."

The prophets were unimpressed. "Venom," they said. "Beware of the venom of Jezebel."

"If you are afraid of fighting because of venom, then you will hand the land over to the serpents." I hated it when the prophets would start tearing their robes in front of me. "Repentance first," they would wail.

I had heard nothing but babble from the stand of prophets King Ahab had herded in front of us. Prophets were not fond of throwing themselves to the wolves for no cause. One of Ahab's commanders, Jehu, stood behind us as the prophets held court. I asked him what he knew of this Micaiah. "He has given good counsel," Jehu replied, "but he is always at King Ahab's throat for dispossessing the poor and for the Baals." From what I heard, Micaiah was the only trustworthy prophet present.

"Micaiah," King Ahab addressed the prophet, "do you see all of these prophets assembled before us. They have to a man advised your King and King Jehoshaphat that we should attack Ramoth-Gilead and take it from the Arameans. They have said that we will be victorious. What say you?"

Micaiah kept his eyes focused on the ground just in front of his bare feet, shifting slightly side-to-side, rubbing his wrists as if he had just had shackles removed from them. He seemed to be mumbling to himself, or talking under his breath to someone who was not there. But he remained silent.

"Micaiah," shouted King Ahab, as if to awake him from sleep, "answer your King. See, King Jehoshaphat of Judah is here also. You have nothing to fear. Shall we attack Ramoth-Gilead?" Micaiah kept mumbling to himself, rubbing his wrists and swaying slightly. I looked from Ahab to Micaiah and back again several times. Ahab was incensed at being ignored while he sat on his throne. I was wondering how I would intervene if Ahab ordered him struck down.

Then, with his eyes still focused to the ground, Micaiah, in a droning, rapid monotone, answered, "Attack and be victorious for the Lord will give it into the King's hand." It convinced no one. He was obviously reciting a line someone had fed to him on the way to the threshing floor. The other prophets had been exuberant in their utterances. He spoke as if recounting the number of toes on each foot.

Ahab was not about to be mocked. He rose from his throne and yelled at the prophet, "How many times must I make you swear to tell me nothing but the truth in the name of the Lord?" This time Micaiah raised his eyes from the ground and looked directly at King Ahab. His sing-song drone was gone. In a firm, deep voice Micaiah answered, "I saw all Israel scattered on the hills like sheep without a shepherd, and the Lord said, 'These people have no master. Let each one go home in peace.'"

King Ahab threw up his hands and turned to me, "Didn't I tell you that he never prophesies anything good about me, but only bad?"

But Micaiah was not done. He continued, "Therefore hear the word of the Lord: I saw the Lord sitting on his throne with all the multitudes of heaven standing around him on his right and on his left. And the Lord said, 'Who will entice Ahab into attacking Ramoth-Gilead and going to his death there?' One suggested this, and another that. Finally, a spirit came forward, stood before the Lord and said, 'I will entice him.' 'By what means?' the Lord asked. 'I will go out and be a deceiving spirit in the mouths of all his prophets,' he said. 'You will succeed in enticing him,' said the Lord. 'Go and do it.' So now the Lord has put a deceiving spirit in the mouths of all these prophets of yours. The Lord has decreed disaster for you."

As I listened to Micaiah's words, I was certain King Ahab would reconsider and hold a council to determine how to deal with Ramoth-Gilead and Aram. Instead, Ahab was intransigent.

"Take Micaiah and send him back to Amon the ruler of the city and to Joash the King's son. Put him in prison and give him nothing but bread and water until I return safely."

I turned to look at Ahab when he decreed "until I return safely." Ahab realized his slight, and turned to me.

"These prophets! Some are not happy until they find something to condemn. Four hundred prophets say return in victory, and one says you will die. If I waited to act until all of the prophets agreed on the same thing, I would still be waiting to be born. Brother, you have heard the prophets. They speak with one voice. One braying jackass will not deny us our victory."

I nodded in assent; assent to Ahab passing judgment on himself. What an idiot this Ahab is. He wants my army to assure his victory at Ramoth-Gilead. "Where was Elijah?" I wondered. "Does Ahab have no memory of who saved him from the Arameans when they besieged Samaria four short years ago?" A prophet of the Lord had decreed his death if he goes to fight at Ramoth-Gilead, and he is eager for battle. I could not understand what Micaiah had told us about a deceiving spirit before the Lord, but whatever a deceiving spirit is, it had done its work with Ahab.

I had had my fill of the sights of Samaria. I was sick of the fawning viper Jezebel. Ahab did not know how to save himself. He had heard the prophecy as clearly as I had. Then I thought of the children of my son Jehoram ruling the Kingdom of Israel. I would not take any action to topple the House of Omri. But if Ahab died, his childless, besotted son Ahaziah was the heir to the throne. How long before his crown fell to the dust? Then the people of Israel would be eager for a new king. We would bring Jezebel to Jerusalem for her own protection, and keep her in one of my palaces where she could spend the end of her days. I thought of all of this as the gaggle of prophets was ushered off of the threshing floors, and preparations were made for the fires which would soon be lit for a continuation of the never ending feasting. The battle for Ramoth-Gilead would be worthwhile. Should Ahab survive, the Kingdom of Judah would still claim a benefit with trade through Ramoth-Gilead. But should Ahab fall and Ahab's son Ahaziah be unable to maintain his hold on his kingdom, all of Ramoth-Gilead, if not all of Ahab's kingdom could fall to the Kingdom of Judah.

THE PROPHETS RIDDLE

Jehu

If a liar and deceiver comes and says, "I will prophesy
for you plenty of wine and beer," that would be just the
prophet for this people! Micah 2:11

T HE prophecy of Micaiah was met with stunned silence. Prophets
from old had recounted their dreams and visions; they had shared
their wisdom and insights. Sometimes they said nothing more than to
recount the law. Sometimes they simply shared common sense when
common sense had fled. But what Micaiah said had never been heard
before. Moses had heard a voice from the burning bush. At Mount Sinai,
the Lord spoke to Moses in a thick, dark cloud. Samuel as a child had
heard the voice of the Lord in the tent of meeting. Elijah had shared that
the Lord spoke to him in a gentle whisper. The Lord had spoken to his
prophets in this world before. But Micaiah saw something that had not
been heard of before, "I saw the Lord sitting on his throne with all the
multitudes of heaven standing around him on his right and on his left."
Who had seen the throne of the Lord before? Who had seen the multitudes of heaven? What kind of thing was this? And this was a vision for a
message to King Ahab?

This vision of Micaiah was so astounding to those who heard it, that
many of his audience failed to comprehend the rest of Micaiah's message to Ahab. It seemed to them that the way in which the vision was
delivered to Micaiah was so frightening and wonderful and shocking that
the message could not overtake the means by which it was delivered. In

Jerusalem, only the High Priest was allowed to enter the Holy of Holies of the Temple, into the presence of the Lord, once a year and then only after meticulous rites were observed. Who had been taken into the abode of the Lord?

I stepped back and spoke to Jehonadab. "This is something new. Is this prophet deranged?"

"I have heard Micaiah many times. I have seen him in the dungeon in Samaria, and I have spoken to him in the wilderness. If Micaiah says it, it is so," replied Jehonadab.

"Then what does this mean? Who has seen the throne of the Lord?"

"Only the prophet would know. Perhaps the Lord does not only speak from the Temple in Jerusalem."

"So the temples in Bethel and Dan are as good as the Temple in Jerusalem?"

"Don't be a fool, Jehu. The Lord will never speak from those hovels in Bethel and Dan. The Lord may be taking a different path, but it will not go through Dan or Bethel. Perhaps the Lord is no longer impressed with the Temple worship in Jerusalem. Maybe he is saying he is greater than his Temple."

"But what does that mean to the Kingdom of Israel, that the Lord has taken this different path to speak to King Ahab?"

"It cannot be for Ahab that the Lord has taken this different path. It is for his people, for Israel and Judah. He would not bend for the likes of Ahab."

"You are too devout, Jehonadab. Perhaps this means that the Lord will not reside in the Temple in Jerusalem. Maybe the Lord is coming over to our kingdom."

"Have I called you a fool already today, Jehu? Have you seen our Kingdom? Have you walked the streets of Samaria? Do you see anything in the palaces in Samaria or Megiddo or Jezreel, or in the temples in Bethel or Dan for the Lord to abandon his Temple in Jerusalem?"

"But the Lord still sends the prophets to this land, we have not been abandoned."

"The Lord will not abandon his Temple in Jerusalem, Jehu. Will he abandon this Kingdom of Israel? The Lord abandoned King Jeroboam, the Lord abandoned King Baasha. Do you think the Lord cannot abandon your King Ahab?"

"I will serve the kings of Israel until the Lord abandons the King, Jehonadab."

❀   ❀   ❀

After the menagerie of prophets had finished their exhibition, the kings and people retired to rest during the heat of the day to resume their feasting and festivities as the sun began to set. As I was resting, Bidkar came to my quarters.

"Commander, the old prophet has been seen outside the gates, well beyond the threshing floors."

"Elijah?"

"Yes. One of my soldiers saw a young prophet from Elijah's group near the threshing floor when Micaiah was prophesying. He followed the young prophet to a grove of trees where a group was resting and says Elijah was in the group."

"I am going to find him. Why would we attack Aram if our King is to be killed? With all these prophets babbling, how can the kings hear the word of the Lord? Old Elijah will be able to tell me."

I had Bidkar's young soldier lead me out to the grove of trees where he had seen Elijah. There were only three figures under the trees when we reached the trees, but the recognizable form of the old prophet rose and walked toward me as I approached.

"You have not had your fill of prophets today, commander?"

"My fill? How can so many words leave me so empty?"

"Now you answer my questions with more questions?

"You do not approve of questions?"

"Are there any answers to these questions?

"Would anyone listen if there were?"

"They worship idols that cannot hear, is it not part of their religion not to hear?"

"I have a question."

"Have you asked Queen Jezebel's lord Baal your question? He is deaf but his priests prattle on with many words."

"Have you seen my sword, prophet? It is silent, but its testimony is convincing."

"If your sword is as dull as your wits, I fear only that I will be badly bruised."

"Do you enjoy provoking me, prophet?"

"Would that I could provoke your wits to be as sharp as your sword. Do you have a question, soldier?"

"Yes. Micaiah said he saw the Lord's throne in heaven. Have you seen the throne of the Lord?"

"The Lord shows me what he shows me."

"So was Micaiah shown the throne of the Lord, or is he like the prophets of Baal with their tales of the glory of their lord Baal?"

"Soldier, I do not know what Micaiah saw, other than what he said he saw. But the Kings were on their thrones, surrounded by their multitudes of adoring retainers; perhaps Micaiah wanted to remind the kings who it is that sits on the throne, or perhaps he saw the throne of the Lord. I do not question what Micaiah saw."

"Then tell me one thing, prophet. If the throne of the Lord is in the heavens, what use does he have of these kings?"

"And now you seek to riddle me. Have you become a prophet too?"

"Enough of a prophet to see foolishness attracting followers."

"What makes you think the Lord's throne is in the heavens?"

"Isn't that what the prophet Micaiah said, prophet? And isn't that what the Psalms sung in the Temple in Jerusalem say."

"What do you know of the Psalms sung in Jerusalem?"

"The One enthroned in heaven laughs; the Lord scoffs at them. From heaven the Lord looks down on them. The Lord answers from his heavenly sanctuary."

"So you are a psalmist also, will wonders never cease?"

"Yes, prophet, the Psalms are sung, even in the temple in Dan. They are sung to the golden calves and to the people, but they are still sung. My grandmother would sing the songs she had heard in the Temple in Jerusalem."

"You went with your grandmother to the Temple?"

"Not with my grandmother. She went as a young girl, before Jeroboam."

"You've seen the Temple?"

"I have, prophet. I thought you knew everything?"

"I know whatever the Lord wills to show to me, nothing more. How did you come to see the Temple?"

"I went with my father, who was selling purple dye from Sidon."

"So you are a merchant and a psalmist."

"My father was a soldier under Commander Omri. Omri was a wise man. I have seen Jerusalem, Tyre, Sidon, Damascus, Ashkelon, Rabath-Ammon, and others. My father was sent to measure city walls, to inspect the gates, to learn the height of their towers, to plumb their watercourses, to locate their armories. It would be too late to find these things out once we found ourselves in battle with one of those countries."

"Not only a merchant and a psalmist, but Joshua the spy as well."

"That I was, prophet. But Omri was looking for lands that looked promising, not the promised land. But you have not answered my question."

"God is in heaven, you are right about that. But he dwells on the earth also."

"Through his prophets?"

"You have already answered your own question. You visited God's dwelling on earth."

"The Temple?"

"The Temple. Built on the threshing floor of Anaunah that David purchased for the Ark of the Covenant. Built on bedrock. How much closer to earth can you get?"

"If the Lord dwells on earth, in the Temple in Jerusalem, which kingdom is his? Judah or Israel?"

"The Lord has not told me. But he has sent me here, so he claims these people. Does the Lord claim this Kingdom? I do not know."

"But you spoke to King Ahab in the years past and twice we routed the Arameans. Ahab is the King of Israel. Is the Lord not for this King also?"

"And yet the King freed King Ben-Hadad from his hands and a prophet condemned the King for it. All I know is that the Lord seeks to preserve this people."

"And the Lord preserves his people with the army of the Kingdom of Israel."

"Do not become too proud, soldier. The Lord has used the Arameans and the Philistines for his purposes."

"Are you telling me the Lord a god of war?"

"Another question? I thought my questions bothered you."

"You bother me, prophet. But if I go into battle with King Ahab, am I fighting for the Lord? When King Baasha fought King Asa for twenty years, who was the Lord fighting for?"

"The Lord fights with his word, with his law. You have heard the Psalms about the Lord's law?"

"I know the Psalms, prophet, 'Blessed are those who keep his statutes. I ask for bread and you give me thorns to chew on. Micaiah prophesied that if King Ahab goes into battle at Ramoth-Gilead, he would die. Do you prophesy the same thing?"

"That has not been given to me to say. I know Ahab will die some day. Did not a prophet already condemn the King for releasing King Ben-Hadad? Did not the Lord condemn Ahab for killing Naboth? And yet the King lives. Ahab has not learned anything from the prophets, have you?"

"What good are the prophets then, If Ahab still lives?"

"Listen soldier, how many prophets do you need to hear? If I said I agreed with Micaiah, would you ask for a third prophet, or a fourth, like these kings? If you were king, which prophet would you believe?"

"If I were king, prophet? I am only a soldier; it is for the King to listen to the prophets."

"And if your King is as deaf as Baal, you would choose to go into battle blind?"

"Should I disobey my King and not bring my chariots into battle? Will you provide me with lands, houses and wives the King will take from me if I do not go into battle with him? Will you restore my life?"

"Commander, I have been told of Micaiah's prophesy. The Lord did not forbid King Ahab from going into battle. You will not be disobeying the Lord if you go into battle. Micaiah's prophesy was that if the King does go into battle he will die."

"A commander is to protect the King's life. How am I to protect my King's life if he goes into battle?"

"The King is ordering you into battle even though Micaiah has said the King will die. The King would be his own regicide. You saw how your King Ahab went around in sackcloth after he was told he would die because of Naboth. The Lord relented. If Micaiah truly delivered the word of the Lord to Ahab, then the Lord is allowing Ahab to pass and execute his own sentence. 'Listen to the word of the Lord and live, or refuse to listen and die.' You could save the life of your King if you rally the other commanders and bar the King from going into battle."

"Then all of the commanders will become regicides if we allow the King to go into battle."

"Every person is responsible for their own actions. Would you have the King die?"

"I would have the King die if he scoffs at the word of the Lord."

"Then all will have a hand in the death of the King."

THE ARAMEAN ARROW

Jehoshaphat

I will enter the battle in disguise, but you wear your royal
robes. Ahab, I Kings 22:30

A FTER the prophet fiasco and the ensuing feast, I consulted with
my commanders. Yes, we could attack Ramoth-Gilead with Israel.
There was much discussion of the prophets, which I dismissed, except in
discussion with a handful of my closest advisers. The commanders always
had a contingent strategy for either staying on the field or withdrawing
from the field in the event the King is disabled, and who would command in the King's absence. In campaigns with allied kings, we always
had strategies for command if one of the kings were disabled. But these
possible developments were always discussed as contingent strategies,
and were always developed in consultation with our allied kings. This
time we discussed the possible loss of King Ahab in our own councils and
we discussed it as one of our primary strategies. What did the prophet
mean? When would Ahab be stricken; on the field against Aram or ten
years from now?

It took more than two weeks for the armies of Judah to be assembled
and brought up to Ramoth-Gilead. By the time they arrived, the army of
Israel was at Ramoth-Gilead and was facing the armies of Aram. As we
waited for my army to arrive, there was much time to discuss strategy and
tactics with King Ahab.

"Listen, King Jehoshaphat," said Ahab, "you heard the ramblings of
the maniac Micaiah. His group has been haranguing me for years. They

are just looking for an opening to raise another Zimri against me. Micaiah and his lot hope that by saying 'the word of the Lord,' they can incite some malcontent or madman to reach for my crown. You and I have been in many battles. Remember King Saul who fell in battle against the enemies of Israel. We do not enter into battle lightly, nor do we as Kings watch on the hillside as our armies ride into battle. The Lord forbid that any one of us be struck down, but if an arrow finds me while we battle Aram then that maniac Micaiah will claim that he is the only true prophet out of four hundred. He will try to anoint himself with his own sweat. Then his kind will afflict my family for generations. My son Ahaziah will not stand a chance if Micaiah's pack can raise the hue that I was struck down by the Lord and that the Lord decreed my entire house should fall. But for that madman Micaiah I would never dream of asking you this."

"But for this one battle, King Jehoshaphat, I would desire that I enter the fray dressed as one of my commanders. You know that any force will try to attack a king if there is an opening, but that never happens since the king is so well-guarded. If I do not wear my robes, that threat to me will be removed. But if you are not in your royal robes, then the Arameans will know that we are not in our robes, and will search for me among the commanders. If they see one King on the field, they will just think that we are led by one King, and will not search for me among my command-ers. In your robes, King Jehoshaphat, we will hold you well behind the front, well out of range of any threat. I will not be in my robes, but will be closer to the front, closer to danger, but will not be singled out by the Arameans."

I had seen perfidy before, but it had never been as transparent as with Ahab. Perhaps his court had always agreed with all of the lies that he had told in the past. No one would dare call him to task to his face for his lies. His court may have trained him to believe that he could paint a lie as the truth and everyone would believe him. Ahab looked me straight in the eye. His hand on my arm pulled me close to his face as sincerity oozed from every pore. I returned his sincere gaze, taking the opportunity to study my assassin as he was plotting my death.

Maybe he was concerned with Micaiah's prophecy, but if that were true, he had plenty of opportunities to call off the attack on Ramoth-Gilead. Maybe he was driven by a desire to prove the prophet wrong. If he could do that, then he would have license to strike down any prophet of the Lord who would dare prophesy against him. But I believed that Ahab and Jezebel had conspired together and had come up with a scheme to have me killed on the battlefield. My son Jehoram was now married to Athaliah, the daughter of Ahab and Jezebel. How wonderful it would be to have me out of the way.

To have two kings go into battle and only one wears his royal robes? Only a fool of a king would agree to that. Ahab the King was a regicide. He could not strike me down himself; the entire Kingdom of Judah would pledge to wipe him from the earth, Athaliah or not. So I agreed. Perhaps at heart I was a regicide myself. I would not strike Ahab down, but if Micaiah was a prophet of the Lord, Ahab would be struck down in this battle. If I were not a regicide, I would have told Ahab to withdraw from this battle. But if the only way Ahab would enter the battle was in disguise, then I would wear my royal robes. I had seen Ahab's son Ahaziah drink his weight in wine every night at the festivities. How long could he hold on to the throne? With Ahab's daughter Athaliah in my court, should a usurper try to oust Ahaziah, we would heed every call to set things right. Many things would have to fall in place, but the death of Ahab could open the door to reunifying Solomon's kingdom.

Many of my commanders on hearing King Ahab's proposal wanted to withdraw from the field. "We will not sacrifice you King Jehoshaphat because that serpent will not listen to the word of the Lord." That was usually considered reckless language to use in the presence of the King, since if the speaker considered one king capable of being a viper, he may expose himself as thinking that all kings are vipers. But with Ahab it was different. All of my commanders had now heard of the events of my stay in Samaria. They had heard of the many temples in the city, of the widespread slavery and the lavish royal palaces. They had imbibed the wonderful wine from Jezreel and heard of Ahab's boasts of the great vineyards of Jezreel that he had built with his own hands. Some had heard from their guards of discussions with the slaves bringing loads of wineskins to the palace of their former work as foremen under a man named Naboth. All agreed that they would take no action to expose King Ahab to harm, but that all of their formations would have as their primary focus my protection. Battle would be waged against the Arameans, but only if I was protected. If a company had to withdraw from an Israelite position to protect me, the Israelite army would be left to its own devices.

On the day determined for battle, I was in the van of our formation as we approached Ramoth-Gilead and the Aramean formations. This was for show, far out of the range of their archers, to satisfy Ahab that I in fact would go into battle in my royal robes. Ahab was not far behind, leading one of Israel's chariot formations, but dressed only as one of his chariot commanders. As we approached close to Ramoth-Gilead I swung to our right and fell behind our lines, leaving Ahab in the center. He also faded toward the rear. As my guard swung with me to our right, an alarm rang out. "Pull the King to the rear, to the rear!" All of the chariots that had been scattered as pickets throughout the Aramean lines had left their detachments and were charging our right. As I fell further back, our Judean chariots met the advance by assembling in front of the right of our line, supported by several detachments of Israel's chariots. Ahab's chariot contingent remained in the center, but fell even further back. When the Aramean chariots saw they would not be able to break through our advancing chariots, they broke off and reformed on our right, as several of their foot platoons formed behind them. My commanders ordered my guard to move me toward the center, as they began assembling troops to meet the mounting threat on our right.

As I moved toward our center, I could see the charioteers in Ahab's contingent swing to the left side of our lines. He was neither moving toward the right of our lines to meet the imminent advance of the Arameans, nor joining with me. "That Ahab will have nothing to do with you today my King," shouted my driver. But as we watched Ahab fade into the dust, an alarm was raised by a rider coming from our right. The Aramean chariots were now racing back toward our center, raking our leading footmen as they went, followed by their rushing footmen chasing behind them, as horsemen charged out of their center to join the attack. It was not a full frontal attack, but a concentrated push against a narrow portion of our line, directly in front of me. As our advance footmen fell back into defensive groups ready to do battle, the Aramean chariots and riders rushed by them, not offering to do battle with them, but pushing into our center directly toward my position. I could not retreat without leaving a hole in our center which would allow the Arameans to breach our line. We formed up to repel the advance. It was obvious by now that the Arameans were aiming at the royal robes I was wearing. I began to think that Ahab had outwitted me. If the Aramean strategy was to fell a king rather than rout an army, I had presented myself as the only target. As the Aramean first wave was reaching our lines, immediately in front of me, we could see another group of Aramean chariots riding to our right. I yelled out to our commanders, "Judeans, bring up the reserves to support our right, they are trying to flank us!" As I yelled out other orders, repeated by my commanders, the Aramean advance suddenly pulled up.

"It's not him. It's the Judean King. It's not King Ahab." The Arameans wheeled around, forming up not to continue their charge, but regrouping their chariots to protect their footmen as they dashed back out of the opening they had just created.

The Aramean advance melted back into its lines. We had formed up to begin a broader advance to see if we could get a portion of their line to waver, when another raiding group, like the first, rode out to strike the left of our line. Ahab pulled back, and moved to our right flank, not willing to expose himself to this second, dagger-like strike the Arameans were making. By quick maneuvering, we bolstered our left side, and the Aramean advance retreated again. Groups of the Aramean chariots and horsemen dashed in and out of our lines, striking where the opportunity arose, but never forming up at any one point to attempt a major blow. The entire battle through the rest of the day was a repeat of these first two Aramean feints. We continually formed up to repel these sudden strikes, which they threw at us one after the other, which in turn prevented us from mounting our own offensive strikes. However, the Arameans never mounted a major strike either.

"They are hunting for King Ahab my lord," one of my commanders shouted to me after the fourth or fifth attack was repelled. "None of their attacks after the first has been directed at any position you have been in. They are charging in and out of our lines like they are looking for someone. They battle briefly with each strike, but if their target is not there, they withdraw. The fighting is not so heavy to force them to retreat. They withdraw when they see that their target is not there. They identified you with their first strike. If you were their target, they would mount a major strike, but they keep up these quick strikes all over our lines."

The commander was correct. They were hunting Ahab. He had routed them two years in a row, even capturing King Ben-Hadad, and now Ahab was pushing toward Ramoth-Gilead. They would not be humiliated a third time and they would erase the humiliation of their King being captured by killing or capturing Ahab. Ahab may have come to the same conclusion. The few times I could pick out Ahab's position in the field he was well back from the front and always moving away from the repeated strikes from the Arameans.

The Aramean chariot charges became less frequent and smaller. They had spent their horses. Their footmen, having been held back to rush into any breach the chariots may have been able to create, began to move forward, and our footmen began to advance to meet them. Now the bloody, grotesque part of the battle would begin. Sudden, swift strikes by chariots and horsemen having proven inconclusive, our armies would now try to hack and cudgel each other into submission. This battle provided standard fare. Small pockets of footmen would prod, the enemy line would throw up a larger force of footmen, we would respond, and after a few minutes of desperation to the point of exhaustion, both lines would withdraw to reform and carry away their wounded. Then the process was repeated; constant prodding and pushing to try to create a break in the Aramean line and their prodding our lines, with no stomach for constant, sustained combat.

If a line began to waver, commanders would funnel more men into that sector, risking the Arameans pouring men into another section of the line where the reserves had been taken. Major counterstrikes using all of a commander's men were avoided; a collapse of the strike with no reserves left could lead to a collapse in that section of the battlefield, and if a panic develops, a total rout.

As the battle devolved into furious skirmishes flaring up and burning out from one section of the battlefield to another, my principal commanders would race me from one side of the battle to another, as we moved archers, slingers and footmen over valley and plain and sent couriers dashing over to detached formations, and talking to furious riders bringing us news from our scouts of the Aramean formations.

We had lost sight of King Ahab hours ago. We had tracked Ahab's position early on in the battle by the furious attacks the Arameans launched against him, but after the first maddening hour of pitched battle the fight had been reduced to heated skirmish after skirmish where the position of every unit was in question. Long after mid-day, an Israelite courier raced up to us with news.

"King Ahab has been struck by an arrow."

"Is he alive?"

"He is still in his chariot, but the arrow is still in him and he still bleeds."

"Who commands Ahab's army?"

"King Ahab from his chariot, but he weakens."

We sent our own rider back with the Israelite courier to gain more information, but soon after they departed the battle began to deliver its own news. Advances and feints by the Israelites halted, and soon they began ceding positions on the field without contest.

We ordered our own withdrawal. Our army was being left in the advance positions on the field, and without support from Ahab's army was becoming exposed. We slowly began to pull back, covered by our archers and slingers. Our chariots were called back up to make threatening charges against the Aramean positions as if to announce a major thrust. The Arameans pulled back to ready their defenses against what we made to look like a last-ditch attack, giving us enough space to march away in force. By the time our major units were moving away from the battle, Ahab's army had melted away. As we moved toward the west, a cloud of dust rose from the ground ahead of us filtering the light of the sunset. It was Ahab's chariot commander Jehu racing the light of the setting sun. As he approached we could see that Jehu had the reigns. As he pulled to a stop, his driver looked green from the ride.

"Withdraw as best you can," were the first words out of Jehu's mouth.

"We are. What news do you have?"

"Our army is in flight. Each man flees to his own village. We can offer you no support, there is no one left."

"And King Ahab? What news?"

"He had sunk to the floor of his chariot as I left. He rests in a pool of his own blood. There is no life left in him. There will be a new King in Israel by the time I return."

"What word did King Ahab leave us with?"

"As I bent over him he said, "Now Jezebel reigns.""

"Strange words," I replied, "He leaves a son, does he not?"

"Ahaziah is his son," Jehu answered, "but he remains in Samaria, enchanted by the fermenters. It does not matter what son sits on the throne, Jezebel will rule."

Looking back, I thought it unusual that this army commander would be so blunt about the royal house he served when talking to me, the King of Judah whose son had married Jezebel's daughter. But he passed this information on to me as if he spoke of positions on the battlefield.

The battle had ended. It was night before the Arameans could think of pursuit. They had been sufficiently bloodied and exhausted in the battle that they would not be able to offer a fight even had they caught up with us. We retired from the field for the season. The Arameans had their victory over Ahab. They gained no territory, villages or slaves, but they had killed the scion of the mighty King Omri.

Somewhere in Damascus words are being pressed into clay regaling the great Aramean victory at Ramoth over the son of King Omri. Etchings are being struck for a great pillar showing the army of the Kingdom of Israel being crushed, and, no doubt, showing Jehoshaphat of Judah fleeing the field.

King Ahab's tomb will depict his many victories over Aram.

My stonecutters will be silent.

No monument of any kingdom will praise the powerful words of the prophet Micaiah, cutting down the King on his throne and routing his army.

AHAZIAH THE SOT

Joram

Woe to those who are heroes at drinking wine and
champions at mixing drinks. Isaiah 5:22

A HAZIAH, my brother, was a fool, a drunken fool. Two years as King,
but what did he accomplish? Nothing. He stayed in his palace and
drank. Father Ahab had been killed in battle, so Ahaziah was afraid of
even mounting a horse.

The Queen Jezebel, I could not address Jezebel as "mother" unless
we were in the private quarters of the palace - she was always the Queen
- ran the palace in the two years Ahaziah was King. Ahaziah did not
marry, so there was no wife of the King for Jezebel to contend with. As
for my wives, none of them dared show their face in the royal rooms of
the palace if Queen Jezebel was there. I certainly would not refer to any
of my wives as "Queen," or by any other title suggesting royalty, or any
claim to the throne. Jezebel is Queen, it is her dynasty and only her sons
will rule - or her. If I or my brothers do not survive, there is no doubt who
will be Queen.

I think Ahaziah was paralyzed by Queen Jezebel. Of all her children,
I think Ahaziah hated Jezebel the most. He was horrified by Jezebel's actions, her temple worship, her debauchery, her willingness to murder and
usurp. Or maybe he was just ashamed. Or maybe he just went along because that's what the sons of Jezebel did. Whatever it was, he kept his own
counsel. No, wine was his counselor. He did not say, but he did drink. He
would honor Queen Jezebel. He would proclaim her the daughter of the

Kings of Sidon, Queen with King Ahab; trumpets and processionals and feasts to honor her without end. She was so blinded by flattery she did not see the mockery in it that I saw. All the feasts and banquets and festivals were excuses for Ahaziah to drink, and to drink to excess, and then to drink more. He would recover in between revelries, but at every occasion he manufactured to honor Queen Jezebel, he would arrive drunken and then proceed to drink more. I saw what he was saying; Jezebel has all of us reeling with drunkenness, we cannot stand straight in the presence of Jezebel; the only way to keep our minds is to drown them in wine.

And a wife for Ahaziah. Oh how Jezebel lusted after a royal princess from Edom or Moab or Aram, or anywhere. Another dynasty in her name! But how can you peddle Ahaziah to the neighboring royalty when he can't stay sober. If he was sober when leaving on his journey, he will be drunk by the time he arrives. And if he arrives sober, he will demand wine as soon as he arrives, before he can dismount. And he will keep demanding and keep demanding. Some initial visits had been arranged for courtiers from other kingdoms to take the measure of the prince, but if he wasn't drunk when they arrived, he would be drunk for the duration as soon as he knew the purpose of the visit. After several visits ended with excuses and apologies, Ahab and Obadiah and Jehu insisted that there be no more. To let a neighboring kingdom know that the heir to the throne of Israel is a habitual, falling down drunk, would be to invite an invasion the minute King Ahab passed.

Oh how Jezebel screamed and ranted. "An heir! I need an heir! I need an alliance!" Oh how she dreamed of an empire. Finally Obadiah prevailed upon her by convincing her what she would do if she found out that a neighboring King was an incompetent, drunken fool. "I would send him a caravan loaded with the finest wine and have his kingdom by the time he drained the last skin." She blanched the moment those words left her mouth, and took to wine within the hour. The next several weeks she spent going from temple to temple with her favorite prophets, sending back to the palace for more wine.

"What can I do," she would wail. I don't know if she had hatched a plan before her son Ahaziah died, but I suspect she had.

Ahaziah's ascension was precipitous and unexpected. King Ahab was killed in battle, and suddenly Ahaziah was King. For Ahaziah, such unwelcome news called for a drunken revel without parallel, at least up to that time. A king without a queen and without an heir; I think Jezebel had given up not just on a marriage of Ahaziah to a princess, but had given up on the thought of any marriage at all. Ahaziah was consumed by wine. Even encouragements and enticements to engage in debauchery could not ply Ahaziah from his wine. He was not interested. If it was not wine, he did not care.

As a drunken fool, Ahaziah did everything Jezebel ordered. He had no spine. He ignored Jeroboam's golden calves. He followed Jezebel around like a dog to her temples of Baal. I did not, but then, as long as Ahaziah was King, I did not matter. Myself, am I not an Israelite? Isn't Abraham my father also? I saw my father relent after Elijah had dressed him down. Even though it was Elijah, Elijah was an Israelite. Jehu said there was nothing wrong with giving a fellow Israelite his due. Saying something Jezebel would take as treason was a thing one would not say lightly. But we could talk freely in camp. Jehu was a valued commander. He had led Ahab's chariots into battle; he was loyal to the army and capable. Talk of gods had nothing to do with command of the army.

But the army was quiet and restless under Ahaziah. No commander desired to lead his men into battle with a drunken King. If Ahaziah was not drunk when a battle was being planned, he would be drunk by the time it began. If he was not drunk when a battle began, he would be drunk before the chariots could overtake the footmen. When Ahaziah was drunk he would scowl and frown when he was told something he did not want to hear. "Get out of my sight," would be his only response. If there was a raid or a skirmish, commander Jehu would deal with it with as few men as possible. I would ride with Jehu often. It kept me out of the palace, and besides, my grandfather was King Omri, the army commander under King Baasha.

"Your brother the King must not hear of this," Jehu would say. And I would agree. Jehu was not being disloyal. He was confiding in the brother of the King. If the matter was serious enough he would say, "You must tell Queen Jezebel about this." He was artful in what he said I must and must not tell Jezebel. And never did I disagree with Jehu's assessments. Never did I want that sot Ahaziah to issue orders to the army. And never did I want Jezebel to decree that all the inhabitants of a town or village be slaughtered, from oldest to youngest, for an imagined slight to her royal sensibilities. And yes, it let me be king after a manner. A commander of the army was confiding in me, and we made our decisions jointly. And having a commander of the army confide in me could not hurt the brother of the drunken King.

So there was peace during the short, ignominious reign of King Ahaziah, my brother, if you can call it peace. It could not have lasted long. Word would spread fast. "The men of Israel did not pursue us," - "we made off with all of their grain, and they did not send their own raiding parties." Soon, our enemies, maybe even our friends, would determine, "Israel will not fight." Then we would be meat for the jackals. Weakness. A king cannot tolerate weakness. But drunken Ahaziah would tolerate anything, as long as he had enough wine.

Then Moab rebelled against Israel. They would not have dreamed of rebelling against King Omri. King Omri had been the commander of the army and looked forward to a good battle. When my father King Ahab succeeded Omri, perhaps Moab did not want to test the son of Omri. Besides, they had seen Ahab lead his army as Israel and Aram battled King Shalmaneser of Assyria in the battle of Qarqar and respected him. Now that drunken sot Ahaziah was King. King Ahab did not expect to die when he did. Ahaziah was just an embarrassment that needed to be addressed. And yes, we would hear rumors if the son of the King of Edom or Aram was an imbecile or a rebel. So Ahaziah was not a secret from our neighbors. Now Ahaziah was not just an embarrassment, he was our King. Moab had been paying King Ahab tribute of 100,000 sheep and the wool from 100,000 rams a year. It was an onerous requirement. But King Ahab pressed them hard. He would ride behind Jehu and his chari-oteers into Moab at the time of the tribute, as if conducting a raid; just to demonstrate what would happen if the count fell short. The first year after Ahab died, the tribute stopped. And from Samaria? Silence. Moab held its breath and fortified its border towns. Aram watched. What would the son of Ahab do? The best strategy was silence. Let them think that we are filling our armories and stocking our supplies for an invasion.

And then it came to an end. Two years as King and he was gone. Obadiah rode out at night, long before dawn, with the news. Ahaziah had fallen through the lattice work around an upper room overlooking a courtyard in the palace and fell to the ground. We didn't have to ask. Of course he was drunk. What we knew for a fact was that Ahaziah was drunk, that he had been in the upper room, and that his body plum-meted from there to the ground. Anything else is conjecture. Not baseless conjecture, but conjecture nevertheless. Supposedly he was alone and no one saw how he fell. We had seen him many times before leaning over the decorative lattice work after a bout of drinking. Was it for the view, for the breeze, or to vomit? Often he would fall asleep with his arms leaning on the lattice work, his head hanging down. The workmanship, especially in the private upper rooms of the palace, was exquisite. A terrified servant had brought Ahaziah another skin of wine more than an hour before his bleeding body was found on the marble floor below by another even more terrified servant. Jezebel had both of them killed anyway. It was a bad omen to be in the presence of recently deceased or soon to be deceased royalty. One can never be too cautious in stamping out a potential regicide. I have always wondered where the Queen and her prophets were while Ahaziah was drinking in the upper room. But no one has ever asked. To make such a suggestion would doom the luckless idiot along with his wives and his children.

And then he lingered. Even while he lingered, he drank. But I think at the end he regretted his life. Was there hope? He sent messengers to the prophets of Baal-Zebub in Ekron. "Bring sacrifices to the temple of Baal-Zebub. Ask Baal-Zebub if I am going to recover." I knew of the Philistines of Ekron. When the Philistines captured Israel's Ark of the Covenant in a battle, it went from Ashdod to Gath to Ekron. Each city became more terrified of the Ark than the last. Finally, the Philistines sent their war trophy back to Israel with gifts of gold, to make sure the Ark would not be returned. I know something of old Israel. Ahaziah only knew what Jezebel knew, and Jezebel knew there was a powerful Baal in Ekron.

JEHONADAB

Jehu

We have lived in tents and have fully obeyed everything
our forefather Jehonadab commanded us. Recabites,
Jeremiah 35:10

"I AM through with this fellow, Jehu, absolutely through."
Jehonadab presented himself as a country bumpkin, but not a
bumpkin you would ever want to cross swords with, either on the battlefield, or in a discussion of the Law of the Lord. He was a driver of oxen,
a forger of iron and bronze. He could control a team of six oxen better
than anyone I had ever seen. You would think it was because of his size,
he was at least half of a Goliath, but he was also the most gentle ox driver
I have ever seen. He was always the one called on to lift, move and carry
the heavy loads, so maybe he understood the work of oxen, maybe they
understood him. Yet if an ox was a bully, he could bully it right back.

I had seen him in many campaigns. When a baggage train was stuck
with a broken axle, a shattered wheel or a lame ox, he was the one called
on to wheedle, cajole and bull the wagon, freight or animal and get the
train underway again. If iron needed forging in the field, he would hew
the trees, mount the bellows, and hammer the metal into submission.
If the army was mounting a major campaign, I always summoned Jehonadab to the field. His silent, forceful labor would inspire soldiers to
attempt to do at least half of the work Jehonadab would do to keep from
embarrassing themselves.

He was a man of the earth. Crops and animals were without guile. He understood them. He did not understand our royal family, or maybe he understood them all too well.

"They are the most perverse, mean-spirited litter of vipers ever hatched in this land."

"Worse even than the Moabites or Philistines?"

"They would hold their own with the worst of them."

"Yet you serve the King."

"I serve the nation of Israel. It is my inheritance. Kings live and die. My wife and my children and my kin live under the King. If the King does poorly, so does the nation. So yes, I serve the King also. And you? Do you admire our royal family? The house of Omri wedded to the Sidonians?"

"Yes, I serve."

"Hah! You serve you say. Since when is Jehu a man of few words?"

"I have whipped the hide off of my words and left them bleeding on the roadside and I am no further along than I had been. There are times when words do not fit the harness, when more than words needs whipping."

I have decided to unharness my words, Jehu. I have decided not to serve the land anymore."

"Serve the land?"

"If you thresh grain or tend grapes or press olives or gather figs, the King will take a King's tithe of your pittance, and demand silver and gold besides. If you do not pay, they will pull your house down or smash your press. If you own what comes from the land, you are at the mercy of the King's men."

"Is that not how it has been?"

"Is that how it was under Joshua or Samuel? I do not believe it. We served the Lord then."

"It was a different time."

"Who do we serve now? The Temple is in Jerusalem and Jerusalem has a different King. We have prophets, but the prophets are living in caves while our kings have put up so many temples and altars and high places that the people don't know who to serve. And all these priests of all these new gods say that we must bring offerings to them too. While the poor? The poor sell themselves and their children. If the King's favorite priest says he wants your house or your servant or your olive press, he will take it. None of it goes to the poor. They have it worse than dogs."

"So you have decided that you will complain about the King. That can be more dangerous than being a soldier in battle."

"No, I have decided to wait; to wait and serve myself. Jehu, I am selling my house and my fields and my barns. All of it is going except my flocks. I have told my household that we will live in tents. We will follow the sheep and goats and rams. We will have flocks and tents we can move as we wish and serve no one. If the King wants my house he will not find it. If he wants my flocks we will move. I have made all my household pledge that they will live as nomads, that they will live in tents, that they will not drink strong drink. My household is in agreement. We will not be part of this land. My kin will take our land, and we will take to our tents."

"But you will be nothing but wanderers; blown across the wilderness by tribes and armies out for plunder. You will be living on the edge of the sword. Do you wish to be like Cain?"

"Whose land are we in, Jehu? We thought we were in the promised land, but we still wander. We might as well be in the wilderness with Moses. He at least knew he was going to the promised land. But now we are in the promised land, and we are following a king who is lost. Is this our lives? Following a king and doing whatever the kings tells us to do because he is the king? Does that make me an Israelite? I might as well be in Moab or Edom or Aram. They have kings. What difference does it make what king we follow? The prophets say we were delivered from Egypt to come here. For what? My household will live in tents as Israelites and serve the Lord, and we will serve only the Lord. What good does standing rooted in your land do? You were at the vineyard of the winemaker Naboth. Where is the land of his forefathers now? And where is Naboth? He is certainly rooted to his land now; planted by Jezebel and fertilizing the very wine she drinks. She imbibes a little of Naboth at each meal, much to her delight, I am sure."

"You are a hardheaded man Jehonadab, and I can no more change your course than a blind ox on the way to water. So you will leave the army then."

"Not until I have fulfilled my pledge to the King to serve. But tell me Jehu, why do you serve?"

"It is my trade now. I have not felled a tree in a generation. I am good for nothing but the chariot and the bow. I am waiting too, Jehonadab. But I have to wait where I am. I am of no use anywhere else."

"And what do you wait for, Jehu? Another king? Another battle? Or pillage from the defeated?"

"Another king will come along, but I fear the children of Joram. I have seen them behead a beggar child in the streets and contest the head of the child on their horses through the market place. I wait, but I know things will become even worse. After Ahaziah, Joram will be king, and after Joram, Joram's son, the terror of the marketplace. I can outwit and outpace any foe in a chariot, but it gives me no pleasure if my King is just as evil as the King of my foe. Of pillage I have no use. I have seen the pillage of kings, and have seen how it festers their minds."

"And yet you wait."

"I wait, and look for a reason to wait. What will you wait for out in the wilderness and deserts of this land, Jehonadab?"

"I may give up waiting. I will serve the Lord."

"How are you serving the Lord by playing the shepherd?"

"I will live by my own flocks, by my own hands. I will not steal from the merchants, I will not crush the poor, I will not deal in slaves, I will not drink wine from the vineyards or fields or pastures of the dead. If my children live rooted to the land of their inheritance, they will either be victims of the children of Joram, or be complicit in their crimes. I will have neither. Their inheritance will be the rains from the heavens and the grass on the plains. Let the sons of the King try to wrest that from them."

KING AHAZIAH AND ELIJAH

Joram

Her hand reached for the tent peg, her right hand for the
workman's hammer. Judges 5:22

WHILE Ahaziah was waiting for word from Ekron, the old prophet
mother Jezebel called the potter shows up. The potter - Elijah
- had killed the Queen's prophets of Baal when Ahab was King. Jezebel
had conducted a frenetic manhunt for Elijah. It was only a matter of time
before he was ferreted out; anyone who may or could have helped Elijah
escape or hide paid the price. Then King Ben-Hadad of Aram invaded.
With King Ahab's army fully occupied battling Aram, the King was happy
to brush off his Queen's demands for punishment, and Elijah was all but
forgotten. When we did not hear of him after our two years of warring
with Aram had come to an end, I had assumed the old man had died
someplace out in the wilderness.

It must have been Ahaziah appealing to Baal-Zebub of Ekron that
woke him from his slumber. Elijah shows up in the flesh and confronts
Ahaziah's messengers on the way to Ekron with a message for Ahaziah.
"Tell your master he is going to die for consulting Baal-Zebub of Ekron.
There is a God in Israel." Twice Ahaziah sends an armed contingent of
fifty soldiers to bring Elijah in. Twice word comes back from the countryside, "Your soldiers were destroyed - burned to a crisp - obliterated."
Jezebel is incensed, but frightened. She had warred with gods from other
nations before, but fire falling from the sky was something none of her
prophets of Baal had been able to conjure up. She respected, even feared,

a god with this unusual power, and decided to keep herself closeted and see how Ahaziah fared when her avowed enemy Elijah entered her city. She would wait for some powerful omens before confronting the potter head on. Ahaziah on his own ordered a third contingent to capture Elijah. My brother had never set foot on a battlefield, but being King gave him the power to send men to their death. Petrified, the commander of the third contingent reaches Elijah and cries and begs for his life. I guess Elijah felt he had made his point.

I was amazed at the recklessness of Elijah. He strolls into Samaria with his walking staff and marches right into the royal palace. Did he forget that Queen Jezebel lives here? But the third contingent of solders followed Elijah all the way to the palace. "Hands off this fellow." They were afraid they would pay the same price as the first two contingents of troops if Elijah did not receive safe passage.

So there is Elijah, in the royal palace, and face to face he tells King Ahaziah, "You will not recover. There is a God in Israel, but since you sent for Baal-Zebub, you will die in the bed you are lying in." I had to follow Elijah in. I had to see what Jezebel would do. But nothing happened. Ahaziah stared at Elijah for the longest time, but Ahaziah did not speak. He stared at Elijah expressionless and motionless. Old Elijah with his goat-skin vest tied with a length of weathered leather, hand on his staff, long beard moving slightly in the breeze stood before the silent Ahaziah for as long as Ahaziah was silent. "What are you waiting for old prophet," I thought. I expected him to deliver his judgment and turn on his sandals at his last word and run out of the palace as fast as his bandy legs could take him. But he stood as a judge after pronouncing his decision and imposing the penalty, waiting for a plea of mercy from the condemned. But none came. He looked steadily into Ahaziah's eyes. But Ahaziah's eyes were vacant. I don't know if Elijah saw anything in Ahaziah's eyes, but I didn't.

Maybe this is what Ahaziah wanted. The wine did not kill him soon enough. Maybe he did go over the lattice work voluntarily. Maybe the clasps were not removed. Maybe he was not helped over in a drunken stupor. Whatever happened, I believe it was what Ahaziah wanted to happen. "There will be no heir for you from me, mother Jezebel." But he followed Jezebel around so willingly to the temples of Baal. He never sought out any word from a prophet of Israel's god. Where were you Ahaziah? Your father Ahab had gone around in sackcloth and ashes after Elijah issued his judgment against Ahab. But Ahaziah? Nothing. He had been hollowed out. Maybe by Queen Jezebel; maybe by himself. Maybe he was still waiting for some word from Baal-Zebub, and just didn't care what Elijah was saying.

I was not surprised that Elijah pronounced some kind of condemnation on Ahaziah. But I was startled to hear him say Ahaziah would die. Not that the Lord would take his life, not that Elijah would kill him, just that he would die—for consulting the wrong god. As I watched Elijah who continued to silently gaze at Ahaziah, I began to realize that I would soon be King. I thought that Elijah would turn to me, the next King of Israel, and issue some type of warning or condemnation. At first I wanted to say something to Elijah, but King Ahaziah was holding court. It was not my place. Yes, Ahaziah was my brother, but I had spent years watching Queen Jezebel hold court, afraid to blink at the wrong time. But Elijah did not pay me any notice. I had seen this old man briefly before when I was still a boy. He did not miss anything. There was less spring in his step, but his eyes were clear and sharp, and his voice was like a quiet knife. So he chose not to speak to me.

There had been prophets and priests and diviners and sorcerers in the royal palace before. Most of them earned their living trying to inflate the king's ego, or by heaping praise and adoration on Queen Jezebel, prophesying great things that her sons and daughters would accomplish, the nations they would subjugate and the wealth they would bring to Samaria. Those seers would perform wonders, real stagecraft. We would argue afterwards who was the best diviner, using their performance to support what our plan was, debating whether a particular sorcerer had been able to foretell events in the past. If the prophecy was about war, the army commanders would chime in. "That man is a lunatic! It is not possible that anything like that will happen. He has no idea what the plains of Moab are like." But with old man Elijah it was different. So many tales had been told of him. He lived out in the wilds, dependent on no one. He went to the market for nothing. He did not live off of some temple, and he certainly was not on the payroll of the palace. He had no favorites in the royal household. No one was on his side.

I could see that the keeper of the royal household, Obadiah, was struck dumb when Elijah strolled into the palace that day. It was like he had been struck by lightning, or expected to be. His mouth fell open; his arms limp at his sides. Obadiah is not quite as old as Elijah, but I can tell that some of these old Israelites feel that old Elijah is the "word of the Lord" walking around. They were not old enough to remember Solomon's kingdom, but as children they had heard stories from their parents of the glories of Jerusalem under Solomon. The Temple in Jerusalem still meant a lot to them. They would not go to worship the golden calves in Dan or Bethel. And Obadiah would do anything short of getting his head cut off to avoid going into a temple for Baal.

But Elijah strode past Obadiah without a glance. You could only hear the wind blowing through the curtains. None of Jezebel's favorite prophets tried to shout him down or interrupt him. He did not bow to the King, there was no "Oh great King live forever," and no, "Oh great King your renown sweeps over the lands like a mighty flood." It was just, "Ahaziah!" Then he told Ahaziah his fate. Baal. That was the problem. But who in the royal family did not serve Baal in one way or another? Queen Jezebel is in one Baal temple or another almost every day. Even though Jezebel was considered the Queen in Samaria, she did not reign as King. Ahaziah was King and, according to Elijah, that was what mattered.

And then Ahaziah died. Not right then. But everyone knew it was coming. In two weeks he was dead. Killed by the ribs shattered in his fall, not by Elijah, not by any god. Had Elijah's god won this battle against Baal, or did Ahaziah kill himself with his fall? Whatever happened, Jezebel redoubled her offerings to Baal in temples throughout Israel over the next month.

GRISTLE AND BONE

Jehu

The King would have my head because of you. Ashpenaz,
Daniel 1:10

W ORD came quickly to me that the prophet Elijah had entered the
royal palace.

"That old fool," I commented to Bidkar, "how many times has he
fled from that palace? Is he so old he feels he has no life left to preserve?"

"If the word of the Lord tells him to go, he will go, palace or not."

"Jezebel is at the palace, she has not forgotten her prophets he had
killed."

"What can we do? He delivered himself to the palace. He was not
summoned."

"Bidkar, go to the palace. If he is ordered struck down, step to his
side and take him to the city gates, I will meet you there. If there is still
any life left in him when you reach the gates, I will take responsibility for
his life."

We parted, both shaking our heads at our half-cooked plan. But
what could we do? As Bidkar said, Elijah had delivered himself to the
palace.

As it was, Elijah did not need our help. The third set of Ahaziah's
troops escorted Elijah up to the royal palace, past the palace guard and
directly into King Ahaziah. Elijah did not spend much time with the King.
Once he was done, I think the troops wanted to get Elijah off their hands
as soon as possible. By the time Bidkar reached him, Elijah was walking

out of the palace, his troop escort still following him, but hanging back as if he were a wandering bolt of lightning seeking out something to strike. Bidkar took the old prophet by the arm and moved him to the gate of the city faster even than the prophet's normal rapid gait.

As he approached the gate, the old man looked like he didn't like being hurried, but still appreciated being moved away from Jezebel's abode speedily.

"Prophet, I am Jehu. I am going to get you away from the city. Where are you going?"

"I know who you are soldier. We have talked before. I have lost a few steps but not my mind."

"No, you have not changed."

I enjoyed talking to someone who did not call me "commander." A soldier who would talk to me as Elijah did would be whipped. But this man had condemned kings to their face, and the lashings he held in store for me I sometimes enjoyed, but not always.

"Perhaps if you were more diplomatic, you would not have to flee the palace so quickly. Baal's prophets eat at the King's table." Elijah's sidelong glance at me was that of a teacher chastising a student for forgetting a lesson.

"Where in God's law does it say to build ivory walled palaces? Where in God's law does it say to build terraced gardens and temples to strange gods? Where in God's law does it say to use slaves from your own people to build these things?"

I am not a prophet, prophet, I am a soldier. How should I know of those things?"

"Yes, you are a soldier. The men under your command enjoy hearing you say such things."

"And it is true."

"But you are a soldier that has the King's ear. You are more than a soldier."

"I may have the King's ear, but I do not have his tongue."

"But the King's ear can sheathe many a sword. Why does Israel have an army, soldier?"

"An army, prophet? Should all Israel be like Ziklag with our houses burned and wives and children taken captive? Shall we all have our right eyes gouged out by the Ammonites again? Shall we beg the Philistines for iron weapons as in the times of King Saul? Must we drool and act like a madman as David did before the King of Gath? You see prophet, I have questions for your answers as well. Did not our father David have an army?

"When a Moabite or a Sidonian or an Aramean comes to Israel, he sees an army. Does he see the army of the Lord?"

"He sees the army of Israel. Was not Israel the son of Isaac and Isaac the son of Abraham? So is this not the army of Abraham's children? Is that not a good question for a prophet?"

"Your wits awaken from slumber. That is a good thing. And is that why Moses brought Israel to Canaan? Because there were not enough armies here already? Were the Canaanites not slaughtering enough Amorites? Were the Edomites not slaughtering enough Moabites? Did the Lord need the children of Abraham to increase the slaughter? What is the purpose of this army of yours, soldier?"

"Prophet, the sword does not question its master. That is why I am a soldier and not a prophet. I would rather slice your words from the air than chew and digest them. They are full of gristle and bone."

"Your dull wits you use as a weapon. Your dullness is a feint, a false sally you dispatch to avoid a pitched battle with God's will."

"Tell me God's will then, prophet. If I say I do not want to hear it, you will tell me. Perhaps if I ask you to speak, your contrary mind will strike you dumb."

"I know God's law; I trust that his will is in his law. I know the law does not say, 'Build me an army to do my will.'"

The old man was silent for a moment, his gait slowed as he paused to peer into the sky for a moment "And yet we have an army. It has saved us from the Arameans and the Philistines, but it has also been used to oppress. It was used by King Baasha against King Asa when they slaughtered thousands of their kinsmen in battle. I know Baasha and Asa's slaughter was not the will of the Lord. Yet the army was used by Omri to overthrow the murderer Zimri. Was that a good thing soldier? Was that the will of the Lord?"

"Oh prophet! You are now asking a soldier what the will of the Lord is? Next you will inquire of a school of shepherds, or maybe a council of lepers."

"I did not ask that question of a shepherd because a flock of sheep never overthrew a king. I asked the question of you, because you are commander of the King's chariots, Jehu."

I stopped walking as if his words had pierced me. The old man kept up his pace; he must have been walking when he left his mother's womb. I shouted to his back, "That is a dangerous thing you say!"

The old man kept walking as if he was being borne by the tides, saying nothing in reply. We were well away from the city thanks to his pace. I turned and began walking back to the city.

MIRACLES

Elijah

His word in my heart is like a fire. I am weary of holding
it. Jeremiah, Jeremiah 20:9

A ND what did the people of Israel want to see? Miracles! Of course! A wonder to entertain them, something to talk about. An event to fill them with wonder as an earthquake or a windstorm. Something to boast about with their neighbors; something to tell their children. And what did they mean, these miracles? No one knew. Oh, they knew alright, but they didn't care. It was like the sacrifices in the Temple in Jerusalem. Let's go to be entertained, to see the big bulls slashed and cut apart, to see the priests work their wonders, the ceremony, the crowds, the markets. Maybe it was just as well the people of Israel stopped going to Jerusalem for the old festivals. What did they go to see anyway?

But the miracles only lasted so long anyway. Like last year's floods remembered during this year's drought, they no longer bring any water. And the priests of Baal were wonder workers when it came to miracles anyway. Raise the dead? The prophets of Baal could raise the multitudes. Litter after litter of lifeless bodies were carried into their temples, covered with grievous sores and lesions, with grave wounds and gore, accompanied with wailing mourners. And then the ablutions, chanting, incantations, the cutting and slashing, almost as if they were to produce more dead, and wonder upon wonder, their dead were raised, and in such good health it was as if they had never been dead in the first place. Produce an endless supply of food; feed a hundred with a few loaves? The prophets of Baal called forth banquets of succulents and rivers of wine from the rocks, so powerful was their god.

Of course, just like the miracles done at my hand, sooner or later the miracles of the priests of Baal will cease. I do not know why the miracles by my hand ceased, just as I could not tell you why they were put in my hands in the first place—although I have my ideas.

I do know why the prophets of Baal got out of the miracle business; the demand for their miracles exceeded their ability to produce. Crowds would throng the temples insisting on the next feeding. Many more miracles and their treasuries would be exhausted. They learned, as I already knew, that no matter how impressive the wonder, it was the crowd's stomach that dictated their hunger for miracles. Rather than adoring devotees, they garnered angry petitioners insisting on a miracle banquet greater than the last. The real problems began when their devotees began dragging cadavers of dead family members to the temples insisting that they be brought to life. Tempers flared, fights broke out, sacred lights were knocked to the floor starting fires, and sacred objects were flung at the priests and prophets. "Why will not your god raise my child from the dead? I saw others raised." The blame had to be placed squarely on the survivors. They had not done as Baal had required, they must do more or they will meet the same fate. Perhaps your child should be sacrificed to make amends. After much shouting and recriminations, the demand for resurrections plummeted.

The real miracle? That I was not murdered by the kings. How I have outlasted that tyrant King Ahab, I do not know. He did not outlive Queen Jezebel, but the fact that he had survived her for so many years was a wonder in itself. Despite their miracles, one wonder I did not see the prophets of Baal perform was to prophesy to the King that he was going to die. The prophets of Baal had seen the prophet Micaiah in the King's dungeon. Their god was not stupid. It was a rare prophet of Baal that would dare challenge the King.

I would rather perform my miracles with stiff mud on my wheel. That was creation. I can call forth something from nothing and put it through the fire to give it life. If the form does not please me, I can take it off my wheel, meld it back into mud and refashion it to please me. That is what I had hoped the Lord would do with this Kingdom of Israel. Perhaps that is what the Lord was trying to do with these kings and princes, queens and princesses. We spent many days and nights when we would gather at our meeting place along the Jordan River reading our worn scrolls back to each other, searching to understand this kingdom of ours. "We are not just another kingdom," some would argue, "we have been called into being by the Lord." Others would say, "but our kings have turned their back on the Lord." "Yes," others would shout back, "but the Lord has not called on us to anoint another king," while others would rejoin, "the people called for a king, not the Lord, why should we hope for another king?"

I would leave to turn some pots when these young prophets would start shouting at each other. Even prophets need to trade for goods. We would ply our trades in our home villages, but after we returned from Jerusalem, if any of us were able to sneak off to Jerusalem in the off season, we would meet to discuss what the Lord was doing. The young prophets knew when I was at the wheel that I felt that their words were sand and dust that would never hold bread, figs or wine.

I was not convinced that the Lord's heart was held captive by these kings and the people that shouldered their way up to the King's table to engorge themselves. I held to the words of David, "The ends of the earth will remember and turn to the Lord and all the families of the nations will bow down before the Lord." The nations will bow down to the Lord, not to these kings in their palace in Samaria, not even to the King that lives in Jerusalem.

The Lord had sent me to the town of Zarapheth, in the region of Sidon, to stay with a widow during the famine of King Ahab's reign. I was sent to King Ahab and King Ahaziah of Israel, but to tell them that they would perish. And I am being sent to anoint Hazael, an aide of King Ben-Hadad of Aram as King over Aram. Ben-Hadad is still king of Aram, so I do not know when I will be sent. I will go where the Lord sends me. I have trod on the soil of Israel and the soil of other kingdoms; it is all the Lord's land, and I see no difference. I heard the Lord's whisper on Mount Horeb. Kings and queens announce themselves with thundering drums, crashing cymbals and blaring horns; it is not the Lord they are announcing, it is not the sound of the Lord's voice.

Rather than kings, I believe the Lord has cast his lot with his word. It is up to the nation of Israel and it is up to the nation of Judah if they follow the word of the Lord. I have cast the Lord's word into the face of these kings and into the face of these people, and they only sputter, as if it is only water. It drips off their faces and they tread it underfoot.

As for me, my time is short. I have anointed my successor, Elisha, an ox of a man. I found him driving twelve yoke of oxen. Even with his helpers, there are few in Israel capable of the task. It requires stamina and determination to control the beasts, along with an ability to reason with the seemingly irrational sensibilities of the beast—a task much like that of being a prophet to the Lord's people. I believe it was with his flaming spirit, a spirit of fury and zeal, that he kept the oxen in check; it seemed as if the oxen recognized Elisha's flame, fury and zeal as he drove them down furrows he willed to be as straight as a plumb line. After I anointed Elisha, he sacrificed the twelve yoke of oxen he had been driving as an offering to the Lord, something it would have taken a family of Levites all day, and something many prophets believed would be a fitting end for many of their listeners.

Elisha's flame, fury and zeal will carry on the word of the Lord. But will the Kings listen? Will the people listen? Whether they do or not, the word of the Lord will travel on with the flame, fury and zeal of Elisha until it finds a listener.

I know of the Lord's will for Hazael, commander of the army of Aram, and for Jehu, commander of the army of Israel. They will be instruments of the Lord should events already in motion not be stopped by those who have put them in motion. They will be instruments of the Lord to execute judgment. Jehu is a soldier with zeal and fury, but not the flame. He will drive his chariot headlong into battle, far ahead of the charioteers he commands, with one word from his King. Yet he rails against his King, and his King before that, and his King before that. Yet he still drives his chariot with the same fury. He seems to bend the course of battle with his fury, just as Elisha's fury bent the will of his oxen.

Perhaps my own flame and fury has dimmed. I have flashed the brilliance of the word of the Lord into the faces of kings and princes and they have remained wet, sodden and dull. It has chilled my zeal. I have run for my life. I have hidden in caves and deserts. I have been sheltered by widows. I have visited the widows and children of the prophets cut down by Jezebel the Queen. I have seen the Lord's altars torn down. But still I am sent.

THE MOAB REVOLT

Joram, Jehu

I have heard the insults of Moab. Zephaniah 2:8

Joram

So that blight on the House of Omri, my beloved brother Ahaziah, is history; a history that will not be recorded. But to erase Ahaziah, we must erase what we lost due to Ahaziah. My first task is to bring Moab back in line. The loss of Moab's tribute has strained our treasury, true. But what is Moab doing with the tribute it is holding back? Paying its metal workers to make swords and shields? Sending gifts to Aram to form an alliance against us? Other kings are watching to see how weak Israel has become.

We sent an emissary to Moab:

> Do not think that Ahaziah was the House of Omri. Do you re-
> member King Omri? Do you remember the wrath of King Omri
> over your land? Would you prefer that wrath to a few of your
> sheep? Do you remember King Ahab? Do you remember how
> King Ahab repelled the Assyrian hordes at Qarqar; how King
> Ahab led the armies of Aram and Hamath and eight other king-
> doms against the Assyrians while the King of Moab lay whim-
> pering and shaking in his bed, counting out his treasury and his
> wives to give to Shalmaneser? Where is Shalmaneser now? Will
> he help you?

Do you remember how King David took your measure and slew two out of every three of your warriors as they lay prostrate on the ground before him? Do you think the House of Omri is more merciful?

I, King Joram, son of King Ahab, of the House of Omri, will not take your measure. There will be no one left to measure. I, King Joram, will not spare one out of ten.

Restore now what rightfully belongs to the House of Omri. The army of King Ahab stands ready. Had King Ahab not saved you from the Assyrians, you would now be a eunuch serving the Queen of Assyria, and your sheep would be scattered over a thousand hills. Do not continue your insults to the House of Omri.

King Mesha of Moab had our emissary sacrificed to their god Molech. His charred and hacked bones were sent back with the emissary's blinded servant in an ox cart. It was a sign that Moab had made good use of the tribute they had withheld. The Moabites thought I was another Ahaziah. Within a year one of our neighbors would be invading, seeking to carve a piece of Israel off for themselves, and then another. We swiftly sent messengers to King Jehoshaphat of Judah, and, separately, to Queen Athaliah, my sister and Jezebel's daughter. An alliance is one thing, family is another.

To Jehoshaphat, King of Judah:
Most esteemed King Jehoshaphat!
You have now heard of the abomination practiced by those pagan Moabites. An Israelite sacrificed to Chemosh! Is that not a rebuke to the great Temple in Jerusalem? Are we not brothers? If one descendant of Abraham has been sacrificed to their detestable god, will there not be others? Does not your great God of the Temple in Jerusalem demand that this spilled blood be avenged? Are not the actions of that swine Mesha the Moabite a call to arms to the ruler of every walled city with a statue of a god who is still jealous of the great kingdom of Solomon? Will not that slave Mesha now seek to rally all our neighbors into an alliance against us? I beseech you, my brother, let us join our armies against the followers of the detestable Chemosh. Let us make Moab an answer to all who would do us harm.
Your brother, King Joram of Israel.

❉ ❉ ❉

To Athaliah, wife of Jehoram, the King's son:

Daughter, heir to the throne of Judah, daughter of the Queen of Israel, and descendant of the mighty King Omri: A courier has been sent to your husband's father Jehoshaphat, the King of Judah. The King of Moab has done violence to the name of our father, King Omri. Now the jackals will seek to assail us from every side.

Many in Jerusalem would love to see our blood spilled. They will say King Baasha fought against King Jehoshaphat's father King Asa for years. They will say King Omri enlarged his own domain and did nothing to help Judah. They will say your father King Ahab blasphemed the god of their temple in Jerusalem. Remind your husband that your father King Ahab died while fighting the King of Aram with his father, King Jehoshaphat. My daughter, King Joram is your brother. King Jehoshaphat and your husband cannot refuse King Joram's request. Save us!

My daughter, kings die in battle. Should the sword take King Joram or King Jehoshaphat, we must think of our royal line. Think of the Queen of Judah and the Queen of Israel united; our two nations as one. Think of your sons and daughters married to the Kings of Aram or Edom or Egypt!

I will be sacrificing in the house of Baal every day until I receive your answer

Your Mother, Jezebel, daughter of Ethbaal I, Queen of Israel, Queen mother of King Joram, son of King Ahab, son of King Omri.

Jehu

Warfare and revelry. There is something obscene about the way kings celebrate the beginning of a new season of battle. Since our objective of Moab was to the south of the Kingdom of Israel and on the eastern shore of the Dead Sea, opposite the Kingdom of Judah, it was agreed that King Joram would lead the army of Israel to Jerusalem where their council of war would be held. The Kingdom of Judah controlled Edom and King Jehoshaphat appointed the governor of Edom, so the army of Edom was enlisted to join Judah and Israel in the expedition. The armies would proceed from Jerusalem in their campaign against Moab. The armies encamped outside Jerusalem and the kings set up their pavilions in the center of the encampment, after which a full week of feasting, boasting, races and diversions were observed. Old King Jehoshaphat preferred to tell war stories than create any new ones, and young King Joram simply preferred revelry to anything else. The soldiers of Israel were steeled and determined on their march from Samaria, but after a week of idleness they had everything on their minds but battle.

For some reason King Jehoshaphat felt that he had to match the revelry that King Ahab had staged when King Jehoshaphat had encamped outside Samaria before the disastrous campaign against Aram. From what I learned from the commanders from Judah, King Jehoshaphat still believed that Ahab had schemed to have him killed at the battle at Ramoth-Gilead. But Jehoshaphat's gamble at Ramoth-Gilead had paid off. A stray arrow had found Ahab, and the prophet Micaiah's prophecy of Ahab's demise came to pass.

It took several days for the commanders of the army to get the kings to talk strategy. Riders from Jehoshaphat's border outposts brought word that Moab, aware that Israel's army had marched out of Samaria, was assembling forces on their northern border to the East of the Dead Sea. Jehoshaphat made the determination that the armies should go around the south end of the Dead Sea and attack through Edom's arid desert at Moab's undefended southern border.

I was relieved when neither King asked to consult with the prophets. Perhaps King Jehoshaphat recalled the debacle of prophecy on the threshing floor of Samaria before the campaign against Aram. I preferred to determine the order of battle based on the number of our horsemen and chariots, not on the whims and imaginations of those people who preyed on a king's indecisiveness.

Although not summoned, Elijah's successor Elisha had joined the army on its way to Jerusalem somewhere south of Jezreel. Perhaps Elisha could see that these two Kings would sooner or later find themselves wandering blindly through the wilderness and seek some illumination. Elisha the muscular ox driver looked nothing like his predecessor Elijah the famished potter. Old Elijah would look like he was being blown over the ground by a whirlwind. The hulking Elisha looked like one of his yoked oxen, furrowing the earth under his feet as he went. But the mind and tongue of Elisha had the same frightening flash of lightning, with perhaps more thunder, than old Elijah. Talking to the new madman was just as irritating as talking to the old madman.

BATTLING FOR THE POOR

Elisha

Is it not enough to try the patience of men? Will you try
the patience of God also? Isaiah, Isaiah 7:13

I HAD known of the kings of Israel through my teacher Elijah. King
Joram was the first King of Israel I met face to face. I do not pretend to
know the ways of the Lord, but I could not understand why I was directed
to follow the armies of Judah, Israel and Edom as they sought to exact
retribution on Moab. Were the followers of Chemosh worse that the followers of Baal? God's people were scattered throughout the Kingdom of
Israel, but they were no better than the Israelites during the times of the
Judges. It was as if God's people once again had no chariots, no weapons
of iron, no walled cities, no ruler and were reduced to hiding in the hills
coming out only at night to harvest wheat and pick grapes, if there were
any left.

So I followed the camp of King Joram in his folly against Moab. It
would seem that the last place the word of the Lord would come to me
would be in the middle of an army camp, but it was better to be out in
the desert where the King was concerned only with the army than to
be in Samaria where Jezebel would have the run of the countryside. I
had decided to travel alongside the baggage train with one or two of my
brother prophets in order to keep out of sight of the King. Commander
Jehu put us in one of the carts carrying food and equipment following a
detachment of his chariots on the flank of the column.

Dust, dirt, sun and wind were all we saw. We rode for seven days through the dessert of Edom on our way to Moab. Jehu could not stand the pace, although his pace was not the pace of the expedition. He would constantly drive his chariot from the scouts in front of the column to the flanks to the rear guard and back again. He knew the army well, from the soldiers to the metal and leather workers to the cooks to the baggage train, stopping to talk to everyone, and then rushing on to the next.

The kings constantly sent patrols out and waited for them to come back before deciding to march on. We saw only shepherds and traders, no one that looked like they may be a Moabite picket or scout. Then we would halt while the Kings sent riders to retrace our steps to make sure a force was not creeping up on us from behind. "Forward, my lords, forward!" Jehu would exclaim, "We are giving them notice we are on our way, we must move before those shepherds bring word back to their army!" But King Joram was either too cautious or to scared. "They may be laying in wait. They may have withdrawn their forces and are waiting to encircle us once we are well into Moab." But then he would lace his caution with boasts of how he would crush those upstarts from Moab.

King Jehoshaphat listened to Joram's boasting and could only think of going to war with Joram's father King Ahab against the Arameans years ago, and how Ahab had boasted so much before he took an arrow between his shoulders. King Jehoshaphat was not so eager for battle that he was given to boasting. He had spent his early years as King putting the Philistines and the Arabs under his thumb and collecting tribute. By now Judah had been at peace for years, feared and respected by all of Judah's neighbors, with a strong kingdom that was looking like King Omri's of Israel at his peak.

Jehu and I would talk while we waited and waited for the scouts to return. I felt like I should be a teacher to him, but he was not a willing student and it felt like the words I spoke to him were said to chastise and irritate him. He had many questions about Elijah and the way of the Lord, and many questions about the Kingdom of Israel. We had spoken of these matters before, but as an army commander of Israel now marching alongside King Jehoshaphat's army of Judah he thought of tactics and strategies for the combined armies of Israel and Judah, which opened up broader questions about these two separate nations so closely related. He was an intense, hard-headed soldier who would run the world his way if he could. I tried to get him to see the world, and especially the kingdom he served, from some other viewpoint.

"Then tell me, prophet, if the Lord's Temple and the Lord's priests are in Jerusalem, why do you prophets roam our land, far from the Temple in Jerusalem? And let me prophesy, prophet; you will answer with a question."

"Were not Miriam and Aaron the Lord's first prophets?"

"I am truly a prophet, proven by my prophecies! You tell me, prophet. We hear little of Miriam and Aaron in the temples in Bethel and Dan."

"That's because there are no Levites in Bethel and Dan. They all fled to Jerusalem when your King Jeroboam built the temples in Bethel and Dan."

"That I know. So how are we supposed to know all of the things you speak of, prophet?"

"You are an Israelite. The Lord has claimed you. The Lord is your birthright. You owe your breath to the Lord. You are required to seek him out."

"How are we to seek him out if the priests in our temples in Bethel and Dan are ignorant of his ways?"

"Miriam and Aaron were the Lord's prophets well before your temples to the golden calves were built, even before the Temple in Jerusalem was built. The Lord's work is not kept captive in the Temple. There are prophets in the land, soldier. Are you ignorant of this?"

"I am ignorant of many things, prophet. And sometimes I wish I were ignorant of you. But it is not my lot to be ignorant of the prophets. You prophets nip at the heels of the King like curs. How can I, a commander of the King's army, be ignorant of you? But what of the people who go to the temples at Bethel and Dan. How can they help but be ignorant?"

"Are they not Israelites?"

"They are, prophet. And now you will say that they must seek out the Lord. That is a heavy burden to place on them. Jezebel has scattered the prophets, and those she has not killed she has put in prisons. So the people are to go out to the wilderness or to the prisons to hear the word of the Lord? They will be chased into the wilderness next."

"You answer your own questions. Maybe you are ready to become a prophet."

"I am enough of a prophet to know I will not become a prophet."

"The heavy burden was placed on your people by your kings, soldier."

"It is still a burden regardless of where it came from."

"When the prophet struck Jeroboam with leprosy for building his temples for his calves, did the people not think they should take notice?"

"That was a long time ago, prophet. That generation is gone and the temples to the calves are still here."

"When the prophet Ahijah, the same prophet that anointed Jeroboam King, told Jeroboam's wife that Jeroboam's son would not recover from his illness because of Jeroboam's temples, and the son died, did the people not notice?"

"Why didn't the priests in the temple die? Why the King's son?"

"When Ahijah on that same day told Jeroboam's wife that the entire house of Jeroboam would be burned in the fire like a pile of dung because of Jeroboam's temples, and when that came to pass, did not the people learn of the Lord's anger over Jeroboam's temples?"

"Old stuff prophet, old stuff. And where is that written? Where is it proclaimed? How are the people supposed to know of these things that happened before their parents were born?"

"Are you listening soldier?"

"The Lord has cursed me with ears so you can afflict me with your haranguing. So yes, the prophets. They could listen to you prophets."

"When the prophet Jehu bar-Hanani told King Baasha that his house would end because he continued the temples of Jeroboam, and when Zimri wiped the house of Baasha from the face of the earth, did not the people think that was important to notice? And that brings us to the house of Omri. Is that old stuff too, soldier?"

"You tell me it's the temples, prophet. But Elijah told me it was the slaves and the impoverished. So which is it?"

"Don't play the fool with me, Jehu. The Lord strives for the poor; 'Because the poor are plundered and the needy groan, I will now arise.' The Lord will be worshiped and the poor will be served. What does Baal have to do with the poor, other than to crush the weak? To serve the Lord is to serve the poor."

"I am a soldier, prophet, I serve the King. I do not proclaim the word of the Lord, I do not serve in the temples, I do not serve food to the poor."

"But who do you serve? Were things better with King Baasha than they were with King Jeroboam? Were things better with King Ahab than they were with King Baasha? I have walked the streets of Samaria. I could have been in Sidon. There are beggars in the streets outside of the temples of Baal. The land of the poor has been taken from them. They sell themselves into slavery, while caravan after caravan of ivory traveled through the same streets to make King Ahab's palaces even greater than could be imagined."

"I am a soldier, prophet, a soldier."

"You are a son of Abraham, soldier. Have you abandoned the Lord?"

"I have not."

"Why do you think I keep talking to you, soldier?"

"You keep talking because I have not taken out my sword yet."

"I would not be the first prophet to meet my end at the edge of a sword of the Houses of Omri and Ethbaal."

"I have not raised my sword against any prophets. King Ahab knew I would not."

"And the answer to my question, soldier?"

"You keep talking because you cannot be silent."

"That is very true, soldier. Maybe I will make a prophet of you yet. I do keep talking soldier, but my riddle for you is why do I keep talking to you?'

❊   ❊   ❊

Then a more immediate theological issue arose. At least King Joram thought it was a theological issue. After seven days of all but sitting still in the desert, the army had run out of water. To lead an army you should know how much a horse drinks each day; you should know how many hours it has been since we crossed the last brook or left the last wadi. But no, it was now his commanders' fault, and as his commanders pointed fingers in all directions, which started to lead back to the King, it now became the Lord's fault. The Lord had apparently called the Kings of Judah, Israel and Edom together to hand them over to Moab. I have no control over what prophets King Joram listened to in his palace when he decided on this venture. I'm sure his palace prophets were feeling the pinch from the reduced revenues from Moab. What prophet doesn't like to swell in oratory and receive generous gifts when his predilection proves right? Sometimes all it takes is good grasp of the situation to appear brilliant.

The prophets in King Joram's train melted away as far as they could from the King as they feared being called to account. They had been in the van with the King, smelling an easy victory and a beneficence of plunder from a King thankful for their supporting prophecies.

"Those damned prophet have so many answers while standing on the soft carpets of the palace sipping wine and pomegranate juice," groused King Joram, who had been more than happy to listen to his favorite prophets go on glowingly about the mighty victories their deities would deliver into his hand. "Did any of them declare to me that we would run of water?"

Suddenly the King felt he had a revelation. It is that god of the temple in Jerusalem. Joram suddenly explodes, "Has the Lord called us three Kings together only to deliver us into the hands of Moab?"

King Jehoshaphat rolled his eyes. I heard later that in his camp that night King Jehoshaphat lamented ever undertaking this adventure in combination with King Joram. "And to think that I married my son to the sister of that fool. What has happened to the mighty House of Omri? One day he thanks Baal for the rain, and then curses Molech for the flood. One day he thanks the Lord for the sunshine and the next day he curses Chemosh for the wind."

King Jehoshaphat wanted no part of one of Joram's rages tearing our camp apart as he takes his wrath out against whatever god he thinks is to blame for his own stupidity. King Jehoshaphat asked, "Is there no prophet of the Lord here, through whom we may inquire of the Lord?" This was the second time King Jehoshaphat had asked that question of a King of Israel. The first time was to Joram's father King Ahab, shortly before Ahab was cut down by an Aramean arrow. If he had not before, I imagine King Jehoshaphat began wondering how he had agreed to allow his son to marry the sister of this dolt.

Jehu answered, "Elisha son of Shaphat is here. He is the successor to the prophet Elijah."

Jehu may have been risking his life in volunteering this information. King Joram no doubt was aware of word in the camp that I had been following the army. King Joram took every occasion to defame me as the ox driver who pretends to be Elijah. It was not that he could stand Elijah. Elijah had discredited his father Ahab, claiming credit for lifting the siege of Samaria that Ahab was helpless to lift. He did not want any god, Baal, the golden calves or that deity of the temple in Jerusalem claiming credit that was due the King. One thing that King Joram had learned from his mother Queen Jezebel is to never look weak, and never allow anyone to make him look weak, and he felt that Elijah had made his father Ahab look weak. He was too great a coward to defame Elijah, who was held in high regard in the countryside, so he contented himself with claiming I was a charlatan pretending to be Elijah.

Once Jehu told the kings that I was in the camp, King Joram had no choice but to seek me out. King Jehoshaphat said, "The word of the Lord is with him." So Jehoshaphat, Joram and the King of Edom followed Jehu back to the baggage train to search me out.

My attendant Gehazi arrived at my tent breathless. "The Kings are coming to speak to you."

No sooner had he said these words when the Kings' guard could be seen coming down the path to my tent, soon followed by the Kings and their retinue. Some of the Kings' guard entered my tent first, with some of the Kings' retainers on their heels, when the guard had to back out, realizing that they were entering a soldier's tent, and not a royal pavilion. After a few moments of embarrassed shuffling, King Jehoshaphat and King Joram, each with an attendant and guard crowded into my tent. Gehazi had to stand outside to give them room.

Royal protocol may have required me to stand outside my tent to bow to my royal visitors, but there was no real protocol for a king entering a soldier's tent to hold an audience with a prophet. Whatever the protocol, I thought it fitting for the kings to be forced to exercise some humility if they were seeking the word of the Lord, bowing unavoidably as they ducked their heads to enter my tent.

I knew that whatever answer they sought, it was King Jehoshaphat who had brought them to my tent. King Joram's mother Jezebel had never inquired of a prophet of the Lord, except to ask where the other prophets were hiding, and Joram's brother King Ahaziah on his death bed had sent for word from the prophets of Baal-Ekron. King Joram himself had always been convinced that in the battle between the gods, the Lord of Israel constantly contended against the House of Ahab.

It was fitting then that King Joram was the first to speak.

"Prophet Elijah, the people seem to think that you are a great seer. And yet you have been following our armies for these seven days, and have not sent word to your King that the wells and springs that flow in Edom this time of year were dried up. Does not your god tell you these things?"

I waited to see if King Jehoshaphat cared to redress Joram, but he remained silent. So I answered Joram.

"Why do you want to involve me? Go to the prophets of your father and the prophets of your mother."

"No," Joram answered, "because it was the Lord who called us three kings together to deliver us into the hands of Moab."

I said, "As surely as the Lord Almighty lives, whom I serve, if I did not have respect for the presence of Jehoshaphat King of Judah, I would not pay any attention to you. But now bring me a harpist."

It was a strange request, but I knew that King Joram brought musicians with him even on a campaign with the army. King Joram little appreciated that I was requisitioning one of his musicians, but with King Jehoshaphat present he had no choice but comply. After a few minutes the harp player was given a chest to sit on outside my tent. King Joram was accustomed to conjurers who were adept at thinking on their feet and spinning thorny riddles for princes who insisted that their gods answer to their every whim. I was buying time. I felt that the Lord was telling me that Joram and Jehoshaphat would leave without victory, but felt restrained from telling them that.

While the harpist was playing, I had a stronger feeling, one I had difficulty accepting, but one I felt the hand of the Lord guiding me to deliver to the kings. How it comes I do not know. Sometimes it comes with insight and understanding. Sometimes it is so simply stated in the Law of the Lord that it can be no other way, one would think that even a king could see it without a prophet. This time the Lord spoke and I opened my mouth. I cannot explain in any other way.

So I told them what I saw, "This is what the Lord says: 'I will fill this valley with pools of water.' For this is what the Lord says: 'You will see neither wind nor rain, yet this valley will be filled with water, and you, your cattle and your other animals will drink. This is an easy thing in the eyes of the Lord; he will also deliver Moab into your hands. You will overthrow every fortified city and every major town. You will cut down every good tree, stop up all the springs, and ruin every good field with stones.'"

King Joram stood staring at me. Perhaps he was stunned that I would be giving him good news instead of condemning him. More likely, he was affronted that a prophet of the Lord was maneuvering to take credit for saving him from an enemy he had proven too inept to defeat by himself. He probably was thinking that Elijah had been given credit for lifting the siege of Samaria, and now I would be given credit for defeating Moab.

So I gave King Joram some pure nonsense. At least it seemed like nonsense to me when I opened my mouth. "Dig ditches," I said in wonder and amazement, wondering whether I would keep my head and amazed that the King listened to this drivel without running me through. "Dig ditches from here to there, and in the morning your foes will be ripe for the plunder." This would give King Joram something to do, some grand gesture he could make, so he could claim that his ditches brought about a turn in the battle.

I have spoken to kings before about military matters beyond my comprehension, but in those times, after I spoke there seemed to be some logic in what I said. This time, it was sheer stupidity. Jehu stood at the side of King Joram his mouth wide open. He would tell me later that he thought I was trying to make the King look like a fool in front of his commanders. When the King ordered the ditches dug, his mouth dropped open again.

THE SACRIFICE TO CHEMOSH

Jehu

Where now is the Lord, the God of Elijah? Elisha, II Kings
2:14

W ANDERING in the desert of Edom for seven days allowed every sheep herder and nomad to get a good look at our army and bring word back to the Moabite royal palace in Dibon. Having sacrificed King Joram's envoy to Chemosh, Moab certainly expected a battle and had sent its army north to meet Israel's advancing army. Word of three kings attacking from the south caught Moab by surprise. Moab was dug in and fortified against an attack from the north. It takes time for an army to pull up stakes, load everything for transport and move the entire length of the country from North to South to meet this new threat.

In a panic, Moab sent riders and chariots racing to the South, stopping in every village and pasture and ordering every man and boy capable of standing and holding a pitchfork to advance to the south to meet the invading armies. Our scouts who had ridden ahead of us into Moab at first found the southern border all but undefended. By the time we began our advance across Moab's frontier, our scouts brought reports of the roads leading South from Dibon to our positions becoming clogged with men and boys walking toward us with a few riders prodding them on their way. Later, scouts brought reports that initial contingents of horsemen and chariots from Moab's army were just beginning to make their way past the Moabite capital of Dibon toward the south, about to overtake its conscripted mob.

It was here that the mob of hastily assembled farmers and the ditches dug by slaves by order of King Joram came together. When the kings consulted with Elisha, their sole concern was the lack of water. Joram had dug canals, entrenching the dry creek beds and wadis surrounding the armies' encampment. How these canals filled with water in the night and flooded the creek beds and surrounding lands I do not know. Elisha had tilled his land for years. He knew how water reached his fields. Did he know how water flowed in arid southern Moab, or was this water from the Lord?

The mob of Moabites impressed to defend their land from our attack had no scouts, no advance battalions and no commanders. Men and boys from each small village were led by their own headman, whipped on by some scattered soldiers sent to move them to the South. Each headman made his own decision and followed his own path. How each small group made its decision when reaching the water that had flooded the land was impossible to determine from the few survivors we were able to round up. One handful of stragglers from a tiny village said that their headman, seeing the sun beginning to rise over the reddened water, concluded that the water was red with blood and shouted, "That's blood! Those kings must have fought and slaughtered each other. Now to the plunder, Moab!" Their small group began to run headlong toward our encampment, with other small groups following. Whether the other groups reached the same conclusion, or found some other reason to throw themselves headlong into our lines or simply followed the example of the first groups thinking some order had been given we could never determine.

The greatest threat the accelerating mob of untrained farmers and herdsmen posed to our forces was wearing our forces out with a constant slaughter. It was not possible for such a force to stand up to trained charioteers and horsemen covered by overarching archers and slingers. The untrained horde from Moab became herds of sacrificial lambs running headlong into our lines of trained soldiers, thinking only of plundering our camp, with no thought of any opposing army until our arrows and stones pierced and cracked their ranks at close range. With no commander to order a reversal, the Moabites kept coming. It was up to each individual to see the slaughter for himself and realize he should retreat.

Slowly Moab's headlong rush for plunder came to a halt, and slowly the survivors turned, realizing their only hope was to begin fleeing back down the same paths that had brought them to our front lines. Once the reversal started, it became an avalanche, a wave sweeping away the other groups of clansmen rushing behind them for the plunder, now clogging the roads leading to Dibon, and all but blocking our efforts to attack the rear of the retreating Moabite hordes.

We sent our fastest chariots and riders to bypass the fleeing Moabites, but there were few level plains in that part of Moab to give them an advantage. The sight of our chariots racing toward the Moabite rabble increased the speed and chaos of their retreat. Most of the Moabites by now had dropped their weapons and were scattering over the country-side to bypass the clogged roads and trails. Seeing the Moabites panicked flight, our chariots did not seek to engage them, but simply swept past them again and again to maintain their panicked retreat. We were almost within sight of Dibon when the first panicked wave of retreaters crashed into the first organized units of the Moabite army advancing to do battle. It was exactly at that point that we stopped our sweeps along the panicked mob, and charged all of our chariots directly into Moab's colliding forces.

It was impossible for the Moabite army to turn the mob around and face our chariots, and it was impossible for their army to form into an organized front line as the mob crashed into them. Although they were only untrained villagers, their panic confused and unnerved the soldiers. Some units began to melt away, and their commanders, seeing an orga-nized attack bearing down on them with their forces in disarray, turned their forces around and raced the mob to the gates of Dibon.

We thought a major battle was in the offing when King Mesha and a large force surrounding him tried to form up and advance against us out-side of Dibon, but it turned into less than a brief skirmish at the city gates as King Mesha's force was jostled and disorganized by the last of Moab's army racing into the city. Many chariots and wagons were broken up and dumped alongside the road to the gates when they were overturned in the rush to safety. The Moabite soldiers scrambled through the city to mount the walls, and the fight at the gates was fierce until a handful of archers reached the top of the wall and we had to withdraw to escape the arrows.

We were moving to the walls of the city. As the carpenters began hurriedly constructing siege ladders to scale the walls, battering rams for the gates of the city and covering shields to protect us from arrows and rocks from being hurled down on us from the walls, there was already griping in the ranks. "This will be just like Ramoth-Gilead with King Ahab, I tell you. We captured King Ben-Hadad in the city and King Ahab let him go free in exchange for a trade treaty and we saw none of it." "Why should I take an arrow in the neck so the King can fill his treasure chests?" "If I have a spear in my hand there will be no king walking out of this city upright."

We allowed those from the unorganized mob who did not make it into the city gates to melt away into the hills and fields, as we chased down and captured a sizeable number of chariots and wagons that had scattered over the countryside. We had the King of Moab trapped in his capital with less than half of his army. With only a small force needed to keep any of Moab's army from trying to break out of the gates, we sent the main body of our army to chase away detached groups of the Moabite army that had not been washed away by the retreating mob. Reports came back that none of the Moabite army had chosen to stand and fight. Moab is a rugged country, and their army had melted away into concealed ravines. While they stayed hidden there was no threat that they could organize into a fighting force to offer any threat.

The King Mesha of Moab could see from the towers on the walls of Dibon that to the north his army outside the walls of the city had disintegrated. To the south, Mesha could see the armies of Israel, Judah and Edom, unbloodied and in battle formation approaching his capital. Catcalls, jeers and threats issued over the walls in both directions, but gradually the bravado of the Moabites fueled by desperation petered out. Soon there was a siege of threats and challenges hurled against the walls of Dibon. "Throw us down your King and you will live." "Throw us down your wives and children, save us the trouble of killing them." "Throw us down your daughters, they will be ours soon enough."

We were in the process of putting up a canopy for the kings to use during the siege when King Joram, King Jehoshaphat and the King of Edom arrived with their escorts. As the Kings approached, our archers were preparing lighted brands to shoot over the walls, although I felt they were too far out of range at the time, and footmen were dashing between ridges and ditches exploring the ground close to the walls of the city, seeing how close they could approach.

The kings had no more than dismounted when we heard trumpeting coming from on top of the walls followed by an uproar from both our troops on the ground and the Moabite troops on the walls of the city. Looking toward the city we could see banners being raised above the walls and towers and traces of smoke beginning to rise from the walls as fires and torches were lit.

"Send a rider out," I commanded, "See if they are asking for terms."

While we were waiting for word from the riders that were sent out, other riders came to us from close to the walls.

"They are asking for the kings to approach. The King of Moab is on the walls. They say the King is going to offer a sacrifice to Chemosh and the King of Moab wants the Kings of Judah, Israel and Edom to witness it."

"What sort of nonsense is this," I replied, "this is not the time for sacrifices. He is too late. He should have offered his sacrifices before the battle began."

"That may be so, Jehu," answered King Joram, "but let us see what this is all about. We have heard from your prophet Elisha. Let us hear what their gods have to say."

"Master, they are trapped," I replied, "we should see if we can force our way into the city."

"You can do that, Jehu," replied King Joram, "in the meantime, while your commanders prepare for the assault I want to see what my brother the King of Moab thinks his god can do for him. Are we in any danger if we approach the walls closer?"

We turned to the rider who had brought us the news. "They say that they will have no archers on the walls for the sacrifice."

"What about the gates?" I asked.

"We have riders, chariots and troops near the gates. They could not get enough fighters out of the gates at any one time; they would be cut down before they could mount an attack."

"Then to the walls," decreed King Joram, not bothering to turn to King Jehoshaphat or the King of Edom. In what was probably insubordination, I turned to King Jehoshaphat and simply said, "King Jehoshaphat?"

King Jehoshaphat continued looking at the walls as a new trumpet blast rang out from the walls. Sizeable fires were now burning on top of the walls. "It will not slow down our assault," replied King Jehoshaphat, "and if the King of Moab is offering sacrifices instead of preparing a defense of his city, it will not hinder us. Maybe he will make a plea for mercy." King Jehoshaphat nodded to the King of Edom, "Your majesty, shall we accompany King Joram to the walls?" This was a courtesy to the King of Edom, not a request. The King of Edom was bound by his treaties with King Jehoshaphat to support Jehoshaphat's army.

Along with one other commander and a body of chariots and horsemen accompanying the kings we approached the walls. A line of archers was assembled in front of the kings ready to let fly in the event the Moabites had plans for something other than a sacrifice. We were close enough to the walls to see that it actually was the King of Moab standing exposed on the walls surrounded by a handful of soldiers and what I assumed were priests of Molech. No sooner had we stopped at the foot of the wall when a voice boomed out down at us.

"Kings of Judah, Edom and Israel, you have advanced to the walls of our city because our Lord Molech is not pleased with our land. But Molech is mighty and will save us from destruction." With each statement the spokesman, standing next to the King of Moab, paused, letting us digest what was being said, but not long enough to invite a response.

"Molech will show his power if Moab is devoted to him. Our King will show his devotion. Our King will sacrifice his first born son, his heir to the crown here on the walls of this city to Molech. Then the wrath of Molech will rain down on you."

A gasp ran through the group standing below the wall with the three kings. It was not the thought of another death that caused the gasp. We had butchered our way to the walls of the city, and as we prepared for our siege, we prepared for more butchery. It was the total surprise. We expected oxen to be sacrificed, not the King's son.

"It is to rouse his army," I sneered, "We should not be here listening to this drivel. He plans to fight and we are giving him his chance."

Before anyone could answer me, another gasp rose from our company. A man tied to a scaffold was being raised up on the wall. His arms were stretched out from his sides and raised slightly higher than his head, lashed to the wooden framework.

"This is the son of the King of Moab; first born of the King; heir to the throne of Moab," boomed the voice from the top of the walls.

"Father, father, no! I beg of you! Spare my life," screamed the figure lashed to the framework.

"To the mighty Chemosh, god of Moab and god of these lands," boomed the voice as water was hurled in the face of the figure, choking out some of his protests, "accept the King's son, great Chemosh. No greater sacrifice can be made, oh great Chemosh!"

"No! No! Father! Release me!"

A handful of priests standing alongside the King and the doomed figure began chanting, "Blood for the mighty Chemosh. Life for the mighty Chemosh. Power for the mighty Chemosh." One of the priests handed the King of Moab a dagger and the King took a few short steps to the figure. The scaffold to which the King's son was lashed raised his chest to the height of the King's face. Without hesitation the King slashed at the chest of the figure with two short, hard chops. Then with two hands on the dagger, the King thrust the dagger under the figure's ribs and violently ripped the dagger upward to separate his ribs. Blood gushed down the King's arms and ran down his elbows. The King began cutting and thrusting with his dagger, then raised his bloody hand over his head with a bright red clump I took to be his son's heart. The priests and soldiers on the wall erupted with shouts and cheers, and in their exuberance some of the soldiers on the wall hurled their lances toward our soldiers on the ground. The spears landed harmlessly far from our men. This had to be answered.

"Archers!" I screamed toward the line of archers in front of us, ready to order them to let fly.

"No!" shouted King Joram, raising his hand in the air. He sat as if stunned, still staring at the King of Moab, his bloody, dripping arms still in the air, standing among his cheering priests and soldiers.

The archers had already drawn. "Hold," I yelled, looking back to the King in amazement. King Joram kept his arm in the air silently, still staring as if in a daze. I waited another moment, then ordered, "Bows down."

I looked over to King Jehoshaphat. A look of total disgust covered his face. He had seen and ignored every form of wound and gore and violence on the battlefield, but he had never seen this. "I had heard of this," he said to no one in particular, "my father had told me of this, but never did I think . . ." Jehoshaphat's voice trailed off as he too stared toward the wall.

"My lord," I implored the King, "what are our orders?" hoping to stir some action from the Kings.

"This cannot be answered," whispered King Joram. "How can we resist this? I have none of my sons with me to sacrifice. What offering is more powerful than this?"

"Offering?" snorted King Jehoshaphat. "That is murder. That is an abomination. What kind of vermin are these people?"

"We cannot fight this. How can our gods answer this?" responded Joram.

"Our gods?" shouted Jehoshaphat. "What kind of gods are you talking about?"

Joram was silent.

King Jehoshaphat stared at Joram, as did I. I did not know Jehoshaphat's thoughts, but they may have been the same as mine. King Joram had stood in the temple of Baal as his mother Jezebel and sister Athaliah had offered his infant half-brothers as sacrifices on a flaming altar. What did the world look like to a young boy, a child, after he had seen this, and seen it again and again? When Joram was a boy, tales from around the world had circulated in the royal palace in Samaria of sacrifices of the last resort offered to buy the favor of a god. The more powerful the offering, the more power the deity derived from it. Joram had gutted his mother's temple of Baal in Samaria when he became King, but was that a rejection of the thought of Baal, or a rebellion against his mother, proof that he was the King? Did he still live in the world of battling deities vying for the most extreme measures of obeisance? King Joram had not brought any of his sons with him on this campaign; if he had, would he have sacrificed them to Baal to give Baal power over Chemosh? Had Joram been overpowered by his inability to offer a sacrifice equal to King Mesha's? Elisha the prophet had told him that the Lord would give him victory over Moab, but what was the word of that former ox driver compared to the ultimate sacrifice offered at the height of battle?

King Joram stood up silently, his face ashen. He had been routed. No amount of words, supplications, prayers or incantations could shake his conviction that the world of the gods had suddenly tilted against him. He would not throw his chariots against the impenetrable wall of a deity empowered by the sacrifice of a king's first born.

"Call our troops back from the walls," Joram ordered in a dead monotone. We will assemble at our camp of last night, and from there withdraw back to Samaria. We will fight no more in Moab this season."

We had achieved what we had set out to achieve. Moab lay open to us. A fragment of their army was behind the walls of the city, trapped there with their King. The main body of their army had withered away, running back to their villages hoping to save their homes and families from total ruin.

The army was even angrier as it withdrew from Moab than it had been when King Ahab had spared the life of King Ben-Hadad at Ramoth-Gilead and cheated them of plunder. More than half of the troops simply walked or rode away. Many commandeered supplies and wagons from the baggage train before taking their leave. Other troops were forced to remain, raising their resentment even higher. Some of the soldiers had suddenly become devotees to the Lord. The Lord had delivered Moab into their hands and now the King has undone what the Lord had decreed. That Joram had supposedly been swayed by the human sacrifice of the King's son made their resentment even greater.

With Joram's army withdrawing, over half of the attacking force against Moab was gone. King Jehoshaphat and the King of Edom decided to withdraw as well. The battle had been started to regain Israel's tribute from Moab. Now Israel was abandoning the fight. The soldiers of Judah and Edom could not be counted on to fight valiantly to regain Israel's tribute after Israel deserted the field.

Our troops exacted their revenge against Moab as they retreated. Every village, home, winepress and sheep pen unfortunate enough to be on the path of our retreating army was plundered and burned to the ground. All the wells were plugged up. Even the sparse trees on our route were not spared. Our soldiers gave vent to their rage over this needless retreat by attacking every tree they came across, hacking it to the ground a burning it.

We beat a slow, reluctant retreat from Moab. Their army had scattered and the remnant hiding behind the bloodied city wall was not large enough to threaten us. The King of Moab was content to let us wreak our vengeance in the southern fringes of his kingdom as we retreated back through Edom around the southern tip of the Dead Sea and into Judah. He had kept and prospered off the tribute that Moab had been required to pay Israel since the reign of King Omri. It was to recover that tribute that King Joram had started this war.

Knowing that our army was retreating south, he mounted the bloodied corpse of the son he had murdered standing up in a cart as if leading the army, minus his heart that had been burned as an offering in the temple of Chemosh, regrouped his army that had fled north, and marched north to Israel's undefended border and fed his army on the plunder and slaves he captured as he cut a swath through southern Israel. Israel plundered southern Moab in a hurry as they retreated. Moab exacted its vengeance in a leisurely manner, delighting in telling King Joram's subjects that their King had retreated in a panic upon witnessing the power of the mighty Chemosh.

Moab, having withstood our onslaught and survived, decided two years later to form an alliance with Ammon and attack Judah. Fighting alone, King Jehoshaphat routed them, but they continued to raid, and Jehoshaphat had to be constantly defending his borders. The campaign against Moab was the last time King Jehoshaphat showed any interest in joining forces with the Kingdom of Israel. His dreams of reuniting the two kingdoms based on his son's marriage to King Joram's sister Athaliah died a sudden death when he saw Joram wilt under King Mesha's bloody sacrifice. He now wanted no part of that kingdom to the north, and was happy to let them reap the whirlwind in their battles with Aram.

For his brash attempt to humble Moab, King Joram was repaid with new aggression from Aram. Aram became bolder now. Knowing that the Kingdom of Judah was tied down with its contests with Moab and Ammon, Aram could risk probing Israel without fearing that King Jehoshaphat would come to Israel's aid.

With King Jehoshaphat's loss of interest in closer relations with the sister kingdom of Judah, Jezebel and Athaliah were forced to bide their time until Athaliah's husband Jehoram succeeded King Jehoshaphat.

THE BESEIGED

Elisha

Give up your son so we may eat him today, and tomorrow
we'll eat my son. A mother of Samaria, II Kings 6:28

I T was like war - it was war - a siege, and the siege engines were at
my door trying to batter it in. It was no accident that the door to my
courtyard was of heavy oak. King David's rebellious son Absalom found
himself hanging from an oak tree when Joab plunged javelins into him,
his rebellion dying with him. If the oak stopped one son of a King it may
stop another. It was my wife that convinced me to move into Samaria.
The raids by the Arameans had become more and more forceful, and
reached closer and closer to Samaria, and she spent so much time looking
fearfully to the horizon that she began to waste away, even at that time
when we still had enough scraps of food to keep us from starvation.

The siege at my door had been going on fitfully since midday.
Chunks of plaster had fallen to the floor and great cracks in the wall and
ceiling threatened more and greater destruction. Dust filled the air, and
great crashes and booms shook us to our cores, but the door held fast.
I wondered at the energy and force of the assaults on the door. We had
had our last meal of roast pigeon mixed with sawdust, clay and the last
handful of weeds plucked from the cracks in the roof two days ago. What
food these pigeons thought they would find in Samaria I do not know.
Perhaps they were sent by the Lord like the ravens that visited Elijah at
the brook in the Kireth Ravine. Unlike us, the pigeons could scale the
walls of Samaria and find abundant food in the countryside. I thought of

the words of the psalmist, "Oh, that I had the wings of a dove. I would fly away and be at rest."

My besiegers were fellow Samarians, brother Israelites, not Arameans, and I wondered what food they subsisted on to give them the energy to keep assaulting my door. The last of the mules in Samaria had been slaughtered for food weeks ago, and their skulls and hooves discarded. But now that the food was gone, the people had begun digging up the rotting skulls and hides for food. The wealthy, at the price of all of their household goods, could secure an entire putrefying mule skull to give them enough strength to witness their poorer neighbors faint and die in the streets.

The Arameans had descended like locusts on Samaria and within two weeks were at the gates of Samaria. What had started out as a drought on the plains of Jezreel had turned into a famine. Aram was dry but not desperate, and on learning that the army of Israel was no threat to Aram this year saw their opportunity. The people in the countryside fled to Samaria seeking shelter from the Arameans and food, reducing Samaria to a state of desperation in a few short weeks. With food not abundant even for the Arameans, rather than a full-fledged onslaught to breech the walls of Samaria the Arameans settled in to let starvation wage its war inside the walls of Samaria.

While the Arameans sat outside the gates of Samaria occasionally flinging burning sacks of pitch over the walls, King Joram's men began their assault on my oaken door. The siege had brought Samaria to the point of desperation, and had driven King Joram beyond desperation. The King had been crawling along the wall of the city with a few of his commanders looking for any new tactic by the Arameans that might speed the collapse of the city. While his mind was occupied with the siege, he was called to adjudicate a case between two residents of the city. A woman watching from the street below cried out to Joram on the wall.

"Help me, my lord the King!"

King Joram did not take well to this supplication. Could not this woman see that Samaria could fall within the week, that the palace could be put to the torch, that half the city was on the verge of being slaughtered or sold into slavery? Did she think she was entitled to a special dispensation from the King? King Joram's response was dismissive, almost mocking.

"If the Lord does not help you, where can I get help for you? From the threshing floor? From the winepress?" Everyone in the city would like some grain to eat, some wine to drink, but the threshing floor and the winepresses were underfoot of the Arameans. Then the King asked her, "What's the matter?"

It was the woman's plea that led to the pounding and battering against my oaken door that day, "This woman said to me, 'Give up your son so we may eat him today, and tomorrow we'll eat my son.' So we cooked my son and ate him. The next day I said to her, 'Give up your son so we may eat him' but she had hidden him."

King Joram stood glaring down at the woman, his face flushed. Suddenly he tore at his robes again and again, leaving his robes in shreds, and showing the sackcloth he was wearing under his robes. When he had no more strength and no more fabric left to tear, he shouted over the city to no one, "May God deal with me, be it ever so severely, if the head of Elisha son of Shaphat remains on his shoulders today!"

King Joram had not waged war against the prophets as his mother had, but Queen Jezebel was still in the royal palace in Samaria. Jezebel was still fighting the battle of her Lord Baal against every other deity, and her constant advice to her son King Joram was to strike out against the prophets of the Lord to appease Lord Baal and regain his favor for his kingdom. I never learned what King Joram believed in, but in his rages he would lash out at the prophets.

To King Joram's credit he had not yet slaughtered any of his sons on the walls of Samaria as King Mesha had done. Maybe things were not desperate enough. Maybe he was only capable of being cowed at the sight of such a sacrifice, but without the determination to take the action himself. Perhaps he was simply a coward.

My oaken door had been barred and barricaded many times during the siege of Samaria. I knew at some point the King would issue his judgment against me. The King's petitioner at the wall had asked that the King order the other woman to deliver and cook her son so that the women could eat their last meal. Instead, he passed his sentence on me.

I was meeting with a few of the elders gathered in Samaria when King Joram passed his sentence. I suddenly rose and said, "That that son of a murderer has sent someone to my house to cut off my head. Look, when the messenger from the King comes, shut the door and hold it shut against him. Is not the sound of his master's footsteps behind him?"

Moments later, the King's men were over the wall from the street into my courtyard and were at my door, pounding on the oak timbers, demanding that I show myself. The elders were terrified, thinking that the

King's wrath would extend to anyone consorting with the condemned. It was only the fear for their own necks that kept them from opening my door and delivering me to the King.

Finding that the door would not budge, the pounding stopped, only to hear King Joram shouting at the other side of the door, "Release the prophet Elisha to me. This disaster is from the Lord. Why should I wait for the Lord any longer? This prophet has called this disaster down on our heads, why should he live in his house in peace while the entire city suffers?"

The elders with me stared at the door in silence. They wanted to obey their King. They were willing to look the other way while other prophets were being hunted down, but were fearful of the thought of having the blood of a prophet on their own hands. They hesitated long enough to allow me the shout back through the door.

"If this is the Lord's doing, where was your army as the Arameans marched across the border of Israel?"

This was met by the sound of fists pounding on the other side of the door, which could only have been the fists of King Joram. Then the voice again of King Joram, his mouth all but pressed against the door.

"It was you, prophet, that had me feed the Aramean army in this city when you led them here by one of your tricks. You had me return them to Aram unharmed. If I had killed them all then, they would not be besieging the city now."

"The Arameans were blinded by the Lord. It was the Lord that had me lead them to Samaria. You were feasting on a fattened calf, drinking the wine from Naboth's vineyard when I led them in the city. Your army did not capture them; they were not your prisoners. You had no claim on them. Did you not see the power of the Lord?"

"Where is the power of your lord now, prophet, now that the Arameans are trampling our threshing floors and eating the little grain we had stored there?"

"Where was your army, Oh King, when the Arameans were on the road to this city? Did they not know how to put grain in sacks and baskets? Did they not know how to load grain onto carts and bring it into the city?"

This was met by more fist pounding on the other side of the door.

"It was you, prophet, who healed Naaman, the commander of the army of Aram. If he had died he would not be outside our walls waiting to sell your children as slaves."

"Oh great King, it was you who sent the mighty Naaman to me. Was I to tell him the Lord God of Israel was powerless to heal him? How is it, Oh King, that Naaman of the army of Aram heard of the power of the Lord, and you remain ignorant of it? How is it that Naaman's slave, a young girl he had stolen from your kingdom, could tell Naaman of the Lord's power, but no one can tell you? Has not Naaman been sent to you twice now? Once when he had leprosy, and now when he is besieging our city. Has not the Lord sent Naaman to you because you chose to remain ignorant of the Lord?"

This was followed by more kingly fists battering the door. I had hoped that the door had been made from the oak that had ensnared Absalom, and that it would continue its service by falling onto King Joram and crushing him, but it stood fast. The fist pounding stopped, followed by shouted, kingly orders. Moments later, the violent pounding against the door began, and my person was under a very private siege.

This was the senseless, mindless rage of King Joram. Mother Jezebel could rage as well, but hers was an artful, devious rage with a purpose. There was not one of the King's subjects in Samaria that was not slowly starving to death. Fires were raging outside the gates and walls of his capital city as the army of Aram waited for their fires to turn them into charcoal and chalk. Messages sent by Jezebel to her brother the King of Sidon had gone unanswered. Tyre and Sidon were happy to be aligned with Israel if Israel would protect its borders from inland powers, but if Samaria was about to fall, they did not want to start a war against Aram by coming to the aid of Israel. No help would come from the Kingdom of Judah. King Jehoshaphat had his fill of fighting with Joram after the rout in Moab.

King Joram had not adopted the strenuous devotion to Baal of his mother, so the gods blew him over the countryside like the desert winds. Chemosh had outmaneuvered that god in the temple in Jerusalem when he was attacking Moab, and now that the Arameans were at his gates, it was the doing of that god of the temple in Jerusalem. If a god was seeking to end his reign, he would fight back by striking down a prophet of that god.

Almost all of the plaster had been shaken off the walls and the ceiling surrounding the Absalom-dismounting oak door, but the door, at least from the inside, was unmarred. I had the craftsmen make the door of several thick layers of oak, the grain of the timbers criss-crossing each other, and pegged tightly together, with the door jamb even thicker than the door. It was the only way I would agree to live in the same city as Queen Jezebel. I was a prophet, not a fool. Perhaps the soldiers stopped their ramming and pounding out of embarrassment for lack of progress, or maybe they were weak from lack of food. In the sudden silence, dust continued to drift down from the plaster-freed walls and a few loosened chunks of plaster fell to the floor. While the silence continued, a thought assailed my mind as forcefully as another blow to the oak door. I knew what was going to happen.

I walked quickly to the door and shouted into it, "Hear the word of the Lord. This is what the Lord says: 'About this time tomorrow, a seah of the finest flour will sell for a shekel and two seahs of barley for a shekel at the gate of Samaria.'"

My ears were still ringing from the battering on the door and I felt my throat burning from the force I used to deliver my words into the door, trying to hear my own words over the ringing in my ears. I stood half a hand's breadth from the door, cringing at the renewed battering I expected to hear in answer to my own unexpected words and at the same time mortified at the words I had heard myself say. No one in Samaria had seen half a seah of barley in the last month. Every pigeon dropping on every roof in Samaria had been scraped off and traded for treasures, and I was promising fine flour at the price of straw. But I was gripped by a convincing certainty that what I had just said was as certain as the wind and the rain.

Just as unexpectedly I heard a firm voice faintly through the door. "Man of God, this is your King. Open the door."

My servant Gehazi was standing behind me. I turned to him and said, "Open the door."

Gehazi stared at me for a moment and then said, "Master he will slaughter us all." I continued to look at Gehazi a moment longer, saying nothing. Gehazi was not protesting, only voicing his fear, knowing that I would not change my mind. Slowly Gehazi stepped past me and began to lift the solid timbers binding the door to the jambs. With the timbers on the floor, Gehazi began to pull with full force on the heavily hinged door. Bright sun flooded into the doorway. Standing in the sun was King Joram, his royal robes in tatters, rough, raw sackcloth showing underneath. The King was leaning on the arm of one of his captains.

"Man of God," said the King, "I heard you tell my brother King Ahaziah that he would not get off of his sick bed, and that came to pass. Will what you just said come to pass?"

I did not understand why I had said what I said, but on hearing the King's question, I was gripped by the same certainty as when I spoke the words. "It is the word of the Lord."

Then the captain spoke up, "Look, even if the Lord should open the floodgates of the heavens, how could this happen?"

"You will see it with your own eyes," I answered, "but you will not eat any of it!"

King Joram looked at me quietly. Maybe he was calculating whether my words would still stand if he had me run through. There was no condition placed on my words; nothing the King was required to do. He was probably certain I was playing a trick on him; promising something impossible to keep him from breaking down my oak door. I was waiting to hear the King order me put in the royal dungeon as his father King Ahab had ordered Micaiah after the threshing floor debacle. But why imprison me? Where would I go? The Arameans encircled the walls of the city. Perhaps he was thinking that I would get to share in the excruciating death the Arameans had planned for him once they broke down the gates of the city.

"We will see, man of god. We will see."

With that the King turned around and walked out of my courtyard and down the street in the direction of the royal palace. A line of soldiers standing behind the King with their swords drawn and daggers in their hands stared at the back of the retreating King, and then turned to stare at me, amazed. The King had won the siege of the door from the oak that had defeated Absalom, and now was retreating from the field. The gaunt, starving soldiers were drenched in sweat from their labors in assaulting my door. They looked at me enviously, swords in hand, sizing me up as if I could have been a fitting last meal for them but a meal which the King has now denied them. Slowly the soldiers sheathed their weapons and turned to follow the King.

THE BESEIGERS RETREAT

Jehu

Why stay here until we die? Leper of Samaria, II Kings
7:3

I WAS in the stables when word came to me of King Joram's assault on Elisha's door. I was taking my turn on watch guarding the last handful of horses in Samaria capable of pulling a chariot. With no horses to pull their chariots, many of my charioteers had been sent onto the wall to defend the city. We had begun slaughtering our horses in the second week of the siege. We were not that hungry yet, but there was not enough grain and straw for all of the horses we had with us in the city. The pounding the Arameans were able to deliver to us sent us reeling into the city in a panic. We had underestimated the number of their chariots, and they had launched assault after assault that we were unable to stop. Had we been planning for a siege, we would have sent some of our chariots to Jezreel and Megiddo, but the Aramean chariots were flanking us, leaving only the road back to Samaria open to us.

In the first week of the siege, we had to guard our grain for the horses from theft. Then even the straw became a commodity on the streets. No one had been able to get their hands on any of our horses, but there were plenty of hungry people who would mill outside the stable, hoping maybe someone would get up the courage to storm the doors and they could follow. We resorted to jabbing our spears out through the gates of the stable to dissuade any thought of breaking down our gates. As the weeks passed, our soldiers were jabbing their spears at the crowd in earnest. In the stables we limited ourselves to a few handfuls of the horses' grain, and found ourselves chewing on the straw for sustenance. On the streets, a pile of fresh horse dung would bring a hefty price, and our soldiers were not above marketing this food stuff of last resort.

I was not shocked when I heard the story of the mothers who had cooked one of their children to eat. I had already seen a father outside the stable parcel out a handful of fresh dung to his children, who fought over the last scrap. Nor was I shocked at the rage of King Joram against Elisha.

I had thought about sending someone out from the stables for a report of what was actually happening, but decided that by the time a messenger would go and bring back news, Elisha's fate would have already been decided. Anxious to keep a prophet of the Lord from being struck down while we were in a bitter siege, I hurried through the streets of Samaria toward Elisha's house, both for the sake of Elisha and to reduce the chance of being confronted by a desperate citizen pleading for relief or seeking to relieve me of something that could be bartered for food. I was less than half way to Elisha's house when I met the King and his contingent walking towards me on the way back to the palace. I stood still as the King approached me and then I asked. "What of Elisha?"

The King did not stop walking and said as he passed me, "He says we will have wheat tomorrow. Yes, fine flour he said. Maybe the Arameans will start hurling cakes of figs and dates over our walls tomorrow."

I watched as the King and his men walked past me. I thought of asking after the king what had happened to Elisha, but thought that had he been murdered the King would have gladly announced that. I turned and went back to the stables. Whatever was going to happen to Elisha had already happened, and I was needed at the stables.

That night, there was pounding at the stable doors. I was being summoned to the royal palace. When I arrived, several other commanders were already there. We had been hunkered down for several weeks with little to confer about. Most news was sent by couriers scurrying like rats over the detritus of the siege. Had the Arameans issued an ultimatum? Had a tunnel been discovered? Were we about to capitulate?

Upon entering the throne room, my first thought was that I must reek of manure and horse urine after having been locked in the stables for weeks. But the stench of rot and death filled the city, and it was no different in the throne room. In the throne room I recognized the King's regular attendants and a smattering of commanders. To one side I saw one of the gatekeepers, looking out of place.

"Tell them what you have told us," the King directed the gatekeeper. Although the gatekeeper's job entailed yelling at the top of his lungs about anything urgent that could not wait for signal banners to be waved or script to be scrawled on parchment and thrown down, this gatekeeper's voice was hushed, either at having to deliver his message in front of the King, or at embarrassment of the message he was delivering.

"The lepers out by the city gates—well, they were closer to the gates than they should be—but—with the siege we did not go out and chase them—and the Arameans would have nothing to do with them—well—so they could come and go as they pleased—except for in the city—so the lepers - "

"Out with it man!" shouted the impatient King, "tell them the message."

"Oh yes, my lord, the message. One of the lepers told us this through the gate. He said, 'We went into the Aramean camp and no one was there—not a sound of anyone—only tethered horses and donkeys, and the tents left just as they were.'"

"A rabble of lepers would have us believe that the Arameans abandoned their camp and left all of equipment and horses behind. What do you make of that," asked the King to all of us.

Bidkar spoke up, "There is no reason for the Arameans to leave. We are dead men here in the city, and before we closed our gates there was no word of any force that would be challenging the Arameans."

We all stood silently, listening for the first time someone put into words what our situation really was. Finally King Joram spoke up, "I will tell you what the Arameans have done to us. They know we are starving; so they have left the camp to hide in the countryside, thinking, 'They will surely come out, and then we will take them alive and get into the city.'"

By now I had heard of Elijah's words of late afternoon to the King. I wondered if anything would come of them, but never imagined anything would happen so soon. I did not want to bring up Elisha's words to the King. They had been spoken directly to the King, but the only thing the King could believe was happening was a trick being played by the Arameans.

But I was sick of sleeping on weeks-old hay coated with fine manure powder and living on a handful of grain each day. "My lord," I said to King Joram, "We have five horses left in the city capable of pulling a chariot. By next week, there may only be two. Let's send some men out to see for ourselves. Their plight will be like that of all the Israelites left here—yes, they will only be like all these Israelites who are doomed. So let us send them to find out what happened."

The King agreed. I was to select the horses and charioteers, so Bidkar and I drove the chariots out of the city. The dim light of dawn was just beginning to light the sky as we approached the city gates. The gatekeepers called down from their posts that the campfires in the Aramean camps had dwindled down to embers toward the end of the night and that no new fires had been started for the morning as had been normal. They had seen no movement in the camp, and had not seen any movement in the Aramean entrenchments close to the walls.

We held our chariots as far back from the gates as we could as the gates were opened, and waited in the silence once the gates were opened. If there was a force close by, we could expect them to rush the gates immediately and fight to hold the gates open for a main force to breach the city. Inside the walls, a few doors and gates could be heard opening, the beginning of some far off murmurings, perhaps even a subdued wail of a mother finding another of her children cold and dead from starvation.

We waited long enough for even the sleepiest commander to rouse his troops and begin a charge up the ramp to the gates, or for a few sappers to crawl up to the gates to peer in. Hearing nothing from the watchmen on the wall or the gatekeepers, I raised my whip over my horses and brought it down without a word. We reached a good trot going through the gates, and were at full speed at the bottom of the ramp. If there were archers in the trenches waiting to let fly, I would not make it easy for them. If troops or riders rose out of the trenches to give chase, I would have a chance to wheel around and race back toward the gates.

Nothing met me but the wind. I kept lashing my horses past the Aramean trenches, then past the small camps set up beyond range of our archers on the walls. My horses had not been run in more than a month, and had been on less than half-rations for several weeks. They pulled with great release going down the ramp from the gates, but by the time I was past the range of our archers I could tell the horses were straining. I reined them back to half speed and began making a long loop, turning back toward the gates. If Aramean chariots appeared out of the dawn, my horses may not have the speed to outrun them back to the gates at this distance.

Bidkar brought his chariot alongside mine and we came to a stop, looking in every direction for Arameans.

"Our horses are spent, Bidkar. Let them get their breath if we need to retreat."

We stood on our chariots as the sun broke the horizon, our horses panting and shaking their bridles as if to question why we had stopped. I listened for the whisper of an arrow in flight, but only heard birds singing.

"We are fools, Bidkar. The Arameans have good archers."

"You are the fool, Jehu, this was your idea."

"At least we have escaped starvation. If we are not dead, we must have survived. Did you see anyone in their trenches?"

"No one, but then I had my head as low as I could get it."

"The gates are closed behind us. Let's go on toward their camp."

"Did you see any lepers outside the gates?"

"I only saw the backside of my horses. If what the lepers reported is true, they would not be waiting at the gates."

By now our horses had found a stand of grass and we were hard-pressed to urge them back on the road. We finally got them to cantor toward the Aramean encampment, stopping half way to let them graze again. When we resumed again, we had them walk toward the Aramean camp. There was no sign of life. No smoke from any fires, no riders visible and no one on foot, yet their tents and banners stood, rustling calmly in the wind.

We passed through the entire camp to find it deserted. A few horses and mules stood grazing, tied to posts driven in the ground; a few others were seen wandering aimlessly in the surrounding fields. We ripped open a basket holding grain to let the horses feed then continued our ride on the road to the Jordan River fords. The roads were strewn with the clothing and equipment from the Aramean camp. It looked like they had been routed and had retreated in a panic.

We rode as far as our weakened horses could take us without seeing one Aramean or a camp follower. By now the watchmen on the walls of Samaria would have seen our progress and sent out troops to cautiously explore the Aramean camp. We harnessed fresh horses abandoned by the Arameans and continued on toward the fords at the Jordan River. The entire day we saw not a horse or a traveler. Close to the Jordan we over-took a young boy driving a cart filled with clothing, weapons and utensils the Arameans had abandoned at the ford. He watched us curiously as we approached.

"Are you the Hittites and the Egyptians?" he asked us.

"We are Israelites from Samaria. Have you seen the Aramean army?"

"I had brought honey from home to trade at the ford of the river. I was asleep last night when I heard a great uproar. It was a great body of Arameans, throwing themselves over the river, not even caring if they were by the fords or not. Some drowned. Their bodies are still lying downstream. They said the Hittites and Egyptians were pursuing them. Are the Hittites and Egyptians coming?"

We saw a glut of carts and wagons on both sides of the river, with cloaks and baskets and sacks strewn along the banks for as far down-stream as we could see.

"Hittites and Egyptians, Jehu?"

"If there are Hittites and Egyptians, Bidkar, our starving horses just out ran them."

"There was grain and flour in the wagons we passed on the side of the road."

"Fine flour, just as Elisha said. But Hittites and Egyptians? My fa-ther told me legends of the old Hittites from before his time, and the last Egyptians raiding this far North were during the times of Jeroboam and Rehoboam. I thought Elisha had gone back to his madness when he said we would be eating fine flour today. Perhaps Elisha imparted some of his madness to the Arameans if they fled from the spirits of old and dead Hittites and Egyptians. Only madness can explain why the Arameans fled in a panic."

We did not cross the Jordan. Even our new mounts were exhausted and the sun was setting. We saw no more Arameans that year.

A DISH OF SCORPIONS

Jehu, Elisha

Your father was an Amorite and your mother was a
Hittite. Ezekiel 16:3

Jehu

The year after the siege of Samaria was lifted there were no campaigns for the army. It was a year of refilling the granaries and buying and breeding horses for the chariots. The Arameans had bypassed the Israelite city of Ramoth-Gilead to the east of the Jordan when they crossed the Jordan to besiege Samaria. Outposts the Arameans had established to the north and east of Samaria to support their siege were left abandoned or defenseless in their panicked withdrawal. I led small detachments against the remaining outposts to see what force it would take to overrun them. A few choice words scrawled on a piece of parchment while the outpost was ringed by our chariots were sufficient for the Arameans to agree to abandon their outposts. My summer was occupied riding between Jezreel, Samaria, Ramoth-Gilead and the small outposts we had recovered from the Arameans.

On one trip back to Samaria, my chariot overtook a lumbering pilgrim being followed by three quite smaller fellows. The square, walking cedar tree could only be Elisha, being trailed by three of his followers. I had my driver ride up alongside Elisha and I dismounted. Unlike my walks on the roadways with the old Elijah who never stopped walking,

Elisha stopped and turned around as the chariot approached and stood and waited for me to get down from the chariot.

I would not pass up an opportunity to butt heads with one of these fellows. They were fellow Israelites and followers of the Lord, yet as I stepped down from my chariot I felt like I was entering battle. They would hurl their bolts and shafts at me as I struggled to wrest the truth from them. Elisha was much more animated than Elijah had been. Elijah would just shake his head and grit his teeth. He had butted heads with so many people in Israel that he had lost hope of convincing us to his way of thinking. Elijah had smoldered intensely, a burning chamber of a furnace buried under the ash of indifference from his people, with much heat still under the surface, but he had no longer flared and flamed like Elisha did.

"Commander, are you on your way to someplace?"

"I am on the same road as you, prophet. Do you trust your door to withstand another battering in Samaria?"

"I trust neither door nor king. I was sent to the King's brother Ahaziah when he was King and the Lord disposed of him. The King should have learned to fear the Lord from that, but he did not. Moab was delivered into his hands, yet he bowed down to the wrath of Chemosh, a god that can neither feel nor touch. Then the King saw the army from Aram delivered into his hands and he did not learn. As if delivery from the army of Aram was not a great enough sign for the King, he was delivered when Aram's siege of Samaria had a death grip on his kingdom and he still does not learn. The Lord has pummeled and pelted him with signs, but he is deaf and dumb to them. His hearing is worse than his mother's lord Baal on Mount Carmel. Do I trust the King? I trust only that stone does not see and wood does not hear."

"And yet you are on your way to Samaria again. Will the King hear you this time?"

"The King? What about you commander Jehu, do you hear?"

"I have heard of your works, prophet."

"They are not my works, soldier. I do not conjure them up. It is the Lord's doing. I do not know how the Lord moves. If you hear, soldier, why are you on your way to serve a king that is deaf?"

"I am a soldier, prophet. I am paid to serve the King."

"A soldier who serves a king that cannot see and cannot hear might as well serve his mule."

"Must you be as difficult as your teacher? He was an obstinate old fool."

"My teacher could hear and see. He taught me to hear and see. Has your King taught you to be deaf and blind?"

"I serve my King because he is the King of my people. I serve Israel."

"And what is Israel?"

"Now who is the blind fool? Is not the Lord the Lord of Abraham, Isaac and Jacob? And is not Jacob Israel?"

"If this is Israel, then there would be no poor in the land. Are there poor in Israel, man of war?"

"Of course there are. There are poor everywhere."

"And why are there poor in Israel?"

"There are poor everywhere, prophet. Should Israel be any different?"

"Should Israel be different, soldier?"

"Didn't I just say that, prophet?"

"Have you loaned money to the poor?"

"Another question? I thought you prophets knew the mind of God."

"Have you forgiven your loans to the poor?"

"Since I do not loan to the poor, I have no loans to forgive."

"Have you set the poor free in the Year of Jubilee?"

"If we freed the poor who would dig entrenchments for the army?"

"And are they paid to dig your trenches?"

"They are poor before they dig. They are poor after they dig. They are not harmed, and the King has his ditch."

"For a ditch the poor are sold into slavery; sold into slavery so they can serve the King and forget the Lord."

"I am a soldier. I fight for the rich and poor in the nation. What battle are you fighting, or do you just enjoy prattling?"

"My battles? Has your sword hunted down prophets, you soldier for the rich and poor?"

"Not my sword, prophet. Never!"

"The sword of many a soldier has."

"None of my soldiers, none, I forbid it. And I have told the King I will not."

"So the King finds other soldiers who will do the bidding of that Queen in Samaria. What good does your refusal do?"

"Would you would prefer I join in the hunt then? My sword is sharp, prophet. You should not talk to me this way."

"Then you should whet your wits with it."

"I should run you through with it if that's your opinion."

"Pierce me as often as you would like, you shedder of blood. You will still remain a dullard."

"A dullard! A dullard! I cannot count the times I have saved you and your kind from the sword, and you call me a dullard!"

"You have saved me, have you saved your nation?"

"By the name of Abraham, Isaac and Jacob, can you tell me why I am talking to you?"

"Maybe you will learn something that is a cure for the dullard in you."

"If I am dull, it is from scoring my edge against that block of granite that is in your head."

"With all your scoring you have not told me why there are poor in Israel."

"If I were a prophet, I would tell you. But I am a soldier. I do not know why there are poor in any land."

"You have heard of the Year of Jubilee?"

"I know the name."

"Have you heard of it spoken in the Temple?"

"If I went to the Temple, Jezebel would call me a disloyal, you know that."

"You have heard of the Law, of the laws Moses taught Israel east of the Jordan?"

"I know of Abraham and Moses and God's Law. I am an Israelite, you know. I am sure you will tell me of the laws from Moses."

"Moses spoke to the Israelites, but they were deaf then and you are deaf now: 'If anyone is poor among your fellow Israelites in the land I am giving you, be openhanded and freely lend them whatever they need. Give generously to them. Do not think wickedly that the seventh year, the year for cancelling debts, is near so you show ill will to them.'"

"Is that wise?"

"It is God's Law. Is God wise?"

"I am a soldier. You tell me, prophet."

"Other nations think it foolishness. Does that make it foolish if the Lord says it is wise? Why did Moses lead the twelve tribes to this land?

"He followed the pillar of fire; I have heard that at least, so the Lord led them here."

"Why, soldier? Why? Because the wind was blowing in that direction? Is the Lord as mindless as a stray breeze? You are a soldier. Do you lead your troops or do they follow the morning breeze?"

"Prophet, chasing your answers is like chasing the breeze."

"Why are we here, soldier? To fight endless wars? To entertain your kings with battle and bloodshed?"

"We battle to live, prophet. Or would you rather have King Ben-Hadad build a temple to Rimmon in Samaria?"

"Would that be worse than Queen Jezebel's temples to Baal? What do other nations see when they come to our land? Do they see the sons of Abraham lending freely to the poor? Do they see the debts of the poor forgiven every Sabbath of years? Do they see the poor harvesting the land every Sabbath of years? Do they see freedom restored to those sold into slavery every Sabbath of Sabbath years? Is God so vain that he needed his own people to sing his praises? Did he lead us here so we could build a temple and offer endless sacrifices? Do not the other nations have their own temples and their own sacrifices? Why would the Lord lead us here just to do what other nations already do? The Lord did not need another people to do that."

"But we are God's chosen people! I know the Law says that!"

"Chosen soldier? Chosen? You were not chosen, you were rescued. An Israelite? No, not an Israelite. Your father was an Amorite and your mother was a Hittite. On the day you were born your cord was not cut, nor were you washed with water to make you clean, nor were you wrapped in cloths. You were thrown out into the open field, for on the day you were born you were despised. You were kicking about in your blood and the Lord said 'Live!' That is your birthright, Israelite. You were rescued and you were rescued so you in kind could show mercy to the poor, to show justice to the foreigner, to show this to the nations. That is your birthright. And when the nations come to Jerusalem, do they see this? When they come to Samaria, do they see this?

"Prophet, talking with you is like harvesting scorpions. You delight in stinging, but produce no crop."

"Maybe you are harvesting the crop you planted. Maybe you are being stung with your own thoughts. You think your kings are providing delicious fare, but your mouths are tormented with stingers. Tell me soldier, if the Lord will have us lend freely to the poor, tell me about Naboth."

"Curse you prophet! I am a soldier!"

"You are a soldier. You are the very soldier that broke open the gate of Naboth's vineyard for King Ahab."

"What would you have me do? Am I a Baasha? A Zimri? Your teacher Elijah was there on that day as well. Why did Elijah not ask for my sword? Now you will tell me that Elijah was a prophet and not a soldier. Well I am a soldier and not a prophet."

Elisha

We walked on silently for quite some time. It was the longest I had ever seen Jehu walk silently without rushing off some place, asking a question or giving an order. Being a prophet gave me no clue as to what he was thinking. I surmised he was thinking of Naboth. I know it troubled him deeply. Or he was forming some explanation about following the orders of his King, or his revulsion of Queen Jezebel. But it was not like Jehu to ruminate silently. His thoughts always leapt off his tongue as quickly as he drove his chariot.

"Tell me prophet, you would not have me serve this King, but you would have me serve this kingdom, and yet the King lives. So you are telling me another riddle, are you not prophet? But is this not a deadly riddle prophet? Is this not a riddle that calls forth death once it is uttered?"

Now I was silent. I had never feared Jehu like I did then. Would he take my head off with one blow if I suggested anything against his sensibilities? I knew he hated riddles, so I told him a riddle from our history. "King David struck down the young Amalekite when he learned that the Amalekite had struck down King Saul even though Saul was in the throes of death and asked for the sword. Then King David killed Rekab and Baanah for beheading Ish-Bosheth, the son of Saul. Since the prophet Samuel had already anointed David as King, did not Saul have to die?"

"Your riddle does not answer my riddle, prophet. What is your answer to my riddle?"

"Sometimes answers from the Lord sound like riddles."

"Don't toy with me prophet. That is not my question. When does the Lord say a king may be killed?"

The heaviness of the question again silenced both of us. Knowing Jehu, had a citizen approached him on the streets of Jezreel and asked him the same question, he would conduct a swift trial at the point of a sword, with the only issue being whether there was any mitigation to delay the sentence. But Jehu had asked the question, twice.

"The Lord says do not murder."

"The Lord said kill the Hittites and the Canaanites and the Ammonites, the Perizites, Hivites, the Jebusites when we enter this land."

"It would have saved them the trouble of killing themselves off. You know their descendants. They are warring continually. Did the Ammonites give Israel a day of rest from war, from raids, from kidnapping our wives and children, from stealing our flocks, from burning our grain? You tell the Lord the good that these people have done. But we refrained. They were not killed. Instead they lurk like jackals, waiting to rip us open. Death upon death. The bodies of generations that have been scattered over this land by their descendants would overwhelm the handful of people Joshua saw."

"It sounds like you would kill all readily, prophet, like Elijah killing the prophets of Baal."

"We all have blood on our hands, soldier."

"The question, prophet, seems to be not whether or not to kill, but who and when to kill."

At this I held my tongue, but Jehu continued to probe.

"Our history is a bloody one. When Zimri slew King Elah, he did it on impulse. But no one followed him. Should he have first found supporters in the palace and allies in the army, maybe adherents in the temples? But building a revolt is like laying foundation stones in quicksand. The palace and the army and the temples shift and slip and flow. Do they not, prophet?"

I knew Jehu was willing to be silent as long as it took me to answer.

"One should wait on the Lord."

It took some time for Jehu to digest this. I was not sure what I meant in any event. Finally Jehu fashioned an answer.

"Wait," he said, and then, after a pause, "but not forbear?"

He was probing deeper. Was he going to say I spoke in favor of regicide?

"Waiting means waiting. Even while the crops burn, our children are sold, our flocks scattered. Sometimes we just have to wait."

"Nothing good comes of an army when it waits."

"But every good commander knows he has to wait for the right moment to strike. Not every day is a good day for battle."

That answer seemed to satisfy Jehu, although I myself was not sure what it meant.

JEHORAM ASCENDANT

Jehosheba

What is the meaning of all of the noise in the city? Joab, I
Kings 1:41

I WAS barely out of my childhood. My father Jehoram was thirty-two
years old when he succeeded King Jehoshaphat and became King. I
had only begun to realize, perhaps only shortly before the death of King
Jehoshaphat, my grandfather, that every child did not live in the Palace
of Solomon or that army commanders and governors of cities were not
visitors at everyone's home for the evening meal. The grandeur and solemnity of my grandfather's funeral observation opened my eyes, just
days before I realized that the world I had lived in was being swept away.

King Jehoshaphat's funeral observation was an extended and intense period of national mourning and remembrance, led in large part by
my uncles, the six younger sons of King Jehoshaphat. These sons, princes
in their own right, encamped in Jerusalem with their large retinues and
courts. Each son of Jehoshaphat was well remembered and loved by the
citizens of Jerusalem, recalling their youth as popular denizens of Jerusalem before departing for their principalities. Jerusalem and environs
were packed during these observations with numerous processions, re-
membrances and commemorations held throughout the city.

Many in Jerusalem, including my grandmother, King Jehoshaphat's
wife, were unsettled at the prospect of my father Jehoram becoming King,
especially after more than ten years of marriage to my mother Athaliah,
the daughter of the infamous Queen Jezebel, my other grandmother, or

"your grandmother from the north," as King Jehoshaphat's wife referred to her. All of the mourners were reassured by the presence of the six royal sons. Although none of these six would assume the throne of their father Jehoshaphat, they each had been granted substantial patrimonies, with their own independent treasuries, palace guards and fortified cities with their own garrisons. The heir to the throne, my father Jehoram, had been married to the daughter of King Ahab, giving him, or at least any future heir, a potential claim to the Kingdom of Israel to the North.

I remember snippets of rumors that circulated in the household of my grandmother. Although she still resided in the royal palace in Jerusalem, her quarters were a separate domain. My mother Athaliah despised her, probably because my grandmother despised Athaliah. It may have been my own little rebellion to favor my grandmother and break the unspoken ban against her by visiting her quarters almost daily. I would hear things there that I would not hear in the household of my father Jehoram. I also came into contact with officials and priests from the Temple, people who rarely if ever frequented the quarters of my parents Jehoram and Athaliah.

It was the time spent in my grandmother's quarters, in contact with representatives of the Temple, probably maneuvered by my grandmother, when I first came in contact with my husband Jehoiada, a priest from the Temple in Jerusalem. My Judean grandmother had pressed King Jehoshaphat to have me pledged to marry the priest Jehoiada. Mother Athaliah was at first disgusted with the plot, but as she began to conspire against it, she reconsidered. My marriage to a prince of a neighboring kingdom would be less useful to her plans than potential influence in the Temple. With her daughter married to a priest who may be in line to be High Priest some day, a means to finally control the Temple in Jerusalem had suddenly opened up to her. The Temple would find Athaliah's plan for an empire based on the northern and southern kingdoms conjoined with Tyre and Sidon highly objectionable, but until now she had no influence and no access to the Temple.

My Judean grandmother related how she had been troubled with the tales that had come from the domain of King Ahab and Queen Jezebel, but King Ahab had died in the seventeenth year of King Jehoshaphat's reign. Ahab's son Ahaziah, well known for his love of wine even in the Kingdom of Judah, had a short reign of two years, and was succeeded by his brother Joram, who was now in his fifth year on the throne of Israel. King Joram was not admired in Judah, but he had not exhibited the virulent Baal and Asherah worship exhibited by his mother Queen Jezebel.

I was a young child when Ahab's son Ahaziah became King of Israel. I remember feeling some pride that one of my mother's brothers had become King of a neighboring kingdom, while not fully realizing how few kings in this world there were. I would later learn that during Ahaziah's reign both Israel and Judah held their collective breath, not certain what direction Ahaziah would take his kingdom. But Ahaziah had no direction and the Kingdom of Israel stagnated, the commanders of its army concerned solely with preserving their borders. King Ahaziah cared for nothing other than his drinking, and had little interest in his mother's devotions to her gods, except perhaps at the last moment when he was on his death bed. Queen Jezebel maintained the primacy of her temples, simply because there was only apathy coming from King Ahaziah. The prophets of the Lord also held their breath with Ahaziah on the throne. Jezebel's threats no longer had the power of the King behind them, but she still yielded great power in her own name.

I was only slightly older when King Joram of Israel assumed the throne after the unfortunate or questionable death of King Ahaziah. I was shocked as a youth that a king could die so young, but somehow reassured that another of my mother's brothers had become King of our neighbor Israel. I later learned that many in Judah were relieved when Joram became King of Israel. As King, Joram was no champion of Queen Jezebel's religions. Many people in Jerusalem wondered if there would be some softening in the Kingdom of Israel. Would Jehoshaphat's son, my father and the brother-in-law of King Joram of Israel, have an opening to bring the two kingdoms together? My grandmother in Jerusalem was not optimistic. She had had her fill of her son Jehoram and his wife Athaliah. She feared that if the two kingdoms were brought together it would be under the sway of my grandmother of the north, Jezebel.

Listening to the priests that would visit my grandmother, I learned of the great anxiety that had hovered over the land after King Jehoshaphat agreed to the marriage of his son and heir to the throne Jehoram to the daughter of Queen Jezebel. I sensed that same anxiety returning and reaching a crescendo in Jerusalem within days of King Jehoshaphat's death, but it seemed to ease as people began to hope that something good would come out of this marital alliance with the Kingdom of Israel. Jerusalem had the Temple and the Palaces of Solomon. But more, Jerusalem had been the heart of Abraham's descendants for hundreds of years, while

Samaria, the royal seat of the Kings of Israel, had been built on a rocky outcropping less than forty years ago and even today seemed as if the plaster was still drying. As Jerusalem mourned King Jehoshaphat it also relived its history as the center of King Solomon's empire, and began to convince itself that its restored greatness under King Jehoshaphat may be on the verge of being enlarged under new King Jehoram.

In all of the solemnity and pageantry, few noticed that the new King Jehoram and his wife Athaliah were absent from the observations. To the casual visitor to Jerusalem during this period of mourning, if the King was not at this palace or that observation, it was easy to believe he must be fulfilling his duties elsewhere. There were so many solemn observations and processions, that Jehoram and Athaliah could have been anywhere. Meanwhile, in this procession or the other was one of the other sons of King Jehoshaphat, or the High Priest, or a detachment of charioteers, or a house of prophets or the embassy from Edom or Philistia or Sidon paying their respects. The crush was so great that it was impossible to keep track of anyone. I hoped for word that the King was coming to the Temple. The Law did not require that the King present himself to the Temple, but the Law had been written before we had a king, and Solomon and many kings after him had come to the Temple in thanksgiving.

"He will not be here, Jehosheba," Jehoiada chastised me, "do you think your mother Athaliah will let him come?"

"But he is King now. This is the Temple of Jerusalem. How could he not present himself this one time to the Temple."

"And who will he bring with him? Where he goes Athaliah goes, and with her, her mother's prophets of Baal who accompany her everywhere. Do you want them gawking and pointing while they stroll through the Temple courts. Can you think of anything more unclean? Do you want me to stand at the gate and tell them they cannot enter?"

"All of my uncles have been here, most more than once."

By now the sun was fading behind the hills. King Jehoshaphat had been buried two days ago, and the foreign dignitaries were on their way back home. My uncles, I had heard from those of the royal household who had made their way to the Temple that day, would be at the royal palace for one last banquet before they returned to their provinces. A chill went through me when I knew I would not receive an invitation. I was the wife of Jehoiada, a priest in the Temple in Jerusalem. As Athaliah restored the temple to Astarte, known here in Jerusalem as Asherah, my parents Athaliah and Jehoram ceased accompanying Jehoram's father

King Jehoshaphat in his visits to the Temple. My steady alliance with my grandmother, King Jehoshaphat's wife, who had spoken heated words against the marriage of my father Jehoram to Athaliah and had never changed her tone, made me less than loyal in the eyes of the royal palace. But tomorrow promised to be a quiet day in Jerusalem. It would be the first normal day under our new King Jehoram.

As the streets and the markets quieted down with the approaching evening, we could make out a faint noise, as if in a distant quarter of the city one last celebration was getting underway. Maybe it was the coming from the banquet at the palace. I imagined my brothers, with a little wine, reliving the battles they had waged against each other as children with wooden swords, when their retainers would act as their horses or their siege engines. If it was the banquet at the palace, it must be a rousing banquet I thought as the gentle hubbub grew. Then there were shouts, even yelling, so it must be more than the palace banquet. Then the shouting grew into the streets. And yelling. But was that screaming? Wailing? What place did that have in this evening? We left our quarters, with others, looking at each other for some explanation for the uproar that no one could give. As we got closer to the streets, the maelstrom grew closer to us. As we went through alleys, passageways and streets, it was filling the city. Screams, wails and shouts we could not make out, flooding into all of the streets, then the sounds of horses' hooves, of chariot wheels skidding across paving stones, of heavy blows against wooden timbers. And screaming, more screaming.

Jehoiada took me by the shoulders, stopping me.

"Jehoiada," I said, "there is no enemy. What can this be?"

Jehoiada did not answer and did not look at me as he turned me around.

"To the Temple. We must go to our inner rooms at the Temple," he said as he started to guide me down passageways away from the streets.

"But why? What is this?"

I do not know if Jehoiada was going to answer me, but before he could, we heard the closest wail we have heard, a piercing shriek.

"Death! Death! Azariah has been struck down! Death! Jehiel has been struck down! They are dead! Murdered! The sons of Azariah, the sons of Jehiel, dead! All dead!"

I stopped. Jehoiada still had ahold of my shoulders, but he stopped, staring into the void, trying to understand the words. My knees collapsed and I fell to the ground. Now it was my wail, my scream adding to the growing cacophony.

"No! No! Oh Azariah, my uncles, my cousins! No! No! Jehiel! Oh, Jehiel!"

Jehoiada knelt beside me, his hands still on my shoulders, struck by the same blow that felled me. Then footsteps. Three figures, from what Jehoiada told me later, two priests and a Levite, came running toward us and pulled us up from the ground.

"Quickly, to the Temple! They are upon us!"

Jehoiada and the priests dragged and carried me down an alleyway toward the Temple.

"What is this?" asked Jehoiada breathlessly.

"All have been struck down in the palace, all!"

"And the King?" Jehoiada already knew the answer.

"The King pursues us all, he has slain all his brothers, and the swords still dance."

The word "slain" struck me like a hammer, but knocked the panic and the grief out of me.

"All dead?" I asked, "All?"

"All and more. And they are coming. We must get you to the Temple."

"It is Athaliah," I replied, "She has done this."

As I said this, a horseman appeared in the alleyway behind us, filling the entire passage with his mount.

"Come here, all of you. Come forward."

The Levite walked toward the horseman, as we slowly edged backward.

"Where are you from?" asked the Levite of the horseman.

"From the King," answered the horseman, drawing his sword out of its sheath as if to vouch for his authority, "and who is that woman? Bring her forward."

"Go!" shouted the Levite, as he stepped forward.

As soon as the Levite shouted, I was shoved by the priests and Jehoiada into a small passage way, too small for a horse, as the horseman advanced on the Levite. The Levite leapt to catch the sword, which he did, but caused the horse to stumble to its knees. By the time the horseman righted his horse over the moaning Levite, we were through the passageway and into another alley, and another, and then on the street to the Temple. The streets were not crowded, but seemed filled with people running in all directions, running into and out of doorways while the screaming and yelling continued. In sight of the Temple we halted. There were more horsemen, even up to the steps to the Temple. One of the priests threw his cloak over my head and told Jehoiada to cover his head. They wedged me between them as we advanced on the Temple, looking for our horseman.

The horsemen we saw were going up and down the steps of the Temple, but not searching the streets. As we passed, I glimpsed a figure, no, three or four figures, being pushed out, down the stairs. "The High Priest," I gasped, as one of my priests shoved my head down and shoved me forcefully to walk faster. More I did not see, other than to hear the metallic song of the swords, the rending of flesh and fabric and thuds of lifeless bodies on the stairs. Quiet, startling noises amid the snorting of horses, the clatter of hooves, the slap of leather, curt, shouted orders, and the constant background of a people wailing for their kingdom.

I saw no more until I was brought into a small antechamber, deep someplace in the Temple complex. The priests deposited us there and left without a word. There were at least ten people crammed into that little nook. Some familiar faces, distorted with fear, but with no greeting, no questions. They saw me, Jehosheba, the sister of King Jehoram, as if they were seeing their own death.

"You are alive?" they asked in wonder, but also in the fear that the murderers of my uncles and cousins would be also seeking me out.

"My family!" I wailed, "I must go the palace."

The others gasped at the thought. "No," said Jehoiada, "to show your face at the palace would be seen as a challenge, you'd be swept away."

I struggled against Jehoiada's grasp but he refused to release me.

I do not know why I was not taken that night. Was the horseman that confronted me looking for me, or did he just see a woman in the streets on a night of plunder and blood? Many priests and Levites were cut down that night. No one was captured or chained. They were killed in their homes, on the streets, and in the palace. Many were well known advisors and counselors of King Jehoshaphat. Many were not. Many were simply well known, well respected, well thought of people in Jerusalem. Anyone who could speak out in the market or square or at the city gates, whose words would be considered and weighed carefully was cut down. Any voice against the terror was cut down in the terror. The survivors could feel outrage, but were not equipped to speak out against the terror and the fear. Silence became the byword. It was as if the people had had their tongues ripped out.

Although there had been rumblings against Athaliah at the time of her marriage to Jehoram, several years had passed. There was concern about what actions Athaliah may try to take once Jehoram became King. But that night, we knew how deep the roots of the House of Ethbaal reached, and how strong the hold of Jezebel's daughter was on Jehoram. I had removed myself from the palace, and had been removed, so I had not seen the change come over Jehoram. But it was clear how closely Jehoram had held his plans secret. King Jehoshaphat took great care to provide for all his sons, my uncles. He would have been at table with Jehoram and Athaliah, talking of all that Jehoshaphat had done to advance the kingdom, while Jehoram and Athaliah whispered in their bed chamber how to tear it down.

THE REDUCTION OF JEHORAM

Jehu

We are given no signs from God; no prophets are left, and
none of us knows how long this will be. Psalm 74:9

AFTER King Jehoshaphat's funeral, a flood of Samarian merchants
and traders fled from every city in Judah. They brought with them
tales of a slaughter of King Jehoshaphat's sons in Jerusalem, which was
then repeated in city after city. Some fled immediately after the bloodshed in Jerusalem. Others waited, hoping things would settle down after
Jerusalem. Those that had stayed hoping to weather the storm witnessed
the slaughter spread to every city in the kingdom. Anyone who had supported King Jehoshaphat's sons became targets. King Jehoshaphat had
begun to rule his kingdom through his sons. Each exercised the King's
authority in their assigned regions, and the entire kingdom reported to
the King through his sons. Every army commander, priest, controller of a
household, controller of a palace, administrator of a granary, overseer of
the city's armory and walls, tax collector and supervisor of the city's market place dealt in one way or another with the sons of King Jehoshaphat.
All came under suspicion, and most of them fell to the sword. Those
without power, but who protested the deaths of these able people also fell.

Jehoram's purge of Judah was successful. No elder, merchant or
priest that survived the purge had enough power to challenge the throne.
Every ruler of a city or province whose people were loyal to the King's
sons was struck down. Every judge or administrator who received popular acclaim at the city gates was removed. No one who was left had any

following. No one wanted a following, since it was a good way to lose one's head. King Jehoram began withdrawing military commanders from the fortified cities that had been granted to King Jehoshaphat's other sons and based the entire army in Jerusalem where he could keep it firmly under his control.

After the slaughter, Kingdom of Judah went silent. We had regularly received news of Judah from many of our citizens travelling between Samaria and Jerusalem, or from traders and travelers who had passed through some part of Israel. But the news stopped coming. After several months, a few of our traders ventured back to Israel to try to reopen connections. The reports we received from many of the cities in Israel was that some of their markets were almost deserted. No one seemed to be in charge, and if someone was in charge, they did not seem to know what they were doing. The people our traders had dealt with before were gone, and when our traders asked for them by name, they were hauled before some suspicious magistrate they had never seen before and accused of fomenting rebellion against the King. Few traders were tempted to return to risk their necks a second time. Only from Jerusalem did word come back that markets were booming. King Jehoram had decreed that certain types of trade from the cities had to pass through Jerusalem, the better to tax and control and to prevent anyone not approved by the King from getting rich.

Besides the market in Jerusalem, the only other thing that seemed to be booming in Judah was temple construction. In his later years, King Jehoshaphat had allowed some minor temples to be built in out of the way places. We had all assumed this was done to please his new daughter-in-law Athaliah. But the new temples King Jehoram was building were major edifices with substantial courtyards and surrounding buildings to support the temple operations and house its priests and other devotees. Tradesmen based in Jerusalem were traveling all over Judah to erect these new temple grounds. It was again assumed, just as in the times of King Jehoshaphat, that Athaliah was the motivating spirit behind these new temples. The little news we received seem to echo the temple construction that had started as soon as King Ahab had succeeded his father King Omri. Queen Athaliah seemed to be following in the footsteps of her mother Queen Jezebel.

We tried to sort through the fragments of information we received from Judah as seers and diviners straining to interpret the strange dream that Judah had become. What was left of King Jehoshaphat's mighty army now that the commanders we knew from our joint battles with Aram were gone and their regiments assigned to Jerusalem? Would the revenues from the market taxes in Jerusalem be enough to supplant the revenues we assumed were no longer being collected from the markets that were all but shuttered in cities throughout the realm? What was left in the King's coffers after all of the temple construction was completed?

We were not the only neighbor of Judah asking the same questions. King Jehoshaphat collected substantial tribute from Philistia, Edom, Arabia and other realms large and small. The amount of tribute received by King Jehoshaphat had not been seen in the land since the days of King Solomon. We knew that the envoys from these powers were hearing the same things we were hearing when they travelled to Jerusalem to deliver their tribute and pay their respects to King Jehoram. We had known from King Jehoshaphat's army commanders that a large portion of the tribute received went directly to the fortress cities controlled by King Jehoshaphat's sons. If the markets of those towns had been denuded by King Jehoram, we speculated that this tribute now went directly to Jerusalem. Then we wondered if this influx of tribute to Jerusalem was paying for King Jehoram's new temples being built throughout the land, and if it was being used to build temples, was any of the tribute going to support the outlying fortress cities on Judah's frontiers?

Under Omri and Ahab in Israel, the new temple building, the widening of city walls, the building of the towers at Jezreel, and even the construction of the new capital of Samaria was supported with slave labor. We wondered if the poor in Judah were now being auctioned off for their debts, and put to work to build King Jehoram's temples. We did not know this, but we had seen this festering sore grow in Israel under King Ahab. Taxes on herds, market stalls, gate passage, wine vessels and doorways became oppressive. The tax collectors extended loans with interest, and then called the loans due when it was obvious the debtor could not pay. The debtor, his goods and property and family would be auctioned off to pay the overdue taxes. The King's overseers would frequently outbid all bidders, increasing the debtor's debt, and creating a pool of free labor to build for the Kingdom. This was something foreign to Israel. I had heard our Queen Jezreel hector King Ahab about taxes and slaves; "Do you want your people to cower in ravines and mill their grain on rocks as they had done for generations before your kings? Do you want your armies to go out on donkey carts wielding axes made of stone as your people did against the Philistines for generations? Kingdoms need slaves. Without slaves you will be king of the nomads while Aram rules from Samaria."

King Jehoshaphat's strong kingdom created a great amount of security for Israel. The marriage of Athaliah to Jehoram only increased that security. There was no threat to Israel from the South. King Jehoshaphat's dominion over his Southern and Eastern neighbors kept any threat from that direction at bay. If Israel had to contend with Aram and also fight invaders from our South, we may have been overrun. We tried to strain every bit of information received from Judah. If this is what we are seeing, what are the Philistines and Edomite seeing? We did not have to wait long for an answer.

Edom was the first to revolt. Judah's governor of Edom was whipped raw and lashed to a donkey and sent back over the border. A detachment from King Jehoram's palace guard sent to Bozrah to collect reparations was made to bow down to the newly acclaimed King of Edom. King Jehoram led his newly appointed army commanders to invade Edom, but he barely escaped with his life. King Jehoshaphat's army commanders had been dispatched in the purge, along with any commanders serving Jehoshaphat's sons. King Jehoram's new commanders were accomplished in raiding villages to proclaim an imaginative horse, mule and donkey tax, but not much else. The newly reborn Kingdom of Edom had no chariots, and at the time of its revolt against King Jehoram did not have anything I would have called an army. Edom had been under Judah's thumb since the times of Kings David and Solomon. They had staged a serious rebellion against King Jehoshaphat, in league with Moab and Ammon, but had been crushed. The remnants of Edom's ragtag army had been picked over for plunder. But King Jehoram had been so busy crushing anyone he thought was a threat inside Judah, he had given no thought to controlling his dominions.

King Jehoram rushed into Edom with his entire contingent of chariots against a new kingdom that had no chariots. But chariots cannot fight alone. Chariots cannot rush into caves or crevices or ravines. Charioteers who dismount to chase their harassers from their hiding places are nothing more than foot soldiers unsupported by riders. After the King of Edom had learned how to lure a good number of Jehoram's charioteers off of their chariots, Jehoram found himself encircled by carefully concealed archers, javeliniers, and slingers. Jehoram and most of his chariots were only able to escape by dashing away at night when the arrows, spears and stones could only follow the sound of retreating hoof beats.

That was the first blow against King Jehoram. Why he did not immediately return to Edom with a properly balanced force, I do not know. I suspect that the army commanders he had left simply did not know how to mount a proper campaign, or did not want to risk explaining to King Jehoram that his strategy did not succeed because it was foolhardy, while theirs was not.

After Edom shook off King Jehoram's yoke, tribute to Jerusalem dwindled to a pittance. The tiny city of Libnah was next. It was not even a kingdom. It was a walled trading center with rich commerce and was one of the main sources of grain in the region. It had accepted the dominance of the Kingdom of Judah because it did not have any army that could contest Judah's army, but principally because the Kingdom of Judah would protect it from domination by the Philistines. When Edom stopped paying tribute to Judah, Libnah withheld its grain shipments to Judah, and instead traded to hire some mercenaries from Edom, Philistia and Arabia. It mounted its own minor revolt and waited to see how Edom fared in its revolt.

The revolt of Edom may have encouraged other dependencies of Judah to test the waters, but the revolt by Libnah opened the flood gates. Philistia had paid King Jehoshaphat substantial tribute in silver, supplemented by shipments of wine, beers and olive oil. From Arabia King Jehoshaphat received sizeable yearly herds of rams and goats, sufficient to keep slaughterhouses, tanneries, looms, weavers and dairies busy year round.

Having seen King Jehoram flee for his life in the night from a detachment of shepherds with slingshots and a few archers in Edom, the Philistines and Arabians mounted separate raids against King Jehoram. The Philistines had an army that could hold its own in the field. They appeared ready to strike at Jerusalem, so King Jehoram threw every reserve he had against the Philistines. While King Jehoram marched out in good order against the advancing Philistines, the Arabians advanced unnoticed from the South, encouraged and aided by Edom. My own suspicion from the reports we received after the battle was that the Philistines acted in league with the Arabians. There were Philistine commanders riding with the Arabians.

When the Philistine threat seemed to be at its highest point, pinning down the entire Judean army, the Arabians struck between the rear of King Jehoram's encampment and Jerusalem, throwing Jehoram's army into a panic. The Arabians raced through the gates of Jerusalem, brushing aside the old men and children left to guard the gates of the city, and rioting through a meagerly defended Jerusalem to the point of looting the gold from the very Temple, while ripping through the city, sacking, pillaging and raping. It did not last long.

It was the rape of Jerusalem that led to my order to heighten the towers of Jezreel so that raiders even a day's march over the plain of Jezreel could be seen by our watchmen. Jerusalem was ripped open. The Arabians did not pillage for pillage's sake, but their plundering was thorough. Their many trips to Jerusalem to deliver their tribute to King Jehoshaphat gave them great knowledge of the treasures of Jerusalem. Jerusalem even supplied the bulk of the livestock, wagons and slaves needed to haul away Jerusalem's treasure. And the slaves? Citizens of Jerusalem. All of King Jehoram's wives and children were captured and divided between the Philistines and Arabians, except for Queen Athaliah and her youngest child Ahaziah. It was rumored that Athaliah bargained with the Philistines for her life and the life of her youngest son by revealing where the palace treasuries and her other sons had been secreted

King Joram of Israel, the brother of Queen Athaliah, was not willing to send troops into the catastrophe that had become the Kingdom of Judah, even though Jezebel prevailed on Joram to send chariots and horses to Judah to replace those that had been lost. Queen Jezebel's master plan to unite Israel and Judah under the House of Ethbaal had received a heavy blow. Jezebel's time was waning, and we hoped that the disaster her son-in-law Jehoram brought down on his own head would end her scheming.

The silence out of the Kingdom of Judah deepened as the misrule of King Jehoram went on. Word reached Samaria that King Jehoram had a disgusting bowel disease of some sort; that he could not keep from soiling himself. But that sort of message could just as easily have been born from off-color stories told by the King's detractors. Other rumors swirled around Samaria that the prophet Elijah had sent King Jehoram a letter. This letter from Elijah supposedly said that the Lord would strike King Jehoram's wives and daughters with a heavy blow and Jehoram would die from disease because he was causing Jerusalem to prostitute itself to Ahab's gods and had killed his own brothers. But Elijah was gone. Elisha said Elijah had been taken by the spirit of the Lord, and Elisha had taken Elijah's place while King Jehoram's father Jehoshaphat was still King of Israel. With only rumors and gossip escaping from Jerusalem, it was hard to tell what was happening in that now strange land.

It would not be until King Jehoram finally died of his disease that contact was reestablished between Samaria and Jerusalem. Emissaries were sent to Jerusalem for King Jehoram's funeral, but they learned that there had been no observation of his death. The people were afraid to rejoice, fearful what revenge the now widowed Queen Athaliah may exact, so they showed their joy at the death of King Jehoram by ignoring it and going to market. There were no weeks of observation as had been the case with the death of his father King Jehoshaphat. There was no observation at all. He was buried, but as a final insult to his memory, he was not buried with the kings of Judah. That would have been unthinkable had Queen Athaliah remained in charge, but even Athaliah's vengeance had lost its purchase after the failures of her husband King Jehoram. The kingdom had been hollowed out and gutted; there was a gray pall hanging over the palace.

It was not long after we received news of the agonizing death of King Jehoram and the ascension of his sole surviving son Ahaziah as King that we began receiving regular dispatches from Jerusalem. The Kingdom of Judah had been reduced, but not as much as I had expected. Judah's treasuries were all but exhausted, but its territory was mainly intact. It was only the rigorous health of the kingdom under King Jehoshaphat that had allowed it to survive under the scourge of King Jehoram.

THE MADNESS BEGINS

Jehu

They sow the wind and reap the whirlwind. Hosea 8:7

MADNESS is something one gets used to in the army. Waging war is madness with strategy and tactics. An armed Aramean on the battlefield will be trampled by my horses as quickly as I can whip them into madness, and I feel joy and exaltation as his blood spins off my wheels, splatters onto my face and drips off my beard. Yet I have met Arameans in the market in Samaria and greeted them in their own language and wished a blessing on their house.

There was a time when I knew that I would meet this madness only when I was driving my chariot at the head of my troops. Then there was a time when this madness started to bleed off of the battlefield and show itself everywhere I turned. The lives of the kings seemed more tenuous that ever. Hazael, King Ben-Hadad's closest advisor, had murdered the King with his own hands on the king's sick bed and promptly assumed the throne. King Joram was incensed. He ranted around the palace grounds, his sword unsheathed swinging randomly in every direction.

"Aren't there enough Baashas? Enough Zimris? Who will kill their master next? Learn from Zimri, will you. After the king, you will be the next to burn."

It was King Ben-Hadad who had besieged Samaria a few short years ago. I thought King Joram would derive some pleasure from his death. But Joram's feigned anger masked his fear. As far as the House of Ahab was concerned, Hazael was but another Zimri; a common person with no royal blood, made treacherous by a position granted him by the king. For invading kings, Joram had his loyal army. Yes, loyal to the King in part, but loyal to its own fear; fear of being overrun, fear of pillage and rape, fear of lands and crops being taken, of entire towns being sold into slavery. But for a Zimri, what was the defense? The aspiring regicide had already entered the land, breeched the gates and scaled the palace walls and was standing face to face with the king in the throne room with an unsheathed sword. Joram had been taught the dangers well. Queen Jezebel made certain that for each trusted advisor, for each commander of the army with access to the King, there was an unknown detachment of soldiers assigned to storm his house and cut down his entire household should he lift his hand against the King. I knew who was assigned to my household. I had commanded or been assigned to almost every detachment of soldiers from every corner of the nation during my years in the army. There are many soldiers loyal to me, they trust me more than the King, and as soon as the name was known it was passed on to me.

Sworn enemy or not, the assassination of King Ben-Hadad was a threat to all kings. What better lesson to anyone contemplating treachery than to descend on the regicide Hazael in force to bring the royal palace down on the assassin's head? Of course, the only greater threat to a king than a disloyal advisor are other kings seeing blood on the ground. A regicide on impulse will leave the royal household in disarray. King Joram and King Ahaziah saw their chance, and they acted almost on impulse. Jezebel, the Queen mother of Israel and Queen Grandmother of Judah saw her progeny's impulse as an opportunity.

"Let us ride against that assassin Hazael while the blood is still fresh on the ground," was King Joram's message to King Ahaziah, rushed off on impulse the same day as the news of Ben-Hadad's death reached the palace, without consulting his palace advisors or army commanders. "Commanders of Ben-Hadad's army chosen for their loyalty to Ben-Hadad will have to be weeded out by Hazael. Hazael cannot turn his back on anyone in the palace. Many will seek to avenge the death of their King. If we attack now, he will be guarding against assassins in his own ranks."

As days passed, a more troubling fear arose. Word had filtered back that King Joram's subject Elisha had been behind it all. It could not be fathomed. Many in the army felt it was Elisha who had prophesied the lifting of the siege by the Arameans. King Joram would respond that the ramblings of a mad man did not determine the actions of great armies. One of our prophets upsetting the throne of the King of Aram? How is that possible? But my men told me the very improbable tale. No one could keep track of Elisha. He often travelled alone, and sometimes at night. But however he left Samaria, he returned with his prophets and servants leading forty camels loaded with grain and dates and cloth and wine. No one can keep that amount of treasure secret. The wife of the soldier who has my name is from Elisha's village. Why Elisha chose to wander to Damascus at that time, no one knew. As it happened, King Ben-Haddad was sick. Word came to Ben-Haddad that Elisha was in the country, so Ben-Haddad sent his second-in-command Hazael to Elisha with the forty camels loaded with gifts.

"Inquire of Elisha if I am to recover from this illness," was the instruction Hazael was given by his King. Why was Elisha even in Aram at the time? The only way King Ben-Haddad would know that Elisha was in his kingdom was if Elisha made it known to someone in the palace in Damascus. What made me pause was that the King of Aram had sent for Elisha, a prophet of our Lord, to inquire whether he would recover from his illness. Did our King Joram pause for even a second to consider this? King Joram was at the palace when Elijah told his brother, then King Ahaziah, that he would not recover from his injuries because he had sent to the prophets of Baal-Zebub to inquire whether he would recover.

But the truly startling part of this strange tale was that when Elisha met with Hazael, he told Hazael, "The Lord has shown me that you will become King of Aram." Some versions of the story went on to say that Elisha anointed Hazael King over Aram. No one could believe it. The prophet Samuel had anointed David to overthrow King Saul, and the prophet Ahijah had anointed Jeroboam to take the kingdom away from Rehoboam, but one of our prophets anointing the King of a foreign nation? We discussed this rumor around our campfires long into the nights. "Isn't the Lord the Lord of Israel?" "How can a prophet of the Lord anoint a follower of Rimmon" "If we fight against a king anointed by one of the Lord's prophets, how can we win?" I kept my own counsel, partly because I did not have the answers, and partly because I have wondered ever since I was old enough to lift a sword why two different prophets anointed two different kings, both descendants of Abraham, whose kingdoms would war against each other; why the house of Abraham, Isaac and Israel was divided.

King Joram's impulse to strike against the usurper Hazael to gain an advantage over Aram was now steeled by news that one of his subjects, a prophet of the Lord and a sworn enemy of the House of Omri, had gone over to Aram and had deposed the King. If Elisha was anointing a King over Aram, it could only mean that Elisha was plotting against the House of Omri and the only way to end the plotting was to attack the usurper Hazael.

While the soldiers in the barracks were still disputing the meaning of Elisha anointing Hazael King of Aram, the commanders of the army of Israel were summoned to assemble in the royal palace. King Joram had one of his scribes read to us a missive that was to be sent to King Ahaziah of Judah:

> From Queen Jezebel, Daughter of King Ethbaal of Sidon, mother of King Joram of Israel, prophetess of the mighty Baal;
>
> To my dearest grandson Ahaziah, King of Judah, of the house of David and the House of Omri. Greetings! Kiss your mother Athaliah for me.
>
> May Baal grant you all authority and power over all of your wretched enemies, and absolute dominion over your realm; power, arms, wealth and glory be yours! Death to all who oppose you!
>
> King Ahaziah, your uncle King Joram of Israel has asked that I address this letter to you, and in his name.
>
> King Ahaziah, you have certainly heard by now of the threat that the treachery of that rebellious prophet Elisha has brought to our door steps. That foulest of all creatures has hatched another plot against the House of Omri. Is Elisha not the servant of that miscreant Elijah that brought death upon my son and your namesake, your uncle King Ahaziah of Israel? If we let that vulture brood his plots, there will be no end of the evil he will hatch against us. We must strike now, without hesitation. If you do not join us, and the Kingdom of Israel falls by the hand of Elijah's appointed executioner, Aram will not fail to turn to the south against you. For the sake of the House of Omri, join us in battle against that usurper Hazael.
>
> Remember that your grandfather King Ahab battled the vile Arameans at Ramoth-Gilead, and that in the midst of battle your grandfather King Ahab, while in the vanguard of his army, was struck by an arrow; that King Ahab continued valiantly to command his army in the field as his very life's blood drained from him.
>
> There must be vengeance! Will you let those vile Arameans continue to defame the name of your grandfather King Ahab by their very existence!

> There can be no honor for the House of Omri as long
> as the Arameans remain unpunished for their treachery at
> Ramoth-Gilead.

As commanders, it was our duty to begin sending messages out to our captains to prepare to assemble our reserves after the spring planting for the coming campaign, touring our armories and stables and plotting out our advance against Aram. It was left to us to wonder why the proposal to the Kingdom of Judah to join us in this campaign went out under the name of the Queen mother Jezebel. Ours was to battle for Israel, not for Jezebel's aims, and our griping was done only among close friends. Bidkar and I were of the opinion that Queen Jezebel was maneuvering this offensive for her own purposes. She had been hotly searching for Elijah when an attack by Aram had stopped her search. She was angered that she had not been able to kill Elijah, and believed that her lack of diligence allowed Elisha to pick up the mantle of Elijah.

We did not feel that allying with the Kingdom of Judah in a campaign against Aram was a good strategy. The army of Judah had been savaged in many unsuccessful campaigns under their pitiful late King Jehoram, and their young King Ahaziah had no experience in leading an army. We could see disaster looming if the army of Judah collapsed in the midst of a battle and left our positions exposed.

Perhaps this was part of Queen Jezebel's plan. Had King Joram met with his commanders to discuss a campaign against Aram, none of his commanders would have suggested asking Judah to joining in the attack. By reading Jezebel's letter to King Ahaziah to us, we could see that we were not dealing simply with military strategy, but with Jezebel's campaign against the prophets. Any challenge to the plan on the basis of military tactics would be interpreted as opposition to Queen Jezebel. The thought of incurring the displeasure of Jezebel silenced us.

Not until after the battle with Aram was joined did I discover that there was more to Jezebel's plans than merely her hatred of the prophets.

I had some dread in a foray from Ramoth-Gilead. I had ridden with King Ahab when he was allied with King Jehoshaphat of Judah in battling Aram at Ramoth-Gilead. Yes, it was at Ramoth Gilead that a stray arrow stuck King Ahab under the breast plate, and he bled to death in his chariot that day. Did King Joram share my dread, going to battle with Aram, allied again with Judah, in the same place his father was killed?

I wondered what the prophets would say. Before going to battle at Ramoth-Gilead King Jehoshaphat had asked to hear from King Ahab's prophets and finally heard from Micaiah who had been dragged from the dungeon for the occasion. Ahab was resolute in proving the prophet Micaiah wrong, and proving his prophets right, and what claim does a soldier have to being a better judge of prophets than a king? King Ahab ordered the ragged Micaiah be held in the palace, on bread and water, until Ahab returned from the battle. Ahab was going to settle his score with Micaiah when he returned. Of course he didn't return, but then Jezebel did settle the score anyway. She brought Ahaziah and Joram into the citadel to see Micaiah run through.

But Kings Joram and Ahaziah did not consult the prophets. Perhaps Jezebel did, I do not know.

WAITING

Jehu

Do not pay attention to every word people say, or you
may hear your servant cursing you. Solomon, Ecclesiastes
7:21

I DLENESS. It is what kings seem to do best in battle.
We had had heated feints back and forth outside Ramoth-Gilead.
Lines would form and advance. At one point it seemed as if battle was
about to be joined until King Joram was thrown from his chariot. Joram's driver had wheeled his chariot around to avoid a collision with
three Aramean chariots which had appeared suddenly out of the dust of
battle when he was rammed by an accompanying chariot that veered into
Joram's chariot. It seemed at first as if he was dead. Blood from his head
covered his face in bright red. Immediately before the collision, a stone
slung from one of the approaching Aramean chariots had creased Joram's
temple. He was limp. I jumped from my chariot to attend to the King, and
it looked like there was no life in his eyes. Then he gasped and sputtered.

"Get him in his chariot. Get him behind the lines. How close are the
Arameans? Are they advancing?"

By the time I got back into my chariot, I could see that the Arameans were wavering. They had seen our lines form up to attack, and then
come to a dead stop. Were we only feinting? Or did they think our orders
had become confused? Had they caught us in a moment of confusion? If
so, an able commander would order an immediate attack directly at our
center.

Kings being kings, I had a rider dispatched to our right to seek out King Ahaziah. But as soon as the rider was on his way, a shout went up from the Arameans. They began pounding their shields with their swords and lances, maybe ramping up their courage to attack, maybe just to discourage us from attack.

"Chariots, behind me. All speed! Get word to the archers, let fly over us as we sweep their line. Have the footmen rise up and raise their lances to the sky."

Our chariots dashed out directly toward the Arameans, then we swept along their line, letting fly with arrows and lances, just as the archers and slingers to our rear let loose. As we broke off and drove back to our center, to decide if we needed to sweep again, the Arameans broke off. They were not forming their front lines to repel the attack they thought was coming, they were moving toward their rear to retreat should we attack. Disaster did not visit us.

King Joram was awake as I rode back into camp. He could barely stand. He had some good gashes in his head. He could not move his right arm. He gasped and moaned with each breath.

"Jehu," he wheezed, "attend to King Ahaziah. Review our defenses with his commanders. Do you think the Arameans will attack soon?"

"If they were ready to attack, they just lost their best opportunity. We have been feinting for three days now. I have not seen any sign that they were assembling to attack. They are more concerned with keeping an avenue open to retreat. They are not ready to attack."

I sent a messenger to King Ahaziah. His commander replied that he has only seen the Arameans entrenching and pulling back. He did not think they had enough forces to mount an attack. The handful of Aramean prisoners we captured said that King Hazael was at their army's camp, but none of those prisoners had actually seen him, and none of our men had seen Hazael on the battlefield. We surmised that Hazael's grip on his newly acquired kingdom was not yet secure enough for him to risk receiving an errant arrow in the back in the course of battle. We felt that Hazael would not mount any major attack so late in the season with commanders whose loyalty was not yet assured. We decided to send King Joram back to Jezreel to recover. His mind was too clouded by his injuries to make the decision himself.

With King Joram injured and no threat from the Arameans, we strengthened our defenses of Ramoth-Gilead and allowed our soldiers to rest in camp while wondering if King Joram would recover from his injuries in time to resume the fight. No commander from Israel was willing to fight under King Ahaziah alone. King Ahaziah was a palace rat. The only fighting he had seen under his father King Jehoram were retreats after routs. His throne in Jerusalem hung by a thread. It was only by an uprising by the people of Judah that he held onto his father's crown. His mother Athaliah had been intent on taking the crown, but the House of David had such a hold on the people of Judah, that they were not willing to relinquish that slim reminder of their great past as long as there was one last surviving heir from that line.

The Judean army was a rump of what it had been after the misrule of Ahaziah's father Jehoram. This expedition from Ramoth-Gilead, started as an ambitious attempt to topple the usurper Hazael, ground to a halt after King Joram left the field. Ahaziah had been just as enthusiastic about this war as Joram, but Judah's green commanders were hesitant to fight under the green King Ahaziah, and with King Joram absent, the commanders from Israel were reluctant to go into battle with this untested leader.

After several days where King Ahaziah was able to observe a reconnoitering mission, observe a few feinting probes, and watch a few volleys of arrows at the Arameans as a means of further discouraging any offensive ideas on their part, he decided to go to Jezreel to visit his injured uncle and to discuss whether an attack would be mounted once King Joram had recovered enough to resume the field, or whether we should withdraw.

❊   ❊   ❊

When our armies began our offensive against Aram from Ramoth-Gilead, there were few troops from Aram protecting their border settlements. Several days after we pushed into Aram, Aram's army responded, trying to push us back, leading to the initial and only fight of this campaign which ended when King Joram was injured. With the armies of Israel and Judah encamped against the army of Aram, and neither side willing to renew the fight, the commanders of Israel settled into the walled city of Ramoth-Gilead, awaiting word from Jezreel.

Our soldiers knew that heavy fighting was not in the offing. If King Joram did not return to the field, we would probably withdraw from Ramoth-Gilead until next year. If King Joram did return, it would be too late in the season for the Arameans to mount a successful campaign to

drive us back. It was difficult to convince the troops that they were still on
the battle field. They were more interested in scouting for the fattened calf
and bartering for wine. Command was reduced to maintaining control of
our own troops, a threat now greater than the Arameans posed.

Even so, we commanders had our own time on our hands. We kept
separate from the Judean commanders. Yes, we feasted and drank wine
as well, with our eyes on the horizon, but mainly we talked of kings and
queens, of this new King Ahaziah, and his mother, Athaliah, daughter of
Jezebel. Were the two queens designing to combine the two kingdoms?
And under who? How were the Levites and prophets of the Lord holding
up in Judah?

"The house of Omri is not what it once was," one of us said, and
most seemed to nod or sigh in agreement.

"And who comes after our King Joram? The oldest sons of King Joram are barely as old as Ahaziah of Judah. There are more sons of Ahab
in Samaria, and they have their own sons."

"And what of Ahaziah of Judah? He is Jezebel's grandson."

"Samaria is thick with heirs to the throne. Each one worse than the
other. Jezebel is jealous of her dynasty. She will decide who would be
king, and if Joram fails to please her, he will fall over the same railing his
brother Ahaziah did."

All were silent, motionless, almost breathless, each lost in his own
thoughts. These were thoughts rarely uttered among more than two or
three in the dark of night. It could be considered treason if heard the
wrong way. But with the armies of Israel and Judah on the same battlefield, having seen King Joram seriously injured in battle lent urgency to
what generally went unsaid.

There were many days and evenings when we had nothing to do
but talk as we waited word from Jezreel on King Joram. There was still
a question of whether he would be able to return to Ramoth-Gilead
before the season for battle was over. There was nothing to arrange or
fortify until then. It did not surprise us when King Ahaziah followed
King Joram to Jezreel. The boy had no experience in leading an army,
and his commanders had more experience in retreating than attacking.
All of the Judean commanders that had served under King Jehoshaphat
that we had known from our battles against the Arameans under King
Ahab at Ramoth-Gilead were gone. The new Judean commanders were
tight lipped about what happened to the old commanders. The little they
did talk suggested that many of the old commanders that had served in

Jehoshaphat's fortified cities assigned to his sons did not survive the purge when King Jehoram did away with his brothers and their supporters. The current Judean commanders seemed to have little grasp of tactics. Some of our commanders came to believe that the real reason for this campaign against Ramoth-Gilead was to provide the Judean army, its commanders and King some lessons on tactics and maneuvers. In the small but furious skirmishes we engaged in before King Joram was injured, the Judean forces followed us like shadows, taking no action on their own.

There was some grumbling about the forces of Israel taking the lead in our feints and attacks and the Judean forces holding back to watch before King Joram was injured. When we had days on end with nothing to do but to post pickets, the grumbling took on a more serious tone. "Are we training the army of Judah so they can carry the fight for us, or are we training them for the House of Ethbaal?"

An unhappy army does not fight well, and I was afraid that with days of inactivity, our soldiers would start melting back to their homes if they felt they were being abused.

"Judah is our ally now. With the union of Athaliah and Joram, the years of our kingdoms trying to destroy each other are over. We are a stronger nation for it. If we can help our ally, it makes us stronger." I knew there were many grievances about this campaign, and I knew my comment would flush out the discontent. Better to deal with it now than have it still festering when the kings return from Jezreel.

"I say we are weaker for it. Look how Judah collapsed after Jehoram became King. And why? He killed his brothers when he became King! The entire House of David except for him. Is that not treachery? And by their King? I say we are not helping Judah, we are helping the House of Ethbaal."

"Commander," I said, "that was Jehoram and Jehoram alone, and Jehoram is gone. King Ahaziah is the sole heir of the House of David. And when King Joram succeeded Ahaziah, did he kill his brothers? No. It was only Jehoram and he is gone"

"I think it was more, Jehu. Our Queen would not have her sons kill each other. But killing the sons of Judah's King? I say that was Athaliah's doing. So who do we serve? I fear that we are helping build a dynasty that has nothing to do with either Israel or Judah."

I had no stomach for the talk to continue. I had heard this talk before. I had had these thoughts before. There was a fear that in a generation our children would be serving a Sidonian kingdom.

"Soldiers, you serve your King, the son of King Ahab, the House of Omri. You will do your duty." That satisfied no one, but no one wanted to take the conversation any further. The name of Zimri had been a curse word in Israel for generations. None were happy with things in Samaria, but all were torn between wanting to continue to complain and not wanting to look like a Zimri.

JEHU ANOINTED

Jehu

In my anger I gave you a king. Hosea 13:11

THE next day promised another day of inactivity with no word coming from Jezreel. If the King is not present with his army in camp, it develops a mind of its own.

In the morning the commanders and their attendants assembled as normal to maintain the appearance of order. We discussed things such as the number of our men and horses, the hills and ravines in front and in back of us, and water supplies, almost as a veneer to keep last night's discussion from cropping up.

It started again as someone began comparing the House of Omri and the House of David. Some of the commanders looked back to the time when Israel and Judah were one Kingdom. Others were enthralled with tales of the reign of King Omri and had no interest in the affairs of the Judean kingdom. Someone could not resist bringing up the royal marriage. "What does it mean then that the House of Omri and the House of David are now united in marriage? This has never happened before, not since Jeroboam split the kingdom in two."

"But Jeroboam was anointed by the prophet Ahijah; anointed to split the Kingdom apart. Is there a prophet that will mend the two? "

"And the same prophet decreed that Jeroboam should fall; then our fathers were left with Baasha. Baasha was not anointed by a prophet. There was mourning in every village in the land with each battle Baasha waged against Judah. What kind of King was that?"

"But it was King Asa of Judah that Baasha fought against. It was that kingdom to the South that filled our graves. Should we be united with them?"

"And no prophet spoke when Zimri slaughtered King Baasha's son. And no prophet spoke when Omri dispatched Zimri and then fought Tibni for the crown. Omri enlarged our kingdom greatly. There was no prophet to thank for that."

"But the House of Omri has changed much since the death of Omri."

A long silence followed this remark. Eyes went from commander to commander, searching for an expression, a tilt of the head, a cough, something that could be interpreted. In the palace the comment would have been challenged; it may even have been considered treasonous. In a cramped upper room with too few windows to let the air in, as pickets occasionally came and went reporting on their postings, any type of griping was allowed.

The silence went on too long to suggest that this was just a gripe. I finally said, "So all of my commanders are now seers, interpreting the minds of the prophets. Shall we rip open a pigeon and study its gullet to divine what we will eat tomorrow?"

"If we rip open a pigeon tonight, I fear we will eat pigeon tomorrow."

There was no joking after this remark. Everyone was still lost in thought thinking about the House of Omri.

I added, "Soldiers, you are not prophets or seers. It is for the King to listen to the prophets and decide. We listen to the King."

"What prophets would you listen to commander?"

There was silence again after this remark, and I was the only one that could break it. Was it a challenge? An encouragement? A test? Many of the commanders had been in the palace and seen prophets of various stripes carrying on with the royal family. Some had been present when King Ahab consulted with these palace prophets; they engaged in oratory, poetry, presentations, costumes, drama, and incantations.

"I would listen to a prophet who knew how to lead an army," I finally said. It was a safe remark. A gripe heard before in camp. Were we supposed to lead an army into battle based on what prophet put on the best show?

There was some nervous laughter, some shuffling after my comment, but the House of Omri still captured the thoughts of the commanders. I had spoken with many of these commanders one-on-one about our concern, sometimes our disgust, with our Phoenician Queen.

We had great respect for Tyre and Sidon. We saw the riches their trading ships and colonies around the sea had brought them. King Hiram of Sidon was still remembered for his alliances with King Solomon. But this Sidonian Queen was different. She seemed to have no interest in trade or merchants. Her time was taken entirely with her temples, priests and prophets. It was all she talked about and all she did. People in Samaria seemed to join with her willingly, but many in the army were repulsed. "We are not Phoenicians that we should be serving Phoenician gods." "And those rites. Have you been in a temple to Baal?" "And now that Queen's son is King over Israel, House of Omri or not, we are all being turned into Phoenicians."

There was silence after this remark, each commander weighing any response he would make carefully. Then a captain who had not spoken until now said, "What does it mean that the House of Omri was not anointed by a prophet, but that the prophet Elisha anointed Hazael King of Aram?"

The question was a silent thunderbolt. Footmen around their campfire, ready to face death the next day may be allowed to silently ask the fellow next in line to them if the King should be King, but such talk among commanders could be considered subversive.

The captain who had spoken broke the silence he had created. "If we fight against King Hazael, who Elisha anointed, how can we expect the Lord to come to our aid?" This soldier could not stop talking once he heard his own voice, "Twice it was Elisha that repelled the Arameans. Can we seek to overthrow Hazael and rout the Arameans with a wounded King Joram in Jezreel and with Athaliah's offspring King Ahaziah?"

I could not hesitate to reply. "Elisha does what the Lord directs him to do. If the Lord has a purpose for Hazael who are we to question it? Perhaps Hazael's purpose was simply to kill King Ben-Hadad. I could not disagree with that. If he was anointed for more than that then the Arameans would have chased us from the field by now. As for the House of Omri, have you seen a Jeroboam anointed to take its place? The Lord will do what the Lord will do. My father and I have served Omri and Ahab, and now I will serve King Ahab's son King Joram."

My answer seemed to satisfy all of the commanders, but there was still a weight hanging over us. The questions asked had been too pointed, too direct. If we took this up again tomorrow night, still waiting for the Kings to return to the field, it could go from complaining to plotting.

"Soldiers," I said, "we are not prophets, priests or kings. If I tried to spin a clay pot, it would be dashed to pieces. I am a soldier. My arrows fly straight."

"And your chariot chases them down." The laughter showed that the tension was lifting.

"If I tried to prophesy, the shards of my oracles would make my clay pot look good. The kings will return. When they do, we will talk to them of Ramoth-Gilead. Let the prophets do what prophets do. Let the kings do what kings do. And we, my soldiers, will do what soldiers do. For Israel and the King."

"Israel and the King," was the reply.

The patch had been applied. The strain on the nation and on the minds of my commanders from the policies of their foreign Queen still remained. But at least for this morning, the seam was not going to tear.

We were talked out. We were silent as we sat and reclined, staring at the walls and floor, turning over in our own minds what we had said and heard. There was not a Zimri among us. A generation of us had fought under the banner of the House of Omri. Some of our fathers had served under King Omri. All but a few of the commanders had fought under King Ahab. We had endured under the reign of that drunk Ahaziah. Serving under Ahab's son King Joram reminded many of us of serving under King Ahab. He was more at ease with the army than in the palace. He was a competent King on the battlefield, or at least he was wise enough to trust the advice of his commanders. In the palace they both seemed blown around by the wind of that Queen in Samaria. Her name was not mentioned in our discussion. Even army commanders need to be wise in the ways of the palace, or at least be silent, which, in this case was wisdom.

"I'm going back to camp." I heard someone say, and we all gradually stood and began to walk out. Our silence was broken with talk of bread and horses and metal workers and tent makers as we slowly made through the door and onto the steps to the upper room.

Looking down into the street below we could see a man running toward us with his cloak hitched up as if on a journey. He briefly glanced up in our direction and began up the stairs as if we were his destination. As he came closer, we could see he was not from our camp. He carried no weapon. His hair was matted and clung to the sweat on his forehead. His cloak hung on him as it were a piece of laundry not yet dry. The gray dust of the country side clung to his sandals, feet and legs. He looked like he had been traveling since before dawn, if not earlier. When he got closer, a few small twigs and leaves clinging to his hair suggested he had slept on the ground the night before.

As he approached, he was looking intently at us glancing from face to face. He was breathing as if he had run all the way from the city gates to our upper room. We all puzzled at what message he brought that let him pass through the city gates. There were at least ten of us standing on the steps, a few feet from the door to the upper room when he spoke.

"I have a message for you commander."

"For which of us," I asked.

"For you, commander," he replied looking directly at me, and then walked up the final few steps to the door to the upper room and into the room. We all exchanged glances. A message from King Joram from Samaria would have been expected, but he was not carrying a scroll or tablet containing any message. A messenger from the Arameans would not have been let into the city, and this was not one of our soldiers, it was not a message from our camp outside the city. As I was about to pass through the door, I realized that I had seen this man before following Elisha. I turned to look at the other commanders. They all looked back at me puzzled. I could not tell if any of the other commanders had seen this fellow before or recognized him.

I followed the young prophet back into the room. He closed the door behind us. I had no sooner turned around after entering the room to see what he wanted, when I see he is pulling on a leather strap around his neck, fishing a small clay flask from under his cloak. Without a word he snapped the neck of the flask, and as he began to raise the flask over my head, he started to speak.

"This is what the Lord, the God of Israel, says."

I started backing up and grabbed at his wrist, first thinking that he was pulling a weapon from under his cloak. I hesitated as something started running down my face and neck, my arm freezing as I tried to understand his first words. I was stepping away from him but he matched me step by step, until I backed into the wall. All the while he continued his talking. His words were firm and measured. It occurred to me that he had been repeating these words to himself since he started his journey to Ramoth-Gilead.

"I anoint you King over the Lord's people Israel. You are to destroy the house of Ahab your master, and I will avenge the blood of my servants the prophets and the blood of all the Lord's servants shed by Jezebel. The whole house of Ahab will perish. I will cut off from Ahab every last male in Israel—slave or free. I will make the house of Ahab like the house of Jeroboam son of Nebat and like the house of Baasha son of Ahijah. As for Jezebel, dogs will devour her on the plot of ground at Jezreel, and no one will bury her."

He was looking me directly in the eye as he was speaking, with the intensity as if he were on the battlefield grappling with the enemy. Before I could think of a thing to say, he took the flask down, I could smell the musty odor of the olive oil. He dropped the expended flask to the floor; he was still looking intently at me. Then he rapidly spun around and literally ran out of the room slamming the door open. I could see his back as he dodged around the other commanders who had remained on the steps. The commanders looked at him as he rushed by, half startled by this apparition, not sure if they should grab ahold of him or not. If they recognized that he came from the prophets, perhaps they were afraid that if they grabbed him they would end up like Uzzah after he grabbed onto the ark of God.

They had not expected to see anyone leave the room so soon after we had entered, that they stood frozen. They could see me standing in the room. I stared past them, at the young prophet as he ran down the stairs jumping down the last few steps and running back the way he had come, going twice as fast as he had arrived, as if to escape any hue and cry that may follow him. I found my hands wiping my forehead and passing over my beard, looking at my glistening palms, rubbing my beard again and brushing my hands on my tunic, trying to comprehend the words I had just heard.

As I was silent and did not move, looking again at my hands and the drops of oil pooling on the floor underneath my sandals, the commanders began to slowly walk back into the upper room, one by one, each one looking in my eyes, down to my beard and tunic and down to the oil dripping on the floor. I looked back at each one, bewildered. Bewildered by the words of the prophet, and bewildered at what each of the commanders would do if they had heard the same words I had heard. Would someone strike me down? Would they bind me and deliver me to King Joram? They were now all in the room, all looking at me, waiting for me to say something. Finally one of them said, "Do we give chase?" motioning at the open door and down the street where the prophet had already disappeared. It struck me as a peculiar request. They had all let the prophet pass without a word, and now even our alarm could not race the prophet to the gates. Someone had voiced the question to avoid the obvious question.

Finally one of them asked, "Is everything all right? Why did this maniac come to you?"

I hesitated, trying to digest the words of the prophet. Why did they sound so familiar? Then it came to me. I had heard the same words, "dogs will devour Jezebel at Jezreel" when Elijah confronted King Ahab. It was a message from Elisha. He knew I would recognize the curse Elijah had delivered to the King in Naboth's vineyard. It confirmed that this wild haired maniac who had just drenched me with olive oil was not some possessed mad man. "Word of the Lord," I thought. I was stunned, word-less, astounded. King? King? He had said King! How could that possibly be?

"Jehu! Commander! What did that maniac have to do with you?"

I stared back at the questioner dumfounded, his words not register-ing. I understood what the prophet had said, but was grappling with what it meant. How could it be?

"You know those prophets and where they come from. They are always complaining or praying or babbling or just mad."

"That's not true!" they said, "tell us."

I looked from man to man. Many I knew well, a few hardly at all. They had all fought under me and followed my commands. I had no choice but to tell them.

"Here is what he told me: 'This is what the Lord says: I anoint you King over Israel. You are to destroy the House of Ahab to avenge the blood of the prophets Jezebel has slain.'"

A gasp of shock went through the men. Some stepped back, as if to look me over from head to toe. All kept their eyes fixed on me, looking at my beard, my tunic, the floor, realizing that they were smelling olive oil.

Then one suddenly raised both of his arms in the air. "Yes! Yes! Yes! It is from the Lord! From a prophet of the Lord! Jehu is King!"

"Jehu is King! Jehu is King!" Several of them took up the call.

I tried to understand their shouts. I was still trying to understand the words of the prophet. I wanted to sit down quietly with three or four of them; to talk quietly of what I heard the prophet say; of what they thought it meant; of who I should tell; of when I should speak of it; of what we should do. Instead there were more shouts from more of the commanders, "Jehu is King! It is from the prophets! Jehu is King! It is from the Lord! We are rescued! This is the end of Jezebel, the end of the House of Ahab!"

I wanted to stop them. We had a King, Joram. We were encamped against the Arameans. The armies of Judah were encamped next to us. This was not the time. I started to raise my hand; started to say "no, no, wait . . . ." but they took my hand as I was raising it and led me toward the door they had all just entered. Some started taking off their robes as they went out the door, the fabric billowing in the air as they draped robe after robe on the stairs leading from the upper room. Still holding me by the hand they led me out on the steps leading me over their draped robes.

I was trying to speak, but as they led me out they started shouting, "Jehu is King! He has been anointed by the prophets! Jehu is King! The Word of the Lord! Word of the Lord! Jehu is King. Here is your anointed King! Trumpeter, declare the message! A royal trumpet blast for our new King."

A trumpeter, standing below the steps with other attendants waiting on their commanders, taking in the scene as the commanders exited the upper room with me, raised his horn and delivered a series of piercing chords. I recognized the call. I had heard it as King Ahab and King Joram would enter the camp; I heard it as King Joram would proceed to the city gates of Samaria to hear his petitioners. I had heard it as a victory in battle was announced. It was making no sense to me now. There was no king in Ramoth-Gilead, they had left for Jezreel. And yet the cheers went on, "Jehu is King! He has been anointed." Now the cheers were not directed to me. As men assembled in the street below, wondering what the royal proclamations meant, the commanders were directing their cheers to the crowd in the streets.

I was still stunned with what the prophet had said, stunned again by what the commanders were shouting. Suddenly, it was in alarm, out of sheer terror, I said, "The gates! The gates!"

It did not take a second for the commanders to grasp what I was saying. They immediately took up the call, "Soldiers, to the gates! Close the gates! No one is allowed out. Any one on the road leaving must be turned back."

The commanders had just proclaimed a new King while King Joram was living and breathing in Jezreel. Factions from the army could rush the city walls to put down the insurrection. A horseman could be dashing out of the gates of Ramoth-Gilead down the road toward Jezreel to sound the alarm. A rebellion besieged behind a city wall would meet the same end as Zimri. That name hammered through my head. But then I thought, "The prophet! The words of the prophet! Has he really said that?"

Some of the commanders ran down the stairs to the street, following their soldiers who were already on their way to secure the gates of the city. The remaining commanders herded me back into the upper room, leaving their robes draped on the staircase. There were no more cheers, no more proclamations. These old army hands realized how close to death they were; they may be cut down in the streets as traitors before sundown. The battle was joined. These soldiers had been under attack before. They began calling on the arts of their craft as a sudden shift of the lines threatened to sweep them away. There was no chain of command, no ordered meeting; it was a command under attack throwing up the barricades.

"Post pickets at all the camps. All soldiers are to be restricted to camp. Everyone readied for battle."

"Put detachments outside the city gates."

"Send chariots and riders down the road to Jezreel. Detach scouts ahead of them."

"Anyone coming from Jezreel is to be captured and brought in the city and questioned."

"Place a contingent on the road to Jezreel. No, we need a defensive perimeter around the city first."

"Place pickets by the Judean camp, detain anyone who rides out."

"The Arameans. We need to break off. Send a parlay out to approach the Arameans. Speak of peace; find a way we can stand down."

"Jehu, the Judeans. If they see that we are sending messages to the Arameans without consulting them . . ."

"Yes," I responded, "the Judeans. Send a commander and his lieutenants to the Judeans. The Judeans are sitting in their camp doing nothing just as we have been. Go as bored soldiers to talk about nothing, but listen if any word gets to their camp, keep them at ease, allay any suspicions they may have, buy us time."

Younger commanders were being brought into the room to begin executing the orders. Other commanders were rushing out to assert control over the army. As I digested the orders and commands, I began to realize what was happening, how poor our situation was.

"We cannot be trapped behind the walls, waiting for something to happen." I found myself saying. "Joram has reserves in Jezreel with horsemen and chariots. That much he has learned from us. We cannot let

Joram make the first move. He will push us into the Arameans. Get me my chariot, raise my charioteers. We must ride to Jezreel immediately. Our blow must be struck before they can raise the alarm."

"Our forces cannot keep pace with the chariots," came the protests, "You will be exposed. We need to break camp, assemble the foot soldiers, prepare an advance on Jezreel," came the protests.

"We cannot allow the two kings to barricade themselves at Jezreel or to flee to Samaria," I responded. "We will be a rogue army against two kings. They will raise the countryside against us. They will send to Aram or Moab or Edom for assistance, pledging our treasure. The other kings will rush to stamp out a revolt."

"Jehu, you are the King. You cannot be cut down. All would be lost."

"If I have been anointed as King, then I will ride as King - in the van. If I do not, then indeed all will be lost. Can you ride ahead of me?" I knew the answer, as did everyone else. "Then it is settled. My chariot to the gate, now! Who rides with me?"

Names were shouted out as I strode to the door toward the stairs to the street. I turned at the threshold. "The rest of you, secure Ramoth-Gilead, send horsemen and soldiers to follow. Send commanders familiar with Jezreel to control the army there. Then word to every city and temple, "Jehu is King!"

"Jehu is King!" came the resounding reply. The words caught me by surprise as I uttered them, and more astounding as the echo came back magnified.

THE DASH TO JEZREEL

Jehu

How could one man chase a thousand, or two put ten
thousand to flight? Moses, Deuteronomy 32:3

W E sent teams of our fastest riders out immediately on the roads to
the fords of the Jordan River. They were to question people at the
inns, the watering holes, the towns and the fords to learn if anyone riding
from the encampment at Ramoth-Gilead had been seen on the way to
Jezreel. They were to send riders back to the battalions of chariots following them to report what they found. No one from Jezreel had been seen.

At the fords of the Jordan River, the sentries stationed there were
questioned closely by the riders. They had received no news from Ramoth-Gilead, and their orders from Jezreel were to send riders to Jezreel
if any alarm needed to be raised. The advance detachments held at the
Jordan River waiting for my arrival to learn what our plan would be for
approaching Jezreel. No one had yet advanced toward Jezreel.

My chariot commander Bidkar rode with me. Before we left Ramoth-Gilead we assigned commanders to ride out to our encampments
and assemble their officers to tell them of their new orders. We would
melt away from Ramoth-Gilead silently. Units to the rear would withdraw first, until only a shell of a few banners and tents and horses remained visible to the Arameans. The Arameans did not want this fight
and would not follow us. If any did, our rear guard would alert us. We
sent word to the Judean army that King Joram was too badly injured
to continue the battle and that we were withdrawing. It was up to our

commanders how to answer any Judean questions as to why they had not received this word from King Ahaziah who was with Joram in Jezreel. As we rode, we discussed how we could prevail over two kings behind the walls of the fortress city of Jezreel. Bidkar had kept me from rushing into disaster many times. But many times Bidkar had been too cautious and would have denied us victory by holding back. "Master," he said, a strange word to me since Bidkar would always call me "commander" in the field, "Should we send back word to send a detachment to Samaria as well? We need to know if Samaria sends any forces against us."

"No," I replied, "we are a dagger pointed at the heart of the kingdom. If we send a detachment to Samaria, they will know there is a rebellion. If the King is still alive, no one in Samaria will dare raise a hand to help us. They will fear the wrath of the King. They will close the gates of the city to us and we are not equipped for a siege. The only territory we control is within the walls of Ramoth-Gilead, and the Arameans will happily contest Ramoth-Gilead if they learn Israel is divided. We must take Jezreel. Without Jezreel we can only last a few days."

"Should we wait to assemble the entire army before we move against Jezreel? The force we have with us is only large enough to herd sheep. If the King's guard and chariots ride out against us in force we will be crushed."

"Bidkar, you are right in all respects. As a commander you would never allow your King or your soldiers to rush into a battle with no preparation and no strategy mapped out. But you were there when the prophet of the Lord anointed me. I did not choose the time. I am always thinking tactics, Bidkar, you know that. I would always think, "how would an adversary attack our King? How would I protect the King from an attack? What if a raiding party attacked from here or from there? And to defend the King, I would plan attacks. How would I attack the King on the field? How would I attack the King on the way from Megiddo to Samaria? How would I attack the King in one of the royal palaces?" And the answer was always the same. Only a fool like Zimri would attack now. I certainly could have killed the King any day I desired, But to what end? You have seen his household, his sons, his priests and prophets. They would fall on my household, they would sacrifice my children, they would fall on your household, Bidkar, because you are close to me, they would have a carnival of revenge. And the next king would be worse. More Kings like Ahaziah and Joram and Israel would be swallowed up."

"But now that prophet, Bidkar, that prophet. Do you understand those prophets, Bidkar? I don't. You have heard the prophecies of the prophets of Baal, haven't you? 'Serve Baal and the Master will flood the earth with his vengeance, torrents of gold will flood into your treasuries and the finest women will be your plunder.' On and on and on. Rubbish. That prophet of the Lord? He promised me nothing. He said do this thing. Do this thing, and I am doing it. How will I do it? I do not know. Will I even live? Will my household perish? I have no tomorrow in my future, only this hour and maybe the next. And even that is not certain. The only thing I know, Bidkar, is that the prophet of the Lord chose this hour to anoint me. You may be a fool to follow this Zimri."

"I know that a prophet of the Lord decreed that the House of Baasha would perish, Master, but I never heard that any prophet anointed Zimri to take the throne. Zimri sought the throne for himself. I saw the oil dripping from your beard. If you were anointed for this hour, then you are anointed for this hour. It is for the Lord to dispose of his word."

"But Zimri brought to pass what the prophet said and still he burned. I will bring to pass what the prophet decreed, but I may be King for seven days also. I only know that I will do what the prophet said I was to do, and I will act swiftly, I know no other way. We will strike at King Joram first. If we fail that, we will flee like Jeroboam to Egypt while our households burn. If Joram falls, it will be easier to contend for a kingless kingdom than to strike at a kingdom fighting for its King."

That night, we rode as long as we had light for the horses. We slept curled up in the chariots or on the ground. We lit no fires. As soon as we had enough light to harness the horses we were off again. The troops following behind us were instructed to march through the night, breaking only to rest lightly and eat, and then off again.

Jezreel would be at ease. Aram had shown no willingness to offer a fight, and the main body of Israel's army was between Aram and Jezreel. Since the two kings were present at Jezreel, some precautions would have been taken; some troops would be held in their barracks, enough horses and chariots to mount a counter attack would be kept in the stables to hold off any unforeseen foe. Watchmen would be stationed in the watchtowers of the citadel, able to survey the entire valley of Jezreel. Our advance riders were instructed to stop just out of sight of the main tower of Jezreel, dismount, and advance on foot to get as close as they could without raising an alarm.

The heat of the sun was starting to cool when we met up with the advance riders. Jezreel lay at peace. The royal banners wafted peacefully over the walls. They had made out three. A scout ran back under cover of hedges and trees and reported three indeed: the Lion of Judah, the House of Omri, and a Sidonian banner the scout had not seen before.

"Jezebel is here as well! 'The whole house of Ahab is to perish,' words of the prophet! Is not King Ahaziah of the house of Ahab? Is not his mother Athaliah a daughter of Ahab? Do you see those three flags, Bidkar? They are drenched in the blood spilled by Ahab and Jezebel. That banner of Sidon can only mean that the three houses are united. No one from Sidon is here but Jezebel. She has raised her own banner with banners of her offspring. All three banners must fall."

Bidkar blanched. "Master, you have been anointed. But your master was King Joram. He is from the house of Ahab. King Ahaziah, my Lord, he is the House of David, King of Judah. Surely we are not to strike down the House of David!"

"My friend, I do not understand the ways of the prophets. Elijah played a warrior when he put four hundred and fifty prophets of Baal to the sword on Mount Carmel. If the prophets spilled blood, should I cringe and cower? We have put many to the sword. We have run over those who would oppress us with our chariots. Is this now too much? You yourself heard Elijah condemn Ahab only to relent when Ahab moaned and groaned and put on sackcloth. But Ahab met his end at Ramoth-Gilead, and now this prophet comes to me at Ramoth-Gilead and says the House of Ahab is to perish. He was a prophet, that is all I know. I spoke to Elisha many times, as have you. It was like grinding gravel with my teeth. I do not know his mind. But this prophet said, 'Word of the Lord.' I can have no doubt that this is what we must do. We have the words of the prophet, and we have moved against the King with his army. If we do not strike now, Jezebel will hunt us down as she hunts prophets."

"If you strike down King Ahaziah, the Judean army will become our enemy, and they are already camped on our land."

I could always sense cold feet in a soldier. Bidkar would never turn on me, but he spoke only of me, Jehu, striking down King Ahaziah, not the King of Israel striking down King Ahaziah, not of the army of Israel striking down King Ahaziah.

"Bidkar, are your with me?"

"Yes, master I am with you, even to the point of striking down King Ahaziah. But you were anointed King over Israel. Strike down King Joram and his family, and we may not risk war with Judah. But strike down King Ahaziah, and we could be at war with Judah even before you can secure the throne in Samaria."

"One battle at a time, Bidkar. I only know what the prophet said, and I know that King Ahaziah is of the House of Ahab and is now united here with Joram and Jezebel. If I let Ahaziah go now, he will flee behind the walls of Jerusalem, and who can breach the walls of Jerusalem? As for the Judean army at Ramoth-Gilead, send a rider back to the commander of our rear guard. Let him know that King Ahaziah will also fall, and let him chose the best course for dissuading the Judeans from attacking."

"Their commanders are green. They have seen their predecessors whipped by every minor king that could lay his hands on a chariot. It should not be too hard to bluff them back to Jerusalem."

Bidkar had reassured himself that any threat posed by the Judean army could be managed. I think he was overwhelmed for a moment by the scope of what we had undertaken. In that regard, I was with Bidkar. I also was overwhelmed by what we had undertaken. I had pitched my tent with the prophets; the prophets that lived in caves and ravines and fled from the Kings of Israel. The only path of flight laid out for me was to rush headlong against the King. There was no place left for me to hide except behind my sword.

MADNESS ON THE PLAINS OF JEZREEL
Jehu

The driving is like that of Jehu son of Nimshi—he drives
like a maniac. Watchman, II Kings 9:20

O UR ride to Jezreel was furious. The young prophet who had fled
from Ramoth-Gilead was nowhere to be seen. We needed to outrace any word that may escape from Ramoth-Gilead. Despite the scouts
we had sent out immediately from Ramoth-Gilead after my anointing,
no one knew what happened to the young prophet. He certainly would
not raise an alarm in Jezreel, but if King Joram had set out pickets around
Ramoth-Gilead in his absence, they could have picked up the prophet
and learned of my anointing. Since the pickets would have been to guard
against any scheming by his own commanders, the King would not have
shared with his commanders at Ramoth-Gilead if he set out pickets or
not. I was not sure if Joram would have recalled this tactic of his father
King Ahab. I could only hope that Joram was not smart enough to think
of it, or was too overconfident being in the company of another King,
or perhaps in the confusion attending Joram's injury his plans had been
overlooked.

The towers of Jezreel were visible far down the plains of the Valley of Jezreel, and I knew how far out we would be when we would be
visible to the watchmen on the towers. It was important to keep up a
seemingly fast pace when we became visible from Jezreel. If they saw an
army in battle formation trudging slowly toward Jezreel, the gates would

be closed, and riders sent for assistance to Samaria, Megiddo and probably even for whatever help that would come from Ramoth-Gilead. If we rode at the pace expected from a messenger, they would keep the gates open to receive any messages from the battlefield, and possibly even send out fresh riders to relay the message to Jezreel. I knew how close I could maintain a cantor toward Jezreel, enough to raise a visible dust cloud, but not too fast to outpace those following me, and I knew where I would have to increase my pace as if carrying a message.

I had personally supervised the training of the watchmen. The skills called for were greater than those of an expert archer or a charioteer. How much dust would a single horseman kick up? A chariot? A camel? An oxcart? The difference between a chariot at a cantor and a horseman at a full gallop? How much dust would a troop of fifty soldiers kick up? In the rain, can you tell the difference between the spray kicked up by twenty horsemen racing full speed and three chariots cruising along? We lamed and exhausted countless horses testing the watchmen's acumen. Watchmen were tested every day; they made a call on every cloud of dust approaching on the road from Megiddo, from Samaria, from the Jordan fords.

Jezreel is our armory, our army's supplier, our ready reserves. As the commander of the army, I realized that an enemy could strike a staggering blow to Israel if it could take Jezreel by surprise. The army would be crippled. When Ben-Haddad had besieged Samaria, his big mistake was not striking Jezreel first. As he besieged the court and the temples and the merchants in Samaria, harrying raids were sent out from Jezreel against his besiegers at Samaria.

From the towers, the watchmen were the first line of defense for Jezreel. Pickets stationed along the roads could rush warnings back to Jezreel, but they could be waylaid or overtaken. The watchmen had the sole authority to close the gates of the city at a moment's notice. The watchmen would throw down weighted flags from the tower indicating exactly what type of force was advancing. Woe to the watchman who closed the gates to the city for hours unnecessarily because of a stampeding oxcart or a spontaneous camel race.

It was crucial that I approach the towers of Jezreel in a way that kept the gates of the city open. Because of our mission, speed was the ultimate concern. Along the way I thought of other approaches, but realized that if any word of a rebellion escaped from Ramoth-Gilead before we got into Jezreel, we would be nothing more than a band of well-armed fugitives.

But if we got to Jezreel while the gates were still open - what then? If a sizeable force was seen coming from Ramoth-Gilead with no advance notice, the gates to the city could be closed as a precaution. But if I approached Jezreel without a force, how would we get to the kings?

"Madness," I thought. "The madness of those prophets has captured us. This is no way to start a rebellion. Even Zimri had done more planning than this." We had done no planning; we did not even know if the army we left back at Ramoth-Gilead would support us. We knew that if we did not make it into Jezreel, we would be trapped outside walls and the shuttered gates of Jezreel, and if we were trapped outside Jezreel, the army coming from Ramoth-Gilead may reconsider and turn on us.

We raised enough dust with our three chariots to indicate an important message from the battlefield. If we got too far in front of the horsemen following us we would not have enough men to strike a blow. If the force following us raised too much dust, the gates would be closed until the kings could sort out what was happening. "Madness," I thought, "madness. If they do what they should do they will close the gates." After we had been in sight of the towers of Jezreel for some time, I told the other two charioteers to hang back, while I drove my chariot in a way I knew they would recognize. I had taken the young striplings Ahaziah and Joram on many chariot rides and made it a point of pride that I could make the King's young sons vomit before each ride was over. King Ahab thought it great sport and good training for a future king.

After a short, mad spurt, I had my driver, who by that time was looking like a young Joram, signal to the watchmen a warped or cracked wheel, one of several signals we had struggled with and discarded a few years ago as too confusing. A warped wheel would justify us stopping to get out to hammer and secure the hub for several minutes before resuming another wild spurt. This would allow the following force to keep close without raising enough dust on the road to give them away. We got out of the chariot and walked around a bit to keep up the ruse. As we were getting ready to resume, we could see a rider coming toward us from Jezreel. "Ride on, slowly. Let him come to us."

We rode for a short distance and then stopped. The horseman advanced but then stopped short, as if giving himself room to make a run back to Jezreel, not a good sign. The horseman called out, "Commander Jehu, this is what the King says: 'Do you come in peace?'"

I called back, "What do you have to do with peace? Fall in behind me."

"You bring troops. Do you bring a message?"

This told me that my subterfuge had not worked. The watchmen had spotted the troops behind me. "I repeat soldier, fall in behind me. I will show you how to bring peace to this kingdom."

This time the horseman rode up alongside my chariot. He could take my words only one way. My driver said, "Jehu has been anointed King by a prophet from Elisha's house."

The horseman advised us that the gates to the city remained open, but that King Joram was concerned about what the troops following me meant. The question Joram gave the horseman to ask showed that the King felt I may not be advancing in peace. "What a fool, that Joram," I remarked to my driver. "He sees troops advancing that may be a threat and keeps the gates open."

"Soldier, are both Kings in the city?"

"Yes, and Queen Jezebel."

"Why is Jezebel in Jezreel?"

"She was expecting a great victory against Aram - that I know. She has issued orders for a great procession back to Samaria. I have seen the orders. She wants first pick of the plunder - that is what I think. There will be little left for the soldiers once she has satisfied the demand of her temples in Samaria."

Some of the best intelligence about the state of the army can come from the common soldier complaining.

"Soldier, are the troops loyal to Queen Jezebel."

The horseman spat on the ground. "King Joram is King. I do not know what she is, but her husband is dead."

"If King Joram does not ride back into the city, will the army close the gates to protect Jezebel?"

"If Joram is struck down, they will want to know who the new King is, but they will not take orders from Jezebel."

As we spoke, we saw a second horseman riding from Jezreel. This second rider confirmed what the first rider had told us, and he too fell in behind us. I took that as a good sign. Had one of the riders turned and fled back toward Jezreel, then part of the army in Jezreel may be willing to fight me. Or had I just gained two assassins in my camp, waiting for an opportunity to strike me down once a third rider was sent from Jezreel? What kind of instructions had King Joram given to these riders? Were they just sent to inquire, or did they have further instructions? By now,

Bidkar, seeing two of Joram's horsemen flanking me, rode up to support me.

Those questions prodded me to put the lash to my horses and resume my dash toward the gates of Jezreel. It is better to be the one in motion to keep your opponents off balance. What was King Joram thinking? Had I placed him on alert?

Kings Omri and Ahab had spent time studying plots against the royal houses. Our nations had much to study: would be regicides Absalom and Adonijah, Jeroboam's rebellion, Baasha's rebellion, regicide Zimri. Other plots had been discovered before they could hatch. They concluded that plots with little advance planning were the most dangerous. The careful, organized plotter consulted with too many potential supporters. The more supporters, the more time spent in planning, the greater chance of betrayal. Zimri acted almost on impulse, but succeeded only in killing King Elah and taking the capital of Tirzah, but he ended up burning the palace down over his head.

I know Joram had been present with his father King Ahab as we had spoken about the rebellions of the past, and how they could be repeated, but Joram's father and grandfather had ruled so successfully for so long that I could tell that Joram took these only as interesting tales of old men. He had not seen kings ripped open or beheaded in his presence. His father and mother, the King and the Queen, had so cowed the entire kingdom, and driven any opponents so far out into the wilderness that it was hard for him to conceive that there could be any real threat to his kingdom or his life.

Had Jezebel's talk of building an empire so blinded Joram to any threat from within? Could he only see an army commander that had been loyal to him and his father advancing toward him?

THE KINGS RIDE OUT

Jehu

Have you come in peace, Jehu? King Joram, II Kings 9:22

THE answers to my questions came riding toward me in chariots from the gates of Jezreel. Neither Joram nor Ahaziah were skilled tacticians. They rode out of Jezreel accompanied by their own guard, but they had no one riding behind them to secure their path back to the gates. We could not see the gates of Jezreel yet, so we could not tell if the King had placed a detachment at the gates, either to secure the gates or to ride out to support them if necessary. If they had doubts about my mission, they had taken no steps to overwhelm me. Had their arrogance prompted them to brush aside concerns of their commanders, or had their commanders allowed them to ride out unprotected?

The kings had ridden out just beyond the vineyards King Ahab had wrested from Naboth. I did not want to meet the kings close to the city gates and give them a chance to retreat back into the city, so I held back and let them advance toward me. I did not need to give any orders to my commanders behind me; they knew our mission. I glanced back as I waited for Joram to advance. Several of my chariots were flanking us on the right, riding along the outskirts of the surrounding vineyards. I hoped that this would not look suspicious to the kings. It would have been a standard maneuver on a battlefield to keep all of the chariots from being bunched up in a group. But there was no enemy present, and no reason to spread out the chariots except to launch an attack. I was not certain that either Ahaziah or Joram would be thinking enough about tactics to be concerned or not. Their fathers would have called both of them fools.

As soon as we fell on Joram, who was in the lead, the road would be clear for Ahaziah to dash back to Jezreel and close the gates in our faces. If the remainder of my chariots remained behind me, they would not be able to race through my position and through Joram's guard to catch Ahaziah before he made it to the city gates. By flanking the vineyards, and moving forward slightly, they could cut off Ahaziah before he reached the gates. If Ahaziah got back to the city we would be tied down in a siege of Jezreel, which held all of our army's provisions and supplies, with King Joram's court and his heirs safe in Samaria, and the Judean army of the besieged Ahaziah behind us at Ramoth-Gilead. We had brought no supplies with us on our race to Jezreel. All of our supplies, equipment and transport wagons were still at the army's camp in Ramoth-Gilead, sitting alongside the supply wagons of the Judean army. By the time we would have been able to go back to retrieve our supplies from Ramoth-Gilead, word would have reached the Judean commanders that we were attacking their King in Jezreel. There would be a fight for the supply wagons, at least part of the Judean army would race to Jezreel to rescue King Ahaziah, and messengers with news of our attack would be sent to Joram's court in Samaria.

As I waited for the puzzled King Joram to slowly advance toward me, I sent back one of our advance riders who had caught up with us with a message to secure the road from Jezreel to Samaria.

My commanders had to be as anxious as I was about our mission. Despite the haste we had shown in our race to Jezreel, there was plenty of time for them to consider what hung in the balance. As we had started out for Jezreel, I considered how to hold those following me in check. The exhilaration of the sudden acclamation after the prophet anointed me could fade if they had time enough to think of the retribution Jezebel would exact against those swept up in this rebellion.

The thought occurred to me that if both of the kings were able to make it safely back into Jezreel, I would probably be struck down on the spot. My most trusted commanders were very loyal to me, but if we became trapped outside the walls of Jezreel they may scatter.

King Joram rode down the road to me in his chariot as he had done dozens of times before in the field. My chariot commander Bidkar was with me in another chariot, along with a third chariot behind him as Joram advanced. "Bidkar, what would you do if you were Joram?"

"I would not ride out here if I were Joram. Make us come to the gate, where he can rain down destruction from the walls."

"But he is out here now. Will he retreat or attack?"

"The King, he will run for the gates. He is not a charioteer, even though he drives one. He has ridden against us in drills. He knows he is no match. The chariot with him may attack, to cover the King, but if we drop the King before he can run, they will fall back."

"King Joram is mine. It is my duty. The blood of the King cannot be on your hands."

"Then you must be quick. If you miss, he will be mine. He cannot get back to the gates. What about King Ahaziah?"

"We will not be able to make it through Joram's chariots to get to Ahaziah. We have to trust that our rear guard has found a way through the vineyards to get behind him."

We held our chariots in place and simply watched King Joram and his guard approach and stop in the road in front of us. I did not speak or give him any form of greeting. He could see the two horsemen he had sent out from Jezreel riding behind us. King Joram and his chariot stood still in front of me as some light dust from the chariots behind him washed over him. He looked slightly puzzled, perhaps surprised that I was the first face he saw. I wondered what he thought would have brought his army commander from the battlefield instead of a messenger. He recognized that this was unusual, but could not make out what it meant.

In this strange moment of silence, I realized that I was beyond the point of no return. I could have dismounted from my chariot, approached him unarmed, bowed before his chariot, pledged my fealty to him and tell him that I wanted to be the first to report to him that a deranged prophet had tried to anoint me as King, but that it meant nothing to me. But I had already accepted the acclaim of the commanders of the army and sent out orders designed to advance the revolt. Joram would probably order arrows into my chest for such a confession.

Finally King Joram asked, "Have you come in peace, Jehu?"

My hand was resting on my bow, held below the front shield of my chariot where King Joram could not see it, an arrow already notched in the bowstring.

Finally I spoke, "How can there be peace as long as all the prostitutions and sorceries of your mother Jezebel abound?"

I wanted to make my response significant, not just to King Joram but to the members of his guard riding with him. Had I announced to King

THE KINGS RIDE OUT

Joram that a prophet had anointed me King, they would see a usurper, a commander who would be King. To call the Queen Mother and the wife of King Ahab, a prostitute and a sorcerer to the face of the King, did not announce a new King, but declared the unfitness of the current King.

I knew the King's guard. I had ridden with them a few short days ago at Ramoth-Gilead. I knew their distaste for what the Kingdom of Israel had become under Jezebel. None of them would see any basis to question my statement about Jezebel. They would see Jezebel's son standing in the chariot next to them, not the King. I had chosen my words carefully. Life in Samaria now centered on rites, celebrations and observances in the many temples in the city. The soldiers were not theologians, but felt that their lives and the lives of their families had been degraded. They did not want their children performing in any of the temple rites they had seen. They did not want to see the children of their poor neighbors being forced to perform. They did not feel like Israelites any more. They felt that Samaria had become a foreign city.

King Joram must have had his suspicions about my mission as he stood in his stopped chariot. He raised his reins as soon as he heard "How can there be peace," but continued to look at me as I uttered "prostitutions and sorceries" while he was wheeling his chariot around. King Ahaziah had hung back some distance, probably out of ear shot.

As Joram wheeled his chariot around and whipped his horses, he yelled to King Ahaziah, "Treachery, Ahaziah, treachery!

Joram had a supporting chariot on his right side, with two other chariots flanking King Ahaziah who had followed behind Joram. The charioteer on Joram's right looked stunned. He neither wheeled his chariot around to follow the King, nor advanced toward me. I had said something no soldier would have ever said to a King, but nothing to announce a revolt. But hearing the King's alarm of treachery, had I given chase, he would block my path, and then there were the chariots escorting Ahaziah. From a chariot letting an arrow fly was easy. I was stopped; my chariot was a stable platform. Joram's chariot had just completed turning around, his horses straining under the whip, their hoofs still slipping to gain traction. Joram's back was square to me. He was not turning around to offer an arrow at me. Joram's escort chariot was stopped, a look of wonder on the charioteer's face, but he was not reaching for a weapon. I raised my bow and leveled my arrow at Joram. My arrow followed a slim arc straight into Joram's back. He dropped to the floor of his chariot. I realized then that he had ridden out with no armor on. Joram's charioteer pulled his chariot to a stop, and bent over Joram's body.

Ahaziah's chariot had wheeled around at the same time as Joram's chariot, with his two escorting chariots wheeling around behind him. As I strung my second arrow for Ahaziah, Joram's chariot and the two chariots following Ahaziah were blocking the path of my arrow. In battle I would have offered five or six arrows arching over the following chariots, but I did not want to kill a soldier to get at Ahaziah while we were still outside the gate of Jezreel.

"Ride," I ordered my charioteer. We dashed around Joram's escorting chariot, and then around Joram's chariot. I recognized both of the charioteers, and they recognized me. I looked directly at them as I passed. They knew King Joram was dead, and that I had killed him. If they did not offer an arrow, they were with me.

Ahaziah was well ahead of me, and the two chariots supporting him could delay us from getting to Ahaziah before he got into the gates of Jezreel. We had just made it to a full run behind them when they veered off the road leading to the gates. We followed off the road as arrows from Ahaziah's chariots flew past us. With that I strung up arrows and let fly, with Bidkar behind me letting fly as well. These flights were not the straight flight leveled at Joram. Our wheels were bouncing over the field, their chariots were veering side-to-side to dodge our arrows, our charioteers were doing the same and they were racing away from us. Arrows were dotting the ground in all directions.

Careening over the hillside, I saw three other chariots racing off the road from Jezreel. They were the chariots that had ridden with us from Ramoth-Gilead. They had cut off Ahaziah's retreat to the gates.

"Chase them down," I yelled at Bidkar, pointing to Ahaziah's chariots, and then grabbed our reins and turned our chariot to the gates. With Joram dead, Jezreel was less ominous, but only for a moment. Jezebel would be in the fortress, if she was wise. I did not know what other family members she may have brought with her from Samaria, including any of Joram's brothers. But with King Joram having ridden out of the city, no one in the city could countermand my orders. I did not know if the watchmen could tell from their vantage point what had happened to King Joram. If they could tell an arrow had felled him, word would have been sent to the gatekeepers.

As I raced toward the gates, I realized it was a mistake sending Bidkar to chase down King Ahaziah with the other three chariots. My force attacking the city gates of Jezreel was one chariot, holding me and my charioteer. The horsemen and footmen behind me had been held back to avoid alarming the watchmen. Even if they were racing forward now, if I raced through the gates by myself, the gates could be closed behind me and I could be captured and separated from my troops. When in doubt, attack. Your foe will think your attack may be backed by force, and by the time they discover it is not, it is too late for them.

As our chariot mounted the ramp leading to the city gates, we could see that the gates were still open. Three footmen with lances were standing on the ramp, with other footmen with swords behind them. I lashed the horses to keep their speed up the ramp.

"Jehu! Make way for commander Jehu, make way!" shouted my driver waving the footmen off the ramp. The leading lancers wavered and lifted their lances, quickly stepping out of the way. We raced through the gates and had to put our horses back on their haunches to keep them from crashing into a body of troops who looked like they were just assembling to rush out of the city. I recognized their commander as he rushed forward to me. I had heard the footmen at the gates yelling back into the city, "Jehu! Jehu!"

"Who is in command of the city?" I directed at the commander.

"King Joram is here."

"King Joram has left. Who commands when the King leaves the city?"

"King Ahaziah . . ." he started to say, when I broke in.

"I am in command of the city now. Assemble your commanders, immediately."

"Commander Jehu, there is a large body of troops advancing from the fords of the Jordan. That is why we are assembling."

"It is the entire army of Israel; they are with me, they are under my command. Joram has fallen in the vineyard that his father Ahab purchased with the blood of Naboth. Did you not hear the prophet of the Lord tell Ahab that the Lord would make him pay for that land? That price has now been paid. Even now commander Bidkar is chasing after the fleeing King Ahaziah. The end of the House of Ahab is at hand. Are you with me?"

Before the commander had a chance to reply, my charioteer shouted, "Jehu is King! Jehu is King!"

The commander and his troops looked stunned, trying to understand what he was shouting. My charioteer kept up his chant, "Jehu is
King, Jehu is King, Jehu is King!"

"Jehu is King," came the reply from several of the troops, and then
all of them and then their commander. I had taken the fortress of Jezreel
with one chariot.

"Commander," I shouted over the troops, "Send the chariots and
horsemen you have to chase after King Ahaziah, it will be your pledge of
fealty. Your watchmen will know where they are headed"

"Yes, commander, right away." He immediately turned to his charges
with orders to the stables and watch tower. He did not call me "King"
yet, but it was important to have him relay my orders. Their acclamation
would only last minutes, but as soon as they executed my orders they
were under my command.

THE FALL OF JEZEBEL

Jehu

Have you come in peace, you Zimri, you murderer of your master? Jezebel, II Kings 9:31

A s the commander's charges left on their missions, the commander walked up to my chariot while I was dismounting. "Commander, Jezebel the Queen is in the city."

"Yes, we saw her banner over the tower. Is anyone else from the House of Omri in the city?"

"No, just Queen Jezebel."

"Show me where she is."

"She is in the royal quarter. The streets are too narrow for your chariot."

"Bring up horses for me and my charioteer. Lead me to her."

The commander of the city and the three lancers we had met at the city gate walked ahead of us to the royal quarter. By the time horses had been rushed to us, word had spread quickly through the city that the forces advancing to the city were the army of Israel, and that King Joram had been slain. Windows that had been shuttered tight were reopening. Soldiers that had been running to their stations to prepare for an attack were now standing in the streets buzzing with news of the death of King Joram and a new King.

I did not know if there was a body of troops hiding in some barracks or alley still loyal to the House of Omni or Jezebel, ready to strike at this new usurper. Bidkar was outside the walls, chasing down King Ahaziah, but I could hear what his advice would have been, "Wait at the city gates. Assemble a detachment to defend the gates if some troops from inside the city assemble to try to push you out of the city. Don't rush in without support and fall into an ambush. They will close the gates behind you, and you will be trapped fighting inside the city with no support."

I am sure Bidkar would also have expected my response. If I waited at the gates, I would give anyone loyal to Joram or Ahaziah or Jezebel time to organize a force to rush out of the gates and overwhelm me. I could not give them time. If they were assembling, they were assembling now. I had struck a dagger directly at King Joram, and now I would direct my dagger at Jezebel. If Jezebel were dispatched, there would be no one in Jezreel for the House of Ahab to rally around.

The gate into the royal quarter was open as I rode up the street. Servants and attendants milling around outside the gate to the royal quarter quickly ran into the gate as they saw us approaching. There were no soldiers in sight. No one attempted to close the gate before we reached it. I had been to the royal quarter in Jezreel before. It was not large compared to the royal palaces of Samaria. There was no room to house any large detachment of guards. As we passed through the gate into the main courtyard of the royal quarter it was deserted. Unlike the streets in the city leading up to the royal quarter, all of the windows facing the courtyard were shuttered. Balconies on the second level overlooking the courtyard did not have shutters, but they were vacant. None of the servants who had disappeared into the gate as we approached were in sight. Drapes and curtains wafted along the balconies, some draping over the railings to the balconies. The clacking of our horses hooves on the mosaic tiles of the courtyard echoed around the courtyard, along with the slap of the soldiers hard battle sandals and the jangle of their belts and scabbards.

I wheeled my horse around to look up at the balconies lining the four walls surrounding me in the courtyard, but saw no one.

"Where is Jezebel?" I shouted.

The riders and soldiers entering the courtyard after me ringed the courtyard, waiting for an order to go here or there. Suddenly a figure walked toward the railing in the balcony immediately in front of me. It was Jezebel. It was not Jezebel preparing for flight. She was not dressed for a quick dash from the city by horse or chariot. She had her royal robes on. Her hair was freshly braided through a jeweled headdress. It was Queen Jezebel in her most austere, regal bearing. It was the Queen Jezebel that could make elders of the city lose their bowels and fall down faint with fear when called to appear before her. Behind her on the balcony were three of her eunuchs that were never far from her side. They were not soldiers, but they had dispatched unfortunate petitioners in Jezebel's presence if that was her will. It was Jezebel who just an hour before had been holding court with two kings, King Joram and King Ahaziah, her son and grandson. Jezebel the mighty, the ruthless. Jezebel the unchallenged. Only unfortunate prophets of the Lord had ever dared to challenge her, and those she had not killed were hiding in caves in the desert.

Queen Jezebel knew how to rule. She was raised in the court of a small but powerful and wealthy kingdom. She had seen how her father King Ethbaal literally ruled over his subjects while holding court. She had visited the courts of other kingdoms and seen a wide variety of kings exercising authority over all aspects of their kingdoms. When Queen Jezebel spoke, she spoke to intimidate and overwhelm. She would conciliate and accommodate only to explore weaknesses, and when having obtained conciliation and accommodation she would go in for the kill. She looked directly at me from her position high above me on her balcony, festooned in her royal robes, surrounded by her eunuchs, but her words were meant to be heard by the commander and his soldiers surrounding me and my charioteer mounted on our horses.

"Have you come in peace, you Zimri, you murderer of your master?" Her voice was commanding, accusing - threatening judgment. Her words were masterful. A murderer does not come in peace, and I, the murderer, was not bringing peace. And "Zimri," the most foul creature known to the Kingdom of Israel, was a byword for dishonesty, greed, avarice, disloyalty, and treachery. The House of Omri was established by rising up and destroying that foul murderer of kings, and the soldiers surrounding me in the courtyard had served the House of Omri all their lives. Forgotten were the horrors Jezebel had brought into the Kingdom, now she was the defender of the honor of the great House of Omri against a disciple of Zimri and his god of destruction.

I had heard from afar many soldiers around campfires arguing over the merits of Omri, Ahab, Jezebel, Zimri and Joram, and the soldiers around me in the courtyard probably all had strong, conflicted opinions of each. But this was no campfire, and the edge of a sword listens to no rebuttals. I could feel the moment slipping away from me. I had been in many battles and skirmishes where the moment turned on a handful of soldiers losing heart; of advancing, yelling warriors turning abruptly to retreat under a sudden flight of arrows or with a horseman breaking through their line. And Jezebel's artful words had cast them all as devotees of the treacherous Zimri.

I did not dare look at the soldiers around me; that would be to confess doubt and cast my success with their waning approval. All of the soldiers with me had seen or heard of the results of someone coming under the condemnation of Queen Jezebel, and it was a training that could lead them to lash out immediately to remove themselves from that condemnation. It was a moment where I was expecting the commander accompanying me to the courtyard to order, "Seize him," or for one of the lancers to spear me through, or a foot soldier to slash at me and take off my leg.

I only had with me a short dagger in my belt, and I did not know what my charioteer mounted next to me carried. We could not make it out of the courtyard without both of us receiving grievous wounds if the soldiers turned on us. I had failed my anointing. Out of desperation I raised my small dagger to the skies and yelled toward the balcony holding Jezebel, "Who is on my side? Who?" I knew the answer, no one. I could not overwhelm Jezebel. It was a prayer, a plea, the last words of my short reign, the epithet of a new Zimri.

As the soldiers in the courtyard with me looked at me, as if to see if anyone would respond to my plea, on the balcony the eunuch standing directly in back of Jezebel stepped forward and grabbed Jezebel forcefully by her gracefully braided hair and roughly jerked her head toward his face. Then another eunuch standing to Jezebel's right stepped toward Jezebel and grabbed her right arm. Jezebel's look of terror could not be described. The eunuch held Jezebel by her hair, and they looked squarely at each other without words. The soldiers now were looking entirely at the eunuchs and Jezebel standing on the balcony, as if I was no longer there.

I was more surprised than the soldiers and Jezebel at what the eunuch had done. If Jezebel were overthrown, her loyal eunuchs would have been the first put to death after her. If anyone would support Jezebel it would be the eunuchs. But this was a strange battle on a strange field, and the flow of the struggle had taken another unexpected turn. A commander has to be prepared to seize any fleeting opportunity. "Throw her down!" I shouted. I did not know what grievance the eunuchs harbored against Jezebel, but one could not expect to touch the Queen and live. He had no choice but to cast his lot with me. My words were the only weapon I had to get past the soldiers surrounding me. Jezebel gasped and looked even more horrified than before. Jezebel always had words; she was never at a loss. But at the exact moment when her entire realm hung in the balance, some unimagined specter from the past stuck her dumb.

The eunuch who had Jezebel by the hair grabbed her under her neck with his left hand and raised her up for a brief moment with her feet barely scraping the ground. As he held her aloft, he issued one word to her face, "Mother!" Jezebel attempted to shout out, but her words were strangled out as the eunuch lifted her clear off the ground, and with one sweeping motion, flung her off the balcony, her body flying directly at our feet. The horses I and my charioteer were riding reared up as Jezebel the Queen was flung down at us and crashed on the pavement with a muffled snapping of bones. The panicked horses reared and bucked as we tried to control them, but as we did, they trampled the lifeless body of Jezebel, her blood splattering their hooves. Soldiers reached up to grab our reins to control the horses, but backed away to avoid the calumny of stepping on the Queen.

As we finally calmed our horses, all stood staring at the crumpled royal robes strewn on the pavement of the courtyard, the stain of Jezebel's blood seeping into the hems. All eyes were fixed on the body. My dagger was lying on the pavement, feet from the body of Jezebel. The eunuchs on the balcony stood staring down at the spectacle, motionless. None of the soldiers looked up to the balcony at the regicide, or at the commander who would be King mounted on a horse who had ordered the regicide. The battle had been won. Had they been for Jezebel, they would have pulled me off my horse and raced up to the balcony to capture the eunuch. But their Queen, if she had been their Queen, was dead. There was no one else in the city to rally around. As the blood oozed out of Jezebel, the fight flowed out of the soldiers. There was no acclamation of King Jehu, no shouts of the death of Jezebel, only silence as each one in the courtyard began to realize what had just happened. Jezebel was no more. From reclining in peace, holding court with her two kings Joram and Ahaziah, to lying trampled on the courtyard pavement in less than one watch of the day.

Then I looked up to the balcony, to the eunuchs still leaning over the railing of the balcony gazing down to the courtyard at their handiwork, and then to the one eunuch who had grasped Jezebel by the hair and rasped the word "mother" to Jezebel before he flung her down to her death. Rumors, too fantastic to believe, even for Jezebel, had been whispered for years, but only between the most trusted compatriots. Rumors that she may have sacrificed bastard children she had borne seemed to have been conjured up by those who hated her so viciously that they would say anything to rouse hatred against her; or perhaps it was manufactured from within the palace to rouse up a dread and fear of a ruler that would stop at nothing to please her gods. But the other rumor? That she had saved one of her bastards, sacrificed his virility to her gods, and raised and groomed him in the palace to be one of her eunuchs, never telling him that he was her son? Even her most virulent foes hesitated to believe the tale. Was it true? Or was an unfortunate eunuch tormented, baited or deluded into believing it? True or not, it only took the one eunuch to believe the rumor to turn the battle.

I turned my glance from the balcony to the soldiers still around me, turning my horse around the courtyard as I looked from soldier to soldier. They all were still taking in the scene, looking from Jezebel's lifeless form, her robes, her blood, to the balcony, to me and my charioteer. The lancers held their weapons at rest. None of the others had any of their weapons in their hands. The commander looked over the same scene, issuing no orders, and then looked up to me, saying nothing, as if expecting to hear an order from me. I obliged.

"Commander, my charioteer and I have had a long and hard journey. We are going into the royal quarters for a meal. Detail five of your men to serve as guards and sentries as we enter. Post your sentries at the gates of the city with couriers to send messages up to me. Also send a rider to the army advancing from the Jordan. Tell their commanders that Joram has fallen, that Jezebel is no more, and that Ahaziah is in flight. Close the gates of the city. No one is to send any word to Samaria. If word is sent to Samaria, it is your life."

The commander and the soldiers listened to my words, as if needing confirmation of what they had just seen. Then the commander snapped to, "Yes master, as you direct." He then began detailing his soldiers to follow my orders. I started into the royal apartment with my charioteer and then turned back to the commander, "And commander, take care of that cursed woman, and bury her, for she was a King's daughter."

SAMARIA CAPITULATED

Jehu

Choose the best and most worthy of your master's sons
and set him on his father's throne. Then fight for your
master's house. Jehu, II Kings 10: 3

A s the army withdrew from Ramoth-Gilead, scouts remained outside
of Ramoth-Gilead and at the fords of the Jordan River to ensure that
the Arameans did not probe to determine if our sudden withdrawal gave
them some opportunity to advance. Our commanders had left envoys
with the Judean army to relay messages and give them guidance on their
withdrawal. Having few experienced commanders to oversee an attack
or a retreat, their oversight was welcomed and not questioned. They willingly accepted our couriers to relay their messages to King Ahaziah, and
accepted the messages we placed in the hands of our couriers from King
Ahaziah without question.

Even had the Judean commanders at Ramoth-Gilead learned of our
attempt to fell King Ahaziah, it was doubtful they would advance toward
Jezreel to attack. With King Ahaziah in flight, there was no one in the
army equipped to take his place. King Ahaziah was just twenty-two years
old with no heirs capable of governing, and none of his brothers had
survived the raids of the Philistines and Arabians on Jerusalem. Only
Athaliah remained in the palace, and she was days away in Jerusalem.
Who would take the place of the fleeing King Ahaziah would have to be
determined before any commander would take it upon himself to lead
the Judean army against Israel.

In Jezreel, only a handful of Judean soldiers remained. All but one of Ahaziah's commanders who were with him in Jezreel had ridden with Ahaziah to meet me outside the city. The Judeans were confined in a house next to the royal quarters.

From Jezebel's eunuchs we learned that Jezebel had come to Jezreel with a small contingent, and with none of her other sons or palace officials from Samaria. It was Jezebel's way of maintaining control, even if she did not rule. No other faction or interest from Samaria - only Jezebel - would confer with the King of Israel and the King of Judah as the kings took a reprieve from their battle at Ramoth-Gilead and King Joram recovered from his injuries. When the Kings returned to battle at Ramoth-Gilead, any word from the Kings at Ramoth-Gilead would be routed to Samaria through Jezebel in Jezreel; Jezebel would be the only one authorized to send word and royal decrees back to Samaria. Jezreel was the supporting base for the army at Ramoth-Gilead. By remaining in Jezreel, should anything more serious befall King Joram, she could maintain control of the army at Ramoth-Gilead and the reserves in Jezreel. It also left Jezebel with an unchecked communication route to Jerusalem should she need to send any communication to her daughter Queen Athaliah.

Had Jezebel taken any of Ahab's other sons or nephews with her to Jezreel, taking Jezreel would have been much more difficult. A ready heir to King Joram's throne would have been a rallying point for the troops in Jezreel to resist me. But their absence from Jezreel also indicated that the House of Ahab would not die easily. The entire royal household and their retainers resided in Samaria. We had survived today, but loyalty can be fleeting. Soldiers will stay away from their homes when the army of Israel is in battle against a foreign foe, but to sleep on the ground and risk death while an army commander fights supporters of the King's heirs is something most soldiers would balk at. My strike against Jezreel had solidified support in the ranks. But I had been around enough campfires to know where the soldiers' talk would take them next. Samaria was a fortified city.

King Ben-Hadad and his Arameans had besieged Samaria with no success, even while Samaria had been cut off from Jezreel. The soldiers will be asking, "Can Jehu do what Ben-Hadad could not?"

A forced march had brought the army from Ramoth-Gilead to Jezreel. Another forced march from Jezreel to Samaria was not in the offing. The soldiers and the horses were exhausted. That I had escaped with my life in my rush to Jezreel was no small miracle, but now we had a fortress as our base. Before I took Jezreel, we were an army in the field with no base of support. I had no choice but to race to Jezreel. But recklessness is rarely rewarded a second time. Although we had closed the gates of Jezreel, I did not delude myself into thinking that no one could have slipped away between Ramoth-Gilead and Jezreel to bring word to Samaria. I could not give Samaria time to rally behind an heir to Joram or Ahab, or time to send word for help from Aram or Judah, or time for Samaria to take the initiative and send out their own forces to determine where their battle against me would be fought.

I had taken Jezreel because I was able to approach its outskirts as a friend. Samaria would be different. But who in Samaria would lead them? Samaria was the capital of King Joram, but none of his young sons yet had the experience or following to claim the throne on their own authority. Jezebel would have had a plan for a co-regency - Jezebel would have had a plan for every possibility - but Jezebel was gone. Samaria was the center for Ahab and Jezebel's Baal temples, but her prophets were the agents of Jezebel, and she had made sure that there was no one prophet powerful enough to assemble his own following.

An immediate attack against Samaria was required. The entire royal household - the entire kingdom - was centered in Samaria. If they had time to get over their shock, resolve their disputes, and rally behind a new king, it would be Jehu and Jezreel against the entire kingdom. I knew the army commanders remaining in Samaria, and I knew who the powerful elders, royals and rulers of the city were. The army commanders in Samaria had field experience. They would be able to come up with a strategy to throw their troops at us from some unexpected direction to repel us or blunt our advance, but it would take immediate action. Samaria was a fortress city and could withstand a siege, but the ablest of the army commanders were with me at Ramoth-Gilead, as were the best of our charioteers, horsemen and archers.

The only question was whether the commanders remaining in Samaria could convince the factions in the city and the palace of their loyalty to their faction. Only an immediate attack would save me, but after a forced march from Ramoth-Gilead to Jezreel another forced march to Samaria would exhaust the army and scatter them along the road to Samaria leaving me without the wherewithal to mount a forceful attack.

The walled city of Samaria was fully provisioned, fully armed and fully rested and with time could summons assistance from outside the city. Only the shock of an immediate full frontal assault had any hope of knocking them off balance and creating an opening I may be able to exploit, but I had no means of mounting a full frontal assault. So I resorted to a strategy pulled directly out of a scroll of the law from Moses: when attacking a city, offer it peace first and do not destroy it if they capitulate, but if they resist, destroy it and all of its inhabitants.

My feint was carried out by a show of exhausted charioteers and horsemen, with my siege works written down on a scroll by a scribe. After the racing from Ramoth-Gilead to Jezreel and then from Jezreel to Samaria, the forces were in no shape to do battle, but they could stand to make a display outside of the walls of Samaria. The force sent by me to escort my scroll was to allow those in Samaria to envision a hostile force descending on their city; an unwritten message that the next wave of forces on their way from Jezreel would not be carrying a scroll.

> From Jehu, son of Nimshi, of the tribe of Issachar, Commander of the Army of Israel, anointed King of Israel by the prophet of the Lord;
> To the officials of the City of Samaria, to the elders of the city, and to the guardians of Ahab's and Joram's children;
> You have your master's sons with you and you have chariots and horses, a fortified city and weapons. Now as soon as this letter reaches you, choose the best and most worthy of your master's sons and set him on his father's throne. Then fight for your master's house.

I was not so crass as to threaten with them destruction. They were still Israelites. As much as the incessant laws were tedious if not oppressive, what was instructive had been adopted and used by the army for generations. They had studied the same laws, learning what was valuable in them for warfare. The instruction I had given my commander was to insist that he read my scroll directly to the assembly in Samaria, and wait in the assembly until an answer was handed to him. He was to immediately ride back to Jezreel if the assembly did not provide a response to my message within a watch of a day.

Jezebel had called me "Zimri." I would demonstrate to Samaria by an escort of horsemen and chariot delivering the scroll that I was supported by the army, and would not collapse in a week. The escort would stay far enough away from the city walls to keep the Samarians from seeing that the soldiers and horses were exhausted and in no shape to offer battle. I would demonstrate that I had honor, unlike Zimri, by offering them an honest contest for the throne. I would also demonstrate that, unlike

Zimri, I had been anointed by a prophet of the Lord. My anointing would only carry weight with a small faction in the city and the royal household, but enough of a faction to lend my words weight. But I did not offer to talk to them, or to negotiate, or to set terms for their surrender. Either they would prevail, or they would perish. There are some words that do not need to be written on a scroll.

While we were waiting for a response from Samaria, Bidkar returned from chasing King Ahaziah. Bidkar's horses, already exhausted from our dash from Ramoth-Gilead could not keep up with Ahaziah's fresh horses as they raced toward Israel's fortress town of Megiddo to the west. We sent out fresh riders with instructions to Megiddo.

My commander reported that there was silence in the royal palace in Samaria after my scroll was read, each elder weighing his own strategy. When they asked to retire to consult before delivering an answer, they broke away into larger and smaller groups, not consulting together as one body, a sign they had much to conceal from my commander. There were many heirs in the House of Ahab, and many factions in the palace. With King Joram and Jezebel gone so suddenly, there was no center of power. They might tear themselves apart in selecting a successor to King Joram. They had many questions as to how I had overcome two kings in the field while the kings were leading their armies; King Ahaziah had escaped his pursuers outside of Jezreel, but this was not shared with Samaria. My commander was instructed not to provide any answers to their questions, other than I had been anointed by the Lord.

My chariots and horsemen encamped outside of the gates of Samaria as riders brought Samaria's answer back to me in Jezreel. I did not want to give them the opportunity to send messages out to anyone else. I expected the answer from the royal palace to be devious, and it was:

> To Jehu, son of Nimshi, with the army of Israel at the fortress at Jezreel;
>
> From the palace administrator at Samaria, the city governor and the elders of Samaria, and the guardians of the heirs of King Joram:
>
> We are your servants and we will do anything you say. We will not appoint anyone as king; you do whatever you think best.

They were not going to capitulate. They did not address me as king. They would not appoint anyone as king because they could not agree on anyone. Their message was clear; they were not prepared to fight today.

But tomorrow was another matter. "Whatever I think best," was obvious. They were to submit to me as King, but they had not. It was in the honeyed language of palace connivers holding daggers behind their backs.

But their words only conveyed part of the message. I asked my envoy to describe the scene in the royal palace in Samaria when he read my scroll. "They were terrified. Their words were brave, but their faces were from the grave, their voices trembled. I heard it said more than once in their councils, 'If two kings could not resist him, how can we?'"

The envoy's description made it sound like I had Samaria trapped on a balcony, just as Jezebel had been. But I knew that a delay of a day or two would allow palace intrigues to work their wiles and temporarily overcome palace jealousies to allow for some temporary accommodation. The guardians of the heirs of King Joram, the elders and governor of Samaria, and the palace denizens had all been in the service of the House of Omri and Ahab for generations, under Kings Omri, Ahab, Ahaziah and Joram. To acknowledge me as their new King - a new dynasty - would eliminate the power of those who had put them in power. "We will do as you say," was an expression foreign to the city of Jezebel. This was a new battle, much like the tides of emotion that swept through the courtyard in Jezreel as Jezebel held court from her balcony.

My next scroll to Samaria was delivered by an even larger and better rested contingent of troops than had delivered my first message. They joined the encampment of the first contingent still keeping vigil outside the walls of Samaria. My army was slowly recovering from the march to Jezreel. The encampment was to discourage any thoughts of a force breaking out of Samaria.

Although Samaria's delay was designed by them to buy time to develop a strategy, it also worked against Samaria. Samaria had waited too long. Samaria's fear of my army, and shock at learning that King Joram and Jezebel had been slain, paralyzed them from acting. I learned later that a handful of captains in the city, who had served under me, when asked how they should respond to my message, had urged, "Strike now! Send all your troops to slaughter Jehu's troops outside the city; then advance immediately against Jezreel. We cannot be trapped in this city. Push Jehu behind the walls of Jezreel. Then Jehu will hold only Jezreel, and we will hold the rest of the country." But my message had its intended effect. If Samaria came out to fight, I had promised to raze the city. To advance in force against an enemy already in the field required a single commander in charge of the entire force from Samaria, and to select such a commander would give that commander a powerful voice over who the next king would be. Had I hesitated a day at Ramoth-Gilead after being anointed, word from a fast rider coming out of Ramoth-Gilead would have sent the entire force from Jezreel to crush my handful of chariots racing toward them. Now Samaria hesitated.

It did not take long to provide my reply to Samaria. I had my second message prepared on a scroll as my first message was still on its way to Samaria. Then I sent Bidkar down the road to Samaria, with my second scroll in hand, to intercept the reply from Samaria, and instructed Bidkar to send off my second scroll to Samaria if their response was anything but total capitulation. If Samaria hoped that it would take a day to deliver their message to Jezreel, a day for me to decide on a reply, and another day to deliver my reply, they were mistaken. Bidkar was directed to insist that my second message be read by him in their assembly the moment he arrived. This time my attack by scroll would be a broad sweep of a sword and would cause many casualties:

> From Jehu, anointed King of Israel;
> To the Rulers of the City of Samaria:
> If you are on my side and will obey me, take the heads of your master's sons and come to me in Jezreel by this time tomorrow.

My message was designed to dismount anyone in Samaria about to clamber into a saddle and ride. Perhaps in the time it took for my reply to their message to be delivered, the factions in Samaria would be close to agreeing which adjuncts would accompany any new commander they could provisionally agree on to keep the commander from siding with a single faction. All of the factions would not be able to agree on a future king in a day, but they could agree to a truce in order to put down a rebellion. But my second message brushed all their factions aside. With factions, to live is to select the faction that will prevail. Jezebel was no longer there to protect all of her sons. Once a new king was selected, after defeating me the factions would fight it out for supremacy and supporters of the defeated factions would be seen as a disloyal threat to the crown. With my second message, there were only two factions that mattered; either support Jehu and live, or support your own faction, hope to survive your battle with Jehu, and if you survive Jehu, die if you are with a faction that did not support the person chosen as the new king.

Loyalty dies an ignominious death. Bidkar reported the same silence that followed my first message, but there was no request for a time
to retire to consider the message; the factions still intact and negotiating
with other factions froze in their tracks; they hesitated. Instead there was
a period of intense whispering and short, animated discussions among
people standing next to each other in groups of two or three.

Finally, Amon, the governor of the city rose at the head of the
assembly.

"Citizens of Samaria. King Joram has been struck down. Queen Jezebel has been struck down. Jehu, the commander of the army of Israel,
has done this. Now the army of Israel is at the gates of our city. You have
heard the heirs of Ahab shout 'treachery' in this assembly. But word has
reached our city that Jehu claims to have been anointed by a prophet
of the Lord. Can there be a claim of treachery if a new king has been
anointed by the Lord?"

"Have your fathers told you of the war throughout our realm for
seven years while Omri battled Tibni for the crown? Fields and homes
were burned, the sword devoured our land, and mothers mourned their
sons lost in battle. King Joram is dead. Shall we battle Jehu for years? Shall
we starve as Jehu besieges us in this city? Shall we burn as Jehu breaches
the walls and puts the city to the torch? Shall we all be sold into slavery?
And for what? Because these sons of Ahab cannot agree who should be
king? Shall we devour each other over these sons of Ahab and leave our
survivors to fight Jehu?"

"Israelites, Jehu has prevailed. We have a new king. The sons of
Ahab clamor that they should be king. Where is their army? What have
they done to protect us from the army of Jehu? While the sons of Ahab
were reveling, Jehu was on the battlefield. We have a King and we have
our lives. Shall we forfeit our lives so some child raised in a palace can
continue to eat the choicest foods and dress in the finest linens? If they
were fit to be king, they would have protected us from Jehu. But they
have failed and put us in jeopardy of our lives. No, citizens of Samaria,
we have not forfeited our lives, they have forfeited their lives. They have
been routed in battle with Jehu, and they have fallen in the field. What say
you citizens of Samaria? Shall the sword of Jehu claim these vile men who
would have us all slain?"

"Jehu is King! Jehu is King! Death to the traitors! Behead them! Do
as Jehu bids!"

As the hubbub slowly quieted down, individuals quietly slipped out of the assembly, leaving for the doorways. Then a different hubbub ensued, individuals walking out of the assembly were stopped by other individuals grabbing at their robes and arms and questioned, followed by pleading and louder and louder speech. Soon yells of treachery, treason and betrayal ensued with yells and howls of protest. As the demonstration of protest grew louder and stronger, two, then three, then many soldiers entered into the assembly and bound the protesters, herding them roughly out of the doors.

The entire assembly filed out to the courtyard in front of the royal palace. Heirs of the house of Ahab were being assembled. Tallies were made of the family tree of Ahab and soldiers were sent to houses throughout the city to bring in any heirs not present; the sons of Ahab, the sons of Joram, the sons of Joram's brothers. The "vile men" cursed by the governor of Samaria in the assembly included men, youngsters, children and toddlers. Screaming mothers and wives trying to enter the courtyard were roughly pushed back by soldiers. The governor of the city went through the court yard with his attendants and soldiers separating the victims by groups, fathers and sons, making a tally.

When satisfied with his tally, the governor went to the captain of the guard signaling which group was to be dispatched first. It was impossible to conduct an orderly beheading, one prisoner at a time; the group of heirs was so large, the courtyard so crowded with the assembled dignitaries, and the screeching and wailing of relatives from outside the courtyard was so loud. Finally the governor ordered the captain of the guard to send in groups of soldiers to dispatch each group of heirs. Each group of soldiers was to stand guard over their slain victims to make sure the tally stayed accurate, and once the entire group was dispatched, the soldiers would begin beheading their victims.

As the soldiers waded into the courtyard to begin their assault, the screaming in the courtyard and from without became almost deafening. After countless blows had been struck, the tumult in the courtyard slowly descended into a chilling silence, and the wailing and sobbing outside the courtyard was reduced to a subdued groaning and sobbing. Few of the dignitaries surrounding the courtyard had ever been in battle. As blow after blow landed, streaks of blood and gore splattered against the witnesses. Several fainted, some vomited, many turned away; few watched the carnage from first blow to last. Once the victims were collapsed and silent on the courtyard, more of the spectators collapsed, overcome by

grunting of the soldiers wielding their heavy swords, and the slashing
and hacking of iron blades ripping into human flesh. Their butchery
done, the soldiers picked up the heads of their victims while Governor
Amon matched each head against his tally, throwing the dripping, lifeless
orbs into large, woven granary baskets.

The soldiers in the courtyard of the royal palace at Samaria spilled
more blood that day than had been spilled at Ramoth-Gilead against the
Arameans or at Jezreel as King Joram was struck down. The courtyard of
the royal quarter in Jezreel had been spotted and stained with the blood
of Jezebel. The courtyard of the royal palace in Samaria flowed red with
the blood of the heirs of Ahab. And yet, I did not strike a single blow in
Samaria.

My envoy brought with him the governor's tally roll as he accompanied the bleak caravan of mules and donkeys under a bright moon on
his way transporting his shipment of severed heads to Jezreel. Wolves
were seen in the hills, attentive to the aroma of the blood of Ahab's heirs
wafting in the night air.

A contingent from the small army divisions that had accompanied
my scrolls to Samaria were allowed to pass through the gates of Samaria
to mark my presence in the city. But the captain of my forces held most
of his men in a camp outside of the city, awaiting a larger force that could
safely occupy the city. Samaria was silent that night. All of the shutters
were drawn and closed. No light escaped onto the streets. Only occasional wailing could be heard behind walls, along with murmurs trying
to quiet the wailing so as not to attract attention. There were trails of
blood along many of the streets, coming from the main courtyard of Samaria and leading to the closed doors where the intermittent wailing was
heard, identifying the houses from where the bodies of the heirs of Ahab
had been dragged.

THE HEADS OF SAMARIA
AT THE GATES OF JEZREEL
Jehu

It was I who conspired against my master and killed him,
but who killed all these? Jehu, II Kings 10:9

A T Jezreel, when my plunder of heads was delivered to me, I had
them stacked in two piles on either side of the city gates, outside the
walls of the city. Many of my soldiers had not seen as much carnage as
this on the battlefield. The effect of the severed heads standing as silent
sentinels at the city gates on the citizens of Jezreel was palpable. Word of
the piles of heads spread rapidly throughout the city. An old priest who
had grown up in Jezreel tried to lecture me on leaving the dead exposed
overnight. "Unclean," the old man hectored me, "it is not allowed by the
law." But the law was the least of my concerns. Residents of the city gradually wandered toward the gates of the city. No one wanted anyone else to
think that they were leaving to gawk at such a grotesque spectacle, but
they all had to see it for themselves. If anyone in Jezreel was harboring a
thought of resisting my rule or waiting for some signal from Samaria to
rise up, the severed heads debated effectively against that impulse.

As an army commander, I would have been revolted by this pagan
display of victory by a king. But as King, I found it necessary. The kingdom
was not yet mine. The only thing I had secured in the few days since my
anointing was Jezreel, and that was because the army commanders had
acclaimed me in Ramoth-Gilead and their soldiers had followed their
orders. In order to cower Samaria, I had sent two small detachments of

my troops there. But the effect of sending troops to Samaria was that the army directly under my command in Jezreel was reduced. Samaria had capitulated to my demands, and a small contingent of the army under me was now outside Samaria, but I was not there yet, and until I appeared in Samaria in force, there could still be factions considering whether they would support me or not.

It could not be certain that all of the royal heirs had been dispatched. I suspected that the more devious royal heirs would have had contingency plans in place to have available a servant in their household that would be held out as the heir. Several heads in the two piles at the gates of Jezreel probably belonged to slaves or servants who protested the ruse as they were run through. Until I could make it to Samaria in force and take control of the royal palaces and household, I was still a distant entity garnering no personal loyalty from anyone in Samaria. I needed to proceed to Samaria immediately, but first I needed to ensure that Jezreel was securely in my grasp. The time of greatest risk would be as I traveled between Jezreel and Samaria. I could not afford to have the gates of both cities locked against me as I was travelling. There was no rumor of any faction conspiring against me in Jezreel, and I hoped that the display of heads ripped from their bodies would cause any potential opponent in Jezreel to soberly consider the value of resisting my rule, at least overnight, before deciding to act.

During the evening, Queen Jezebel's eunuchs and the army commander that had met me when I arrived that morning at the city gates were questioned closely but separately. Who was in the city from the House of Ahab, its main supporters, its chief administrators? Who had accompanied Jezebel from Samaria? Who had come down from Samaria to counsel with the King? The lists were compared and more questions asked. Before dawn, detachments of soldiers were stationed around the city, close to, but not in front of, the houses of those whose names appeared on the list.

After the residents of Jezreel had a night to consider the display of beheadings from Samaria at their gate, I roused the entire city at dawn with drumming and horns, directing the populace to assemble at the gates. To avoid any panic, the soldiers tasked with rousing and assembling the people carried no weapons, and outside the gates there was no show of force. I could not have the people think it was time for a round of beheadings in Jezreel.

As the city filed out of the gate to answer my summons, soldiers at the gates with the lists prepared that night noted who on the lists made it out of the city. The names of those on the lists that were not seen filing out of the city were passed back to the soldiers in the city. While the populace was assembling outside the gates for my address, the contingent of soldiers stationed throughout the city, following the lists compiled in the interview with Jezebel's eunuchs and the army commander, broke down doors and gates, searching for anyone on the list who had decided to avoid showing their face in the streets. A handful of those on the lists found by the soldiers in the city were dragged out of their houses and struck down in the streets.

Once every household was represented, and all the officials and priests of the city were assembled, I made my way out of the city. I took my time, to impress on my subjects the gravity of the situation, and simply to make them wait for me, their King.

I was escorted to the gates by my royal guard, and wore my royal robes which had been stitched together from Joram's wardrobe in the night. My procession was announced by more horns, trumpets and drumming. After gazing over the silent crowd, I addressed them.

"You are innocent. It was I who conspired against my master and killed him, but who killed all these? Know then, that not a word the Lord has spoken against the house of Ahab will fail. The Lord has done what he announced through his servant Elijah."

There were those in Israel, trained by the House of Omri and Ahab, and those trained by the House of Ethbaal by Queen Jezebel that revered power. The gods of Jezebel were the gods of power, advancing the cause of the powerful and crushing the weak. These people I did not need to address. The voiceless tongues in the pile of severed heads each delivered their own prophecy. The power of Jehu provided its own exhortation. There were others in Israel who still valued the prophets, the word of the Lord, and the law of God issuing from the Temple in Jerusalem.

There was not a person in Jezreel who had not heard over and over again the tale of Elijah's condemnation of Ahab over his murder of Naboth and the theft of Naboth's vineyard. Each time they left and entered Jezreel through the city gates, they passed through Naboth's vineyard, still known by some by that name, as if a rebuke to Ahab and his son Joram. The vineyard repeated Elijah's prophecy each time they passed through it, or each time they tasted its wine. To them my message said "you may resist the power of Jehu, but you will not resist the power of the

Lord." I was an instrument of the Lord in destroying King Joram, but the mounds of heads in front of them came from Samaria while Jehu was in Jezreel. It was the Lord's doing. I had carried out the prophecy of Elijah, the most revered prophet of the Lord.

After my address, as the people began to file back into the city, the soldiers pulled out of line those people on the lists compiled with the eunuchs and commander and pulled them to the side outside the gates of the city. There were protests and pushing and shouting. But the soldiers reassured the reluctant citizens that King Jehu had need of them. Those not on the lists were ushered back to their homes by the soldiers and told that those detained would return to their homes by midday.

After everyone not on the lists was ushered back into the city, the gates were closed and the soldiers began to usher their charges toward Naboth's vineyard. Perhaps their destination was too obvious to those devotees of Jezebel. By the time the assemblage reached the end of the ramp leading from the city gate, they began to recognize who was included and who was not. It did not take them long to make their calculations. They all had close dealings with each other and with the lifeless heads that no longer looked like men. Once one of them spoke up and stopped walking, they all began to protest.

"That Zimri you serve is a bloodthirsty madman! He intends to murder all in Jezreel and Samaria who served our King. Are you soldiers or murderers? We are all Israelites, why would you harm us?"

They began hectoring and pushing individual soldiers, pointing fingers and gesturing. The soldiers' captain had been well-selected. He did not leave it to his individual soldiers to debate their captives or to consider their words.

"Do your duties here and now and be quick about it. Extra grain and wine for death blows."

A captain's order is not something a soldier has to weigh or assess. The shouts and protests of the condemned were confusion to the soldiers, and a blow of a sword ended the confusion. The ears of the beheaded did not hear the bodies of their friends fall to the ground. The blows were so sudden and forceful that the doomed had little time to cry out as they sought to avoid the swinging and thrusting blades. Fresh, new blood trickled on the ground toward Naboth's vineyard, following the last breaths of the deceased.

A few birds fluttered away as the swords swung, but they resumed their morning songs from a stone's throw away as the soldiers waited for a cart to pile their morning's work on.

An older soldier spoke to the captain.

"I know these people, captain. I am from Jezreel. That man there ran the granary. The man next to him dealt in linens. Why were they struck down?"

"Did you ask the Aramean you struck down outside of Ramoth-Gilead if he was a shepherd or a priest?"

"They were soldiers in battle. These are Israelites."

"You marched in the army under Jehu to Jezreel. If we did not prevail it would be your bones the birds would be picking clean. The good and the evil die in battle."

The captain and the soldier continued to look at the lifeless forms lying at their feet. The captain continued, "It is a harsh judgment, but Jehu has been anointed King by a prophet of the Lord. If this was a sin it is Jehu's sin to answer for."

"Would that kings had to answer."

ENTOURAGE OF RELATIVES

Jehu

We are relatives of Ahaziah, and we have come down to
greet the families of the King and of the Queen mother. II
Kings 10:13

W ITH Jezreel secured, I began my march to Samaria to claim my
capital and to take my place in the royal palace. While we were
still in sight of the walls of Jezreel, we could see black smoke rising from
outside the city gates. Logs and timbers soaked in pitch had been hauled
outside the city and set ablaze. The bodies of those slain outside the city
gate had been tossed onto the conflagration. The piles of severed heads
from Samaria were added to the fire. Bodies of those slain inside the city
were dragged out and increased the inferno. We could still see the black
smoke rising on our march when we were out of sight of the towers of
Jezreel.

We were less than half a day on our march from Jezreel to Samaria
when sentries on our flank and from our rear guard sent riders advising
us of riders advancing toward us from both Jezreel and over the plains
of Jezreel from the direction of the fords of the Jordan. We halted our
march immediately to set up defenses in the event these were an advance
guard of an attack against us. My commanders and I believed that we
had a clear path to Samaria with no threat against us. Now we tried to
assess the worst that could happen. Had the army of Judah rallied from
Ramoth-Gilead and decided to advance against us? Had hidden factions
in Jezreel rallied the army against us?

Sometimes, seeking to anticipate the worst threat conjures up enemies that do not exist. Our sentries at the ford of Jordan had been racing toward Jezreel with news of a Judean contingent travelling from Jerusalem toward Ramoth-Gilead whom they had barred from crossing the river. When our sentries sent riders to Jezreel, they arrived at Jezreel to find we had departed for Samaria. New riders had left from Jezreel to forward the message to us. Thus there was no threat from Jezreel. The riders from our flank had ridden ahead of the Judean contingent to track their progress when the Judeans started heading toward Samaria after the Judeans had been rebuffed at the fords of the Jordan.

I did not want to delay my march to Samaria, but I needed to be certain of what these Judeans were up to before I continued on. We resumed a slowed march toward Samaria, while sending out a contingent to intercept the Judeans and bring them to us.

It was after midday when the haggard Judeans were brought to us, covered in the dust of a hard ride, several on horses reined to our horsemen's horses, several riding mounted with our horsemen on our horsemen's mounts, several more clinging onto the sides of chariots, and a few packed two and three onto a chariot. They were not willing passengers, and a few looked as if they had been roughly handled along their journey, well beneath their accustomed station, to encourage their unwilling participation in the journey.

Our sentries had intercepted an embassy of forty-two Judeans who had come directly from Jerusalem toward the Jordan fords, on their way to Ramoth-Gilead. I could tell immediately that while it contained a handful of soldiers, this was not a military contingent. They had come from the palace in Jerusalem. I would expect four or five riders to transmit messages between Jerusalem and King Ahaziah in Ramoth-Gilead, not an entire group of forty-two. Nor was this group carrying any supplies or weapons to the army in Ramoth-Gilead. In my years of fighting alongside King Ahab and King Joram, even in our battles while allied with King Jehoshaphat of Judah, I had never seen an embassy such as this sent to a king engaged in battle. What was their purpose?

"We have come to see King Ahaziah. This is the second time we have been turned away. Who is your King, soldier?"

I had approached the dismounting Judeans flanked by two of my commanders with a detachment of guards following. The handful of soldiers among the Judeans, providing the embassy an escort I assumed, had not been disarmed. Despite their rough treatment to encourage their quick journey, our riders had been told to treat them as the allies they still assumed they were. The young, agitated Judean barking at me had just stepped off the back of a chariot, straining to stand up straight after his ride.

An older Judean just behind him put on a diplomatic smile, while quickly putting his hand on the shoulder of the younger Judean.

"We are relatives of Ahaziah, and we have come down to greet the families of the King and of the Queen mother."

"Elder," I replied, imitating his diplomatic gloss, "we are in battle. This is not time for family visits."

The younger Judean, brushing the other's hand from his shoulder, shot back, "What battle are you in, soldier? Our forces are in Ramoth-Gilead but you are on the road to Samaria."

I dropped my conciliatory tone and turned to the young Judean, "What is your mission?"

"Israelite, we come from the royal palace in Jerusalem to see King Ahaziah. What business do you have interfering with our mission?"

I turned to the charioteer who had brought the Judean in, "What is their mission?"

"They will not say. They only say they came to speak to King Ahaziah."

"Do they know of King Ahaziah?"

"No. They talk of King Ahaziah."

With this the Judean reddened. "What is your meaning? Take us to our King!"

I ignored the Judean. I asked the charioteer. "Are they carrying messages?"

"This one has a packet around his neck."

"Judean, hand me your packet."

"This packet has been sealed in the palace in Jerusalem and is only to be delivered to Queen Jezebel. I will hand this over only when I see the face of Queen Jezebel"

"You have heard him." I motioned to an archer in the guard escorting me and my commanders. "Deliver him to Sheol!"

Before the Judean had the time to understand what I had said, my archer drew an arrow, strung it and let fly. Only a flash of the arrow was visible before it plunged into the chest of the Judean, cutting clean through his body, then flying a looping path behind him and clattering on the ground like a stick in a breeze.

The Judean gave a faint gasp, with a look of wonder on his face, before crumpling on the ground, his robe billowing around him.

"Let me see what the Judean was hiding from us."

The charioteer rolled the Judean over and cut the leather cord off of the neck of his lifeless body. Attached to the cord was a leather wallet. The charioteer lifted a flap on the wallet and drew out a scroll.

"Charioteer, bring the scroll here. Hand it to my commander. Commander, read the Judean's scroll."

My commander took the scroll from the charioteer. The scroll was bound by cords wound around it, and the cords impressed by wax seals along the rolled edge of the seal. Both ends of the scroll had also been dipped in wax to seal it. The commander took his dagger out, cut the cords and scraped off the seals and the wax along the edges and slowly unrolled the scroll. It was tightly flattened, as if to be concealed. My commander scanned over the scroll, reading passages to himself, then glancing at me, as if asking for guidance.

"Commander, read the scroll to all of us, read it aloud as if a proclamation. If I have acted rashly, then it will proclaim judgment on me." The commander lifted the scroll in front of him and began in a slow, loud voice,

> To Queen Jezebel, of the House of Ethbaal, House of Omri and House of David . . . .

"She is not of the House of David!" protested the commander. "Silence. Read all of the scroll. Read it!"
The commander continued,

> From Queen Athaliah, of the House of Ethbaal, House of Omri and House of David, mother of all descendants of the House of David, from the Royal Palace of King Solomon in Jerusalem.
>
> Mother: My emissary who has delivered this message to you is my most trusted advisor. He will deliver your response to me without delay.
>
> My embassy has delivered my message to King Ahaziah at Ramoth-Gilead as you have directed. By the time you receive this scroll, King Ahaziah, depending on the vicissitudes of battle, will be arranging to meet you in Jezreel, away from the influence of the royal palace in Samaria.
>
> I agree wholeheartedly with you that action must be taken immediately if we are to have any chance of obtaining our agreed upon objective in our lifetime. My brother Joram has wandered

from the ways of the House of Ahab and the House of Ethbaal, and has adopted the Israelite's golden calves. I fear that the successor of the old conjurer who condemned my brother King Ahaziah for seeking the counsel of Baal-Zebub of Ekron has corrupted his mind. As divined by your prophets and priests, I fear that it is only a matter of time before Joram will empty the Temples of Baal in Samaria. Should Joram exile your priests of Baal from Samaria, our hope for a dynasty would be lost.

As I have assured you, my son Ahaziah, as King of Judah, has received with respect the counselors of my father King Ahab of Israel. As they had counseled my unfortunate husband Jehoram, they have counseled Ahaziah. He has wisely restrained the influence of the denizens of the Temple here in Jerusalem. He has wisely recognized the power of the mystique of the mighty King David to suit our agreed upon purposes. He has elevated the tales of King Hiram of Tyre supplying the lumber and artisans for the building of the Temple in Jerusalem. He has retold the stories of King Solomon's wives from Sidon and put their Sidonian temples on display.

One thing is lacking, due to the misfortunes of the late King Jehoram, and that is a strong army.

With the dedication of Ahaziah and the resolve he has shown that is necessary to rise to the head of a great dynasty, combined with the strength of the army of the Kingdom of Israel, this may be our last hope to achieve our aims.

Would that my son Ahaziah was older than his twenty-two years, but to wait would risk Joram taking more action to reduce your influence in Samaria.

As for the present King, your son Joram, I will entrust him to your disposal. He has shown weakness in the face of the incessant prophets of your land. He has reduced the Temples of Baal, thus weakening your devotees. Whether he can prevail, or whether we should look to another, I entrust to your judgment.

Our lands, united in purpose, united in dynasties and united in alliances with our native lands of Sidon and Tyre will stretch from Assyria to Egypt and beyond the great sea. Why should we cower to Assyria or Egypt? Our Empire is there for the taking, the time is ours for the taking. I am ready to strike here in Jerusalem. Upon receipt of your reply, after you have accomplished what you need to accomplish in Jezreel and Samaria, I will bring all of Jerusalem to its knees.

Mother, success in all of your undertakings.

My commander had read out each word of the scroll clearly, slowly and without hesitation, as a judge pronouncing his sentence. When he finished he looked up at me without expression. All of the Judeans had been brought in front of me as the scroll was being read. I stood gazing out at them in silence. I waited to see some expression of amazement, some protest, even some feigned denial, but none came. This whole large embassy stood in front of me, convicted of the indictment that had just been read out.

"Vipers," I cried out, "Scorpions, lice and vipers! The city is nothing but a pit of vipers!"

The eyes of the Judeans widened as I spoke, thinking I was speaking of them. But in my mind I was thinking of the nests of vipers still lurking in Samaria. This plot was not just hatching, it was full-fledged. Jezebel had gone to Jezreel to strike down the King of Israel. She had gone to Jezreel to conspire with her grandson King Ahaziah to establish the dynasty of Ethbaal over both Israel and Judah. Her household in Samaria was waiting for her to spring her trap. No wonder they had so willingly sacrificed the heirs of Ahab at my demand. Queen Jezebel's household and retainers, her supporters from the Baal worshipers she had imported from Sidon, they were the ones supporting Queen Jezebel as she built her dynasty. And they were still entrenched in Samaria, ringed by a thin line of my troops waiting for my arrival.

I thought back to my anointing. I had wondered why this young prophet had run all the way to Ramoth-Gilead, to the point of collapse, to anoint me. I had spoken to Elisha many times on the road and in camp. Why had he not anointed me then? Why had the young, exhausted prophet dashed out of the room, down the stairs and out of the city gates after he anointed me? Why did he not stay to rejoice with me? His speed, his panicked rush, had unnerved me and inspired me as I had ridden to Jezreel, trying to rush ahead of an unseen onslaught. And now I understood why.

The harried, sweating prophet had been sent on his way to anoint me in Ramoth-Gilead as Queen Jezebel sat down with her scribe in Samaria and composed her message to Athaliah in Jerusalem. I had been anointed and made my rush to Jezreel, then exchanged ultimatums with Samaria as Jezebel's message made it to Jerusalem and as this royal embassy was being sent out from Jerusalem with Athaliah's concurrence in Jezebel's plan to strike down King Joram. Had they reached Jezreel before I had, it would have been Jezebel who struck down her son Joram. They had made a slow, royal progress to Ramoth-Gilead, to belie any urgency, any danger in their message. King Ahaziah did not know they were on their way, so no message had been sent to Jerusalem to tell them their King was resting at Jezreel, and I had barred any messages from leaving Ramoth-Gilead once I had been anointed, so they had continued their procession to Ramoth-Gilead.

I thought I had struck hasty blows at the House of Ahab, but I discovered I was only dashing ahead of a rushing torrent I had not seen coming. An unseen threat still prowled the streets and darkened alleys of Samaria, forming into groups, making alliances, peeling away anyone they could from my small advance guard sent from Jezreel.

I did not know what my commanders standing on either side of me thought as I cried out "vipers." I had been in many maneuvers with them, both on the battlefield and in skirmishes in villages and the open field; I knew how they thought, and what they thought about, and they had heard the same words read from the scroll that I had. The boulder teetered on the precipice, ready to crash down on us all.

I turned to the few archers standing behind us. "Archers, let fly!"

The archers had seen the one Judean felled. They did not hesitate. As they strung and drew, the horsemen and charioteers who had been escorting the Judeans leapt and scrambled to the side, out of the way of the oncoming arrows. The first few Judeans fell. Having seen the scroll bearer fall, they knew what was coming. Some had time to turn or throw themselves on the ground, with some arrows glancing off of them, other arrows striking legs and shoulders but not killing. Those not impaled by arrows ran into the horsemen and charioteers that had brought them to me. The few swords and daggers these palace Judeans carried with them had barely been unsheathed when the soldiers regrouped behind them and slashed one after the other to the ground.

"Finish them all," I directed.

The last few blows were being struck as I turned to my commanders, "Now you have heard why we were sent to battle the Arameans at Ramoth-Gilead when there was peace in the land. Now you know why no emissary was sent to the Arameans at Ramoth-Gilead ahead of us seeking to avoid battle. It was all an artifice. Jezebel and Athaliah have bled their realms dry of troops, having sent us to Ramoth-Gilead with the main body of the armies to leave little force to resist them while they slaughtered whomever they wished, family and all, to take control of the kingdoms. We were sent to battle as Uriah the Hittite to die before the enemy while they prostituted our kingdoms to them."

THE RACE TO SAMARIA

Jehu

Come with me and see my zeal for the Lord.
Jehu, II Kings 10:16

O UR measured march to Samaria had come to a complete stop as
we had waited for word from our riders and then confronted the
Judeans.

"Enough delay. You have heard the perfidy we face in Samaria.
Mount up. We must make it to Samaria. Light torches if you must. Follow
me if you can."

Now we resumed our dash from Ramoth-Gilead. Chariots and
horsemen raced with me to Samaria, hoping we could reach the city before the schemers could finalize their alliances and close the gates of the
city to us. I could no longer consider what the watchmen on the walls of
Samaria may see as we approached. The Samarians knew I would be on
the way. Let them puzzle over what they may see coming. I could only
count on breaching the gates by speed. If I had to, I would race through
the streets of the city in my chariot flailing my sword at them while my
army approached the walls.

The sun was on the horizon when we spotted a rider coming toward
us on the road from Samaria, approaching us almost as fast as we were
driving. I slowed slightly enough to allow my outriders to overtake me
and intercept the rider from Samaria. My riders rode up to the approaching rider and all stopped in the road. There was no struggle or contest
with the rider, so I drove up in all haste. The rider was Jehonadab, the

rustic, now the sworn nomad, detached from the kingdom and its taxes, and still devoted to the Lord.

"Jehonadab, my friend, what breed of sheep are you herding that requires you to ride so fast?"

"I am herding the Lord's kingdom; it has broken the fence and roams the hills without a master."

"I am searching for the same thing my old friend. Are we too late? Have you come from Samaria?"

"I have. I brought a flock to market this morning and then learned of the head tax that a new King had levied against the House of Ahab."

"I thought you were living in the mountains and deserts, staying away from the cities."

"Old habits, my friend. It is quicker to trade rams for iron and bronze than to smelt it myself."

"Are the gates of Samaria open?"

"They were as I left, but guarded. Your name is a byword there, whether friend or foe I do not know. There were enough mutterings that I chose not to inquire. If I was found on the wrong side I may not have made it out of the city. And the anointing I heard so much of?"

"The Lord has herded me off, Jehonadab, to slaughter or for a scapegoat or to green pastures, I do not know."

Jehonadab was silent for a moment, searching my eyes.

"You are troubled, my friend. What is in your soul?"

"Master, you have been anointed. Your master King Joram was from the house of Ahab. But I have heard that you also pursued King Ahaziah as well. My lord, Ahaziah is of the House of David. Surely you were not anointed to strike down the House of David?"

Only an old friend like Jehonadab, a man who had turned his family into a caravan wandering over the hills, would dare to ask such a question to the new King with the blood of the old King still dripping from his sword. I realized that many of my own soldiers could be wondering the same thing, and wondering how much blood was yet to be spilled to secure my throne.

"My friend, I do not understand the ways of the prophets. Elijah played a warrior when he put four hundred prophets of Baal to the sword on Mount Carmel. If the prophets spilled blood, can I say, 'Too much! Too much?' We have put many to the sword. We have trampled those who would oppress us with our chariots. Is this now too much? You yourself heard Elijah condemn Ahab, only to relent when Ahab moaned and groaned and put on sackcloth. But Ahab met his end at Ramoth-Gilead and now this prophet comes to me, once again at Ramoth-Gilead, and says the House of Ahab is to perish. He was a prophet; that is all I know. Is not King Ahaziah a descendant of Ahab and Jezebel? I spoke to Elisha many times, as have you. It was like grinding gravel with my teeth. I do not know his mind. But this prophet said, 'Word of the Lord.' I can have no doubt that this is what we must do. We have the words of the prophet and we have moved against the King with his army."

Jehonadab listened quietly, still studying me. I knew that the old warrior Jehonadab would not dissemble. He would state his mind, and his mind could turn some of his old charges who rode with us against me.

"Jehonadab, I asked, "are you in accord with me, as I am with you?"

"I am," he answered.

"If so," said I, "give me your hand."

Jehonadab reached out to me without hesitation and I pulled him into my chariot. "Come with me and see my zeal for the Lord."

Jehonadab was silent for the first few moments after he stepped into my chariot. He was an old warrior and would want to know what my strategy was for entering Samaria, but he had something else on his mind.

"Zeal for the Lord, Jehu? Is that what we pursue with the sword?"

"Jehonadab, have you become a prophet with your troublesome questions?"

"It is a question I ask myself."

"I only seek peace, Jehonadab, but the sword pursues me. It is a question King Joram asked, 'Do I come in peace?' It is a question Jezebel asked, 'Have you come in peace?'"

"And do you?"

"I killed both of them. Jehonadab, did that prophet come to me in peace? I did not seek him out. I had only two courses. I could have slain that prophet as soon as he raised that flask of oil over my head. Was it not treason against King Joram? He would not be the first prophet cut down by the House of Ahab. But I did not, so I chose the second path. As soon as I did, I have been fighting for my life. Would the House of Ahab have allowed me to live?"

"So your zeal is for your life, and not the Lord?"

"You are indeed a prophet, Jehonadab. You should beware of kings. But my zeal is for both. The Lord has married my life with His zeal and they have become one flesh. It is a crafty thing that prophet did. Jezebel pledged her prophets, her servants, and her officials to destroy the prophets of the Lord. Jezebel is gone, but her work grows and must be rooted out. If not it will sprout up again and again and drag us all down."

It was dark as we approached Samaria. The half moon was low in the sky. A few flickering torches on the walls and alongside the gates laid out the road to the gates of the city. In front of the city, a few small tents surrounded some small campfires of the two groups of troops who had delivered my messages to the elders of Samaria.

As we approached the tents, the light from the torches alongside the gates showed me that the gates were held open, but with a row of guards lined before the entrance, with additional guards posted along the road leading up to the gates.

"Who do those soldiers at the gates serve, Jehonadab?"

"I did not talk to any soldiers in Samaria. I kept my cloak over my head when I was not in the market. No one lingered in the streets. They would dash out of one door, go down the street without greeting anyone, and disappear down the street or into another door. The market was open and there was talk among the traders of keeping the gates open for their trade. Some traders who had said they had talked to soldiers heard that the elders of the city felt that Jehu would not harm them now. But it was possible that an order could come to close the gates at any moment if the city acclaimed a new king. There was much gossip in the market of who would be king."

"And the citizens of Samaria? Were they gossiping or was it just the traders?"

"It was a strange day at the market. The city dwellers came to the market quickly and quietly. They did their business quietly and left quickly. They did not linger, they did not talk. You could hear the traders talking, but the rest of the market was quiet. It was almost like a Sabbath of the old days."

"But you did well at the market? You have no flocks with you."

"I did very well. All the traders did well. It was as if they were all preparing for a festival. Many of us sold out as soon as we set up."

"Preparing for a festival or a siege. You do not describe a city going back to life as normal."

"No. No one seemed as if they were preparing to greet a new king."

"They are still plotting, but they haven't decided yet where they'll lay their traps. Will the soldiers think I am a Zimri?"

"They have word that you were anointed. They would not strike down someone the Lord anointed, unless they already took an oath to another king."

FACTORING SAMARIA

Jehu

Let death take my enemies by surprise; let them go
down alive to the realm of the dead, for evil finds lodging
among them. Psalm 55:15

A s Jehonadab and I talked, a sentry from near the tents approached us.

"Soldier, any news from the city?"

"My lord, no one was expecting you tonight."

"The soldiers posted at the gates, are they with you or the city?"

"They are from the palace guard."

"Have you been in the city?"

"We did not ask to enter, but then we have not been invited in either. We decided to wait for your order. Their garrison could overwhelm us if we entered the city and they closed the gates behind us."

"It does not sound like they are greeting you as brothers."

"The guards at the gates know that you have been anointed by a prophet, but they are wary of the people in the palace and the elders of the city. But commander Jehu, there is more news."

"What news?"

"King Ahaziah may be in Samaria."

"I had received word from Bidkar before I left Jezreel that Ahaziah had been wounded and had fled to Megiddo. What have you heard?"

"After the heads of the princes were sent to Jezreel, two chariots with riders escorting them raced past us and were let into the gates. We could see that the chariots were from the Megiddo armory. We were not expecting any riders from Megiddo."

"This is a war, soldier. You cannot expect the enemy to do what you expect. What if they had fallen on you?"

"Yes, master, it is as you say. But with all of the princes of Samaria being beheaded, we felt that Samaria had capitulated."

"And Ahaziah? Why do you think King Ahaziah was with the chariots from Megiddo?"

"From the commander of the guards at the gate. At first the guards at the gates were struck dumb when we followed the chariots to the gates and asked them who they had just let in. They said they didn't know. We laughed at the gate keepers saying they did not know who they let into the city, while we kept our hands on the hilts of our swords. We asked if it was anyone from the House of Ahab and then one of the guards said they were Judeans. We asked for their commander in the name of King Jehu. When the commander came out the first thing he said was to ask for mercy. He said his post was with the garrison in the city and he had to stay with his post, but the garrison was being pulled in all different directions. He said he feared for his life and the safety of his garrison. A handful of his troops had already deserted and gone over to factions in the city. We walked him away from his guards and told him he would not walk back unless he told us who had just arrived from Megiddo. Then he told us it was King Ahaziah, and that he was wounded. He said a single rider had come from Megiddo earlier telling the city elders that King Ahaziah was on his way to Samaria seeking shelter. The commander was directed by the governor of the city to admit King Ahaziah when he came and escort him to the governor's house."

"I'll decide how to deal with the commander later. Alert your encampment that I have arrived. Tell your commander to assemble the men immediately; we are rushing the gates now. There is no time to lose. If they are not dressed they can fight naked. All they need is a sword. I am going up to the gate now. We will fight our way in if necessary. Your men must be right behind me at the cost of your life. We will then take Samaria."

With that I turned to the contingent that had escorted me from Jezreel. "Form up. We will take the gates and after the gates we will rush the city. The city's garrison will guide you to the houses of the leaders of the city, at the point of the sword if necessary. We will assemble all of the leaders in the courtyard of the royal palace."

I put the whip to my horses and raced up the road to the gates of Samaria followed by my escort, with those in the small camp outside the walls scurrying to strap on their armor and helmets and grab their weapons. As I neared the gates, the group of guards at the gate raised their weapons and began backing into the opening of the gate.

I reined my horses back furiously, skidding to a halt within a lance length of the guards who backed up further into the gate.

"Where is your commander?" I screamed at them, "bring him forward."

The guards held firm, their lances and swords raised, but only defensively. The two archers behind them were not pulling their bows back.

"I am Jehu, King of Israel, anointed by a prophet of the Lord. Who do you serve?"

The question was a challenge. They knew that if they declared for Ahab's House, I would sacrifice my horses to run them over, knocking them back into the archers.

"King Jehu," came a voice from behind the archers, then, "Stand down. Let the King in." It was the commander of the guard. The soldiers pulled back their weapons and stood to the side of the gate.

Without hesitating, I moved between the soldiers and into the gate, passing by the commander and entering into the entrance court behind the gates. There were four streets leading off the entrance court and I knew there could be more troops held back in the streets off of the entrance court. The entrance court was large enough for me to circle my chariot around in the courtyard, allowing me to look down all of the streets, and watch the gate at the same time. A moving chariot is a weapon. A stopped chariot is a target. As I circled, I watched the commander of the gate and his soldiers ringing the entrance court, while my troops began trickling in through the gate.

It was my most foolish move since Ramoth-Gilead. If a faction in Samaria wanted to end my rebellion right there, I had given them the perfect opportunity. A chariot's main advantage was speed and movement. A handful of troops and a few horses could upset a chariot in an enclosed space. A well placed arrow and the prophet who anointed me would become a false prophet. We knew from Bidkar who had brought messages back from Samaria that there were factions in the city still looking for an opportunity to acclaim their own king.

As I was racing up the road to the gates of Samaria, as I squeezed through the narrow gate with my chariot, and as I circled the entrance courtyard in my chariot, thoughts of King Ahaziah flashed into my mind. What did it mean? The grandson of King Ahab had entered the capital city of Israel days after Israel's King, Joram, son of King Ahab, had been killed. Was King Ahaziah a rallying point? Would the factions unite under the King of Judah to bring the two kingdoms together? The scroll from Athaliah the Judeans had been carrying suggested Jezebel would raise Ahaziah as King over both Israel and Judah. Athaliah had been raised in Samaria, but she had been in Jerusalem for years. With Jezebel gone, would the elders of Israel allow Athaliah to execute Jezebel's plan?

It was these thoughts of Ahaziah swarming in my head as I looked for flying arrows that gave me the impetus to race into the gates of Samaria. The factions of Jezebel, Athaliah, Joram and others may have been close to reaching agreement on a new king. The Jezebel and Joram factions may have been ripping at each other upon learning of the deaths of their sponsors, but their calculations of power and survival would have been thrown into confusion when King Ahaziah entered Samaria unexpectedly. I would now sow more confusion in the city to disrupt any alliances against me that may be forming.

As my soldiers entered through the gate of the city and into the streets leading off the entrance courtyard, I brought my chariot to a stop in front of the commander of the gate.

"Who rules in the city, commander?"

"You do, my lord."

The commander mistook my question as a request for a pledge of loyalty.

"Commander, before I entered, who did you report to?"

"After we executed your second message, I asked the governor of the city for direction. He first told me to shut the gates against you, but he was shouted down by people who followed us to the palace. The governor was like a ram being torn apart by wolves; everyone was giving him orders and making demands."

"Then what were your orders?"

"We have no orders. The governor would ask the elders and the priests what he should tell the army, and he got twenty different answers. Some wanted us to advance against you at Jezreel. Others wanted us to prepare for a siege. Others wanted us to secure Megiddo for Samaria."

"But the heads of the princes they delivered, did they not capitulate?"

"Those heads were not all princes. And the heads that were princes were the weak or unpopular ones. And the places of the princes who did die have been taken by their retainers. There is a great lust for power in the city. No one wants the House of Omri or Ahab to die out."

I knew what the commander was talking about. Every elder and official in Samaria owed his position to Omri, Ahab, Jezebel or Joram. It had been that way for almost fifty years now. I was now King, in my royal chariot, talking to one of the officers in my army, but my knees were becoming weak. There were still powerful factions in the city, and now there was another King in the city, King Ahaziah of the House of David and Omri.

"Who is for King Jehu in the city?"

"Few. Those who speak in your favor are spit on and pushed out of the way. The House of Omri and the friends of Jezebel are still very powerful in the city."

"And yet you called me King Jehu at the gate."

"Master, everyone in the House of Omri has their knives out, ready to slay anyone who does not support them. But who do we support? There are ten who would kill us for each one we would support. If you have been anointed by a prophet of the Lord, we will support you."

"I have been anointed. All my commanders who were with me at Ramoth-Gilead witnessed my anointing. Commander, assemble your officers. Find out who took bribes to hide the princes who were not delivered to me. Tell your commanders there will be no penalty for them or any of their men if they reveal who paid the bribes and where the princes are hiding. But if they do not reveal this, tell them it will be death for them and their households when we find the princes and learn who helped them."

"And King Ahaziah? What are your orders?"

"Do you know where he is now?"

"He went to the royal palace first. Then we saw his Judean soldiers take him out of the palace, but they're no longer guarding the place where he'd been taken, so he's probably been moved from there."

"Jehonadab, in the scroll the Judean was delivering to Jezebel, Athaliah said whether King Joram or another, she entrusted to Jezebel. Queen Jezebel was at least considering someone to replace her son King Joram, and it may not have been King Ahaziah. She may have already decided when she left for Jezreel. If not all of the princes were delivered by the elders of Samaria, a successor selected by Queen Jezebel may still be in this city."

"You will not find him out at this time," answered Jehonadab. "There were enough of the princes beheaded that they will point all to a headless body as their late leader."

"Commander, what do you think of this? King Joram was leading the army at Ramoth-Gilead. If the Queen had selected a successor should Joram have been struck down in battle, who would it be?"

"Master, the first word of King Joram's death was your first message to the city. Before that, Joram was King and Jezebel was alive in Jezreel. There was no talk of a successor. After your message was received, there was panic in the city. The army of Israel was at Ramoth-Gilead, many of the reserves for the army were at Jezreel, and you had taken both. Many of the princes asked me and the other commanders if we could attack you in Jezreel. We told them that even if we took all of our forces from the city, we could not match your army—this you know—and if we did that, there would be none left to defend the city. Then there was only talk of a siege, and we had not prepared for that. Any successor would have been a fool to claim he was king. He would be asking for an end like Zimri."

"Jehu, I had sold some of my sheep and goats to people before I had reached the gates of the city," commented Jehonadab. "At the market, my sales were brisk with little haggling. I was planning on driving the rest of my flock to the market in Shechem after Samaria, but I sold the entire flock in Samaria. Only if they were planning for a siege would I have sold my entire flock in Samaria. That is why I decided to go toward Jezreel, to bring word to you."

"So even after they delivered their eighty heads of their princes, they were still planning rebellion. And now we have King Ahaziah in the city."

"If he was injured fleeing to Megiddo, he may have stopped in Samaria only to rest before he continued on to Jerusalem."

"But he would have known that I would advance against Samaria. Why would he not try to rejoin his army in Ramoth-Gilead? He came to Samaria because his family is in Samaria. He is of the House of Ahab."

"But Jehu, to get to Ramoth-Gilead from Megiddo, he would have to pass by Jezreel. It would be too dangerous for him. And Samaria is on the road to Jerusalem."

"It is as you say, Jehonadab, but Samaria is also on the road to the throne of the Kingdom of Israel. He is the King of Judah, and he has outlived Queen Jezebel. Even as we speak, the Judean soldiers with him may be joining with our troops in the city who have left their commanders. Commander, send orders to hold the gates of the city open for my forces coming from Jezreel. We can still be cut down in the streets if they close the gates behind us."

The commander dispatched my orders as directed, but Jehonadab persisted.

"Jehu, King Ahaziah is of the line of David; he is a descendant of King David who was anointed by the prophet Samuel."

"Jehonadab, you are a loyal and faithful Israelite. But was not Absalom the heir of King David when he rebelled and was struck down? Was not King David's first born son Amnon struck down for his crimes? Did not Solomon strike down his brother Adonijah for his rebellion? I will not let these rebels breed and fester in my royal city, sons of David or not."

"My lord, you know I fled the city and went to raise my flocks in the wilderness because of the kings, the kings of Israel and Judah. You have been anointed to put an end to the House of Ahab, and I will not question your anointing. It is the will of the Lord. You were anointed to tear down, to destroy, to erase an entire royal family and I will support you in what you must do. But you have become a King, and I will return to the wilderness when this is done."

"I know you are without guile, Jehonadab, and you see what I must do. You were a respected commander, and your word will be the fire that will temper my sword. If I prevail today in this city, your place and the place of your family will be assured at my table."

"You are a man of your word, but my entire family has already given its oath. We have seen Elijah and Elisha fleeing from our kings and living as nomads. After you will be another king, and then another. 'The word of the Lord,' is what Elijah and Elisha cried out. We will follow the word of the Lord; our royal palaces are not the path we chose to take."

"Then support me as long as you can. The sword has chosen my path for me and I cannot turn back. When Samaria is mine, your entire family will have my peace."

"Then you should order your men to assemble the heads of the entire city at once. It will be better to cut down the entire hornets' nest, rather than let them decide where they will swarm."

I summoned Amon, the governor of the city, along with Obadiah, the master of the royal palace into the throne room. The royal robes I had requisitioned in Jezreel had been brought up to Samaria for me.

Jehonadab and Bidkar stood with me, along with loyal Obadiah. Obadiah, the servant of kings and the protector of prophets would remain in the royal palace until a king removed him. He was skilled in hiding the prophets of the Lord from Jezebel, both in the city and outside the walls and would know where the favorites of the factions of the city would be secreted away. Obadiah was a deep repository of knowledge about the city; knowledge that he shared with no one and that he used solely to further his causes. Because he cloaked his knowledge and his loyalty carefully, he was trusted by the palace and the princes; trusted as if he were but a deaf and unfeeling piece of furniture.

It was Amon who had given the impassioned plea to the city assembly that enabled the city to deliver its shipment of severed heads to Jezreel. I had this history of Amon, along with Amon's other deeds, from Obadiah.

"Governor, I have heard reports that it was your persuasion that convinced the city to respond favorably to my second message to the city."

"My King, live forever. It was my duty, when we learned of your anointing, to obey the dictates of our new King. I remain in your service to do your bidding."

"I understand that your speech surprised quite a few at the assembly; that few in the city expected such an answer to be delivered to me."

"Yes, my lord, there was some surprise, but I felt in my heart that it was the only course we could take."

"On the battlefield, surprise is a powerful tactic. Those not prepared for the surprise are unable to answer it; they are overwhelmed by those springing their trap."

"Yes, my lord, I imagine on the battlefield surprise is a powerful tactic."

"Well, governor, I hear that in the assembly, surprise can also give one a great advantage."

"I imagine it could, my lord."

"I always think that strategy in the assemblies is not far removed from strategy on the battlefield."

"Except there would be less bloodshed in the assemblies."

"That was what I had always thought governor, except when I heard of the banquet given to honor Naboth of Jezreel."

"My lord?"

"You were there, were you not, governor?"

"In Jezreel?"

"Governor, did you not join in the accusation, that Naboth should be stoned for blaspheming the Lord and cursing the King?"

"My lord, the banquet, I was at many banquets, but . . . ."

"And that was a great surprise was it not? How could Naboth answer when two powerful men of the kingdom said they heard that dog Naboth say the exact same thing?"

"There were two witnesses, my lord."

"And there was surprise and bloodshed, as if it were a battlefield."

"But my lord . . . ."

"And did you not earn your position of governor of Samaria shortly after Naboth had been stoned to death upon your accusation?"

"My lord, King Ahab recognized my abilities . . ."

"I am sure Queen Jezebel recognized your abilities as well. But were there not other assemblies and other surprises? At the beheadings in this city, there were many taken by surprise by your speech were there not?"

"As well they should have been, my lord."

"But if you were not taken by surprise, you would be prepared, would you not?"

"My lord?"

"The lists. Of those beheaded. You compiled the lists."

"Yes my lord."

"I am thinking that if I had supported this prince or the other, I would want the other princes taken out of the way. If I knew what the surprise was, I would be prepared to protect my prince.

"My King, live forever. You are on the throne. I pledge my loyalty to you. As you order I will do."

"Then you will be silent now. I have another concern. King Ahaziah. Where is he?"

"My lord?"

"Governor, I asked you where King Ahaziah was, and your answer is 'my lord?'"

I looked over to Obadiah and motioned to him.

"Step forward. Where is King Ahaziah?"

"At the house of the governor of the city."

"Lies," screamed Amon, "lies! Strike him down! My lord, I am loyal to no king but you!"

"Governor. This is not the trial of Naboth. We will not strike in haste, but one of you will fall. Bidkar, send men to the governor's house. Bring me all of royal blood you find there, then I will pronounce sentence."

I was surprised that Amon remained silent as Bidkar dispatched his men to the governor's house. Were his princes and King Ahaziah so well hidden? Had they been moved? Was he protected by soldiers that had gone over to his side? In the confusion of the morning, not all of the city's guard had been accounted for, and the Judean soldiers that had ridden into the city with King Ahaziah had not been located. As the troops that had followed me to Samaria began arriving, they were being stationed first at the city gates and the streets in the city leading to the gates. If any group was thinking of staging an uprising, we had to control the city gates to keep us from being locked in the city and fighting pitched battles in the streets while separated from the army. Enough of the army had not yet arrived to take control of all districts in the city.

I had Obadiah and the city governor held separately while waiting word of the search of the governor's house, although I had no doubt of the outcome.

"Jehonadab, take some soldiers with you and review the governor's list of princes beheaded with Obadiah and those of the royal household. You will know some of these old retainers as well as I."

Bidkar returned with two of the soldiers who had ridden through the city gates with me.

"We have King Ahaziah. He was well hidden in the governor's residence."

"Were there soldiers with him?"

"Only his Judeans and they came out peaceably when we told them they would have safe passage back to Judah."

"Keep the Judean soldiers in custody. They would know what the plan was for Ahaziah. If we just let them wander away, they may rejoin whoever is still in hiding. Had Ahaziah been wounded?"

"Twice. He had taken two arrows, one in the thigh and one in the shoulder. Both in the back. He would have received them outside the walls of Jezreel as he was fleeing."

"Are the arrows still in him?"

The arrow in his thigh went through. The shaft broke off the arrow in his shoulder during his flight to Megiddo, but the head is still in him."

"I hear your chariot was upset, Bidkar. It is not like you to be upset."

Bidkar knew what was coming. He hated to be made sport of in front of his soldiers.

"One of Ahaziah's chariots turned on us as Ahaziah fled. The charioteer along side of me veered to cut him off but lamed one of my horses, my lord. I was not upset."

"So you ran into one of your men in the heat of pursuit."

"It was my arrow that struck Ahaziah's thigh, my lord."

Bidkar's pointed "my lords" were a reminder that a few days ago we were merely fellow soldiers.

"Then you should aim higher next time. Maybe you were out of practice."

"As you wish, my lord."

"Who else did you find?"

"A young son of Joram."

"The horseman of the marketplace?"

"A guardsman of the city said he was well-known and well-feared in the marketplace. The merchants finally petitioned the King; his sword play in the market was driving away people and cutting into the King's taxes."

"I thought he might be someone's favorite. Was he on the governor's list of the heads delivered to Jezreel?"

"He was."

"My demand for heads showed who had the most following by who was not delivered. Hold onto the market place terror and bring in King Ahaziah."

King Ahaziah came in haggard and gaunt, looking much older than his twenty-two years. He limped slightly on his right leg, but he held his left arm to his side and did not move it. He wore a clean white robe, but small spots of blood from bandages on his left shoulder had seeped onto his robe.

"King Ahaziah. You are in the King's city, but you were not at the royal palace. We had to search to find you."

"Tell me, Jehu, does every soldier with a sword think he has a claim to be king nowadays?"

"Ah, Ahaziah, I had forgotten who your grandmother was for a moment. You resemble her in your speech. Tell me, King Ahaziah, did you know what awaited you here in Samaria?"

"Jehu, do you know my grandfather was King Jehoshaphat and his father was King Asa. Have you heard of my fathers King David and King Solomon, or of my father King Omri? Certainly you have heard of King Omri of Israel?"

As he tried to speak forcefully, a wet wheezing rattle escaped with his words, a sound I had heard many times before as I walked through the carnage of a battle that has just ended. The wheeze forced him to bend forward slightly, either out of pain or from the exertion it took for him to make himself heard.

"Yes, King Ahaziah, I have also heard of your fathers, but you did not mention your fathers King Rehoboam, or King Ahab."

"And now I hear that you have taken to pretending to be a king as well. Tell me, commander Jehu, was it your father the renowned goatherd or the revered beggar who qualified you to be King?"

I had to wonder if Ahaziah had not been trained directly by Queen Jezebel. His insults were not directed at me, but at the soldiers and officials surrounding me, just as Jezebel's tirade against me from her balcony. But Ahaziah's youth could not take into account the individual calculations already made by everyone in that room. Jezreel was mine and I controlled the palace and army barracks in Samaria. The army commanders supported me. Joram and Jezebel were dead and their supporters had scurried around to find another scion of Omri to support, only to see many of them beheaded. Ahaziah had met with instant acclaim from some when he had entered Samaria, but he was resisted by some who could only see their kingdom being overrun by Judeans. I suspected that the soldiers standing in the room also surmised what I had surmised; the arrowhead lodged in his chest was leeching the life out of him. Ahaziah probably only had a few painful days left of his life and his reign. And besides, everyone in the room knew that if they rose to stand with Ahaziah they would be struck down on the spot.

"Oh King Ahaziah, my father was a soldier, as was King Omri, and I believe your great father King David was a shepherd. It was not my desire to become King, but a prophet of the Lord came to me unannounced and anointed me King. But more than that, the prophet charged me to destroy the whole house of Ahab. When I rode to Jezreel I rode for King Joram. One of my commanders contested whether I should attack you, King Ahaziah, but when you rode from the gate of Jezreel with Joram I saw that the House of Ahab was reaching into Judah. After you had fled from Jezreel, I had not thought of you again until I had a scroll read to me written by your mother, being carried into Israel by your relatives, and it seemed perhaps that the House of Ahab had overtaken Judah. But even as I sent my soldiers out into the city to search for you, I pondered whether the prophet meant that I was to strike you down. Bidkar and Jehonadab here will tell you that I am not given to pondering. But you have left me with nothing to ponder. The prophet did anoint me King, and anointed me to make the decisions a King must make. When I was pondering, I asked myself whether I would see Jehoshaphat or Ahab brought before me. But I see neither. I see Jezebel before me. You are in Samaria to claim the throne of Joram and to unite Israel, Judah, Tyre and Sidon under the dominion of your lord Baal. Bidkar, strike him down."

Bidkar did not hesitate. Bidkar drew his sword as he strode toward the last seconds of Ahaziah. Ahaziah's injured leg, the one that had taken Bidkar's arrow, buckled underneath him as he attempted to back away from the advancing Bidkar. Ahaziah's uninjured arm reached down reflexively to break his fall. His injured arm remained limp as Bidkar's blade slashed down diagonally between Ahaziah's neck and shoulder, tearing through muscle and bone. The blow pushed Ahaziah onto his knees. Bidkar jerked his blade out of Ahaziah's body, pulling Ahaziah forward onto his face on the floor. Bidkar then thrust his blade through Ahaziah's back, the blade chinking off the marble floor, accompanied by a final, moaning groan from Ahaziah.

Bidkar placed his foot on the body of the King and pulled out his blade. Stepping back a step, his sword in his hand, Bidkar looked at Ahaziah's body for any sign of life, as his blood seeped out of him and dripped from Bidkar's sword onto the marble slabs.

It was silent in the throne room for a long time, as if everyone there was straining to hear if breath had actually left the lifeless body of Ahaziah. I could have let Ahaziah gradually die of his wounds. But to allow him to die of wounds from battle, even though it was only a chariot pursuit, would give him a heroic death and make him a rallying point for those opposed to me. His name could be used to unify the splintered factions making a last, desperate grasp for power. To strike him down as I sat on the throne was to execute the judgment decreed by the prophet, as if he was struck down by the Lord. All that would remain would be the still splintered factions; but then the splinters did remain and they had to be removed.

I looked at Bidkar. "Bidkar, you did the bidding of your King. You are pardoned for the death of King Ahaziah. King Ahaziah was of the House of David and the King of Judah. Summon his Judean soldiers. After we are done here, charge them to escort their King to Jerusalem so he can be buried with his fathers." I was now King of Israel, not a pillager, and to honor a King I had defeated was to demonstrate I had the honor of a King.

"Jehonadab, assemble the commanders of the army, direct them to escort the governor of the city, all the princes of the city that remain here, and the guardians that were sheltering them." Bidkar was to be the commander of my army, and this would be an order I would normally direct to Bidkar, but Ahaziah's blood was still dripping from his blade, and I knew the mind of a soldier after he had been called to commit butchery on the battlefield.

"Bidkar, have two of your men stand guard over King Ahaziah. Do not move the King until I have addressed the officials of the city."

"Jehonadab, as your men bring in the princes and officials of the city, usher them through the throne room, past the body of King Ahaziah. Have them stand by the body of King Ahaziah to honor the dead. Then bring them out to the courtyard where their King will address them."

❁　　❁　　❁

The strange odor of blood still rose from between the tiles of the courtyard. Dark stains showed where the pools of blood had drained just days ago. The governor of the city, the princes, the elders and the guardians of the princes seemed affronted as they were escorted from their houses to the royal palace that a former army commander was ordering them to assemble. Perhaps their affront was masking their fear of another bloodletting.

As they were escorted into the throne room and up to the two soldiers standing in front of the throne, their effrontery changed to puzzlement, until they were close enough to the rumpled pile on the floor between the two soldiers to recognize that it was the bloodied figure of King Ahaziah. As they were shuttled into the courtyard to join the growing crowd they were pale and shaken. As each entered the courtyard, they quickly scanned the other figures already standing in the courtyard, taking a tally of who was present and who was not.

For this assembly, Obadiah's list was thorough. As the courtyard filled up, the later arrivals became less and less willing to appear and were being brought in at the point of a sword, with the final arrivals being dragged in with ropes around their necks. As the city was being assembled outside the city walls at the threshing floor, the leading contingents of the main body of troops following me from Jezreel were trickling into the city. As they entered, more and more of the streets of the city were combed for those still in hiding.

Once all of the prisoners were in the courtyard, I had four of the Judean soldiers carry the body of King Ahaziah out into the courtyard on a litter. I then led a procession out to the threshing floors, followed by the Judean soldiers bearing the body of King Ahaziah and the soldiers bringing up the prisoners.

Although I had sat on the throne as I executed King Ahaziah, this would be my first public assembly, my first court, as King of Israel in the royal city of Samaria. I walked to the threshing floor accompanied by Obadiah, controller of the royal household, Bidkar, commander of the army, and Jehonadab, acting as my personal aide. All four of us were well known to the people of Samaria. I had ridden behind Kings Ahab, Ahaziah and Joram for years. Obadiah was a fixture at the royal palace, and known to many of the supporters of the prophets of the Lord as one who had gone to great lengths to protect the prophets of the Lord. Bidkar was young, strong and vital, a rising and talented new officer of the army. Jehonadab was a rustic, known in both the city and the countryside as having walked away from the army and the House of Ahab to live in the wilderness with his family and to serve the Lord. While Obadiah's familiar presence assured the people of continuity and faithfulness, it was the presence of Jehonadab that made the greatest impression on the people. He had walked away from the House of Ahab out of disgust with their practices and now he was back in the royal city.

Unlike my confrontation with Queen Jezebel on her balcony, or my audience with King Ahaziah in the royal palace, I had no concern that an impassioned plea from one of the prisoners may rally supporters to a final resistance against my anointing. The two Kings and the Queen had been dispatched. A majority of the royal princes and their retainers had been slaughtered. Those princes and retainers who remained stood bound in front of me. Detachments of soldiers who had melted into the city to support the factions that had been forming since my first message to Samaria had melted back into their units. The army commanders being placed in control of the city had all been with me in Ramoth-Gilead at my anointing and had acclaimed me King from the beginning.

For the first time since Ramoth-Gilead, my procession to the threshing floor outside the gates of Samaria was not a headlong rush for survival.

The tents and pavilions for the assembly had been erected in the same arrangement as they had stood for the great festival put on by King Ahab for King Jehoshaphat over ten years ago. The only thing missing were the great throngs of prophets. Unlike any royal procession in the last thirty years in Samaria, the prophets of Baal were not in the lead, and were not in prominent positions escorting the King. Once I was seated on my throne and had received greetings from my commanders, I stepped to the front of the royal pavilion to address the crowd.

"People of Samaria and people of the Kingdom of Israel, it was at this very place, at these threshing floors, that the prophet Micaiah told King Ahab that if he went into battle against the Arameans at Ramoth-Gilead he would die. What the prophet foretold came to pass."

"I have just come to Samaria from Jezreel. It was at Jezreel, while I was riding in my chariot behind King Ahab, that the prophet Elijah told King Ahab 'I will wipe out your descendants,' and that too came to pass."

"I was joined in battle with King Ahaziah and King Joram at Ramoth-Gilead less than a week ago. Yet while at Ramoth-Gilead a prophet of the Lord anointed me King of Israel and decreed that I was to put an end to the House of Ahab. Since that time, I have had no choice but to follow the words of the prophet."

"Just as the words of the prophet Micaiah came to pass, and just as the words of the prophet Elijah came to pass, so also the words of the prophet from the household of Elisha have come to pass, and indeed continue to be executed even today."

"It was for this time that I was anointed King, since at the same time, even though your brothers and sons were in battle against the Arameans at Ramoth-Gilead, the House of Ahab was plotting against the Lord, plotting to raise up a new king, plotting to crown a new king who was loyal to Baal, the god of the Queen Jezebel."

"As I travelled from Jezreel to Samaria, we came across messengers from the House of King Ahaziah of Judah; messengers that were carrying this scroll that I hold in my hand before you to Queen Jezebel in Jezreel. It is a message from Queen Athaliah, wife of King Ahaziah, in Jerusalem, the daughter of Queen Jezebel."

"Let me read to you what it says in this scroll:"

> My brother Joram, King of Israel, has adopted the Israelite's golden calves. I fear that it is only a matter of time when Joram will empty the Temples of Baal in Samaria.

"These are the words of the House of Ahab, Israelites. Queen Jeze-bel and her retainers here in Samaria were plotting to strike down King Joram and establish her own dynasty for the glory of her temples of Baal.

"And there is more Israelites. The scroll goes on to explain what their purpose was:"

> Our lands, united in purpose, united in dynasties and united in alliances with our native lands of Sidon and Tyre.

"Yes, Israelites, Israel would no longer be Israel, Judah would no longer be Judah, and instead, a new nation, drawn from Sidon and Tyre would control your lands and your lives. Is this what Moses led your forefathers out of Egypt to see? Is this what the land promised to your forefathers generations ago was to look like?"

"And how would the House of Ahab accomplish this? The scroll goes on to explain:"

> After you have accomplished what you need to accomplish in Jezreel and Samaria, I will bring all of Jerusalem to its knees.

"Yes, Israelites, Jerusalem, Samaria and Jezreel, were to be brought to their knees. And not just Jerusalem and Samaria, but all of Israel and Judah were to be brought their knees. Indeed, all of you here were to be brought to your knees. And how would the House of Ahab and the House of Jezebel bring Israel to its knees? You and I have lived through those unfortunate times when Queen Jezebel's son-in-law King Jehoram became King of Judah, with his wife Athaliah, the daughter of King Ahab and Queen Jezebel. We remember the horror of that day when Jehoram and Athaliah slaughtered all of the sons of King Jehoshaphat; mere days after King Jehoshaphat had been buried with his fathers. Queen Jezebel and her retainers were planning to repeat that slaughter here in Samaria.

"You have seen the governor of this city order the heirs of the House of Ahab beheaded. You may have thought that King Jehu had begun his reign as another King Jehoram of Judah. I tell you fellow Israelites, the slaughter you saw in the royal courtyard mere days ago would have hap-pened even if I had not been anointed King by a prophet of the Lord. Had Queen Jezebel lived to see this day, she would be standing in the place that I stand now, and would be ordering the same heirs of the House of Ahab to be slaughtered in this place. She would be here today crown-ing her grandson Ahaziah as King of Israel, and you, fellow Israelites, you would be forced to bow down to your new King Ahaziah. And why

would Queen Jezebel choose Ahaziah to be King of Israel? It was because of King Ahaziah's dedication to Jezebel's god from Sidon, Baal. Not
only would you bow down to King Ahaziah, you would be forced to bow
down to Ahaziah's god, the mighty and the mightily cruel Baal. Not only
would you be forced to bow down to Baal, you would be forced to offer
your children to Baal in celebration of the coronation of King Ahaziah to
please the will of Queen Jezebel."

"And an even greater slaughter would be made of the prophets of the
Lord, and all that obeyed and listened to the prophets of the Lord. Israel
would no longer be Israel. Queen Jezebel and the House of Ahab which
she has molded into her own image was intent on creating a royal dynasty
which would exist for the purpose of granting power to the House of
Jezebel.

"I am telling you this my fellow Israelites so you will understand
what is about to happen before your eyes on the threshing floor you are
standing on. I do not have to explain my actions to you, nor do I need to
obtain your approval for my actions. I have been anointed by a prophet of
the Lord, and I am required to execute the will of the Lord, and to answer
to the Lord for my actions. What you are about to witness will appear to
be terrible, but if this thing is not done, this festering, putrid sore that is
the House of Ahab would continue to leech the life out of the Kingdom
of Israel, and bring terror upon terror down on your heads for generation
to generation.

"When I sent a message to the governor of your city, the reply received was, 'Do as you please, we are your subjects,' but your leaders were
seeking to deceive me as they held secret councils to select a king of their
own choosing. They were all in league with Jezebel in seeking to control
this nation, and when word came to them of the death of Jezebel, they
continued to conspire in their private councils to execute the will of Jezebel. The death of Jezebel and the death of King Joram and the death of
King Ahaziah was not enough to stop their intrigues. They have become
so consumed with following the will of Jezebel, and establishing Baal as
the god of Israel, and with wiping out the memory of the worship of the
Lord in Israel, that they have become incapable of thinking of anything
else or doing anything else."

"When a prophet of the Lord came to me at Ramoth-Gilead and
announced that it is the will of the Lord that I put an end to the House
of Ahab, the prophet did not allow me to ask him why he had chosen to
anoint me. The prophet did not allow me to inquire why I was charged

with ending the House of Ahab, and the prophet did not say how I was to do this thing that I was charged to do. But I was given no choice in this matter."

"My fellow Israelites, I am not doing what I am about to do because it pleases me. But I cannot say that what the prophet instructed me to do is wrong. You have heard me read from the scroll sent by Queen Athaliah to Queen Jezebel. You have heard the plans they had for this kingdom. They were not seeking the way of the Lord. You have seen the ways of Ahab and Jezebel and Ahaziah and Joram."

"And yet, even after King Ahab and Queen Jezebel and King Joram had died, the governor of this city and the guardians of the heirs of King Ahab and King Joram continue to follow the plans of Jezebel and Athaliah."

"I have seen many sons of Israel and many sons of our enemies fall in battle. I had been spared from seeing the blood of our sons and our enemies shed in the streets of our cities. It is a terrible thing to see bloodshed in the streets of a city, for that means that the enemy has breached the walls, and what follows is rape, pillage, destruction and captives sold into slavery."

"I tell you Israelites, your enemy has breached the walls of this city of Samaria, and is tearing down your city and your kingdom, and is selling you into slavery, and today you will see bloodshed because this enemy is intent on destroying Samaria. They were given the chance to abandon the House of Ahab and accept the one anointed King by a prophet of the Lord, but they chose to continue their plans to pillage your inheritance and their plans to rape you in their temples of Baal."

"Israelites, the men you are to see brought in front of you today have carried their battle into the streets of the city of Samaria, and they would continue with their attack today if they were not bound. Do not weep for these invaders as they are struck down, but rejoice as you would rejoice over any enemy being struck down as they break down the doors of your house to set it on fire and to sell you into slavery."

I stopped speaking to look out over the people of Samaria to see what they thought of the plans of their new King. As King, I could have brought my captives to the army barracks or outside the walls of the city and have them struck down there without any notice or explanation to the people of the city. Baasha striking down King Elah and the entire house of King Jeroboam, and Zimri striking down the entire House of

Baasha was not lost to their memory. It was something many would have expected any usurper of the crown to do.

Whether I had convinced anyone of the reasons for my actions, I could not tell. Who is going to tell the new King who just announced that he is going to put those opposing him to death that they disagree with his actions? But if I had not spoken to them of the reasons for my actions, they would have no reason to see me as any different from Zimri or Baasha.

"Have the captives brought to the threshing floor," I directed my army commanders. I took my seat on the throne set up under the King's pavilion in the same place King Ahab and King Jehoshaphat had celebrated Jehoshaphat's visit to Samaria; the same place that King Ahab and King Jehoshaphat had heard the assembly of prophets declaim for King Ahab. Now, in place of the cavorting prophets flailing their arms, silent men and boys, their arms bound behind them were led unwillingly by soldiers, one on each arm, as they followed King Ahaziah's bier onto the threshing floor.

Small name tablets were hung around the necks of the captives by thin cords. Commander Bidkar led the column of captives onto the threshing floor, carrying a scroll bearing the names of the condemned, listed in the order the captives were brought onto the threshing floor. Obadiah and Bidkar and Jehonadab had made sure that the captives brought before me were the actual captives listed on the scroll.

Leading the procession of captives was the oldest son of King Joram, followed by Joash, the only surviving son of King Ahab and brother of King Joram, and Amon, governor of the city of Samaria. A powerful clique of heirs had survived the first bloodletting in Samaria. They were a substantial base for any new rebellion and strong evidence of the survival of Samaria's continuing resistance to their new King. These four were to be put to death first, to quell any rising cry of support for these heirs as the executions proceeded. The names on the list and order of the procession were based on the strength of the threat to my rule posed by each of the condemned.

After the surviving heirs came the guardians of the heirs who had protected the heirs during my demand for their heads, several officials of the royal palace under King Joram, several close advisors to Queen Jezebel, four army commanders and captains who held their posts out of their loyalty to Joram and Jezebel, several officials responsible for oversight of the palace treasury, a clutch of elders of the city who were well known supporters of the House of Ahab, and some of the retainers of the wealthy citizens who had been forceful in their support of Queen Jezebel.

Once all of the condemned had been marshaled onto the threshing floor, Obadiah read out my decree:

> Captives, heirs and supporters of the House of Ahab. Know you all that King Jehu has been anointed King of Israel by a prophet of the Lord. Know also that the prophet of the Lord who anointed Jehu King also ordained that he was to put an end to the House of Ahab.
>
> Captives, know also that just as Hazael of Damascus was anointed King of Aram by the prophet Elijah, and just as Hazael put to death King Ben-Hadad of Aram, so also shall King Jehu execute the word of the Lord from the prophet.

"Executioners, proceed with your duties."

Few of the condemned heard anything of my decree after the words, "put an end to the House of Ahab," due to their own strenuous protests and jeering. The soldiers who had broken down gates and doors searching for these fugitives reported that my reputation for unrelenting attack had convinced the conspirators that I would not relent in my pursuit which, they protested, forced them to continue to forge alliances to resist me. I confess to pressing the attack, but found these claims of conspiracy as a form of self-defense unconvincing. I knew the House of Ahab well. I was not the only one with the reputation for attacking without quarter. This was a war that would be fought until the last soldier standing had been felled, and so it was on the threshing floor outside Samaria that day.

The soldiers having custody of the condemned knew their orders, but the uproar kept them from hearing whether my sentence had been pronounced or whether Obadiah had stopped speaking due to the noise. Jehonadab, who had been standing to the right of my throne with a javelin by his side saw the confusion on the faces of the soldiers and stepped toward the row of the first four prisoners, and ran his javelin through Joash, who was standing directly in front of him. Joash collapsed immediately but was held up by the soldiers holding on to each of his arms. The rows of javeliniers and swordsmen took their cue from Jehonadab, and ran the other three prisoners in the first rank through.

As the bodies of the first four condemned were being dragged off the threshing floor, the next rank of soldiers brought up the next four condemned. The next rank of javeliniers and swordsmen advanced toward the condemned and dispatched them in turn, and their bodies were dragged off by their escorts. Row after row of the condemned were brought forward, run through and dragged off.

At the end of the business, the soldiers were splashing through puddles, as if there had been a sudden rainstorm over the threshing floor. Several detachments of soldiers were assigned to the task, so that no one soldier had to carry more than one prisoner, and no one soldier had to dispatch more than one prisoner. If anything, it was an unspoken oath of loyalty to me by each soldier as he performed his tasks. Well over one hundred loyalists of the House of Ahab were struck down that day on the threshing floor.

There was no ceremony or observation that afternoon after the last body had been carried off. Water carriers began carrying their loads on to the threshing floor to try to rinse off the gore and reduce the slaughter house smell. As I walked around the threshing floor with Obadiah, Jehonadab and my escorts on my way back to the palace, stepping over rivulets of blood and water, I marveled at this flood brought on by that small flask of oil poured over me by that prophet in an upper room in Ramoth-Gilead.

Unlike the festivities on the threshing floor with King Ahab and King Jehoshaphat more than ten years ago, no prophets were present. Queen Jezebel's prophets, who had been shunted aside by King Joram but not dismissed, were absent that day, although, according to Obadiah, they had become extremely active after the death of King Joram, dashing through the city as couriers between the contending factions. They held no post or position or authority in the city or Kingdom, other than their offices in their respective temples. No one prophet had a significant following or was the leader of any faction. It seemed as if they acted as permanent attaches and assistants, always hovering on the outskirts, but never taking the lead.

I looked in vain for Elisha or the young prophet who had anointed me, or for any of Elisha's followers, but saw none and had heard of none being in Samaria after the death of King Joram. I had hoped for some word, perhaps some blessing, but none came. King David had the prophet Nathan who lived in Jerusalem and was almost part of the King's court. No prophet of the Lord came to Samaria as my Nathan. But I had my anointing and my charge and I carried through.

That night, as on the morning I rode out of Jezreel on my way to Samaria, black smoke and raging fires lit the skies as the executed men were laid on pyres burning outside the city walls of Samaria.

ALONG THE WALLS OF SAMARIA

Jehu

For my days vanish like smoke; my bones burn like
glowing embers. Psalms 102:3

T HAT night I walked along the top of the walls of Samaria with
Jehonadab and Obadiah. The clear night air and the brilliant stars
would occasionally be obscured by the smoke rising from the glowing
embers of the charnel fires still smoldering outside the walls, along with
the pungent odor of burnt flesh. Guards minded their posts around the
fires to keep anyone from sifting through the ashes for a souvenir, me-
mento or relic. On the wall closest to the threshing floor, the smell of a
slaughter house lingered, providing a strange combination of life blood
spilled out and death being consumed.

Below, in the streets of the city, groups of soldiers walked on their
patrols, visibly reminding the residents that there was a new King, but
also on guard for any sign of messengers being dispatched, or any attempt
to resurrect a plot in favor of the House of Ahab. It was a precaution, but
only a precaution. Anyone remaining in the city who may have sought to
side with an heir of the House of Ahab had been stunned and knocked
breathless by the blows that had felled the House of Ahab. There was
no one in the city left from the House of Ahab; there was no one left to
support. Obadiah knew every intrigue that had swirled and eddied in
Samaria. The House of Omri, the House of Ahab and the House of Ethbaal had consumed all the fires of ambition in Samaria. All of the plotting
and maneuvering had centered around one royal personage or another.

Now all that remained of each royal person, of everyone who had lusted for power, was contained in the bitter stench of the smoke in our nostrils from the fires burning below.

For the first time since I was anointed in Ramoth-Gilead, there was no gate to be breached, no force that may be sent out to meet me. I had been rushing headlong to save my neck, dispatching soldiers securing roads and supplies. Until the last body bled out on the threshing floor outside the walls of Samaria, I was leaning forward in my chariot, ready to strike at the next challenge hurled at me. As the fires were lit and the bodies laid on the pyres, my mind raced ahead to the next attack, but now I was forced to drop my reins, realizing that the battles were all behind me. Until now I had not pondered where I had been.

"Look at this, Jehonadab," I remarked, "death all around. Is this the incense burned to observe a new king?"

"It is the incense burned to preserve the life of a new king."

"Is this what kings are anointed for? To spread death? Why did that prophet anoint a soldier as King, to spread more death?"

"Commander, who but a soldier could do what that prophet asked of you?"

"But a soldier fights for his king, or at least for the kingdom. Now I slaughter Israelites in their own city."

"Commander, you have been racing for your life since Ramoth-Gilead, there was no time to reflect or consider. The prophet pushed you into the mouth of the abyss; you had no choice but to strike. Had you hesitated you would have been cut down."

Obadiah stopped walking with us, put his hands on the ramparts of the wall and leaned over the edge, looking to his side back at the guttering flames of the fires, partially obscured by the rising smoke. Jehonadab and I stopped walking and turned back to look at Obadiah. Obadiah stood still, looking intently at the fires. Without turning from the fires, he said, "The stench from the burning sinews, from those smoldering bones does not offend me. Those disjointed arm bones wielded swords without mercy. Those smoldering jaw bones, that ash that was once tongues spoke of intrigue and malice. Those small, glowing embers that were once the bones of feet and ankles ran to shed blood. You did not know those people as I did, Jehu. You would come to Samaria to hear the King's will for the next campaign, and then be gone to the battle. I lived with them day after day, year after year. They did not pause from their malice, there was no evil they did not shrink from, no horror was enough. More, even more; they could not get their fill. 'What is next, what new evil can we now invent,' - something even their gods could not imagine."

"I am not a prophet," continued Obadiah, but it was the prophets that sought to tell these kings and would-be kings of the will of the Lord. And they would not have it. How many prophets did I shelter, Jehu? And how many were killed by these people? And yet you mourn over these ashes? Jehu, I tell you if these charred cadavers could mend themselves, they would rise up and demand more horrors, more death, more slavery, more prostitution; they would demand horrors as of yet unimagined, they would invent new, unspeakable horrors. And you mourn them? The prophets brought them the word of the Lord. 'Do justice,' they would say. And these bones would scourge the prophets and dash them to the pavement. 'Justice,' they would laugh, 'justice?' Do you believe in judgment, Jehu? Should the prophets prattle on endlessly to the unhearing and there be no justice? It is a true horror that you have done here today, Jehu, and we should all gasp and fall to our knees in terror at what has happened. It is something that no one should ever do. But if you had not done this Jehu, you would be struck down on hearing the unending terror and malice these bones had in mind for this place, a terror and horror you could have stopped but did not."

Obadiah's words were an unexpected torrent, a well-spring in the desert. For decades he had been a silent presence in the palace, speaking his mind reservedly and only to a trusted few, most of whom lived outside of the palace. We knew where his heart was, but it was striking to hear him speak his mind.

There was silence as we stood gazing over the wall, the smoke from the fires occasionally being wafted over us, as if a last protest of their sentence. Then I turned to my companions,

"Obadiah, I must confess I was not appalled by the executions I saw today. I have been in too many battles to be appalled at something as clean and neat as these executions. On the battlefield a clean, killing blow is rare. In battle, a blow is warded off, or it glances off a shield or an upraised arm or is slowed by some frail piece of leather or armor, so it pierces and wounds, but rarely kills. So a soldier falls and bleeds, or loses a hand and is trampled and maybe pierced again, and lies in the filth, unable to get up, and as the battle moves on, is abandoned to suffer and die alone. And what is his crime which brought on his punishment and agony? He served his king, he was simply human. No, what I saw today was mercy. How many of the soldiers that died under my command would have pleaded for a death as gentle, mild and quick as that granted to those who died today."

Jehonadab and Obadiah listened quietly, wondering about the thoughts of their new King. Both were still shaken by the violence they had seen. I added, "What bothered me is that these executions were not new to this land, and my fear is that they were just the same as those that came before and the same as those that will follow. Is this the promised land that Elijah lamented? A promise of violence and carnage? I am King. I have executed judgment. But have I brought justice?"

"If you had not executed judgment, there could be no justice. If you had not struck down the makers of slaves, would they not have risen up to reclaim their slaves? Would not generation after generation of slaves have been born to suffer and suffer again? You struck down the makers of slaves, the dispossessors of widows and orphans, the pillagers and plunderers. You did not see the slaves on the threshing floor today. The widows of those taken in slavery did not join in the procession out of the city. Where were they? They remain huddled in hovels they call their home, wondering when the wielders of swords will come to search them out and impress them to work for the new King. Your judgment did not just fall as blood on the threshing floor. It rained down on the slaves and the poor and the dispossessed while they huddled together, beaten down too much to expect any good to come from this new bloodletting, waiting for the next blow, to see the new terrors to be unleashed by their new master. You have executed judgment; justice awaits its time."

The wind blew the acrid fumes away from us for a moment, revealing the remaining guttering flames below us. Jehonadab then spoke.

"Obadiah is right about the King executing judgment. Obadiah is right about the prophets speaking of the Lord's will to kings. But for the huddling dispossessed, how are they to know the Lord's will if there are no priests in the land?"

I waited in silence, hoping maybe that Obadiah would speak his mind again. But Obadiah's gaze was fixed on the flames below as the fires flared briefly under a freshened breeze. Then I realized that this also was the Obadiah of the practiced silence and steady gaze on the horizon as he weighed the words of kings. I was now the King, and he was weighing my words. I could press him for his thoughts, but I had seen Ahab and Joram press him, and they were left reaping the wind, with a harvest of trailing eddies. I had heard Jehonadab's old saw about the priests of the Temple in Jerusalem since I was a small boy, and it never impressed me. Jehonadab was a devout rustic who had taken his entire family into the wilderness, and I expected nothing less from him. I knew Obadiah had protected the Lord's prophets; I did not know how he felt about the priests of Jerusalem. There were none in the land for him to protect. I tried to draw out Obadiah by questioning Jehonadab about the priests.

"But Jehonadab, Elijah and Elisha and the other prophets were sent to the kings. Why do the people need priests?" Obadiah's gaze and expression remained fixed, but Jehonadab turned to confront me.

"Why priests, Jehu? Why priests? Have you seen the priests prattling in the royal palace and on the streets and in their so-called temples? Weren't you here with me when Jezebel herded her troupes of priests in front of King Jehoshaphat? Who do the people have to listen to but those fools?"

Obadiah lowered his head, looking now only at his feet, as he began slowly stepping along the wall. He had learned keeping physical space between the King and an insistent petitioner as a survival skill. If he did not survive, then the people he was sheltering would not survive. But Jehonadab had already told me what he thought of kings in general. His family was secured away in the wilderness, and he had adopted bluntness as his weapon, just as Obadiah had selected tact. Jehonadab continued his attack.

"Who do these people have for teachers, Jehu? These besotted wretches drenched in the vomit they have the gall to call prophecies? You have seen the Temple in Jerusalem, Jehu. You have seen the sacrifices they offer and were told of the reasons for them. You have learned of the Law of Moses, at least you know there is such a thing. What do these people know?"

As Jehonadab stepped closer to me to make sure I was not missing his point, Obadiah stopped walking, this time turning to look squarely at the agitated Jehonadab.

"All these people know is what they hear from Jezebel's priests," continued Jehonadab. When a prophet of the Lord shows up to condemn their king, they are confused, and their confusion is compounded when Jezebel's priests mock the prophets. And when the Lord's prophets flee from the wrath of their king and the ire of Jezebel, how can the people stand?"

Obadiah stood looking squarely at me, a look I had never seen him give to Ahab or Jezebel. I spoke to Jehonadab,

"The priests and the prophets of Baal turn the people away. And yet the priests of Baal continue to walk the streets of Samaria."

The temples of Baal had been such a fixture in Samaria for so long that it took Jehonadab's words for me to remember that there was a reason why those temples were here, and now that reason was gone. "What claim do the temples of Baal have in the land of Israel?" I asked looking directly at Obadiah. I expected Obadiah to turn away and pretend that my question was directed toward Jehonadab; instead Obadiah maintained his gaze and responded.

"It was by leave of the King," he said, pausing briefly for emphasis, "and of the Queen."

It would have been Obadiah's position in the palace to recite to the King the history of a royal grant without jeopardizing his position, but the firmness of his reply indicated he stood with Jehonadab.

"And it was by direction of the Queen and the King that the prophets of the Lord were expelled," interjected Jehonadab. "And it was the kings who maintained the golden calves in Dan and Bethel."

I pursed my lips and gazed back into the fires. Hadn't I done enough for one day? I was not eager to get drawn into Jehonadab's old gripes about the golden calves or the Temple in Jerusalem. I had never known the land without either the golden calves or the Temple in Jerusalem. I was suddenly exhausted. I knew that after one decision, there would be another one called for and then another. I began to long to be back in the camp with the army. I did not bother to look at Obadiah to see his reaction. I knew of the masks that courtiers wore in front of the King. I drew in a breath, hoping the smoke would remind me of a campfire ringed by army tents, but I could only smell charred flesh.

"Tomorrow," I said, "we will talk of the golden calves."

Jehonadab and Obadiah maintained their gazes on me, waiting for a further word, perhaps hoping that I would include the temples of Baal in tomorrow's agenda, but I remained silent. The young prophet had anointed me to do away with the House of Ahab, and I had done so. Was there more to do? My zeal had been exhausted.

The next day the last smoldering embers of the fires outside the walls were put out and the ashes dug up and loaded onto carts to be hauled far from the city. Even Jehonadab and Obadiah seemed exhausted and were content in dealing with minor affairs and tedium. The entire city was quiet, waiting to see if the next day would see more uproar or peace. I toured the royal palace guided by Obadiah. He pointed out the numerous rooms and niches dedicated to the adoration of one deity or the other, describing in graphic detail the rites demanded by that god or the other. The soldiers' campfire descriptions of these practices proved surprisingly accurate. Jezebel had retained the quarters she had shared with King Ahab, forcing Joram to build new quarters for his rule. Jezebel's quarters could have been mistaken for a most luxurious temple.

After a day of tedium and peace, riders dashed up from Jezreel, bringing news from Jerusalem.

MY ROYAL FAMILY

Jehosheba

Alas my mother, that you gave me birth. Jeremiah 15:10

M Y father was a murderer; that was my heritage. Not only was my
father a murderer, my mother had instigated and planned the
murders. And the victims? All of my uncles in Jerusalem, the brothers
of my father. And had my mother acted on her own? Or had she been
guided by my grandmother of Samaria, Queen Jezebel? My grandmother
of Jerusalem had told me how she had protested to her husband King
Jehoshaphat against the evils of Athaliah, before Athaliah was married
to Jehoram. All of my brothers had been killed by raiding Philistines and
Arabians in a sudden raid against Jerusalem, an attack my father the King
was powerless or too incompetent to prevent. I bluntly told an old priest
that if he had been better at his craft, the Lord would have preserved
my brothers. The old priest was gentle with me. Perhaps he was merely
gracious in dealing with a fool, or perhaps he felt he was protecting the
Temple by not antagonizing the headstrong daughter of King Jehoram
and Queen Athaliah.

I found myself spending more time in my grandmother's isolated
quarters in the palace than with the King and Queen. I still maintained
many contacts in the royal quarters. Servants of the royal household had
raised and educated me and as one of the few surviving royal children
many made known their loyalty to me.

My marriage to the Temple priest Jehoiada had not decreased my
close contact with members of the royal household. The palace had long

established close contacts with the Temple hierarchy, especially under King Jehoshaphat who was intent on extending the influence of the Temple throughout the kingdom. While King Jehoshaphat's interest in the Temple waned in the later years of his reign, many of the channels established during his reign between the Temple and the royal household had a life of their own. There was a strong core group of the faithful in both the Temple and the palace, maintaining their loyalty to the nation as the Lord's chosen people regardless of the winds of change coming from the palace. These contacts allowed me to maintain my friendships in the palace. Other contacts with the members of the palace were maintained during their natural trips to the Temple to worship and sacrifice.

My contacts with the palace during this time were so frequent that admittedly some of the visits descended to gossip. The gossip was such that it was as if I was still living in the royal palace.

The darkness that descended over the kingdom during the reign of my parents Jehoram and Athaliah reduced everyone's strong opinions to whispers, and many who would listen in earlier days would turn away, as if hearing protests against the royal household would somehow implicate them. But several committed whisperers from the palace allowed us to see how close to death my father Jehoram was with his bowel disease, and what to expect during the reign of my brother Ahaziah. We wondered how worse things would get under Ahaziah and feared for the kingdom itself. Ahaziah had been cast in the mold of Athaliah, but had no experience other than losses chasing defeats under his father Jehoram. Having learned nothing of benefit from his father, he was totally in the grip of our mother Athaliah; and being younger than me at twenty-two years of age he had not developed any power base of his own.

Despite the reduction of the realm, the temple of Baal in Jerusalem was enlarged and expanded every year. Houses were torn down to enlarge its courtyards, streets were widened to accommodate the ever-increasing and regular processions to the temple and markets relocated away from Solomon's Temple to better serve the temple of Baal. There were whispers of plans to strip some of the marble work and cedar and juniper from Solomon's Temple for use in a new addition to the temple of Baal. The temple of Baal thus would have marble from King David and cedar and juniper from King Hiram of Tyre, a perfect marriage of Phoenicia and Israel. This would be an unholy sacrilege, but Jerusalem was being remade into the image of Samaria, and the treasury, beggared by the loss of tribute payments that had been made to Jehoshaphat, was emptied to gild the temple of Baal.

Through the Temple guards' contacts with the army commanders in the palace, we knew of the plans of the royal court, probably led by Athaliah, for Ahaziah to join King Joram of Israel in his campaign against the Arameans. The Judean army commanders were in favor of this alliance. The senior army commanders that had not been killed in battle during King Jehoram's many military reverses had been executed at the insistence of Queen Athaliah as an excuse for Jehoram's incompetence. To the junior commanders remaining, maneuvering through palace intrigues became more important to their survival than military tactics. They welcomed the opportunity to learn some actual military skills in league with the experienced army of King Joram of Israel.

The Temple guard was more concerned with the effect of Jezebel on King Ahaziah than were the commanders attached to the palace. The Temple guard was devout and devoted to the Temple. The Temple guard had been created by King David, and was a hereditary position, passed on from generation to generation. The gatekeepers even predated the Temple, having served at the old Tent of Meeting. They protected the Temple, but saw their duty as serving the Lord. They were not attached to the army and answered to the High Priest, not the King and were paid out of the Temple treasury, not the royal treasury. During the rule of Athaliah they were an effective deterrent to any royal thought of asserting control over the Temple.

The priests selected by King Jehoshaphat and dispatched throughout the Kingdom had a strong impact on the population supporting Temple worship. Before the days of Jehoram and Athaliah we would hear of merchants traveling from the northern kingdom who knew little of the Laws of Moses and less about the Temple in Jerusalem. The priests in the Temple had sworn that this would not happen in the southern kingdom, and the Temple guard supported the priests in this regard. How long they would be able to hold out against the program of Jehoram and Athaliah before they may be forced to flee Jerusalem sometimes seemed in doubt, but the base laid by King Jehoshaphat was solid and even Athaliah realized that she would have to bide her time, that a direct assault against all her subjects held holy could result in an uprising.

When King Ahaziah took the army to rendezvous with King Joram at Ramoth-Gilead we all held our breath. Commanders of the Temple guard maintained close connections with a select few from the army, so we knew we would be able to receive reports from the campaign as promptly as the palace. Many thought the Kings' goal of deposing Hazael to be a pipe dream, some looked on it as a practice exercise, with the army of Israel in the van and the Judean army following along, learning how to conduct itself as an army.

Many in the Temple had deeper concerns. What would it mean for the armies of Judah and Israel to be joined for a campaign against a common enemy? The dream of a reunification of the twelve tribes, the reunification of the sons of Israel, had been all but extinguished during the period of incessant wars between the two kingdoms. The first time the armies of Judah and Israel acted in concert was when King Jehoshaphat joined with King Ahab in a battle for Ramoth-Gilead, and King Ahab was killed in battle as a result. Ahab and Jehoshaphat had been two strong kings, and few had any hopes then that the kingdoms would be reunited in the foreseeable future. When Ahab's incompetent son Ahaziah succeeded Ahab, no one expected anything to happen. Now, eight years later, the armies of Judah and Israel were allied for a second time. Now the dream of unification still seemed unlikely but less remote. But in the Temple there was great fear of this happening. Rather than a reunification of Israel's twelve tribes, the Temple feared the reunification of a nation under the sway of Jezebel in the royal palace in Samaria and Jezebel's daughter Athaliah in the royal palace in Jerusalem.

We hoped that at best the adventure at Ramoth-Gilead would strengthen our army and provide a military victory that the kingdom had not seen for years, but there were many other outcomes we feared. The actual outcome we could not have imagined.

A new concern had arisen when news came from the palace that a group that looked like an embassy had been dispatched by Queen Athaliah north. None of my contacts in the palace and none of Jehoiada's contacts through the Temple guard had any knowledge of the purpose of the embassy's mission. Over thirty people from the royal household had been sent out in this embassy, so it was more than a dispatch of messages. It reminded me of the embassies sent out by King Jehoshaphat that I was allowed to occasionally accompany as a child. But young King Ahaziah had not dispatched any embassies during the short time he was on the throne, and we all thought it very strange that an embassy, if this is what it was, was being dispatched from the palace while King Ahaziah was with the army on the battlefield. The only conclusion, but the one we resisted coming to, was that this was an embassy directed by Queen Athaliah, a thing we could not conceive of.

Just one day after the mysterious embassy left Jerusalem for Ramoth-Gilead, we received our first word from the army at Ramoth-Gilead. King Joram of Israel had been injured in the battle and had gone to Jezreel to recover. We thought maybe this would be the end of the expedition for this year. The army would withdraw having gained some positive field experience while suffering no losses, and possibly burnishing its reputation with our avaricious neighbors. The next dispatch that was relayed to the Temple seemed to support that conclusion. King Ahaziah had left the campaign at Ramoth-Gilead to join the injured Joram at Jezreel.

The next day a messenger knocked on our door shortly after dawn with whispered messages for Jehoiada.

"I must go to the Temple."

"What is it Jehoiada?"

"The priests are talking to a scribe from the palace."

"About what?"

"The embassy from the palace."

"What did he say?"

"He told his friend, a young priest, that he prepared scrolls for the embassy."

"Really? So we know what the embassy is for?"

"No. He won't say."

"Fear of the Queen?"

"Exactly."

"I must come with you."

"Why?"

"Why? Jehoiada! Really! I am the King's sister if you have forgotten. I know the royal household. I am coming with you."

When we arrived at the Temple, the scribe was being held in a small ante-room, sweating and trembling. A grey-bearded priest was standing in front of the scribe, arms folded, and two large Temple guards were towering over the pale faced scribe, barely giving him room to breathe.

"What have you learned?" asked Jehoiada.

"Nothing," snapped the old priest.

"I came to the Temple to worship. I came to the sanctuary of the Temple," interjected the scribe, not for the first time I assumed.

"That is all he will say," snarled the old priest.

"What will you do with me?" pleaded the scribe, succinctly putting the quandary we were all in. The Temple had sources in the royal palace, but they were willing and ingenious. This terrified scribe knew if he imparted the information in the embassy's scrolls it would be traced back to him, which led to his refusal to share his knowledge. This made the priest feel the scribe was untrustworthy, and now would not allow the scribe to return to the palace.

I pulled Jehoiada back and stepped in front of him.

"I am the daughter of King Jehoram, the sister of King Ahaziah," I said addressing the old priest, "Step back, I will talk to him."

The guards were truly taken aback. They knew who I was, but I had never asserted my royalty in their presence.

"Your highness," responded the scribe immediately, "Princess Jehosheba. I saw you in the palace. My father was a scribe for King Jehoram. I was younger then."

"We all were. Young scribe, if you know me, then you would have known of my uncles, all killed at the hand of Joram and Athaliah. Truly I understand your fear. You are right to believe that you will die a merciless death if Queen Athaliah learns that you have revealed the message."

"It is not my life I fear for. I have two children, a son and a daughter; they are being held at the palace. Every time I am called on to prepare an important message, my children and my wife are held in the palace until the message is delivered and until there is no suggestion that I have disclosed the contents."

"How does the palace decide when to release your family?"

"It is the palace. The palace decides when the palace decides."

"Can you tell me when you think the palace would be certain you have not disclosed the message you prepared for the embassy?"

The scribe looked back at me helplessly, wide-eyed and silent.

"Something terrible is going to happen isn't it?"

"Princess, my children. My children."

"This thing that is going to happen, it has to do with King Ahaziah and King Joram at Ramoth-Gilead?"

"Princess, princess, please."

"You are not saying anything that anyone doesn't know already. We are all waiting to see what happens at Ramoth-Gilead."

"But the fact that the message was sent out, princess, if the Queen learns that I even said that much, my children will die!"

"But you had already told your friend that much in the Temple before you were brought here," the old priest interjected, "don't tell us you cannot tell us what you gossiped with your friend."

"Priest," I scolded the old man, "this is a matter of the royal household. I am the sister of King Ahaziah. I will deal with this matter."

"What that Queen does in that palace has to do with the Temple of the Lord," railed the priest.

"Are you in the business of sacrificing children also, old man? Is that what your god demands?" I turned back to the scribe.

"Tell me where your children and wife are in the palace. I will go to the palace and bring them to the Temple. They will be safe here."

"But the Queen."

"The woman you call the Queen is not the Queen. King Ahaziah has a wife."

"The Queen is the Queen."

"Young scribe, you are afraid that if your name gets back to Athaliah your children will die. You think we will use your information and then drop you. Let me make you trust us. I will tell you something that would result in our death and our children's death if Athaliah learns of it. That way we will be forced to trust each other. Do you know Maaseiah son of Adaiah?" The Temple guards looked at me with horror.

"The commander of a hundred? I know him and see him every day in the palace."

"Maaseiah is in league with us. We stand against all that Athaliah is for. Now our lives are in your hands. And with Maaseiah we can save your children. Tell us where your children are. I will personally go with Maaseiah to take your children and wife to the Temple. Then you can tell us your message. Once it is safe, you can return to the palace with your children."

"But the Queen will know that my children are gone."

"The Queen knows what the guards tell her. She will not know. She is not your children's nursemaid. Are we agreed?"

"Agreed."

I turned to the old priest. "Summon Maaseiah from the palace. I must go there at once."

"But Jehosheba," protested Jehoiada, "can you show your face in the palace? And how can we trust this scribe? What if his talk is all nonsense? What if the message on the scroll he prepared has nothing to do with us?"

"The palace would not hold his children captive for nonsense. Look at this scribe's face. Whatever the message, it has etched it deeply. And Maaseiah is artful. Another woman tending to children in the palace will not stand out; a soldier carrying away an unwilling child will. And I know the palace. Who else would you send?"

"But is this worth it? Think of the risk. If you are caught, Athaliah will send troops to the Temple."

"You are more worried about the Temple than my life. That is your right. Athaliah's husband Jehoram was the worst King the people have ever known. They cling to the Temple as the only thing she has not soiled. If she attacks the Temple it will be her end."

It took some time for Maaseiah to reach the Temple. With his arrival, the scribe's scroll became more ominous.

"There is news," were the first words out of Maaseiah's mouth. "King Joram has been overthrown and Jezreel taken."

"Taken? Jezreel?" My mind was reeling. The battle was at Ramoth-Gilead. Jezreel is west of the Jordan. "Taken by whom? The Arameans?"

"No. It was the Israelites themselves. They struck down King Joram."

This was as hard of a blow as thinking the Arameans had overrun the armies.

"Joram slain? Who of the Israelites did this? Was it Jezebel? And what of King Ahaziah?"

"We know very little. Word of the death of King Joram came to the palace several days ago. Only a few people in Athaliah's court know of it. A chambermaid of Athaliah was finally able to get word out. Athaliah's chambers had been sealed to keep any word from getting out of the palace."

I turned to the scribe. "Your message. Can you tell us now?"

"Princess, my children."

"Why would King Joram's death be kept secret? I must get to the palace to secure the scribe's children. We must find out why this happened. That embassy must have something to do with King Joram's death."

Jehoiada then addressed the Temple guards in the room. "Secure the Temple. Athaliah should be in mourning for the death of her brother King Joram. Instead she keeps silent, hiding the death from the city. Whatever has happened does not bode well for the Temple."

❀   ❀   ❀

Entering the palace with Maaseiah was without incident. Maaseiah controlled who was admitted to the royal quarters and anyone who was with him was not challenged. Maaseiah had not heard that the wife and children of the scribe were being held, but he only had to talk to two guards to find out where they were. Maaseiah had seen the embassy being organized and sent, but information about its mission was closely guarded. With Maaseiah accompanying a woman to rooms near the royal nursery, we were unchallenged. Queen Athaliah was at one of her Temples at this hour, and would probably not be back until noon.

We found the scribe's wife with her two children in a pleasant room with a balcony overlooking an interior garden. They were being held as security and not as prisoners, and as family of a powerless scribe there was no real thought that anyone would try to secure their freedom. Maaseiah advised the guards that the family was being moved to a lower chamber, as the Queen had use for their quarters.

The scribe's wife quickly stuffed items in a sack for the move when another guard knocked on the door.

"The Queen is returning to the palace. Stay here until she has made her way to her quarters."

"Stay with the scribe's wife," instructed Maaseiah, "I will go out to see why the Queen is returning so early. Then we'll figure how to get you out of here."

Although Athaliah was my mother and I was a royal princess, I was rarely at the palace, and only if invited, and my presence would raise questions I was not prepared to answer.

While I waited with the scribe's wife I learned from her that the royal nursery had been relocated to the other side of the interior garden where the scribe's wife was being held. We could see small children playing on a balcony on the other side of the garden. King Ahaziah had four young children. I had only seen the oldest; the other three were strangers to me.

It was not long before noise from other parts of the palace carried into the small garden; unpalace like sounds, running feet, shouted orders, muffled, confused speech. Footsteps went past our door several times, then a rapping on our door.

"News from Maaseiah," said a voice from outside our door.

The scribe's wife opened the door and a soldier I did not recognize entered. He looked from the scribe's wife to me. I was not as well disguised as I thought as he turned immediately to me.

"You are Jehosheba?"

"Yes."

"There is news, terrible news. King Ahaziah is dead. The army is retreating from Ramoth-Gilead as if routed; they fear the army of Israel may turn on them."

I dropped to my knees. Ahaziah was my brother, as much as I opposed him; he was the last of my brothers. We were the only ones spared during the raids of the Arabians and Philistines into Jerusalem that almost toppled my father King Jehoram. I was now the only child of King Jehoram left.

"Where is Maaseiah?"

"He is with the guard. The Queen is in a rage. You are not safe here. She is in danger also," added the guard in a quiet aside to me, nodding toward the scribe's wife.

"Why?"

"The embassy was destroyed. The scribe's message was the last message to the embassy. They are all in danger. The Queen is not given to lengthy inquiries."

I thought back to the start of the reign of King Jehoram and Queen Athaliah. All of Jehoram's brothers had been murdered. Now Jehoram is gone, Ahaziah is gone, and Athaliah remains. Then it struck me. The only ones left of the line of David were those four young children in the royal nursery and me.

"The King's children; are they safe?"

The guard ignored my question.

"Maaseiah has ordered me to take you and the scribe's wife out of the palace."

"You can see the King's children on the balcony across from here."

The guard continued to ignore me.

"Pick up her children. We need to leave immediately. The Queen may be coming."

"Why would the Queen be coming here? She would not come here for the scribe's wife. Is it the King's children?"

"We must leave. We must leave immediately."

This time I ignored the guard. I picked up the scribe's youngest child, barely a toddler, and walked toward the door.

"We are going to the royal nursery. Follow me."

Even soldiers can be caught unaware. I was out of the door and down the hallway before the guard understood what I had said. As I was carrying her child, the scribe's wife dashed after me with her older child.

The guard had no choice but to follow, glancing up and down the hallway, realizing that now his life may be in danger. We walked down three hallways circling the interior garden and reached the royal nursery. A young palace guard was leaning against the wall in the hallway outside the royal nursery. He was not overly alarmed at two women with two children approaching him with a guard he knew.

"Is he with us?" I asked the guard following us.

Without responding to me our guard spoke to the younger guard, "Into the nursery with us, now."

The younger guard complied and followed us into the nursery. In the nursery there were three nursemaids attending the King's four children.

I spoke to the younger guard, "I am princess Jehosheba. Commander Maaseiah brought us here. We are taking the King's children to the Temple."

The young guard looked at the guard accompanying us.

"As she says," confirmed our guard, "and quickly, the Queen may be on her way up here."

"The King - is he . . . ," the voice of the nursery attendant trailed off as she looked toward the royal children in her charge.

"The King is no more." responded our guard. "The children - quickly."

Neither the younger guard nor the nursery attendants asked why the children should be moved to the Temple. Living in the royal household day after day, they knew the mind of the Queen and they knew what these children represented. The nursemaids quickly took hold of the children. One of the nursemaids struggled, trying to hold the hand of a three year old that was pulling away from her grasp, while carrying a very young child, under a year, who was arching his back, resisting being held.

"Take the child from her," our guard said to the young guard.

"The young child squirmed as the soldier grasped him around his middle, struggling against an unfamiliar touch.

"Let's go," snapped our guard. "Lead the way," he directed the young guard, who had set his lance down to carry his unfamiliar package. With the young guard in the lead, our guard marshaled his procession of five women and six children out of the nursery.

As soon as we were in the hallway, we could hear the shrill alarm coming from nearby, "Murder! Murder! Murder!"

It was the voice of Queen Athaliah, accompanied by the footfall of what must be several soldiers and retainers. I looked toward the direction of the voice and saw nothing. The young guard had rounded the far corner of the hallway and was out of sight, with the nursemaids and their charges following. I turned to follow, but after two or three steps heard Athaliah's voice again.

"Stop! Turn back! Seize them!" She was in the same hallway, her voice accompanied now by running footfalls as her soldiers ran past me and toward the nursemaids who were now rounding the corner of the hallway. Our guard who was at the corner turned around and drew his sword, causing the pursuing soldiers to stop and draw theirs; surprised by a colleague they knew.

"Strike him! Strike him down!"

The Queen's soldiers did not hesitate. Four of them were on the guard immediately, and he was felled by several hard, sickening blows.

"Seize them! Stop them!" screamed Athaliah at her soldiers as they rained their final blows on the guard, pointing to the corner around which the scribe's wife and nursemaids had just disappeared.

"Mother," I turned with the scribe's child in my arms, "the children." Queen Athaliah was now directly in front of me accompanied by at least five more soldiers.

"You!" she exclaimed, "You! Now you come to visit the palace? Have you heard of your brother? Dead! Our dynasty, slain! And you are here for the children? Whose child do you have there, my daughter?"

We were now feet apart as she asked her question. The young boy in my arms stared at the woman who had been screaming. I thought it odd that she asked who I was holding. Then it occurred to me that Athaliah had never seen my children, and never asked to see them, but in our patriarchy my children would not have been considered significant. Had she ever seen Ahaziah's children?

Then I did the unthinkable.

THE RENDITION OF JEHOSHEBA

Athaliah

They have poured out blood like water all around
Jerusalem, and there is no one to bury the dead. Psalm
79:3

T HE embassy had been sent to King Ahaziah in Ramoth-Gilead and
to Mother Jezebel in Jezreel several days ago. We had discussed
these matters in detail over six months ago when I had slipped out of
Jerusalem quietly with a small contingent and made my way to visit
Jezebel in Samaria. King Jehoram was a great disappointment to Jezebel.
He had turned away from Baal and devoted himself to those foolish
golden calves of his kingdom. The final stroke had occasioned Jezebel's
invitation for me to visit her in Samaria; Joram had smashed into rubble
the great pillar to Baal that father Ahab had erected in Samaria. Baal's
pillar had even attracted adherents from Jerusalem.

The hope we had of unifying the northern and southern kingdoms
under my late husband King Jehoram of Israel had grown fainter each
year of his reign. Split between the golden calves of the north and the
Temple of Jerusalem in the south, we would not be able to unify the
people and priests of the north and south. Under Baal, we would be one
nation. United with Tyre and Sidon and in league with Ekron we could
dominate the region and beyond. These fools in Jerusalem with their
Temple could not forge any lasting alliances with any other kingdom that
did not serve their precious god, which none did, so they were doomed to
defend themselves alone against repeated assaults from all sides.

My son Ahaziah was loyal to Baal. He was young and inexperienced and naïve to our purposes, but he was our only hope. My other sons had been slaughtered by the massive raid into Jerusalem allowed by the incompetencies of my late husband King Jehoram. How the House of David had acquired its legendary fame was beyond me. King Jehoram was of the house of David and he was a dolt. How King Jehoshaphat had sired such a fool was beyond me.

The time was short and now was the time.

❁   ❁   ❁

The first word we received back after the embassy had been sent was encouraging but confused. King Joram had been wounded and was now in Jezreel, but whether he had been injured in battle or as a result of some action taken by our embassy was not clear. Our palace guard and the army commanders who had remained in Jerusalem were put on alert, but only as a precaution. If Joram had been wounded as a result of an assassination attempt that had gone awry, the people would expect the royal palace to take precautions since Ahaziah was campaigning with Joram at the time. If Joram died from his unknown wounds, whether from battle or otherwise, we would wait for word from Queen Jezebel before proclaiming King Ahaziah King of a newly reunited kingdom. Yes, even if the Kingdom of their exalted King Solomon was re-established, these Judeans would object to the golden calves of their brothers from the north, to say nothing of the worship of Baal. But once King Ahaziah was King over all, what could they say? Who would dare speak?

The next word we received was also encouraging but still confused. King Joram was dead and had died at the hands of his army. But this did not come from Queen Jezebel. The death of Joram was to be our sign to proclaim King Ahaziah as King over Israel and Judah, but I needed word from the Queen. Once I made my proclamation, there would be no turning back. Upon the first word we would receive from Jezebel of King Joram's death, before it was announced to the public, we planned a royal procession to the temple of Baal in Jerusalem. This had not been done before. Trips to the temple of Baal were made quietly, like my trip this morning, so as not to offend the sensibilities of the inflexible Temple worshipers. A royal procession to the temple of Baal would be my less than quiet way of telling my subjects that change was in the wind.

My procession to the temple of Baal was interrupted at the entrance by a messenger accompanied by a detachment of the palace guard, an unusual development, since my procession already included several members of the palace guard, although they were in the procession as a subtle show of force and not really for security. My world began to unravel as the messenger approaching me scroll in hand prostrated himself before me as we stood on the steps of the temple. No messenger had ever approached me in this manner. In a rage, King Jehoram had the messenger dispatched who brought him news of the raid on the undefended Jerusalem and the death of his children. That image appeared before me as soon as the messenger began to go to his knees, as if his message would cost him his life.

"Get up. What is your message?"

The messenger remained prostrate, not even trying to look up.

"I have a scroll for you, your worship."

"I know you have a scroll, you fool. Stand up and read me your scroll."

The messenger rose slowly, still not raising his head, as if I were going to take his head off if I recognized him. I knew then that this message was more than just a lost battle, cities besieged or treasures lost. My mind, dazed, wandered back to the loss of my children by the raiders.

The messenger, rather than opening the scroll and reading from it, raised in his hand a leather pouch, draw string still pulled tight, offering it to me. I motioned to a eunuch standing just behind me and said to him, "Take the scroll. Open it for me."

The eunuch stepped forward and took the leather pouch from the messenger and tugged roughly on the knotted draw strings until he could open the pouch. I looked away, as if by not seeing the scroll its words would not come true. I could hear the eunuch removing the seals from the scroll.

"The scroll, my lady?"

The eunuch held the unsealed but unopened scroll in his hand, wondering if he should read it or hand it to me. I looked at the scroll for the first time, staring at it, hoping the words on it would melt away. Finally I held out my hand to the eunuch. I decided it was better to see the message myself rather than having the words read in public. I put iron in my face. I would not betray the words of the message on a public street.

The eunuch put the scroll in my hand and stepped back with a bow. The messenger was taking several steps back from me. I unrolled the scroll and shook my head nonchalantly, as if tossing a strand of hair that was not there out of my eyes. The scroll was a mess; passages scratched out, newer passages hastily sewn over on top of older passages. The stained and rumpled piece of hide looked like horses had trampled over it.

To Queen Athaliah of Judea, in Jerusalem

Then there was a patch of a rougher surface rudely stitched over an original message:

This message was on its way to you when the rebel Jehu performed even greater treachery than originally written in this message. All of our cause in Samaria were forced into hiding and this message was hidden. For a time no one would risk carrying this message out of the city, so it was buried until we could find a messenger willing to risk carrying a message to you.

My Queen, in Samaria at this time, to be seen in alliance with the royal House of Ahab is to risk certain death.

If you received our earlier messages, then you know that the rebel Jehu, an army commander of the army of Israel and commanders supporting him have mounted a rebellion. It was at the hand of Jehu that King Joram was killed.

My Queen, great tragedy has followed great treachery.

After the patch, the original message continued on the smooth, still glistening skin:

My Queen, the rebel Jehu has also slain Queen Jezebel in Jezreel.

My Queen, this Jehu has also slain all of the members of the embassy you so recently sent to Ramoth-Gilead.

My Queen, even this treachery was not great enough for this soldier Jehu to commit, so he performed even greater acts of treachery.

My Queen, it is with great sorrow I must tell you that this Jehu has also slain your son, King Ahaziah of Judah.

Even more, all of the royal heirs of the House of Ahab in the city of Samaria and throughout the entire kingdom have been slain at the hand of this Jehu. Your great supporter, the governor of the city of Samaria, was slain because he was harboring and protecting your son King Ahaziah. The rebel Jehu has raced through the entire city of Samaria with the sword, cutting down every supporter of the House of Ahab.

At an assembly of the city called to witness his executions,
the rebel Jehu said he was anointed by a prophet of the Lord to
put an end to the House of Ahab.

My Queen, few supporters of the House of Ahab can be
found in Samaria, and all are in hiding. Those few left that we
know about are with Queen Jezebel's prophets of Baal as they
make plans to flee the city.

Below these words written in the hand of a royal scribe were
scrawled words difficult to read:

Since we first tried to send this message out, we have become
more isolated and our position more precarious. To attempt to
send more messages would put us in more danger. There may be
no more news in any event.

I have been in many public assemblies that called for my presence as
Queen. I knew how to control my expression and demeanor. As I silently
read the scroll, any thought of control or demeanor escaped me, but I
gave no hint of any expression. Each word of the scroll was like a blow,
striking me speechless and mindless. I could not understand how these
words could be so. Each sentence was an unconnected, senseless mumble
of script. I silently rolled up the scroll in my hands. My face was hot and
flushed, my eyes dry. My brother, King Joram of Israel, slain. I handed
the scroll back to the eunuch without looking at him. My mother, Queen
Jezebel, slain. I walked back down the steps of the temple. My son, King
Ahaziah of Judah, slain. Without a word or gesture I turned up the road
to the palace, oblivious to the confusion of my procession trying to reform to follow me to an unknown destination.

I do not recall walking back to the palace. I do not recall who accompanied me. I know I was silent the entire way. I know no one talked
to me. Just inside the royal quarters I collapsed, my body wracked by
sobs, then retching. The entire message of the scroll collapsed on me like
the columns of a temple in an earthquake. Then I began screaming, railing against the message, and with each scream my anger grew. Mother
Jezebel dead. My son Ahaziah dead. Murdered. And a nameless rebel
slaying the entire House of Ahab.

"No, this cannot be, no! The King of Judah murdered when his army
was with him? Queen Jezebel murdered? The House of Omri wiped out?
None of my relatives survive? None?"

I could see my attendants shrinking from me. I did not care. Would they murder me now? Did they see an opportunity to rid themselves of their feared Queen? I did not care. All were dead, all! Would it matter if they struck me down as well? I tried to think of who to summon. Every name I would call on in such an event had been sent on the embassy to Ramoth-Gilead and Samaria. All my confidants, all those I trusted to share my plans with mother Jezebel had been struck down. They were to join in with Jezebel's favorites in proclaiming Ahaziah King of the realm, of kingdoms north and south. They would form a triumphal procession from Samaria to Jerusalem with the captive King Joram where Joram would be stuck down on the steps of the Temple of Baal. Jezebel would control the northern kingdom in the name of King Ahaziah; alliances negotiated in secret with Tyre, Sidon and Ekron would be proclaimed, and in a few short years, our supporters in those kingdoms would proclaim Ahaziah King of an empire. Ahaziah? The weak child, King? And mother Jezebel would not live forever, then . . . then . . . .

I had collapsed somewhere in the palace. I was exhausted by fury and fear, anger and despair. Then the words of the scroll came back to me. The rebel Jehu had claimed that a prophet of the Lord had anointed him; anointed him to put an end to the House of Ahab. A prophet of the Lord, that god in the Temple. That god these Judeans refused to even name. That god and his precious House of David. That god who had said "put an end to the House of Ahab."

Now I knew what I had to do. Did that god want to fight with Baal? Then we will have a battle.

"Guards," I screamed, "guards!"

The guards of the royal palace knew their duties. By now they knew of the contents of that cursed scroll. They knew that their King had been struck down. My guards had been selected and rewarded for their loyalty to me. They knew that my mother and my son had been struck down by a rebel in Samaria.

"Follow me! All of you!"

So that god of the Temple in Jerusalem would wipe out the entire house of Ahab? Then I will battle with that god. Did that god realize what a thin reed his vaunted House of David was? Did he not know that King Ahaziah was the only son of that royal line and his rebel Jehu had struck him down? And his heirs? Did that god know where the heirs of King Ahaziah were? All of them? All of them in one place? I did.

I rushed down corridors and up staircases to the royal nursery. As we reached the hallway by the nursery we could see more treachery afoot. A guard with women and children were rushing away from the nursery. So that god wanted a contest.

"Seize them!" I screamed, "Seize them all!"

The guard fleeing with the women drew his sword, but was immediately struck down. Treachery upon treachery; a guard in the royal palace raising his sword against the Queen's guard.

"Seize them. Bring them all here! All of them! Who are they?"

The five women with the children offered no resistance. Then I saw the source of this treachery. My own daughter Jehosheba was carrying one of the children from the nursery. I needed to question no one to find out what was afoot. They were in league with the rebel Jehu. The House of Ahab would be wiped out and these children would be proclaimed the House of David and claim the throne. Had I not arrived at the nursery the moment I had, I would have been struck down by the end of the day by these protectors of the House of David. Baal had certainly protected me.

"Who is that child? Who are these children?" There were five children before me. Ahaziah had four children.

I recognized one of the women who would on occasion accompany one of the older children when I would visit my son King Ahaziah. I walked directly up to her. She was holding the hand of a young boy

"Are these the children of King Ahaziah?"

That useless milk cow could only stammer. I turned to a young woman holding a young child.

"Who is that child?"

"This is my child, my Queen."

"What is your child doing in the royal nursery? No other children are allowed in the royal nursery while the King is on the battlefield."

The woman was not a skilled conspirator. She had no answer, and looked at Jehosheba. Jehosheba was also carrying a young child.

"You come to the palace now, at a time of great treachery my daughter?"

"Mother," she said, the children, the children of my brother Ahaziah."

"And is that your child also, my daughter?"

"No mother, it is Ahaziah's youngest, Joash."

The young woman I had just spoken to gasped, "No, no. That is my child also. That is my child."

I turned back to the old milk cow, the one I had seen in the palace.

"Speak and live. Are these other four the children of Ahaziah?"

The old hag looked at me terror stricken, speechless.

"Speak or be stricken. Are these the four children of Ahaziah?"

The hag continued to stare at me, but then murmured, "yes."

"Strike them down," I screamed, "all of them! Cut them to pieces. Strike them! All of them! Regicide! Regicide! They are in league with that rebel Jehu. Strike them!"

My guards began their work with my first words. It was easy work. The women and children fell like leaves. My soldiers were masters with the sword. I was showered with the blood of the House of David. The butchery was a gruesome sacrifice.

"Put them in baskets - every last shred of them in baskets! Wash this floor. Not a drop is to remain in the royal palace. Take them all to the temple of Baal and burn them to ashes. Not one last scrap is to remain to be crowned king."

My sandals were soaked in the blood of the last of the House of David. Who had triumphed now?

And my daughter, Jehosheba. Plotting against her own mother. Treachery upon treachery. Why was I not surprised? Married to a powerful priest in that Temple in Jerusalem. I had hoped she would someday be my road to controlling the Temple. But instead she had invaded the royal palace and sought to smuggle out a usurper to the throne. Now she is in that bloody procession to the temple of Baal. Soon all that will remain of those hacked and dismembered body parts will be in the smoke of a dynasty that is no more wafting through the grounds of Baal's temple.

I am Queen. Who can challenge me now? And my dynasty? My empire? I do not know. I will ask Baal for help. I will wait. There may be a time my army will be able to ride against that usurper, that murderer, that regicide, that Zimri in the north.

JEHOHADAB IMPRISONED

Jehu

I have done nothing to deserve being put in a dungeon.
Joseph, Genesis 40:15

THE royal palace was now mine. All of the commanders of the army had pledged their loyalty to me. I had met with the few remaining elders of the city who had not cast their lot with the House of Ahab. I had appointed a new governor of the city. I had visited the dungeons of Samaria to see if any prophets of the Lord were being kept there. I found none.

I had expected that the young prophet from Elisha's household who had anointed me at Ramoth-Gilead, or maybe Elisha himself would visit me in Samaria, but none did. "Strange, those prophets," I thought, "they perform wonders, they antagonize me and confront me at every opportunity while I am serving King Ahab and King Joram, but after one of them anoints me King, and after they task me with wiping out the entire House of Ahab they abandon me. Where is the word of the Lord now," I wondered to myself.

I kept watch during my first few days as King in Samaria, relearning what I thought I knew about the royal city. I had Jehonadab read Athaliah's scroll to me several times as we discussed what we saw in Samaria.

I discovered that there were many in Samaria who had silently served the Kingdom of Israel and not the House of Ahab. They maintained a form of loyalty to the House of Omri for the strength and stability Omri's reign had given to the Kingdom. I knew many who had done unspeakable things to survive in the city under Ahab and Jezebel. Some had the courage to come to me to confess the lands they had taken and slaves they had made at the direction of one royal prince or the other. There was great fear and great shame at the same time. Some had such great guilt for what they had done that they seemed eager to be punished for their acts. There was no one left from the House of Ahab to protect them anymore. Perhaps they felt it was safer to beg for mercy than to be found out later.

I needed to extirpate this great sense of dread of an impending judgment from their new King many of these people had. Anyone who had advanced the scheme of Jezebel had been struck down. There was no one to defend them. If this feeling lingered, it would fester into resentment and hatred of the King. Eventually, some may prefer to strike out against me rather than live in day to day fear of a sudden judgment that would fall and crush them without warning.

There was a large group in Samaria that did not share this sense of guilt or resentment. They had served loyally and diligently. Every day they would be about their duties without fail. They were such an engrained feature of Samaria that Samaria would not seem like Samaria without them. And they were everywhere. Every time I spoke to an elder or official of the city, at least one of them would be present, lingering in the background. They were present in the markets and the courtyards, holding forth on this point or the other. They were such an institution and a fixture in Samaria that they never imagined how out of place they looked.

When Joram became King, they fell out of favor in the royal palace, but with Queen Jezebel in the city, they were protected. Queen Jezebel would hold court in their temples. It was almost as if there were two royal palaces with two royal courts; King Joram in the royal palace and Queen Jezebel in the temple of Baal.

The prophets of Baal were neither princes from the House of Ahab, nor officials of the royal court, nor commanders of the army, and although they administered many facets of the kingdom, they did so in the shadows, acting in the name of titular officials. As such they had escaped both the first beheadings in the city and the final bloodletting. They had no claim to the throne and no powerful office. They could dispatch no soldiers and issue no decrees, but they had been ingrained with each and every faction in the city which had advanced a candidate to succeed King Joram.

While their retainers had been eliminated, the prophets of Baal retained the conspiracies they had furthered. And they were experts in conspiracies. They had all been in Queen Jezebel's service. They were not just in the households of those who had sided with Jezebel, they were in every household. Athaliah's message from Judah indicated that Jezebel would bring to an end the reign of her son King Joram and replace him with King Ahaziah of Judah, who would reign over both Israel and Judah. Other heirs from the House of Omri and Ahab would take exception, and the prophets of Baal in their households had advised Queen Jezebel of their exceptions.

The Samarians viewed me as excessively cruel in my elimination of the House of Ahab. That a prophet of the Lord had given me leave to take such action made no impression on them. The Kings of this kingdom had always found any number of prophets willing to justify any action a royal heart desired. It would do no good to suggest to them that an equally horrible end would have been coming to them at the hand of Queen Jezebel as she put her plan of succession into action. Nor would it matter if I told them that the executioners of the Queen's plan would be her prophets of Baal; that those prophets of Baal they took to be so harmless would bind them and drag them off to the temples of Baal and to be sacrificed there as a cruel offering to Jezebel's god in a great celebration of the ascension of King Ahaziah of Judah to the throne of the House of Omri.

I was speaking with Obadiah and Jehonadab and the newly appointed Governor of Samaria about the prophets of Baal remaining in Samaria. Jehonadab was all in favor of ejecting them all from the city and forcing them to march back to Tyre and Sidon where most of them had been recruited after Elijah had wiped out their predecessors. Obadiah recommended that I assemble a council of the remaining elders of the city to discuss what to do with the prophets. The governor of the city held his tongue. The governor was familiar with all the prophets of Baal, and knew which ones had associated with which faction of the House of Ahab, but expressed no opinion.

"Governor, I do know that these prophets of Baal were running between the differing camps in the city after I had sent my messages to the city. Jehonadab was in the city before it fell, he saw this happening."

"My King, they are like household servants. They are given messages and told to deliver them and they do."

"And these prophet servants were also in the royal palace with Queen Jezebel, were they not? And after the Queen had met her end, they remained in the palace. And after my messages to the city, with no King Joram and no Queen Jezebel, they remained in the palace and they continued to take messages throughout the city."

"A servant remains in the household after the death of the master. Where were they to go?"

"Governor, you heard me read the message from Queen Athaliah of Jerusalem to Queen Jezebel. This new kingdom of Jezebel was to be united in the worship of Baal. Do you see the fortunes these prophets and their temples would reap if Jezebel succeeded?"

"But they are essential to the kingdom," replied the governor. "A royal heir may be in charge of the royal treasury or the granary of the city, but a prophet of Baal and the temple he is assigned to handles the actual transactions. The kingdom continues to function without the House of Ahab because the prophets of Baal are charged with the actual duties. The royal heir charged with running the city's granaries probably knew nothing about the granary other than the bread he shoved in his mouth. It has been this way since the early days of Queen Jezebel. To force them out would weaken the entire kingdom."

"What the governor says is true," says Obadiah. "That is why we need to call an assembly of the elders. We need to make sure that there are people in place capable of carrying on the business of the kingdom before the prophets of Baal are sent away."

I then realized that the battle was not yet over, but my attack had come to a standstill. "It is as if Jezebel's conspiracy lives on after she has died. And if it continues to grow even though Jezebel is gone, then we have won nothing."

"The people worship Baal because they are led by the prophets of Baal," interjected Jehonadab, "and under King Joram some returned to the golden calves in Dan and Bethel. If the prophets of Baal are gone, they will all turn to the golden calves. They need to be led back to the Temple in Jerusalem. We need priests from the Temple in Jerusalem in this kingdom."

Jehonadab had always reminded me of Elijah and Elisha, but never so much as now. We may have been battling Moab or Aram, but those prophets kept harping on the Law from the Temple in Jerusalem. Now we were talking about Jezebel's prophets of Baal still in control of the kingdom, and Jehonadab keeps strumming his tune about the Temple in Jerusalem and the golden calves. I did not have time to consider the golden calves.

"If we call an assembly of the elders, the prophets of Baal will be the first to know what we are considering. And if they hear that we are discussing their fate, they will not be led like lambs. That is a bad strategy. We need to strike first. I have been delivering the first blows since I was anointed. I need to strike the first blow again."

Obadiah, Jehonadab, the governor and I decided to take a casual stroll through the city, to review the barracks, the markets, the armories, the weavers and even the temples of Baal. I needed to see for myself where the prophets of Baal were. The governor was not wrong in his assessment. There were more prophets in the marketplaces than in their temples.

Our tour was cut short when a courier caught up with us and advised me that a rider from Jerusalem had arrived at the palace with news. I was afraid I had been caught napping. I had killed their King, Ahaziah. Sentries at our border would certainly alert us to any retaliatory raid from the South. But from what I saw of their commanders at Ramoth-Gilead, I could not think of any one Judean commander who would hazard a raid over the border without a king.

"Jehonadab," I asked on our way back to the palace, "you were in Jerusalem before the last lambing season. Who will take young King Ahaziah's place? Certainly none of his sons are old enough to mount a horse."

"The scroll, Jehu. The scroll. King Ahaziah had four sons but they are all very young. The Queen in the south is Athaliah, the one who wrote the scroll you have studied so closely."

Jehonadab was right. When we arrived at the palace the courier from Jerusalem was ushered in to see us. He was not carrying any scroll, parchment or tablet, nor was he one of our soldiers. I was relieved somewhat. If the Judean army was advancing, a soldier would be bringing the news. Obadiah whispered to me that the courier was a priest from the Temple in Jerusalem, but an actual envoy from Jerusalem would be carrying a written communiqué.

"My King," he said bowing. I had been King for a few days now and already I was tiring of these royal formalities. I needed to hear the message.

"What word do you bring? You have come from Jerusalem?"

"I have. I have been sent by Jehoiada, priest in the Temple of the Lord in Jerusalem."

"Does this priest have no scribe? You have no scroll from this priest?"

"I know the name of the priest Jehoiada," responded Obadiah, "he is in line to be High Priest one day."

"But no scroll, no writing, no seal? How do I know you bring word from this priest of yours and not from a temple of Baal in Samaria?"

The courier bowed deeply. "I have this word from Jehoiada. If it is not true, you have my life."

"That I do, courier, that I do. What is your message courier?"

"Jehoiada's message could not be written. If I were overtaken before I crossed the border with a message from Jehoiada to King Jehu, Jehoiada would certainly be struck down, as would I, my King."

"I will hear your message then."

"When word reached Jerusalem that King Joram, King Ahaziah and Queen Jezebel had been slain, and that the embassy from Queen Athaliah had been wiped out, Queen Athaliah put to death the children of King Ahaziah, her son. Queen Athaliah also put to death her own daughter, the princess Jehosheba, the only sister of King Ahaziah. King Ahaziah had no brothers. Even more, my King, the bodies of King Ahaziah's children and of the princess Jehosheba were taken to the temple of Baal and burned on the altar there as a sacrifice to Baal."

"Leave it to a priest," I thought, "to include the nature of the funeral arrangements in his message." All I needed to know was that the heirs of King Ahaziah had been killed.

"Queen Athaliah has taken the throne of King Ahaziah," the courier continued, "no one is in a position to challenge her."

"Your nation has no army, courier, no commanders?"

"My Lord, that was my message from the priest Jehoiada."

"Are you a soldier, courier?"

"I am attached to the Temple guard."

"Will the army obey this Queen Athaliah?"

"There is no one else. None of King Ahaziah's brothers survive. And Ahaziah's sons . . . ."

"Yes, I know, children, and dead. But your army commanders, is there not one willing to stand up to your Queen?"

"All the commanders but those in the Temple guard were appointed by Queen Athaliah because of their loyalty. They have no experience in battle in any event."

I turned to Obadiah. "Why is that, Obadiah?"

"My lord," responded the puzzled Obadiah, "why do they have no experience in battle?"

"No. Why did a prophet anoint me King of Israel? Why is there no prophet in Judah to anoint a king over Judah? Now the daughter of Ahab and Jezebel reigns over Judah."

"My lord," chimes the now excitable Jehonadab, "you were anointed to put an end to the House of Ahab. The Queen Athaliah is a daughter of Ahab. Is your work done? Can the House of Ahab be allowed to rule Judah?"

I looked at Obadiah. He was aghast. No, confused, then aghast. "What do you say Obadiah?"

"My lord, I am in charge of the royal household. Armies and war are beyond me. You have erased the House of Ahab in Israel. We were just talking about the prophets of Baal and then the golden calves. And now this news of Athaliah in Jerusalem." Obadiah's palace reserve was slipping. The events were more than he could take in.

"My lord," adds the governor of Samaria, "if this messenger's words are true, Athaliah has performed your task for you. The sons of Ahaziah have been murdered at her hand. Where are the heirs of Ahab other than Athaliah?"

I pondered for a moment. "Jehonadab, I was anointed King of Israel. I have slain the House of Ahab. Athaliah remains, but she is now child-less. Will she bear another heir? I do not know. But the Kingdom of Israel is my charge. One thing I heard of this courier's message. Something neither you nor Obadiah have mentioned. But it is the most troubling thing I heard him say. The sons of Ahaziah have been slain and burned in an offering to Baal. The House of David. Gone. How can that be?"

Jehonadab, Obadiah and the governor of Samaria stared at me, wordless. The courier looked from one to another, hoping for an answer to my question, but none came.

"I am the King of Israel. I do not know what this means either. But I know it must be answered. I will not answer it with an army. I will not rip these two kingdoms apart as in the times of Baasha and Asa. I will not sacrifice the sons of this people to avenge the sins of Athaliah. But I know now what I must do. The priests and the prophets of Baal overrun this city and listen to every conference of the elders of the city, and every whisper in every hidden alley. Now they will hear that the House of David has been consumed on the altar of Baal. Is that a signal from Athaliah to them? The House of Ahab has been slain and in answer the House of

David has been slain. And who remains? Athaliah of the House of Ahab. The House of Ahab triumphing over the House of David? Who will the prophets of Baal in Samaria side with? With Jehu the rebel anointed by a prophet of the Lord? Anointed by a prophet who was trained by another prophet who struck down four hundred and fifty of their brothers on Mount Carmel? The battle has just been joined I tell you, and I am slumbering on my throne. Obadiah, summon the scribes. Make sure the scribes you select are devoted to the temples of Baal. They should not be too hard to find. I will issue a decree. In two days we will hold a great festival for Baal. We will dedicate this city to Baal. Then I will issue a greeting to Queen Athaliah, from one newly crowned monarch to another, congratulating her on her triumph."

"My lord," gasped the startled Jehonadab, "the House of David! She destroyed the House of David! You cannot honor her for that most unholy - - -"

"Guards!" I shouted, "take this man away! Put him in the dungeon. He will answer for opposing the King's word."

"My lord, my lord," protested the befuddled Jehonadab, "honor Baal? How can you honor Baal? It was the Lord who anointed you."

Jehonadab, the rustic without guile was always too straightforward. He was the perfect foil. Obadiah was well versed in palace intrigue. He had seen royals habitually lie, whether merely in jest or to conceal a murderous plot. They could not help it. Obadiah took control. Maybe I was being too obvious.

"I will see that he is well-confined, my lord," volunteered Obadiah. Then turning to the also befuddled governor said, "Governor, come with me, you will help me with the arrangements for the festival once I summons the scribes." Then in an aside to the courier who we had foolishly allow to loiter while we discussed his message in front of him, Obadiah said, "Come with me, I will fetch you an attendant. You can rest before we send you off with the King's message to Queen Athaliah."

Jehonadab was sufficiently enraged that several more guards had to be summoned to drag the bulky rustic out of the King's presence. The display Jehonadab put on would have generally have called for him to be cut down in the King's presence. Obadiah was careful to let the guards know that the King would enjoy seeing the rustic die a slow, agonizing death for his entertainment, so Jehonadab was carefully handled to avoid spoiling the King's enjoyment.

Obadiah had Jehonadab properly endungeoned, sufficient to communicate throughout the palace that the King's favorite had been imprisoned for opposing the great celebration the King was going to stage in the temple of Baal.

THE FINAL FESTIVAL

Jehu

Ahab served Baal a little; Jehu will serve him much. Jehu,
II Kings 10:18

J EHONADAB had toured the dungeons of the royal palace with me
shortly after we had entered the city. The few sorry souls remaining
there then were the forgotten remnants of a rotating crop of prisoners
who had been shuttled in and out of the dungeon as alliances against me
within the city were forged and broken. The dungeons had been stocked
again briefly after my second message to Samaria had resulted in the beheading of eighty souls, many of whom were not of the House of Ahab.
We had crammed the dungeons full again and then emptied them with
the executions on the threshing floor.

As I entered the dungeons with Obadiah this time there were few
noises echoing off the cool, damp stone walls and brick floors. Very few
had been imprisoned for breaching the King's peace since I had taken the
throne. We allowed anyone to wander the streets of Samaria and voice
their feelings, the better to draw them out in the open. An excrement-
covered mad man lay on the floor exhausted from his incessant wailing;
there was no place else to put him. Two enterprising merchants who had
set up stalls in the market, blatantly selling the household goods of a recently executed prince were being held, awaiting a decision of the elders.
Most inhabitants of Samaria, having seen the blood of the mighty spilled
on the threshing floor, kept to their houses and kept to themselves, not

333

knowing what action may offend the new King, thus avoiding any occasion for the dungeon.

We brought with us three soldiers from my personal guard. Jehonadab backed against the wall as he saw the three guards unlocking and unbarring the door to his chamber, ready to offer a fight if this was to be the last day of his life. When he saw me and Obadiah enter his chamber behind the guards, he slumped, puzzled that we would accompany his executioners, and still confounded that I would imprison him.

"Jehonadab," I said, "you must come with us quietly."

Jehonadab stiffened, sensing another betrayal. "Quietly? For what purpose? To the shearing?"

"I needed you surprised and angry. We do not know whether we can trust all of the palace guard. Even the new governor of the city is untested. Your resistance was very convincing. I was afraid I was going to have to jump into the fray. I can still whip horses, but it has been a long time since I was called on to do combat."

"I am imprisoned, my lord. Why?"

"After you were sent down here, I called all the people of the city out to the threshing floor again. They were terrified. They have seen so much bloodshed by my hand; it is all they expect now. Instead I told them that the reason I had overthrown the House of Ahab was that King Joram had refused to serve Baal."

"But my lord, you were anointed by a prophet of the Lord."

"I also told them that King Ahab had failed to serve Baal properly, that he had never decreed a proper regal celebration of the great god Baal. I announced that I will be sending a decree throughout the entire kingdom summoning all the prophets of Baal to Samaria. The sacrifices I will offer to Baal will put to shame the little celebration King Ahab put on for King Jehoshaphat."

Jehonadab looked at me as if I was a madman, incapable of uttering a rational thought. He could not think of anything to ask a madman.

"Jehonadab, I listened to your words about the prophets of Baal. They will all be assembled in one place. I need your sword with me when I execute judgment."

"My lord?" Jehonadab understood my words, but my reversal in his mind left him lost for words.

"The news of your objections to my face and your imprisonment spread through the city overnight. There was great rejoicing in the temples of Baal. When I announced my great sacrifice, it only increased their excitement. They will all be in one place, Jehonadab. We will not have to hunt them down. We will fall on them like wolves. I need a commander I can trust implicitly so no hint of our plan reaches the temple of Baal. I need you with me to lead our forces."

"Then I am with you my lord."

"Good. We are going to put a hood on you, so no one will see you being led out. One of the guards here is going to remain to take your place, so no word will get out that you are no longer here. Obadiah and I will leave ahead of you, then a prisoner no one knows will be led out. You will be brought to the barracks. Obadiah will meet with you there.

In anticipation of the great celebration, the city of Samaria began to fill up with the prophets of Baal. There were processions, celebrations and of course sacrifice after sacrifice and observation after observation in the many temples and shrines to Baal. Many ingratiatingly obsequious delegations from the several temples of Baal in the city came to the palace to invite me to their temples. They were eager for me to join in their temple rites to solidify my new found devotion to Baal. There was such a longing for their heyday under Jezebel before the death of Ahab, that they abandoned all caution. I asked not to be told of the rites they were performing in their temples, afraid that I would go out in the streets against them before we were ready.

The same priests of Baal that were storming into the city from across the kingdom had inveighed vigorously in the city when my messages had been sent to the city shortly after my anointing, encouraging coalitions and conspiracies, looking for a successor to King Joram with whom they could continue their rise to power. When I took the city, they were duly cautious with the new King who had done away with King Joram and his mother Jezebel, but they did not hide the extent of their influence in the city. They hoped that a show of their influence in the city would convince the new King that he could rule his capital city much easier with the help of their influence. Now they believed their own expectations, and could not believe anything other than that they had achieved their objective; the new King was theirs!

One week after my announcement to the city on the threshing floor, I decreed a grand observation in the central temple of Baal in the city. I decreed that all the minor shrines and subsidiary temples to Baal in the city be closed so as not to detract from the magnificence of the King's grand observation. Obadiah had arranged for a herd of cattle be driven through the center of the city to presage the magnificent sacrifices I would be offering and the feasting and celebrating that would follow. Oxen pulled wagons through the city up to the temple of Baal creaking under loads of the finest wines from Naboth's vineyards in Jezreel.

I set up court once again on the threshing floors of Samaria. Garlands of mint and hyssop were scattered over the threshing floors to mask the odor of recently spilled blood. Under my royal canopy I greeted and formally received the prophets of Baal who had already been in the city for days. Obadiah and his scribes sat with me keeping tally of the celebrants to make sure no outlying temple of Baal had decided to forgo the celebration.

On the day of the great celebration, I processed from the royal palace to the temple of Baal. Obadiah had overseen many such processions while Jezebel was Queen and he ensured that the prophets would recognize something they had not seen during the reign of Joram, the same procession that they had enjoyed under Jezebel. The prophets of Baal were entranced by a reverie of things as they had been before Joram neglected their temples and the welling and astonishing expectation that things were being restored to how they had been before Joram became King.

As I had never set foot in a temple of Baal before, I had Obadiah tutor me in the temple rites. Obadiah had the misfortune of accompanying numerous members of the House of Ahab to the temples of Baal to observe their rites, from the mundane to the gruesome to the obscene. As I sat in the seat of honor in the temple, watching the prophets assemble, I realized I was eager to finish my work, but had grown tired of the sword. I had come across bloodied and dazed soldiers at the end of a pitched battle swinging their sword wildly but with no purpose, exhausted, but fearful if they stop they would be struck down. Was I dazed? Was I swinging wildly?

I went through our charade of death with no feeling. The temple was crowded with prophets of Baal. I had seen many in Samaria, but I did not realize how many there were until they were gathered in one place. I was a spent soldier. I had seen so many severed heads, I had seen so many prisoners struck down, I had smelled the stench of so much ground soaked in blood that there was no force left in my sword. I was like a soldier who had withstood wave after wave of horsemen, chariots, arrows and swords swung behind shields, only to face yet another wave. I was weary of the slaughter, but felt that I was still fighting for my life.

I knew that these prophets of Baal had thrown themselves forcefully behind Jezebel's plans to bring Israel and Judah into Phoenicia's realm. With their champion Jezebel dead, they realized that they either had to find a way to survive under the new King or flee for their lives to Tyre and Sidon and abandon their objective forever. I had not received any overture fronted by the prophets of Baal since I entered Samaria. After having been driven by Jezebel for so many years, the prophets of Baal included many skillful sycophants, but no forceful voice capable of speaking for them all. The announcement from their new King suggesting a resurgence of Baal worship allowed them to delude themselves into thinking that the new King simply wanted to step into the shoes of Jezebel.

To this day I do not understand the minds of those prophets of Baal. They had all heard that I was anointed King by a prophet of the Lord. How could they think I would worship Baal? Did they not realize that the young prophet that had anointed me was of the same school of prophets that has followed Elijah, who had slaughtered more than four hundred of their brothers on Mt. Carmel? Yet there they were, line upon line, row upon row of prophets of Baal filing into the temple of Baal under the gaze of their new King.

Obadiah had an in-depth knowledge of who answered to whom in the community of Baal worshipers, and he knew the language they spoke. He had sent out carefully crafted messages, each one tailored to the predilections of its recipient:

> You know that the House of Elisha anointed Jehu. But Elisha's master Elijah also anointed Hazael, a worshiper of Rimmon. This anointing does not favor one god or another.
>
> Listen, Jehu has been a soldier all his life. He struck down everyone from the palace in a soldier's fury. Now he needs skilled people to govern his kingdom. We know you are the most skilled in your art.
>
> Jehu's quarrel was with Ahab and Jezebel, not with this god or that god. He felt poorly treated by Jezebel, and now needs your support. His supporters will be well rewarded.
>
> We know Jezebel wanted to push you aside for her favorites, but we can see your value. Support Jehu and your position will not be challenged.

Obadiah kept the scribes busy day and night, sending and receiving messages from the priests of Baal. Those accustomed to the royal favor believed so fervently in their own value to the kingdom that they were blind to the twisted deceit Obadiah sowed in his letters.

In their world of many gods, they may have believed that the Lord was effective to overthrow a king, but that Baal would be effective to control the kingdom. Maybe they believed that the orgy of rites and sacrifices Jezebel has overseen prior to Joram joining Ahaziah to battle Aram at Ramoth-Gilead had been effective to sway the mind of this Jehu to the side of Baal; that the mighty Baal would prevail even without his champion Jezebel.

Before the rites began, I brought out the ritual robes for these servants of Baal. I knew that a prophet of the Lord, a Levite or a priest from the Temple in Jerusalem would never don such an unclean garment. The laws of the Levites would have required that the robes be burned due to their exposure to the sacrifices to Baal. I did not want an enterprising spy from the prophets or the Temple in Jerusalem get caught up in the maelstrom I would be unleashing.

The temple's keeper of the wardrobe brought out the robes with great ceremony. The excitement in the temple began to swell. This was no mere lip service to Baal; the new King was not just going through the motions to please a group of his subjects. The sacrificial animals were visible in the wings, festooned with flowers and garlands. Incense was pouring into the chamber, torches were lit bringing mid day into the temple. Chanters were in full voice and dancers swirling through their rites. Vines and garlands swept overhead. The faces of the prophets of Baal were ecstatic as they put on their ceremonial robes.

I advanced to the edge of the platform supporting the altar and raised a decorated scepter of a sort I have never seen before and motioned to be heard. Obadiah stood behind me to my right.

"Look around and see that no one who serves the Lord is here with you—only servants of Baal."

The assembled prophets gladly complied. What an honor! Only true, stalwart devotees of Baal are being allowed to celebrate with the King of Israel in the temple of the mighty Baal. No interloper wishing to gain favor with the new King will be allowed to receive the honors reserved for the true, dedicated servants of Baal.

With Obadiah beside me to guide me, I ascended the stairs leading up to the main altar in the center of the temple. The sacrificial animals were brought up their ramp, and with my own hands, I slaughtered two oxen, three rams, three sheep and an eagle. Cheers and chants and yells went up from the adherents with every stroke to the jugular and every thrust to the heart. The fires flared over my head, stoked by bellows underneath the altar, forcing me to retreat from the altar several times, to the cheers of the assembly. A great column of smoke rose toward the opening in the ceiling, swirling around the altar and wafting over the assembly.

"How strange," I thought, "that this is the first time I have wielded a weapon since my arrow felled King Joram in his chariot outside Jezreel."

With great show I handed the sacrificial sword to Obadiah, who then handed it to the chief priest of the temple. I feigned that I had been overcome by the heat and the smoke of the fires, although it took very little pretense. Even those in the assembly standing close to the altar fell back as the sacrificial fires raged. Obadiah guided me by my arms down the steps of the altar, leading me into an antechamber to briefly revive me. The chief priest and his attendants were assured that I would return to the altar for the great conclusion of the ceremonies. I had been advised by Obadiah that on days of a great sacrifice, it was not unusual for the principal priest to be relieved part way through the ceremony due to the exertion of the slaughter and the heat from the flames and the smoke.

My descent from the altar was the prearranged sign for Jehonadab leading the eighty men stationed outside the entrances of the temple. The royal guard that had accompanied me to the temple drew no suspicion. The royal guard assured the prophets of Baal assigned to be gate keepers during the ceremony that they would guard the entrances to the temple so all the prophets could take part in the sacrifices and ceremonies.

Behind the royal guard were eighty of my foremost siege breakers, battle-hardened, ferocious troops that would be the first to hurl themselves from our siege towers onto the walls of the city we would be besieging to lay waste to the defenders on the walls and break through the city to open the gates to our forces. My instructions to them were simple, "If one of you lets any of the men I am placing in your hands escape, it will be your life for his life." This was not a harsh sentence to these loyal men, but, to them, a challenge. In their fight from the walls to the gates, they could leave no opponent behind them capable of wielding a weapon or they would feel that weapon in their backs. Their deadly art was to challenge, overwhelm, slay and move on quickly. Regular troops were reluctant to train with the siege breakers, because even with their weapons

sheathed in leather for training they would knock their opponents senseless and break bones.

Obadiah quickly ushered me out of the temple of Baal. Waiting
for me was the Jehonadab and the siege breakers. He already knew his
duty, but I took him by the shoulders and challenged him, "Go in and
kill them. Let no one escape."

The siege breakers stormed into the temple of Baal while the royal
guard remained posted at the entrances of the temple to make sure no
prophet of Baal got past the siege breakers. None did. By the time I got
into my chariot outside the temple of Baal, the siege breakers had begun
their work. The shrieks and wails slowly died out as the prophets were cut
down and as my horses strained to escape the sounds of carnage.

That night orange flames and black smoke billowed outside the walls
of Samaria once again. As the flames consumed the bodies of the priests
of Baal, their temple was torn down stone by stone. Every inscription,
carving and symbol from every single stone of the temple was chiseled
into dust.

I did not go out on the walls to watch the fires burn that evening as
many residents of Samaria did. I could hear the workmen at the temple
of Baal work through the night pulling down walls and columns. At times
the sound reminded me of siege machinery tearing into the walls of a
city. Fitting, I thought, the city that Jezebel and Ahab sought to build was
being torn down from inside the walls. I wanted all memory of that place
erased from Samaria as soon as possible. I wanted no child to be able to
ask, "What was that place?" It was Jehonadab's idea to turn the site of the
temple into a dumping station for the manure left on the streets of the city
by its horses and oxen. No child would have to ask what that place was.
If any adult pointed out the site to any child as the place of the former
temple to Baal, the name of Baal would be etched into the child's mind
with the smell of excrement. Kings desire to build monuments to regale
their bloated accomplishments. This was my memorial to Baal.

ATHALIAH'S PURGE

Jehoiada

Must the sword devour forever? Abner, II Samuel 2:26

B EING a priest, you may expect that I would remind you of the Law.
"You are to make no graven images, you are not to bow down and
worship them." How can something so simple be so difficult to understand? And yet even as King, Jehu of Israel could not bring himself to
break away from the golden calves of Jeroboam in Dan and Bethel. For
over a hundred years the golden calves of Jeroboam had been established
as the national god of those people of the north. Generation after generation habitually worshiped the calves. We did not think it could get worse
until King Ahab began building the temple of Baal in Samaria. Perhaps
Jehu took comfort that the golden calves were at least built by the people
of Israel. Jezebel had murdered the prophets of the Lord, but Jehu's adop-
tion of the calves blunted the peoples' minds and rendered them deaf to
voices of the prophets.

Athaliah's scroll, if there ever was such a thing, provided the impetus
for Jehu as he extended his slaughter well beyond the entire household
of King Joram. Some have said that they had seen Athaliah's scroll, but
even if they had actually seen a scroll, had Athaliah written it, or had
Jehu had it written for the benefit of the history of his rule? The scribe
we questioned in the Temple before Athaliah's purge had lost his wife
and children, murdered with Jehosheba, who was also cut down in the
palace with King Ahaziah's children. The scribe blamed their loss on the
Temple and Jehosheba, and not without cause, and never to this day has

he disclosed what he wrote in Athaliah's instructions to her embassy. As Athaliah's entire embassy was slaughtered by Jehu there is no one else who would know what was on the scroll. Did the scroll confirm that Jezebel and Athaliah planned to take over both kingdoms and devote them to Baal, or did the scroll just contain talk of a celebration in the event of a victory at Ramoth-Gilead? Did the notable size of the delegation portend a momentous occurrence, or did simply many from the palace want to participate in some anticipated celebration? We have Jehu's word for it, but is that more reliable than any king's idle boasting on a monument erected for his glory? Can anyone trust the annals of the kings?

Only Athaliah remained who would know of the contents of the scroll. But she had caught her daughter Jehosheba in the palace trying to smuggle out King Ahaziah's sons. Since Jehosheba had come from the Temple, Athaliah cut off all communication with the Temple. For weeks, then months, the Temple guard stood at their stations on every watch of the day, as if under siege, waiting for a blow that never came. I believe Athaliah did not know who to trust, or who to strike out against, so she walled herself in, waiting for any new traitors to reveal themselves.

For seven years Jerusalem lived its life in secret. Athaliah made a prisoner of herself in the royal palace. Jehu in the north had wiped out her entire family, and in retribution, to avoid a rallying point for the devotees of the House of David who would threaten to dethrone her, she slaughtered the children of King Ahaziah. She trusted no one. She feared that Jehu would attempt to finish his extermination of the House of Ahab either by invading our country or sending assassins into Jerusalem to kill her. The palace was her fortress; she rarely left it.

The people of Jerusalem lived their lives in stunned silence. Their King, Ahaziah, had been killed. He had left to do battle with Aram, so his death was not inconceivable, but he had died at the hands of the rebel Jehu, who had proclaimed himself King of Israel. The people filled their jars with grain and dates, also fearing an attack and siege of Jerusalem by Jehu. But more, the people were stunned again by their Queen, Athaliah, killing the King's children. The act itself was horrific enough. Although rumors had circulated through the streets for years that in Samaria she had joined with her mother Jezebel in the sacrifice of children in the temple of Baal, even this did not prepare the people for such an act being performed in Jerusalem.

And it was more than simply the death of the young, helpless children. The people had witnessed the uprooting of the House of David.

Every child in the streets of Jerusalem could recite the lineage; David, Solomon, Rehoboam, Abijah, Asa, Jehoshaphat, Jehoram, Ahaziah. Even they had heard the news. With the weeping and wailing that greeted the news of the murder of King Ahaziah's children, it could not be concealed from them. The children looked for answers from their parents. Who was next in line now for the throne of David? Their parents had no answers; none for their children, none for themselves. It was as if their history, their nation, had been torn from them, and they were left with that murderer of children in the royal palace.

In the Temple there was silence also. No one dared breathe a word. Even I did not know who may have pieced together the events of seven years ago. Maaseiah and I even refrained from talking about these events for fear that we would be overheard. We listened to tales of those who had witnessed the bloody procession to the temple of Baal, afraid to ask any questions. We would see soldiers we knew from the palace in the markets and on the streets, but we never asked them if they knew what happened in the palace that bloody day. We feared that our lack of curiosity might make us seem suspicious to them, but they feared even more being asked about that day, and their relief at not being questioned erased any suspicion of us in their minds.

On that day of gore, rending and death, a Levite at the Temple found a dazed soldier wandering through the outer courts. The soldier had just come from the royal palace. He was brought directly to me. He was breathless, aghast. He probably had never been in a battle, but his face looked like he had just been routed. He was panting, blurting out one thought after another.

"Soldier, calm down, take a breath. Here, some wine to calm you. Tell us, what did you see?"

"I was guarding the royal nursery, the King's children. She came— with a soldier—Maaseiah—no it was not Maaseiah—it was one of Maaseiah's men—then the Queen came—she was angry—she was cursing—and there were soldiers too - -"

"Soldier, calm down. Who came with Maaseiah? A woman?"

"Maaseiah? With Maaseiah? Who . . ."

"Yes, the woman. Do you know who the woman was?"

"—it was one of the women—no—it was Jehosheba—she said she was Jehosheba—wasn't she the daughter of King Jehoram?"

"Were there others?"

"Yes, yes, there were others. There was another guard—and the nurses—and the children, the children - - -"

"Whose children, soldier? What of the others?"

"The Queen, she came with soldiers—the children—the women had the children—and I had one—and the soldiers—I was ahead of the soldiers—but the women - and the children. They were all struck down—all of them were struck down."

"What do you mean struck down soldier? What happened to them?"

"They were struck down. All of them. Run through, struck down, I heard their screams, the blows.

"All of them? What of Jehosheba?"

"She was with the women. They were all struck down. All the women. All the children."

The Levite who had brought the soldier in turned to me. "Jehoiada, sit down. There." Then to other priests in the room, "See to him. Go to the Temple guard. Tell them there is a threat to the Temple. Get all of them to their posts." Then he turned to the soldier,

"Look at me. Listen to my questions. The King's children. What happened to the King's children?

"They were all struck down—and the women—all of them."

"Who had this done?"

"We were all leaving the nursery. We were told the Queen was coming. And she came, with soldiers—down the hallway just behind us. She was angry, cursing, "Seize them," she screamed, "Seize them." I was in the lead, I slipped into a stairway. There was a soldier behind the children. He drew his sword, but the guards with the Queen cut him down. The soldiers dragged the women and children back to the Queen, but did not see me. I stayed in the stairway until I heard the Queen yell "cut them down, cut them down," and I heard them scream, and I heard the swords, but I was down the stairs. The palace was in an uproar. King Ahaziah had been killed, the embassy wiped out, Jezebel of the north had been killed. No one noticed me as I fled."

MY KINGDOM, THE WILDERNESS

Jehu

I have been very zealous for the Lord God Almighty . . . I
am the only one left. Elijah, I Kings 19:10

I, Jehu, charioteer, Commander of the Army of Israel, Regicide, became
King of Israel. The House of Ahab was no more. The temple of Baal
in Samaria and the temples of Baal throughout the kingdom were torn
down. Those that were not turned into latrines were turned into stables.
The priests of Baal which escaped the sword fled to Phoenicia or Aram. It
was more desperate for the priests of Baal during my reign than it was for
Elijah during the reign of King Ahab.

Elisha returned to the land of his parents and still tilled the soil with
his oxen until a few years ago. The hard labor wore him out. Just as the
years of plowing left an indelible mark on his frame, his years of prophesying ground him down but left an indelible mark on his spirit. Some
of his followers still roam the land, and occasionally are seen in Samaria.
In the first years of my reign, they would visit the palace. I had seen the
upset and anger of King Ahab when the prophets would condemn him
for Jezebel's prophets of Baal; upset because he knew he would never give
up the worship of Baal, and anger because they challenged him to his
face. I had imagined that I would welcome the visits of the prophets of
the Lord after I had become King. Had I not followed the charge of that
young prophet who anointed me as King in Ramoth-Gilead? Had I not
put an end to the House of Ahab? Had I not removed the worship of Baal
from the land? But the prophets continued their condemnation of the

King for the temples to the golden calves in Dan and Bethel, and now
I was King. I had not torn down those temples, I had not scattered the
priests of the golden calves.

"The Temple of the Lord is in Jerusalem and there he must be worshiped," the prophets would say.

And I would say, "You say I must worship in the Temple in Jerusalem. Have you been to worship in the Temple in Jerusalem? Have you
gone to the royal palace in Jerusalem to tell Queen Athaliah to tear down
her temples of Baal in Jerusalem? Have you told that daughter of Jezebel
to scatter her prophets of Baal?"

Jerusalem had been turned into a fortress by Queen Athaliah. Anyone coming to Jerusalem, anyone coming into the Kingdom of Judah
from Israel, was under suspicion as a spy or assassin. I was not surprised
at this. Every relative of Queen Athaliah, her mother, her son King Ahaziah, her brother King Joram of Israel, every aunt, uncle, cousin, brother
and sister she had had been slain at my hand. She was certain that I would
send my army or my spies or some hired assassin to end her life. Since I
became King of Israel, the whole purpose of the Kingdom of Judah has
been to preserve the life of Queen Athaliah.

All commerce, trade and travel between Judah and Israel has ceased.
How could any worshipers go to the Temple in Jerusalem? And if not
Jerusalem, where would they go? Their temples of Baal have been wiped
from the land. The Temple in Jerusalem is closed to them. I fear that if I
tear down the temples of the golden calves the people will try to rebuild
the temples to Baal. They only know of Baal and the golden calves, and
Jerusalem is closed to them. I have left them with the golden calves of
their ancestors. I had not built those temples in Dan and Bethel, but Israelites had, the descendants of Abraham had. Would the prophets prefer
the people go to Tyre to worship Baal? But the prophets will not listen to
reason. Let them preach to the sheep, but they are no longer welcome in
the royal palace. I had hoped I would be able to talk to Elisha again, or
maybe he could even send that wild-eyed youth he had sent to anoint me,
but I have not seen him. The prophets are stubborn, but their King can
be stubborn as well.

Old Obadiah remained in charge of my royal household until the
end of his days. He would urge me to send raiders to Jerusalem to end
Athaliah's unholy grip on Jerusalem and to open the city to worshipers
from Israel. He listened to the prophets of the Lord to the end. But I
feared for my kingdom. Not only was the Kingdom of Judah now closed

to Israel, Tyre and Sidon and all the cities of Phoenicia were closed to us as well. I had killed their royal princess Jezebel, the sister of King Baal-Eser II, the late King of Tyre and Sidon, and her sons. The Phoenicians did not want to spend the money on mercenaries to punish us, but they cut off their trade and closed their markets to us, crushing our treasury. To the coast of the sea and to the south, all trade ceased.

I had killed the entire House of Ahab. I had killed all of the supporters of the House of Ahab and all the prophets of Baal, and they were numerous. The royal palace and the royal treasuries, the store houses and granaries, the tax houses, were all but empty and silent after that. The markets, the royal stores, the granaries, armories, the threshing floors, the wineries, the embassies, the scriptoriums were all run by the House of Ahab and its prophets of Baal. The few experienced hands remaining were overwhelmed with the inexperienced. Trade, commerce and governance had taken on a pronounced Phoenician tilt, tipped that way by the prophets of Baal trained in Sidon, Tyre and Byblos. Now these experienced hands were gone, their blood soaked into the soil they once governed. Only the army had been unaffected by the infusion of all things Phoenician, and my commanders had little experience with diplomats and merchants. I was left with a nation of farmers, herders and soldiers.

To the north, Aram remained as strong as ever. But we could not trade with Aram either. Aram had been at war with Israel or had been paying tribute to Israel for generations. It only took a few short years for Aram to figure out that our markets had dried up and maintaining our army was becoming a burden. We were striking against the usurper Hazael at Ramoth-Gilead when I was anointed, and now Hazael was well established as King of Aram. Soon their raiding began. We had not been stripped bare, and there were plenty of our youth for the army, but to mount a major campaign to strike back against Aram's raids would cripple our treasury. So Aram would raid and raid again. Somehow we will grow stronger. In the meantime, every season of battle sees the loss of some fields or plains, the stripping of some crops or groves, the theft of some herds, even the loss of a few small towns on the border. Some we recapture, some we cannot, but only rarely are we able to mount a raid against the Arameans to take something of theirs.

I wonder why the prophets never came to our army camps with some miraculous strategy to rid our land of the Arameans. The armies of King Ahab and King Joram had been aided by the prophets, but will they aide their anointed King Jehu? If they do not see fit not to help me, I see fit to maintain the temples to the golden calves.

I wonder at times why I had been anointed King. I saw the justice in bringing to an end the House of Ahab. I have set many slaves free. I restored the vineyards of Naboth to his heirs. But there is no end to the petitioners. Everyone had been injured by that plague of a dynasty. But I cannot raise the dead. I cannot restore fortunes. I cannot track down squandered inheritances. Is there not more to justice than punishment? Why was I able to punish so thoroughly, but restore so meagerly?

And the kingdom was restored meagerly. The mighty kingdom of King Omri was no more. The army of Israel no longer brings fear to our neighbors. Instead, they merely avoid my army and raid where I am not. The broad alliance between Tyre and Sidon and Israel that had increased the stature of Israel with of all of the kingdoms was no more. The Kingdom of Israel was now hemmed in, pressed in on all sides and trembling in the middle. The Kingdom of Judah, which was being raised out of the mire of its King Jehoram, was now sunk into a bitter isolation, totally estranged from its sister Israel. Have I been anointed to rule over this shadow of a kingdom?

But there is a deeper bitterness. In the army camps of Omri, Ahab and Joram, we had mocked the vaunted House of David. Not for what it had been, but for what it had become. We also mocked it out of jealousy, because the Kingdom of Judah claimed the House of David, and we had broken from it. But we remained Israelites. Not the Israelites of Samaria, but the Israelites that had been brought into this land by Joshua, the successor of Moses, and was not David the King of the Israelites? We mocked the House of David out of envy; we were the successors of Jeroboam, Elah, Baasha, Nadab, Zimri, Omri and his family, and now Jehu, four regicides among them, a continuing succession of assassins. In mocking the House of David, we mocked ourselves, because we had sunken so much lower than the House of David.

And now the House of David is no more; the unimaginable has happened. All of the heirs of King Ahaziah have been murdered at the hand of Athaliah. There is no cause for Israel to envy Judah for its royal house. With the House of David, there was something that connected us to the prophet Samuel, the last of our judges who anointed the first of our kings. And now that is gone. It is as if the history of our nations has been erased.

In the dark, hollow, silent nights in the empty passages of the royal palace, and there are many - nights and passages - the cold stone on my feet chills my very soul. I no longer dip my bread in olive oil. The smell reminds me too much of that upper room in Ramoth-Gilead, that wild-eyed boy of a prophet, and of the cries, "Jehu is King! Jehu is King!" And for what? For what was I anointed King? Season after season Israel is being reduced. The Kingdom of Judah is now a shuttered fortress, cutting itself off from the world, awash in fear and hatred. And the House of David is a memory. Is this now better than the House of Ahab?

Jehonadab, my friend of many battles, remains in the wilderness with his family. I would like to see him in the palace, but I know he would not accept an invitation. I am now just another king, that form of humans he fled to the wilderness to avoid. So he drifts and wanders in the wilderness. I do not know what he is waiting for; only that he is waiting for something a king cannot bring him.

Elijah once told me to wait; to wait, not as idleness, but as a tactic, a strategy. So I wait. But for what? I do not know. I have a strategy, but no objective. I am no different than Jehonadab - wandering in my own wilderness.

THE DEPOSITION OF ATHALIAH

Jehoiada

You said, "I am forever— the eternal queen!" But you
did not consider these things or reflect on what might
happen. Isaiah 47:7

S EVEN years after the massacre of the King's children in the palace, I
found myself in the same room as Maaseiah. The High Priest's council had just met, and each of us was attending to different matters. It may
have been the presence of another person that prompted me to move. It
was the silent priest. He had begun his duties seven years ago. He was
directly supervised by one of my assistants. He was not a Levite, but had
been assigned priestly duties, duties which he would perform by himself.
It had been made known that he had made an oath that required him to
serve in the Temple in silence. He was delivering a message that had arrived at the Temple from the market and had to be brought to the Levite
arranging the evening's burnt offering.

As the silent priest walked past me, my eyes met Maaseiah's eyes.
Maaseiah had volunteered to be Queen Athaliah's agent in the Temple, to
prevent another Jehosheba, and we had allowed him to be forced on us
by the Queen.

"Maaseiah," I said, "come with me." Motioning toward the silent
priest I went on, "Bring him with you."

I turned and began walking toward my chambers. The silent priest
went on to deliver his message and then left the assembly room. Maaseiah

followed the priest out. In a short time both of them appeared in my chamber. Without a word, Maaseiah closed the door.

"Maaseiah, it is time."

I turned to the silent priest. "Pull off your hood, remove your tunic, unlock your tongue. You will be a soldier again."

The priest pulled off his hood.

"I am ready. It has been a long time."

"Why this day, Jehoiada?" asked Maaseiah.

"It came to me as our friend walked between you and me in the assembly room. Messages come in to the Temple, but messages also go out. The child has passed seven years from the day of his birth. He asks who his parents are. He asks why he is raised in the Temple. He asks why he does not leave the Temple like other children do. As he continues to ask, others will begin to ask also. He is no longer small. He cannot be confined to a few small rooms anymore. And we grow older. We must act while we still can. And we must act before the people forget the House of David."

I first met our friend the silent priest seven years ago, after Jehosheba had left the Temple with Maaseiah to bring the scribe's children out of the royal palace.

On the same watch that Jehosheba and Maaseiah left the Temple, a young soldier I had never seen before entered the Temple with one small child, barely an infant. The soldier was terror stricken. He entered the outer courts with his cape thrown over his head and over the infant.

"You must protect me," he said to the Levite who grabbed ahold of him as he looked around in all directions, peering from behind columns and walls, "and this child."

The soldier's cape was that of the palace guards—guards who since King Jehoram rarely came onto the Temple grounds. The Levite only knew that somebody had been dispatched to the royal palace, unusual in those times by itself, but did not know why. A terrified soldier returning from the palace with a small child was even more unusual, so he ushered the soldier into my quarters.

The soldier did not fear harm at our hands, but he feared for his life and he showed it. He did not know who I was, and he did not know that Jehosheba and Maaseiah had left for the palace from these same rooms only a short time ago.

Seeing a small child flail out against the cape the soldier had wrapped over the child to conceal him led me to fear the worst, and my fears did not mislead me. I barely recall hearing the words the solder spoke after first telling us that all of the women with him and the King's children had been slain on the orders of Athaliah. I knew then that Jehosheba had been cut down. As a Levite continued to question the soldier, their words were hollow echoes I could barely comprehend.

"You came from the palace, soldier, but where did you get this child?"

"The child - someone handed him to me—it was one of the women—no—it was Jehosheba—she said she was Jehosheba—was that the daughter of King Jehoram? I took the child."

"Were there others?"

"Yes, yes, there were others. There was another guard—and the nurses—and the children, the children—"

"One thing at a time. Who is this child?"

"He is Joash, the King's son."

"The son of King Ahaziah? How do you know this?"

"I have guarded the royal nursery since the King left for Ramoth-Gilead. I know the names of all of the King's children, it was my job."

Since that day, the young soldier who brought Joash to the Temple had become the silent priest. Athaliah had been so furious and the bodies of those cut down at the palace had been slashed so severely in Athaliah's rage that it was hard to tell how many had been killed, much less who they were as they were hauled away to the Temple of Baal and thrown onto the altar to burn. No one noted how many children the scribe's wife had, and the guards that did either did not dare to speak, or decided to remain silent. As for the missing guard, Maaseiah was ready to deflect any inquiry about the guard count, but it never came.

Now we were ready to reap the harvest King Jehu had planted. It was Jehu's slaughter of Kings that had led to Athaliah's slaughter of the heirs of King Ahaziah. Since Jehu had already slain King Ahaziah, at the time of Athaliah's slaughter one of King Ahaziah's sons was indeed the next King of Judah, heir to the throne of David, when he was struck down by Athaliah, so Jehu's regicide was answered by Athaliah's regicide. Now another crop was ripe.

There were at least a handful who knew, and probably more who had pieced together what had happened. In the Temple there were probably others who had their own thoughts about this child escaping occasionally into the Temple courts who was the same vintage as the massacres by Jehu and Athaliah. How the suspicious Athaliah never doubted that she had killed all the children of Ahaziah I do not know. Maaseiah at his post in the royal household never heard any hint of fear from the Queen's quarters that she had not perfected her vengeance.

I turned to Maaseiah, gesturing to the former silent priest, "This is your new adjunct. He is seven years older, his beard is full, no one in the palace will recognize him anymore. Assemble the commanders of units of hundreds. Bring them to the Temple. We must start our work."

The next day, after evening sacrifices had ended, several worshipers made their way back to the priests' quarters. One familiar with the army may have recognized seven men, some stout, some muscular, some sinewy, as commanders of units of hundreds, but in the crowd of worshipers, the smoke of the offerings and in the shadows of the walls, no one stood out. After the priests had ushered the last worshiper out of the inner court, I led the seven to the altar of burnt offerings. I had all seven stand before the altar, a place reserved for sacred vows and refuge.

"Commanders, what some of you may know has been unspoken until now. But now we will speak of it in the presence of the Lord's Temple and around his holy altar. The line of David continues to bear fruit. While King Ahaziah was killed, his son Joash survives. Joash is the rightful King of Judah, the rightful heir of the throne of David. He has been protected in this Temple until now. But now it is time for him to take the throne of his father David. With your hands on the altar of the Lord, do you pledge your lives to King Joash?"

"We pledge our lives to King Joash," responded the commanders, in voices more accustomed to demanding obedience than giving it.

"Seven years ago under penalty of death you were forced to pledge your lives, lands, livestock, wives, children and parents to Athaliah when she claimed to be Queen. That pledge was not valid since it was made under the same penalty if you refused to make the oath. If you feel it is still a valid pledge, then the only one who can forgive you for breach of your pledge would be a new king."

"This is your task then. You and those selected by you are to go throughout the entire kingdom. Go to the Levites ministering to the Lord scattered through the towns and villages of the Kingdom. Go to the heads of all of the Israelite families in the Kingdom. Pledge them to secrecy. Tell them that Joash, son of King Ahaziah lives. Tell them that on this coming Sabbath they are to all assemble in the Temple in Jerusalem. When here, they are all to pledge loyalty to Joash, of the line of David. After they do this, Joash will be crowned King of Judah. Once again a son of David will sit on the throne. It is the Sabbath, but we cannot wait for the next festival. We will restore the throne of David on the Sabbath."

The day appointed was not a feast day and not a festival. A Sabbath Day's throng would be expected in Jerusalem, but not a festival throng. Queen Athaliah would be making her regular procession to the temple of Baal. Her route was well established and the soldiers at the gates of the city directed the crowds coming in to be silent and to avoid streets near the royal palace and the quarter where the temple of Baal was. On the walls of the city the guards could see steady streams of people approaching. Maaseiah had carefully advised the watchmen's commanders and those in the palace he could trust and no word was brought to the palace.

The priests offered their normal morning sacrifices in the Temple while a large but strangely quiet throng waited in the outer courts. I stood at the gate to the Temple in my robes, holding my staff, leaving no doubt that this assembly was not simply called by the commanders of the army. I looked at each person entering and they all looked at me. There was no question in their mind what was to happen.

Queen Athaliah had been to the Temple in Jerusalem on only one occasion before, at the coronation and anointing of her husband King Jehoram. She had witnessed the High Priest in his full vestments proceed from the Temple, followed by a row of Levites bringing out the large scrolls of the Law onto the steps of the Temple and standing beside the great bronze pillar called Jakin, the pillar having a capital encircled with seven interwoven bronze chains, with a row of bronze pomegranates above and below the chains. She had witnessed the priests following the large scrolls carrying the anointing oil. She had heard the oaths, prayers and charges to the King and the people, as old as King Solomon, and the anointing of the King by the High Priest. Then after days of celebration, she had guided her husband's soldiers as they struck down the King's brothers and their families.

Neither the Queen nor the Levites desired to see her step onto the Temple grounds after that day, and she followed her desires. When Queen Athaliah's son Ahaziah had been anointed in the Temple, the Kingdom of Israel had been much reduced and weakened. The anointing of Ahaziah was undertaken as if Jerusalem was under siege. I was High Priest by then, but the priests and Levites participating in the anointing were only a shadow of those present at Jehoram's anointing, and the temple courts were only half full of people. Out of fear of another bloodletting after the anointing of Ahaziah, I had sent most of the Levites out of the city to preserve them in the event Athaliah felt emboldened to use the ceremony to subject the Temple to her control.

Athaliah waited in the royal palace during the anointing of Ahaziah in the Temple, after which she led her son in a royal procession to the temple of Baal for a raucous celebration of the ascension of the son to the throne.

In deciding that this would be the day set aside for the anointing of the child Joash as King, one thought foremost in everyone's mind went unexpressed; what of Queen Athaliah? I do not know what type of end Athaliah envisaged for herself. Yes, there was that strange thought that probably originated in Egypt, but which had seeped into several other lands, of a king or a queen becoming a god upon their death. Was it a delusion of the powerful that their self-deluding grandeur could not be stopped by mere death? Or was it to instill fear; who would dare raise their hand against one destined to become a god in the afterlife? It was the ultimate blasphemy, but I had no idea what reward that Phoenician princess thought was her due.

Perhaps everyone in the Temple had already decided in their own mind what should happen to Athaliah. Was not Athaliah the grand-daughter of King Ethbaal of Tyre and Sidon who had strangled King Phelles with his own hands to claim his throne? Was not Athaliah behind the murder of all of her brothers-in-law at the hands of her husband King Jehoram? Was not Athaliah the murderer of her own grandchildren in revenge for the massacre of the House of Ahab at the hands of Jehu of the north? Perhaps we had been instructed by Athaliah in the means of her disposal.

In my mind, Athaliah had earned death by her attempt to stamp out the House of David. Did she believe she would become a goddess when she died? We could laugh and mock her for her foolishness. Did she think she could contend with the Lord and in her arrogance upset the Lord's plans? The laughter of the Lord can carry a sharp edge. But she was the Queen; be she Queen through violence and avarice, she was the Queen, and regicide is something not undertaken lightly. By our own actions would we just encourage others to regicide in turn? Would we descend into a nation of Zimris?

Seven years of incense had filled the grounds of the Temple seeking answers. For seven years Athaliah had proven the answer to these prayers by her unstinting worship of her lord Baal, turning the holy city into a cesspool. She had claimed she had other sons. Some of these putative offspring she had murdered when they proved too mild, or perhaps even tilted toward justice. Others of her so-called sons were her favorite lovers from her temples. Was she Sarah, capable of producing sons in her old age, we scoffed. But she was intent on putting the worst of her imaginary offspring on the throne, her last act of revenge against this nation she had grown to hate.

"I have been cut off from Tyre and Sidon by that regicide Jehu in the north," Athaliah was heard to complain in the royal palace, "Phoenicia has neither the army nor the will to break through the Kingdom of Israel to save me in Jerusalem. They are sending their ships to meet the rising sun out on the furthest reaches of the Great Sea to build new cities. I am cut adrift; run aground on the mountainous reefs of this barren city of Jerusalem. I will dedicate my life and my being to my Lord Baal. If he will not save me, he will save the dynasty I will establish in my name."

In the council of the Temple, we decided that our steps would not be determined by Queen Athaliah. Our course would be determined solely by doing what was needed to anoint young Joash King. We had the word of the Lord and would act on them. A king from the line of David would rule. And this child growing up in the Temple was of the line of David. How much like the prophet Samuel, I thought, who was raised by the priest Eli at the Tabernacle of the Lord in Shiloh and had heard the voice of the Lord while still a child. If Samuel was old enough to hear the voice of the Lord as a child, then Joash could be anointed King as a child.

We decided that we would ignore Athaliah. We would not hunt Athaliah down or pursue her. Perhaps she would flee Jerusalem and run to her precious Phoenicia where her family still ruled. The council of the Temple determined that she would not be put to death while she was still Queen of Judah. While she was still on the throne, the wife of the late King Jehoram of the House of David, she would not be harmed. Once Joash was anointed King of Judah in the Temple in Jerusalem, he would assume his rightful place as heir of the House of David, and Athaliah would no longer be Queen. If she then chose to oppose the anointed King of Judah, she would be struck down. The murderous Athaliah could then choose for herself between life and death. There was no doubt in my mind the course she would take.

On the Sabbath that we had chosen for the anointing of Joash, I assembled a procession of Levites, priests, the captains of a hundred, the mercenary Carites, and both temple and palace guards to enter the precincts of the Temple after the people had packed into the Temple precincts and the ways leading to the Temple.

Not only was the Temple well-guarded, the royal palace was also cordoned off. There were no obvious barricades, but one-third of the forces at my disposal were posted as sentries around the palace and on the byways and intersections in the city leading from the palace, ready to repel any incursion from the palace.

At the conclusion of the morning sacrifices, a procession of Levites and priests silently ushered themselves out of the anterooms of the Temple, through the sizeable crowd in the main courtyard of the Temple and up to the two great pillars, Boaz and Jakin at the entrance to the Holy Place of the Temple. They lined the inner court of the Temple, facing the courtyard they had just come from, and ringed the large altar for burnt offerings.

The crowd in the surrounding courtyards suddenly silenced itself as the Levites in their ceremonial robes began their procession. The silence continued as a breeze wafted the smoke from the remnants of the embers remaining from the morning sacrifices. The Levites on the steps and the crowd in the courtyard stood motionless and silent as the smoke weaved its way over and through the ranks of the crowd, as if seeking out the mind of the people, as if purifying their motives, as if anointing them for their tasks ahead, as if announcing the presence of the Lord in their midst. There was no restlessness in the crowd. They breathed in the faint mist of smoke from the altar, now mingled with the sweet odor of the incense flowing out of the Holy Place.

Unannounced, piercing blasts of rams' horns and trumpets shook the air of the courtyard. The trumpeters had assembled in the silence at the rear of the courtyard between the pillars of the portico, and in the four corners of the courtyard. The trumpets and horns produced blast after blast, joining the harmony of the echoes reverberating back from every quarter of the city. There could not have been a crevice of the city not drenched in the shrill, piercing tunes. The crashing blasts pushed back the seven years of silence as we had cowered in the back rooms of the Temple in fear of the Queen and the royal palace.

The horns suddenly stopped as the crowds listened to the returning echoes report back from every corner in the city. As the last echo died out, squadrons of drums roared out their beats, as if rebuking the horns for being too restrained. Then, under the continuing crash of the drums, the ordered marching of troops could be heard, as two columns of Levites, armed as soldiers, made their progress through the courtyard and up to the foot of the altar. In the midst of the armed Levites I took my place, holding the hand of the child Joash as he marched with me into the courtyard. As we were midway to the altar, the horns and trumpets now joined the drums, as a roar went up from the crowd upon seeing Joash make his way toward the altar.

As we arrived at the foot of the altar the drums and horns ceased, but the roar of the crowd continued. They had come expecting to see the boy Joash for the first time, but were overwhelmed upon actually seeing him in the flesh, and realizing that in fact a remnant of the House of David was not a fitful dream. As the hosannas continued to ring out, I finally waved my arms over my head calling for silence.

"Israelites! Sons and daughters of Abraham," I began against the noise of the crowd, which suddenly stilled itself as if of one mind. I had resolved that my words would be few. By now feet would be rushing from the royal palace, summoned by the blast of the horns. The Temple guard was instructed to let the Queen and her royal guard pass but no one else.

"The crown of David and Solomon I now place on the head of the sole successor of the House of David." A Levite came forward from the Temple carrying the crown down the steps of the Temple. Without further words I placed the crown on the child's head. A cushion had been fashioned inside the crown so it would rest on the small head.

"I now present to King Joash, son of King Ahaziah, son of King Jehoram, son of King David, the covenant of the Lord." Another Levite now descended the steps from the Temple carrying a scroll of the Law that had been copied by a team of scribes working day and night up to the morning of the coronation. The Levite with the scroll stood between me and Joash; Joash then placed his right hand on the scroll of the Law.

"Do you affirm the Lord's covenant with this people?" I asked Joash.

The youth, looking unfazed at the tumult around him, answered in a strong voice, audible to most of the crowd, just as had been practiced and practiced, "I affirm the Lord's covenant with this people."

"Do you swear, as King, by the altar of the Lord, to be governed by this covenant?"

"I swear by the altar of the Lord to be bound by this covenant," responded Joash, forgetting the words "as King."

I then held over my head a rough clay flask, secured around my neck with a leather strap.

"I, Jehoiada, High Priest of the Lord God of Israel, anoint Joash King of Judah." Holding the flask up, I snapped the neck of the flask and drained the anointing oil over the crown and head of the child Joash.

As the child sputtered with oil flowing down his face and over his mouth, the crowd roared, all but drowning out the renewed trumpet and horn blasts and the rumble of the drums.

"Long live the King," roared the people, over and over, "Long live the King! Long live the King!"

The summons of the people rose up over the walls of the Temple into the surrounding city and into the halls of the royal palace. It was only a matter of time before Queen Athaliah would answer the summons.

Joash was still standing with me beside the altar of the Lord when shouts from the guard announced her presence.

"The Queen! The Queen has entered the Temple!"

A line of guards from the royal palace were seen pushing their way through the crowd. In the streets outside the Temple, the full contingent of the palace guard accompanying the Queen had been barred from entering the Temple by the Temple guard and the mercenary Carites. Only the Queen's personal guard had been allowed to accompany the Queen into the Temple. I wanted to avoid a pitched battle in the streets and hoped that by allowing the Queen and her guard into the Temple she would forgo a struggle if she were allowed to advance to face the challenge.

Queen Athaliah knew our Temple protocol well enough to know that we would not willingly shed blood on the grounds of the Temple. It took great bravery for the Queen to advance with the palace guard through the streets to the temple. She was risking that the presence of her royal person would intimidate anyone from using force against her. It was a significant risk. Once at the Temple, she felt safe enough entering the Temple with just her personal guard. Athaliah would not be a Zimri retreating to the royal citadel to have it burn down around her. She would advance headlong against any challenge. She had learned from her mother Jezebel the intimidating presence of a forceful Queen. She had seen many a willful, belligerent challenger wilt when allowed into her presence. Now she would challenge the entire nation.

"Let them advance," I said to the Levites guarding the entrance to the Inner Court of the Temple. Only Levites were allowed in the Inner Court, but Joash had already been admitted to be anointed, and it was fitting and just to admit the Queen being deposed by the same anointing.

Since the Queen was choosing to oppose the anointing of Joash, it was proper to have the Queen bring her claim to the throne, if she had one, and for Joash to face the person who had slaughtered his brothers and sisters.

As soon as Athaliah entered the courtyard of the Temple she recognized the scene. She had stood in the courtyard of the Temple as her husband Jehoram was anointed by the High Priest standing next to the altar of burnt offering, holding the scroll of the Law as the anointing oil flowed down his face and beard.

But here was a child standing next to the High Priest, an outsized crown on his head, his hand resting on the scroll of the law. The anointing oil was flowing down the smooth cheeks of a beardless boy. And the High Priest? It was Jehoiada, the husband of her late daughter Jehosheba, that betrayer of her mother who sought to sneak away with the children of Ahaziah.

Queen Athaliah with one of her guards on either side of her walked directly up the steps of the altar facing me and Joash. She was not about to let any of her subjects, High Priest or not, address her while standing over her. I waved off the guard in front of the altar allowing her to approach.

"Jehoiada, would you be King?"

I looked directly at the Queen. I had heard of her legendary scorn, her mythic derision. I allowed her to continue on. In her throne room, a petitioner or accused could be beaten or even struck down for interrupting the Queen as she held court. I did not know what response I could expect from the Queen or from her two guards standing next to her should I try to silence her. I did not want to risk bloodshed in the Temple, even if it was my blood. I could only trust in the loyalty of those gathered in the courtyards for the coronation of Joash.

"This child cannot rule, Jehoiada, he has barely been weaned. Who will rule for this child while his nursemaids tend to him? Are you tired of slaughtering oxen, High Priest? Do you want to live in the luxury of the royal palace? Are you tired of your cramped quarters of the Temple, oh mighty High Priest? Is the treasury of your Temple not enough for you? Do you desire to dip into the coffers of the palace as well?"

Athaliah then turned her back on me and faced the crowd assembled in the courtyard of the Temple.

"People of Jerusalem, do you not see what this priest is doing? He has killed the parents of this child of shepherds and would now have you believe that this infant is of royal blood. This priest has always lusted after power. Did not he marry my daughter Jehosheba and then seek to invade the palace to claim the crown? But he failed miserably, just as he would fail as your King, just as he will fail again in this new rebellion. His first rebellion was struck down, even at the cost of my dear daughter Jehosheba, and her blood is on his grasping hands. After the murder of your King Ahaziah by that usurper Jehu, this High Priest invaded the palace and his men slaughtered all of the children of your King Ahaziah. He would have been your King then, but he was unable to overwhelm me then, and he will not overwhelm me now."

"People of Jerusalem! My dear children! I know your god loves mercy, so I showed this priest mercy. I let him live even though he is the cruelest of all rebels. I allowed him to remain as a priest in your temple. Did I ever desecrate the temple of your god? And yet this priest has desecrated this temple every day with the blood of the sons of David dripping from his hands. There are no sons of David who survived this priest's cruelty. They are dead I tell you! Dead! I saw them all struck down by guards from the Temple who forced their way into the palace. And who sent these guards to put an end to the House of David? This same priest that stands in front of you and seeks to proclaim this child as King. This boy is a fraud. Your King will be the blood-drenched priest that stands in front of you."

Athaliah's speech was powerful and convincing, as all of her speeches were. She was cunning and skillful and cruel when the occasion called for it. She had controlled much of the royal court when her husband King Jehoram demonstrated he did not have the skills or guile necessary for the task, and she all but ruled as Queen for the year her son Ahaziah was king. She had controlled the throne and ruled as Queen for seven years in her own name after Ahaziah had been killed by Jehu. I do not know what impact her words were having on the crowd assembled at the Temple that morning, but I knew the losses and privations the people had suffered when her husband Jehoram was King, and I knew the fear the people lived in under Athaliah as she fought to preserve her crown. Whether any of the people were swayed by Athaliah's claim that I was a self-serving usurper, I did not know. I did know that many of the people were ready for relief from the rule of Athaliah and would be willing to support any usurper who promised relief. I also knew who carried the swords in the grounds of the Temple.

Athaliah had determined her own course. She would not relinquish her hold on the throne, and she would strike down all that oppose her.

I did not respond to her charges as any response would just call forth further recriminations from her. She had failed to state any basis for her claim to the throne, so no response was called for. I turned to the commanders of the Temple guard standing closest to me,

"Bring her out between the ranks and put to the sword anyone who follows her."

With this Athaliah tore her robes and screamed, "Treason! Treason!"

It was a condemnation - not merely a charge - from the throne that called for immediate action. Anyone failing to respond by striking down the traitor would be struck down themselves. The only response Athaliah received was the echo of her words against the walls of the Temple, as if the Temple itself was throwing the same condemnation back against her. The surrounding crowd was silent, awed by the powerful condemnation issued by their Queen, and awed by the silence that followed. They sensed the majesty of the moment—of the House of David being restored—and they sensed the terror of the moment—the fatal blow and gushing blood of Athaliah that would restore the House of David.

Athaliah looked accusingly at her two guards standing next to her, incensed at their inaction. They should have struck me down the instant their Queen uttered the word "treason."

"Strike him down! Strike him!"

The Temple guard quietly placed their hands on the weapons of Athaliah's two guards standing next to her, and the crowd in the courtyards pressed against the other royal guards who had followed Athaliah toward the altar, preventing them from unsheathing their weapons. The royal guard, sensing no one in the crowd had been swayed by Athaliah's speech, and being unswayed themselves, offered no resistance. The Temple guard seized Athaliah by both arms and dragged her from the Temple, her cries of "treason, treason, treason," echoing through the courts of the Temple, sounding now as a public pronouncement of her crimes.

The Temple guard took her toward the royal palace and brought her to the entrance to the stables for the palace. There, swift, forceful blows from the soldiers swords ran her through and dropped her to the ground, and the ground, well trampled by horses hooves, soaked up her blood.

JEHU'S CODA

Jehu

He has also set eternity in the human heart; yet no one
can fathom what God has done from beginning to end.
Solomon, Ecclesiastes 3:11

WORD came to us from Jerusalem that Queen Athaliah had been
slain. It had been seven years since anyone from the Kingdom
of Israel had travelled openly to Jerusalem. As far as Queen Athaliah had
been concerned, everyone from Israel was a spy and an assassin. Even
though Jehonadab had sworn off kings and cities, he was helpful in recruiting his fellow nomads in sending an occasional herder to Judah and
even into Jerusalem to talk privately to those in the Temple. He may not
have been all that interested in getting involved in affairs between Israel
and Judah, but he was very interested in the welfare of Jerusalem and the
Temple of the Lord.

I do not know why Jehonadab would have been interested in Jerusalem during those seven years. All the word we had received from Jerusalem was that all of King Ahaziah's children had been slain by Athaliah
and that the House of David had been extinguished. Many gave up hope
in Judah. Without the House of David, the prophecy that the Lord would
maintain an heir of David on the throne forever seemed a hollow mys-
tery, a promise crafted to disappoint, or maybe just the propaganda of
an earlier generation that turned itself into history. But Jehonadab, the
hard-headed rustic, would not accept that the House of David had been
wiped out. He urged his charges to go to the Temple, to the markets, to

the army barracks, to speak to the palace guard for any news. It was a dangerous mission. Athaliah was on her guard. Any inquiry about any surviving heir of Ahaziah was taken as evidence of a plot against her. We had heard nothing that would change our minds.

There was amazement in Samaria when the news arrived that a son of King Ahaziah had survived Athaliah's slaughter and had been crowned King. So the stubborn Jehonadab was proven right. There was amazement in Samaria, but little rejoicing. The House of David and Jerusalem seemed so far removed from us. Only a handful of people from Samaria had dared to venture into Athaliah's Jerusalem in the past seven years. Few knew or cared about the Temple in Jerusalem anymore. They were comfortable with the golden calves in Bethel and Dan. I had taken Baal from them, and many complained about that. I was not going to take their golden calves from them. We are a land of complainers; they line up before dawn to bring their complaints to the King—some to complain of the King to the King. I would rather run my chariot through their lines than listen to them. It is as aggravating as talking to the prophets, but now my petitioners make less sense than the prophets.

Myself, I was perplexed with the news from Jerusalem. I recalled the sweaty, young, nervous prophet in that upper room in Ramoth-Gilead drenching my head with olive oil. "You are to destroy the house of Ahab your master," he said to me. Was not the new King - Joash is his name, - the son of Athaliah, and is not Athaliah the daughter of Ahab and Jezebel? Obadiah, that old servant of the royal palace had died only a year after I became King. Jehonadab will no longer set foot in the city of the King. Bidkar is always in the field with the army trying to repel one raid by the Arameans after another. The counselors of the House of Ahab have all felt the swords of my soldiers. I am left with my own counsel. My arrows are warped. My lances are bent. My horses are lame.

I had not wiped out Athaliah as Jehonadab had urged. I did not need two kingdoms. Perhaps I fell short. But in the end, Athaliah met her end. Had I attacked, would I have killed Athaliah's children also? I did not know what to do, so I waited and left Judah alone. Waiting was what Elisha had told me to do many years ago.

I have read the Psalms of King David. I do not write Psalms, I do not play the harp or the lute. I have always been a soldier; the bow and lance are my instruments, the wheezing of the horses pulling my chariot is my song. I know King David was also a warrior, but I am not King David. David's Psalms say, "the Lord has chosen Zion," and "our feet our standing in your gates, Jerusalem." So what use are these Psalms to a King in Samaria?

I have read the words of the Preacher and the wisdom and proverbs of Solomon, the great King that built the Temple of the Lord in Jerusalem. Wisdom sometimes escapes me. I am left with the wisdom of the army. If you want to attract the attention of the king, drive a chariot. Now I am King and I have lost my interest in chariots. I have little wisdom to impart.

King Omri was a soldier also; a soldier who built a mighty kingdom. My kingdom is being reduced every year. Without alliances with Tyre and Sidon or Ekron or Jerusalem, our trade is reduced and our treasuries go wanting. Aram sees us without allies and raids us continually. Wise King Omri established a strong alliance with the kingdoms of Phoenicia that enriched Israel, but in the end we were almost turned into Phoenicians. Obadiah sat me down in the first month of my reign and told me why he believed I had been anointed King: to preserve the identity of the people of Israel as the Lord's people. I have not heard a better explanation. So my sons and daughters will not marry the princes or princesses of Phoenicia, Philistia, Aram, Ammon or Moab. Without these strong alliances, I will not build a mighty kingdom. Should I attack another kingdom and seize their cities? That would only tempt other kingdoms to join against us, and besides, I have grown sick of war. I am weary of the only talent the Lord gave to me. I am weary.

Even Elisha did not seem to know that a son of Ahaziah had been preserved. He visited me only one time in the royal palace. He brought me a prophecy or a revelation. Maybe it was only a wise prediction. But I will not live to see if it is reliable. If one of my sons is alive when I die, then I will know that part of his prophecy had come to pass. "The word of the Lord," he said, "Because you have done well in accomplishing what is right in my eyes and have done to the house of Ahab all I had in mind to do, your descendants will sit on the throne of Israel to the fourth generation."

I have pondered those words for many years. What do they mean? What will befall my descendants four generations after me? Why four generations? Still, it is better than three generation. The House of Omri ruled for three generations. Is the House of Jehu to be only two generations better than the House of Omri? And what do these generations after generations add up to? So there will be another king after the House of Jehu whose sons will rule this land. Or will there be? Will this kingdom cease after five generations? The prophets will not answer these questions for me. Perhaps Jehonadab has made the right decision. Who can tell the history of kings not yet born?

The prophets of the Lord still inhabit the land. I do not harass them. They would harangue me about the golden calves if I let them, so they do not gather around my table. I have wearied of warring with them also. They still condemn the King who allows the golden calves to stand in the temples in Bethel and Dan, but then they condemned King Ahab for Baal and the people did not rebel against Ahab. I will let them irritate the people just as they used to irritate me. Four generations the prophet said.

So my history, the history of Jehu, son of Nimshi, commander of the chariots of the army of Israel, and now King of Israel, begins with the regicide of King Phelles of Tyre, himself a regicide, at the hands of Ethbaal, father of Jezebel, and ends with the regicide of Queen Athaliah of Judah, the daughter of Ahab and Jezebel, at the hands of the High Priest Jehoiada.

King Ahab himself was killed by an unknown archer of Aram, the archer's random arrow making him an unwitting regicide.

And for me, it was my arrow that cut down King Joram of Israel, my King, as he fled from me outside the walls of Jezreel. While Joram's body was still slumped in his chariot, I ordered the death of his mother Queen Jezebel inside the walls of Jezreel. A few short days later, I had King Ahaziah of Judah, the grandson of Ahab and Jezebel brought before me and ordered him struck down.

Regicide. It was the birthright of the House of Ahab. Regicide was the lot assigned to Ahab, Jezebel, Joram, Ahaziah and Athaliah. And yet a remnant survives in Joash, of the House of David, but also of the house of Omri and Ahab.

Of all the soldiers in the army of Israel, the prophet Elisha sent his young charge to me to anoint as King. I was anointed King to become a regicide. And that is the inheritance I leave to the generations of my dynasty that will follow me.

THE COURSE OF AN ARROW

Jehonadab

Sun and moon stood still in the heavens at the glint of
your flying arrows, at the lightning of your flashing spear.
Habakkuk 3:11

A N oath to the Lord is not lightly abandoned. Before Jehu's arrow
leapt from his bow, I had left the army, the city, the palace and its
kings and had made my decision that my house would live in tents as
nomads. I may have made a different decision had I learned of Jehu's
anointing before my oath, but the present cannot question the past.

Jehu's arrow portended great change in this kingdom as it raced
through the air; even while it flew no one could be certain where it would
strike, and after it struck, no one could be certain of the outcome. I fear
that Jehu believes that his arrow, and the charge of his anointing, is now
spent. Since he is the one chosen by the prophets for anointing and I am
the one who decided on my own to leave Samaria, I cannot question his
thoughts.

But Jehu is given to quick judgments followed by a swift dispatch.
While he always had a firm grasp of strategy, he was the master of the
sudden strike and despised a siege. For myself, however, I believe that
Jehu's arrow is still in flight, and that it had been traversing this land well
before any prophet's oil anointed any child of Israel. As I watch my flocks
grazing from the front of my tent, I am not certain where that arrow will
strike or what the outcome will be, only that it is in flight.

AND JEHU RESTED

J EHU rested with his ancestors and was buried in Samaria. And Jehoahaz his son succeeded him as King.

The time that Jehu reigned over Israel in Samaria was twenty-eight years.

II Kings 10: 35–36

INDEX: BIBLICAL SOURCES
FOR CHAPTERS

The Succession of Assassins, I Kings 14, 15, 16.

Solomon's domination of the region since the time of his father King David, I Chronicles 18:6.

Aram had been a thorn in King Solomon foot, I Kings 11:23–25.

prophets of the Lord, heirs of Moses they claimed, Deuteronomy 18:18.

agent of the rebellion against King Solomon was the prophet Ahijah of Shiloh, I Kings 11:29–39.

Solomon's half brother Absalom murdering his oldest half-brother Amnon for raping half-sister Tamar, II Samuel 13.

Adonijah pronouncing himself king while King David was still living, I Kings 1.

And the power grab when David died that almost left the memory of youngest son Solomon a bloody mar on the floor of the royal palace? I Kings 1.

The Disposition of King Phelles

Ethbaal, King of the Sidonians, I Kings 16:31: See, generally, Josephus, *Antiquities of the Jews*, Book VIII, Ch. XIII, sec. 1.

Ethbaal, as the High Priest of Astarte,

The Jerome Bible Commentary, p194 (Prentiss Hall, Inc., 1968), states, "Ittobaal, the Sidonian king of Tyre (887–856) . . . had previously been the high priest of the Tyrian Baal Temple."

The Historians' History of the World, Williams, ed., Vol. II, p.284 (The Outlook Company, New York, 1904), states, "He was murdered by Ithobaal (Eth-Baal), priest of Astarte."

Ethbaal killing King Phelles, Phelles killing his brother, *The Historians' History of the World*, Idem, p283.

we hired our army from our trading partners, Ezekiel 27:10–11.

Phelles as the last of four brothers to rule after they had killed their father, See, generally, *The Historians' History of the World*, Idem, p283.

Omri's kingdom . . . exacting tribute from Moab, II Kings 3:4

Refashioning Samaria

establishing the city of Botrys . . Auza, Josephus, *Antiquities of the Jews*, Book VIII, Ch. XIII, sec. 3; *The Historians' History of the World*, Williams, ed., Vol. II, p.284 (The Outlook Company, New York, 1904)

juniper for hulls and beams, cedar for masts, Ezekiel 27: 5–7.

trading outposts in Cyprus, Sicily, Utica, Cadiz, Rhodes, Miles, *Carthage Must be Destroyed*, (Penguin Books, 2012), p36.

we would trade for their wheat, olive oil and honey, Ezekiel 27: 17.

Tyre and Sidon relied on mercenaries for its army, Ezekiel 27: 10–11.

King Nadab . . . assassinated . . . while besieging . . . Gibbethon, I Kings 15:27.

besieging Gibbethon when . . . King Elah was assassinated, I Kings 16:10, 16.

Potters, Prophets and Dynasties

Philistines . . . brought [Jehoshaphat] . . . tribute, II Chronicles 17:11

prophets' curses, Deuteronomy 28:15–68.

Asa bribed the King of Aram, II Chronicles 16:2–6.

King Jehoshaphat fortified, II Chronicles 17:2, 12–13.

he [Jehoshaphat] could field an army of such size, II Chronicles 17:14–18.

They will be the head, but you will be the tail, Deuteronomy 28:44.

there will be neither dew nor rain, II Kings 17:1.

Do you wish to be like Cain, Genesis 4:10–14.

This Too Came to Pass

Jehoram, would be married to the daughter of King Ahab, II Kings 11:1, II Chronicles 21:6, 22:2.

Message to Jezebel

Regulations for . . . , Leviticus 7:22–27; Leviticus 11, 12, 14, 18; Leviticus 19:9, 19, 23; Leviticus 20:10, Numbers 13.

King Solomon's Sidonian wife, temple to Astarte, I Kings 11:1, 33.

The Festival for King Jehoshaphat,
I Kings 22, II Chronicles 18.

offerings of pigeons from the poor, Leviticus 5: 7–11.

A Conjuring of Prophets, I Kings 22, II Chronicles 18.

The Prophet Micaiah, I Kings 22, II Chronicles 18.

The Prophets Riddle

Moses had heard a voice from the burning bush, Exodus 3.

At Mount Sinai, the Lord spoke to Moses in a thick, dark cloud. Exodus 19:18.

Samuel as a child had heard the voice of the Lord in the Temple. I Samuel 3.

Elijah had shared that the Lord spoke to him in a gentle whisper, I Kings 19:11–13.

Built on the threshing floor of Anaunah, II Samuel 24:18–25; II Chronicles 3:1.

The One enthroned in heaven, Psalms 2:4; 20:6.

From heaven the Lord looks down on them, Psalm 33:13.

The Lord answers from his heavenly sanctuary, Psalm 20:6.

Joshua the spy, Numbers 13:16–25; 14:6.

Blessed are those who keep his statutes, Psalm 119:2.

The Aramean Arrow, I Kings 22; II Chronicles 18.
Ahaziah the Sot, II Kings 1.

battle of Qarqar, *A History of the Jewish People*, Ben-Sasson, ed., (Harvard University Press, (1976), p121.

Philistines captured Israel's Ark of the Covenant in a battle, it went from Ashdod to Gath to Ekron, I Samuel 5.

King Ahaziah and Elijah, II Kings 1

Shall we all have our right eyes gouged out by the Ammonites, I Samuel 11:2; Masoretic Text; Dead Sea Scrolls, "Now Nahash king of the Ammonites oppressed the Gadites and Reubenites severely. He gouged out all their right eyes and struck terror and dread in Israel."

act like a madman as David did before the King of Gath? I Samuel 21:12–15.

Gristle and Bone

ivory walled palaces, I Kings 22:39.

Shall we beg the Philistines for iron weapons, I Samuel 13:19–22.

like Ziklag . . . our houses burned and wives and children taken captive, I Samuel 30:1–2.

Must we drool and act like a madman as David did, I Samuel 21:12–15.

Miracles

Raise the dead, II Kings 4:20, 32–35.

an endless supply of food, I Kings 17:12–16.

all the families of the nations will bow down, Psalm 22: 27.

the people called for a king, I Samuel 8:4–5.

miracles with stiff mud on my wheel, Job 10:9, Isaiah 29:16, Jeremiah 18:1–10.

ends of the earth will remember and turn, Psalm 22:27.

The Lord had sent me to the town of Zarapheth, I Kings 17:7, et seq.

I am being sent to anoint Hazael, I Kings 19:15.

I have anointed my successor, Elisha, I Kings 19:19–21.

The Moab Revolt, II Kings 3.

King Ahab repelled the Assyrian hordes at Qarqar, *A History of the Jewish People*, Ben-Sasson, ed., (Harvard University Press, (1976), p121.

King David took your measure and slew two out of every three of your warriors, II Samuel, 8:2.

King Baasha fought against King Jehoshaphat's father King Asa, I Kings 15:16.

Ahijah, Jeroboam's son would not recover from his illness, I Kings 14.

house of Jeroboam would be burned in the fire like a pile of dung, I Kings 14:10

Jehoshaphat agrees to assist Joram, Joram takes army to Jerusalem, and after being "sumptuously entertained" by Jehoshaphat, resolved to march against Moab "through wilderness of Edom" for Moab would not expect them to take that road, Josephus, *Antiquities of the Jews*, Book IX, Vol. II, Ch.III, sec. 1, p249. (Bell and Sons, London, 1900).

marble from King David, I Chronicles 29: 2.

cedar and juniper from King Hiram of Tyre, I Kings 5:8.

Along the Walls of Samaria

My Royal Family

The Temple guard had been created by King David, I Chronicles 26:1–26; II Chronicles 8:14–15; I Chronicles 9:17–27.

The Rendition of Jehosheba, II Chronicles 22:10–12.

Jehoram had smashed into rubble the great pillar to Baal, II Kings 3:2.

Jehonadab Imprisoned

The Final Festival, II Kings 10:18–28.

The laws of the Levites would have required, Numbers 8:5–22; Leviticus 5:2–6

Athaliah's Purge, II Kings 11:1–3; II Chronicles 22: 10–12.

My Kingdom, the Wilderness

So Aram would raid and raid again, II Kings 10:32.

I see fit to maintain the temples to the golden calves, II Kings 10:31.

The Deposition of Athaliah, II Kings 11:4–21; II Chronicles 23.

A king from the line of David would rule, I Chronicles 22:10, Psalm 132:11–12.

the altar, a place reserved for sacred vows and refuge, I Kings 1:50–51; I Kings 8:31.

She [Athaliah] had claimed she had other sons, see, generally, II Chronicles 24:7.

raised by the priest Eli, I Samuel 3:1.

two great pillars, Boaz and Jakin, I Kings 7:21.

incense flowing out of the Holy Place, Exodus 30: 1–8.

long live the king, see I Samuel 10:24' I Kings 1:34, 39.

Jehu's Coda

prophecy that the Lord would maintain an heir of David on the throne forever, I Chronicles 22:10, Psalm 132:11–12.

words of the Preacher, Ecclesiastes 1:1.

proverbs of Solomon, Proverbs 1:1.

Psalms of David, Psalms 3–9, 11–32, 334–41, 51,65, 68–70, 86, 101, 122, 124, 131, 133, 138–145.

because you have done well in accomplishing what is right, II Kings 10:30.

'the Lord has chosen Zion,' Psalm 132:13.

'our feet our standing in your gates, Jerusalem.' Psalm 122:2.

The Course of an Arrow

And Jehu Rested, II Kings 10:35–36